Hilo Bay Mystery Collection

J.L. Oakley

Fairchance Press

J. L Oakley/Fairchance Press
Bellingam, WA
https://www.jloakleyauthor.com

Book Layout © 2017 BookDesignTemplates.com

Hilo Bay Mystery Collection/J.L. Oakley. -- 1st ed.
ISBN 13: 978-0-9973237-3-3

To Toby Neal for encouraging me to write stories set on my beloved Big Island and to my many friends when I was a young woman there, especially Mrs. Santo who gave me such *aloha*.

In my nostrils still lives the breath of flowers that perished twenty years ago." — Mark Twain

CONTENTS

Coconut

Island

Memories are Dangerous

J. L. Oakley

Before the first wave came, all the water emptied out of Hilo Bay. Boats were stranded, fish flopped among the sand patches and coral rocks only to be thrown back onto the beaches by a thigh-high wave. A second wave came like a high black wall with boulders and studied force enough to knock homes and storefronts off their foundations and send them back into the buildings on the streets behind. It sucked people, cars, dogs and parts of the train depot out into the bay before the third wave came. A two-story monster, it smashed the cottages at Laupahoehoe School and grabbed four teachers and a score of students. It took out the train bridge in Hilo, the prestigious Hilo Yacht Club and washed away the USO buildings on Coconut Island. When all was done, the sea lay flat for several hours as if to ponder the devastation and the hundred and fifty souls left dead.

Chapter 1

Hilo, Hawaii 1946

Beatrice Takahashi stood at her bedroom window and looked out to Hilo Bay. It was early morning, the day was just waking up but she could see far out beyond the sea break. Beatrice smiled. More than anything, she loved the sea and looked forward to presenting her science project on Honu, the green sea turtle, to her fourth grade classmates. She had spent a week going through old *National Geographic* magazines looking for pictures. Once her big sister, Hillary, took her down to Coconut Island where the turtles sometimes could be seen. When Beatrice spotted one, she took a picture with her Brownie camera. It only showed a ghostly back and head when the film was developed, so Beatrice drew some pictures with colored pencils to go with the-black-and white photo and pasted them onto her board.

A truck horn beeped. On the street below her family's two story apartment, Beatrice saw Mr. Chang's grocery truck pull over to the beachside of the street. Beatrice listened for the train whistle. The palm tree-lined Front Street ran parallel to the train tracks and wide beach beyond—but there was no train arriving in from the Puna district at this hour.

"Beatrice," her mother called. "Come to breakfast. We haven't much time."

"Coming."

There was more than school today. Her brother, Jimmy, was coming home. For the past two years, he had served in the armed forces, fighting with the 442nd in Italy. It was the most decorated fighting unit in the Armed Forces during the war and was made up of all Japanese-American soldiers. Jimmy had two purple hearts and was going to be awarded a Medal of Honor. Everyone in the family was so proud.

Except Uncle Toshi, Beatrice thought. He had changed since the war. Always stern, he seemed angry all the time now. Maybe because he had to go away.

"Beatrice. Please listen."

"Coming, Mama." Beatrice stuffed her books into her school bags, tied her brown and white saddle shoes, and started to go down to the kitchen, when she looked out the window. The water in the bay looked odd, like it was backing away from the beach. Swiftly, as though on little crab feet, the water receded behind the sea break. Down on the sidewalk, Mr. Chang stopped unloading his goods and taking his hat off, stared.

Beatrice dropped her school bag and ran out into the hallway. "Mama! Something funny is going on. The bay is all dry." She rushed to the living room where there was a large window that looked over the street.

There was a commotion in the kitchen. Beatrice's mother hurried down to her. Her teenaged brother and sister, Clarence and Janice, were close behind. They all stared out the window at the empty bay.

"I heard of this, children," Beatrice's mother said.

"Can we go down and look?" fourteen-year-old Janice asked. "I could look for *opihi* and crab."

"Or treasure," Beatrice chimed in. "I could help Honu if he's stranded."

Their mother frowned. "No. The sea may come back and flood the street. But I think we will be safe here for now."

Flood the street? Beatrice thought. Won't it flood the flower shop below us? She opened a side window. The smell of plumeria and sour seaweed hit her, but the strongest thing she sensed was the lack of natural sound. No myna bird or dove called. It was deadly still.

The sea did come back. Beatrice watched in horror at the speed with which it filled in the bay, raced across the beach and spun Mr. Chang and his truck around. The building shuddered when something hit it.

"To the back, children." Beatrice's mother pulled on her arm. "Now."

"Where's Hillary?" Clarence asked as they squeezed down the hallway. "Shall I wake her?"

"She didn't come home."

Beatrice was shocked at the tone of her mother's voice, even more at her determined assault on every window in the kitchen. Mama shattered each glass pane with a heavy iron pan. Through the gaping windows, Beatrice heard someone yell.

"My Honu project." The thought of it getting wet if another wave should strike the front of the apartment made Beatrice sick. "I'll be right back." She dashed down the hall to her room and picked up the large sheet of cardboard. She peeked out the window. Down below, Mr. Chang and a neighbor were assessing the damage to the truck and what appeared to be missing railroad rails on the other side of the street. The little palm trees looked forlorn.

"Beatrice!"

Beatrice snatched a stuffed animal, clamped it under her arm, and then grabbed her project. A roaring noise made her turn her head. Out beyond the sea break, she saw a black wall making its way toward the town of Hilo. It went over the break as easily someone pouring water. Huge boulders twisted and tumbled along with the wave's flow. People started to scream. Beatrice ran.

Halfway down the hall, the apartment shook so violently that Beatrice was thrown to the wood floor. She crab-crawled her way back onto her feet and ran to her mother just as the walls of the building collapsed. The floor tilted, then seemed to push her up as the wave broke open the ceiling, and then the roof to the morning sky. Beatrice grabbed onto the closest thing to her— the glass knob on the door that once led into her parent's bedroom. Her cheek against the door, she rode the wave as it rushed debris and people in toward the red dirt and green hills behind the town. To her horror, as she spun, Beatrice caught a glimpse of the giant wave behind the one that carried her now. It was the biggest thing she had ever seen. Higher than the apartment, it smashed down the remaining structure of the home and neighborhood she had known all her short life. The door caught on a large piece of the apartment's roof and threw her on top of it. She grabbed on, her bleeding fingers seeking anything to hold onto. Somewhere in the din, she heard her mother cry out to her. The last thing she saw was Mr. Chang's truck sweeping past her upside down and Honu from the sea, beating its legs as fast as they could go. Even the turtle's eyes looked terrified.

The last thing Beatrice remembered was that it was April's Fool's Day.

Chapter 2

Hana, Maui, present day

TV reporter Tawnie Takahashi unhooked her microphone and called it a day. "Thanks, Jim," she said to her gangly cameraman. "That was a good interview." She waved again to her interviewee walking back up the hill, an elderly woman who had grown up in the area. The slight woman waved back when prompted by her daughter.

Tawnie put on her sunglasses and looked over Jim Milstead's shoulder to the ocean beyond. There was no direct access to the beach below, but tourists still spread out along the lawn in various shades of swimsuits and sunburn. Further down, a wedding was underway. Here on the bungalow's lanai—one of several at the exclusive hotel—a canvas awning provided cover from the hot sun. Tawnie picked up her ice tea and stirred it around, her purple-painted fingernails squeezing the plastic cup.

"Miss Takahashi, have you finished?" an awestruck voice asked.

"Yes, thank you." Tawnie turned to face a man dressed in an Aloha shirt with a black kukui-nut necklace draped around his skinny neck. "We're all *pau,* Mr. Garcia. Thanks so much for allowing us to use this space."

The man dipped his head. "Anything to accommodate you. What an interesting series. If you don't mind, we'd like to open this up to the public at 5:00."

"No worries." *Of course, you're interested*, Tawnie thought. Famous historic people with connections to the hotel.

Mr. Garcia nodded in the direction of the unseen beach. "My boss says you can go down there, if you like. And the spa is on the house."

"Isn't the surf pretty rough down there?" Jim asked as he put away the KWAI-5 News equipment into their hard pack containers.

"It can be. We put out warnings for that. But it's very pretty." Mr. Garcia's voice softened. "Of course, the ocean can be deadly. There was a tsunami here a long time ago."

"Here? In Hana?"

"Yeah, yeah. The big one of 1946. Killed twelve people here, but Hilo was worse. One hundred and twenty-nine, I think."

"Wow, I never knew about Hana," Tawnie said. *And not much about Hilo, either,* she thought. So many lost. She hadn't thought about that tsunami in years. "We'll be done in a jif." She put away the microphone and helped wrap up whatever cording was left out.

After Garcia left, Jim asked Tawnie if she was going to take the program manager up on going to the spa.

"No. I don't think that would be a good idea. Not professional. I *will* take him up on the two-for-one dinner. I'm famished. How about you? Ready for some eats?

"I hear the *pupus* here are the best. I could go for some *sashimi.*" Jim shouldered his camera and equipment pack. "I'll just take these to the car."

They left the lanai together. The wedding party had dispersed, a colorful flow of white and orchid colored dresses and aloha shirts across the green lawn. Tawnie could almost smell the sweet pikake flowers strung in the bride's hair. The sunbathers were gathering up their chairs. It was after four and a slight breeze stirred in the palm trees.

"Jim, while you do that, I'm going to the hotel lobby and see if I can get on the internet. No cell service out here. Need to check my email. Could you catch me there?"

"Yeah, yeah. See you in a bit."

At the concierge's desk, Tawnie got the wifi code and logged into her email account. There were some pictures from her little niece's first birthday party, a note from her boss at KWAI-5 and a string of emails inquiring about requests for interviews. One subject line stood out:

"Howzit." Tawnie chuckled. The email was from her Auntie Bee, one of her favorite relatives. A few lines later, a chill went down her arm.

Someone is asking questions about Hillary.

Why? Tawnie thought. Hillary Takahashi was killed in the 1946 tsunami in Hilo.

Her aunt went on.

My nice new neighbor Maile Horner— you know the old Santos house – is a historian with the Big Island Historical Society. Someone sent her a packet of letters from the Mainland for acquisition. They talk about Hillary and a haole friend she knew back then.

The words of the post were plain, but Tawnie could almost feel the emotion behind them. Tawnie conjured up the black-and-white photo of Hillary she had seen in a family album. The photo was taken during her senior year at Hilo High School 1945. Wearing a short-sleeve pullover blouse and a simple chain necklace, her black hair was styled in a page boy. Her rosy cheeks and red lips had been tinted by hand.

Tawnie stopped reading and looked for Jim. Out on the lobby's walkway, her cameraman waited, scratching the patchy whiskers on his face. When he saw her, he patted his belly. Tawnie pointed to the hotel restaurant with its stone lanai and lights strung between the palms. "Get a seat," she mouthed. He motioned "drink."

Tawnie laughed, though she felt a growing unease. Something about her Auntie Bee's post disturbed her. Though Auntie Bee was a retired school teacher, she didn't use email that much. She liked to text instead. Knowing that cell phone service here was spotty, the information in the letters must have spurred Tawnie's aunt to send an email.

Tawnie went back to reading. *Maile brought the letters over for me to read the other day. Several of them mention a man named Joe Cameron, a local resident of Hilo. He was a non-commissioned officer stationed there during the war. Letters say this Joe was in love with my sister.*

"Oh," Tawnie said out loud, then looked around the lobby to see if anyone heard her. She knew very little about her aunt, only that she was a lovely person with much promise. People just didn't talk about the 1946 tsunami because so many families had suffered losses. Now these letters painted a new image of her long dead relative.

The email ended abruptly. *Oh, Tawnie-chan. I need you to help me. My poor sister. I'm remembering things after all these years. I think Hillary was in danger before the big waves came.*

Tawnie put the tablet down on her lap. She was an investigative reporter and encountered unsettling stories all the time. But this was family.

Tawnie hit REPLY and wrote:

Auntie, I just finished an assignment here in Hana, but there is no cell service. I'll call you as soon as I'm back in Kahului. I love you.

Tawnie reread the post and then hit SEND.

Tawnie put her tablet into her handbag and slipped outside. She looked down the green lawn to the sea. The turquoise water in front of her looked calm. Further out, the sun turned the water into scattered gold and white diamonds. Tawnie knew this is what the tourists come for, but it was what she loved about her island home too.

But sometimes the sea hits back. When the coconut palms next to the path rustled in an unseen breeze, she thought she heard the sound of waves and voices in distress. Tidal waves were deadly, but she never thought they could cover a murder.

Chapter 3

Annie Moke drove her Subaru onto her driveway lined with tall banana ferns and parked under her carport. As she opened the kitchen door to her 1970s rambler, Annie's big Lab-mixed dog, LaBaie, bounded over to greet her.

"Did you miss me?" The big dog's tail banged against the kitchen table. Annie patted LaBaie's brown head then put her badge and utility belt on the counter. Unbuttoning her police uniform shirt, she went down the hall to the bathroom and turned on the shower. LaBaie followed her in and took a drink in the toilet bowl before laying down on the linoleum floor.

"Silly girl." Annie undressed and stepping into the lukewarm stream of the shower, let the water stream over her aching shoulders. Soon, she knew, the tears would come, always unbidden. She tried to think of her day, the people she met and the cases she worked with her wonderful partner, Kimo Fortes, but in the end, she felt empty. *Maybe coming back to work so soon wasn't a good idea.*

Her cell phone rang out in the living room. LaBaie got up and pressed her brown nose against the flowery shower curtain to let Annie know. To make a further point, she barked.

"I hear it, Baie" Annie let the phone go to voicemail and gave her straight black hair a good washing before turning off the water. She towel-dried quickly, ran some conditioner through her hair and then padded barefoot out to the kitchen in her black silk robe.

At the sink, Annie drank a glass of water and carefully picked a dead leaf off a brown-freckled orchid in the window before checking on her voicemail. She was surprised to see that it was not from her partner, Kimo, but from her father-in-law, Jerry Moke, captain in the Hilo Police Department. She hit the screen for playback.

"Annie. Heard you were back at work at MPD. Give me a call when you can."

The message was short, but Lei appreciated her father-in-law calling her. Hilo was where she got her first position as a police officer and where she met David. Annie decided she'd call Jerry in a bit, but first she raided the refrigerator for a late lunch. Wrapping her robe tight around her, she brought two containers of leftover Chinese food to the counter and sat down on a stool. LaBaie waited patiently for her portion.

Poking her cold food with chopsticks, Annie scrolled through her email and text messages. Friends and family calling, sending their *aloha* and offers for lunch, a movie out. One text offered to take the twins for catamaran ride off of Kihei. Annie finished up the last container of food and gave the least spicy one to LaBaie, then put some clothes on. A final dash of tinted lotion on her face and she was ready to make the call to Jerry at the Hilo Police Department.

Electra Sam at the switchboards was still guard dog against incoming calls, but she was gentle when she realized Annie was calling. "So sorry for hear about David."

"*Mahalo,* Ellie. Thank everyone for the cards and flowers. Could I speak to Jerry?"

"For sure. Take care." There was a pause on the other line and then Jerry's voice.

"Hey, sweetheart," Jerry said when Annie got through to him. "Glad to hear your voice. Howzit?"

"Things are going fine. It's good to be back. Thanks for calling me."

"How are the twins?"

"Auntie took them to camp. They'll be back next week."

"And you?"

"I'm managing. Had a lot of stuff to take care of after the funeral, but—" Annie's voice cracked for a moment. "—but I'm cool."

On the other end, Jerry sighed. Annie could almost see the frown on his brown face that made squiggly lines across his forehead. Jerry was tall with big shoulders. Except for his graying buzz cut, he looked like a famous Hawaiian warrior sketched in a 19th century lithograph. Family always said *alihi* blood ran through his veins.

"For sure?" he asked.

"Really, I'm doing alright."

"I'm glad to hear. You let me know if you need anything."

"Thanks." LaBaie came over and nudged Annie's knee. Annie rubbed her rough coat and swallowed. "How about you? Anything new in Hilo besides the volcano going off?"

"Well, there was one *kine* thing. Some pig hunters found human remains wrapped up in an Army issued poncho and buried under rocks up above the fern forest. Our ME thinks they are very old. Hard to believe, but he found a hair comb, some old fashioned shoes, and a pendant with 'Class of 45' on it. ME's pretty sure the skull and leg bones belong to a young woman."

"Wow. Any idea who it might be?"

"Got someone working on old missing case files. So far nothing in 1945. That would have been the end of the war. You know, WWII. People coming home. Closing down any military operations stationed in Hilo. Murder—and we think it's murder—could have been in 1946 or later, but 1946 was one crazy year. That's when the big tsunami came through and wiped out the shore line and killed over a hundred people."

Annie sat back down on a stool. "Ah, I remember David telling me about that when we lived in Hilo. Wasn't there another bad one in 1960?"

"Yeah, yeah." Jerry's voice got soft for a moment, then he went on. "Anyway, we've got an UH forensic anthropologist working on this. Dr. Clark specializes in remains from WWII. Does recovery for the military in the South Pacific. He's an expert on determining the age of bones, gender in a tropical environment."

"Well, keep me up to date."

"I'll let you know. In the meantime, there could be an article in the local paper in the next day or so. We've been sitting on this for a couple of weeks, wanted a little more information before we went public, but the 'coconut wireless' is already spreading rumors about the remains. There were hard times after the war. Some of our Japanese neighbors were interned. Many served in the famous 442th. Hilo was trying to get normal, trying to forget. Then the tsunami came." Jerry paused as if he was remembering something. "My dad always said the tsunami did bring everyone together—the Navy was terrific with its help—but these bones could open old wounds. We were so small then, just a little town on an island in the middle of the Pacific."

Annie thought of her Japanese grandfather and wondered what he remembered of those times when Hawaii was a territory and the world attempted to turn itself upright again.

Bee Takahashi put on her slippers, wiggling her toes in place next to the rubber straps. She adjusted her wire rimmed glasses, then stepped outside.

"Come, Asami," she said to her little black-and-white Shitzu." The dog bounded out, a flurry of long hair and mincing feet.

The early evening sky was overcast as Hilo's skies tended to be, but Bee always looked for the blue somewhere out there, a gem of hope that the sun would come out and stay and make a beautiful sunset. It was a way of surviving and looking for something to be grateful for. Her father had taught her that long ago.

Bee walked with a slight limp that had never held her back nor threatened her health. At seventy-nine years old, she was as strong as an ox. "I've had a good life," she told her grandson once when he was worried about a job he wanted. "You can do anything as long as you apply yourself and believe in what you do."

Bee was proud when he got the job, but she was proud of herself as well. She had been through the worst thing anyone could imagine and survived. Except for Papa and Jimmy, Bee had lost everyone in the great 1946 tsunami, though Mama had clung to life for a couple of years after, a shell of a woman.

Bee sighed then sat down on the wood bench that curved around her huge breadfruit tree. Occupying over half of it were her beloved orchids. For many years, they were her only children until she met George Peterson, a Bostonian who came to the island in the late 1950s and never left. He didn't object when she kept her maiden name—*to remember those I lost*—and they had a good marriage. Now George was gone too.

Up here on the hills behind Hilo, Bee could sometimes make out a sliver of the ocean, but though she still loved Honu and worked to protect the green sea turtle, she never again turned her back on the ocean. Up here she was safe. Which is why the letters her new neighbor had shown her were so disturbing.

That day, April 1, 1946, was carefully tucked away in her memory and though the new tsunami museum downtown collected stories and pictures of residents who survived that day, Bee did not answer their requests. But the name of Joe Cameron mentioned in the letters brought a surge of little scenes. Bee remembered Joe in the company of Hillary's high school friends, Joe in a uniform, Joe kissing Hillary down by Coconut Island. The suppressed memory, once as cold as her sister Hillary after she was found in the debris of the tsunami bloomed. Yet, all Bee felt toward this Joe Cameron was warmth. He had been very gentle to a little girl who had...

"Oh, my goodness," Bee said out loud. "I had a crush on him." She adjusted the wire rim glasses on her nose and giggled. "What do you think about that, Asami?" The dog cocked her head. The awakened memory made Bee smile.

Then Bee remembered another man. A tall man. Dark hair, piercing blue eyes. Uniform. No warmth there. Bee put a hand to her chest and wished that her great-niece Tawnie would call her soon.

Something had happened. She remembered Hillary being sad, then scared.

***

Tawnie Takahashi got back to her hotel in Kahului around nine at night and debated whether or not she should call her great aunt at this hour. Auntie Bee could be keeping late hours these days. Tawnie's sweet aunt had suffered two losses this year—the passing of both her husband and her brother Jimmy Takahashi. *My grandfather*, Tawnie thought. Auntie Bee would be grieving for sure, but Grandfather always told Tawnie that his little sister was the strongest person he ever knew. He had been in the war, she had beat Nature. Yet, Tawnie felt an urgency in Auntie Bee's email. *I think Hillary was in danger before the big waves came.* The words gave her a chill.

Tawnie took off her high heels and rubbed her feet. A female TV reporter always had to look her best when on air and even in laid-back Hawaii there was no exception. She had been working for KWAI-5 News for five years now. Coming on after an internship in Washington D.C., Tawnie was one of the youngest reporters ever hired there, becoming the chief investigative reporter at age thirty. That was over two years ago. She knew she was good, but she felt she had to earn it all the time. Doing a personal story on Hana, Maui and its people was a new assignment and it made her a little nervous. She liked being an investigative reporter.

"No worries," her station manager told her. "Just getting you to expand your horizons, girl. You still are the best on hard stories."

Tawnie got out of her suit and slipped into jeans and a tank top. In the little bathroom, she removed her makeup. Her sharp almond-shaped brown eyes had slight bags under them.

Gotta get more sleep, she thought. She dabbed some cream under her eyes, then pulled her sleek shoulder-length hair up into a ponytail. She stood at attention for a moment, shrugged her shoulders up to her neck and then slowly relaxed them as she let her breath out.

Back in the room, Tawnie gave her cameraman Jim a call as she cleaned up. He was staying overnight with a college friend in town. After chatting with him for a bit, she said,

"See you in the morning, Jim. We have a flight out at 10:00."

"You're the boss."

Tawnie smiled. Jim was a good guy. And an excellent partner on news stories.

After Tawnie signed off, she padded back into the room and sat down at the little hotel desk. She tapped her phone and put in the words Hilo Bay, tsunami, 1946. Immediately several options came up. She went to pictures first. The devastation of downtown Hilo was extraordinary. Tawnie wondered what that would have looked like if the same waves had hit Pearl Harbor or over down by Queen's Beach in Waikiki. Tsunamis gained power when they went up rivers. The Ala Wai Canal would be bad, but she didn't remember when it was built. Maybe thousands would have been lost back then.

She enlarged one famous picture of the tidal wave hitting Coconut Island, wiping all buildings away. She swallowed. She knew so little about this tsunami that happened nearly seventy years ago, but somehow, it was more than a news story. This one was personal.

She sighed and made the call to Hilo. It rang for a few moments, then was picked up.

"Hello?"

"Auntie Bee. It's Tawnie. Not too late, yeah?"

"Tawnie-san. I so glad you called. Just me and Asami swatting mosquitoes."

"Are you outside?"

"Yeah, yeah. Going in now."

Tawnie could hear something open and close, the clicking of the dog's toes on the linoleum floor.

"Are you OK, Auntie? Your email sounded like you were really worried about something."

Tawnie heard water running, a glass fill and then stop.

"I'm OK. Get down sometimes thinking of George. I miss him. Jimmy, your grandfather, too."

Tawnie didn't know how to answer, except some canned thing like, "I'm so sorry, auntie. I miss them too." She cleared her throat. "You said that you were remembering something. Some letters."

"Yeah, yeah. Talking about that Joe Cameron. I remember him now. He was one *haole* who grew up here in Hilo. Nice man. Nice to me. But now I wonder."

"But you said that your sister—Hillary—might have been in danger before the tsunami."

Tawnie heard Auntie Bee take a sip of water. "Your Auntie Hillary was nine years older than me and out of school when she died. She was sooo beautiful and popular. Lots of fellows wanted to date her, but Joe was the one, I think. When I remember this now, I realize how hard that would be—with the war and all—but I think it's true because he was *haole* and Hillary *sansei*. They were in love. He was the son of a sugar cane manager, but he went to the public school like everyone else."

Bee paused. "Hillary had a best friend—Bessie Whitehall. She was a *haole* too, but they were best friends since first grade. Always together, always over at our place. That's what I'm remembering. During the war, my sister and Bessie both helped out at the USO dances at the naval air station and at the USO recreation center on Coconut Island. Joe was there. He was stationed in Hilo during that time. And then..."

"And then what?" Bee was quiet for way too long. "Auntie?" Tawnie's heart sped up a bit. This was so unlike her aunt.

"It's all right. Just thinkin'. I was just a little girl. Some things I learned later from Father and Jimmy, though most people just don't talk about that time. But I do remember things. More like feelings, ghost-*kine* memories. Bessie Whitehall disappeared some time at the end of February. I remember grownups talking about it, was aware of people looking sideways at servicemen who came into town. Father told me later that the girl's disappearance was very shocking. The police searched all over, even the folks at the Naval Air Station helped too, but they never found her. Some thought she might have run away with someone to the Mainland."

"That must have been very hard on Hillary."

"Yeah, yeah. Hillary was so sad. Cried a lot, then she started acting nervous. Cautious-like. I got worried. I started following her around on my bike. Found out she was meeting Joe in secret. Once, I saw her kiss Joe out by the island one evening. Not just a friendly kiss, but a good kiss with arms and legs. I didn't understand they were making love stuff, but I got shame and left. I saw them later fighting."

"When was that?"

"Two days before the tsunami."

"Do you know why?" Tawnie tried to picture the scene but kept coming up with movie clips from "From Here to Eternity" in her head.

"No, but the next day—the day before the big waves came—Hillary was in her bedroom crying. When I knocked on her door, she jumped. She looked so scared. When I asked why she was crying, she said it was nothing. I asked if she was mad at Joe. She stared at me with such wide eyes, then said she "No, but don't tell Mama you saw us together.'" Tawnie heard Bee take a drink of water. "I never did."

"Auntie, you never told anyone, not even your brother Jimmy?"

"No. Nevah. Hillary, my other brother and sister, Clarence and Janice gone. Why bring up something with so many lost? Hillary told me not to tell Mama. I just let it go."

"Until now." Tawnie rolled her shoulders. It had been a long day and she was getting stiff. Yet she was very focused on the story Bee told. Though this was a family tragedy, her reporter instincts started to kick in.

"Hmmm," Bee said. "Yes, until now. Before the girl disappeared, I'd see her and Hillary out with a whole gang of girlfriends and servicemen. There was one *haole* who was always with Bessie. He flew planes. He was good looking, but I never liked him."

"Are you thinking this man might have something to do with Bessie disappearing?"

"Maybe."

"Did Auntie Hillary say anything else to you that day? Was she afraid of this man or Joe?"

There was dead silence on the other end. Tawnie walked over to the hotel window, closed the drapes for the night and waited for Bee to answer. Finally, her aunt spoke.

"I don't know. What do I know? I saw Joe and Hillary fighting. Maybe because this guy was moving in on her. Jimmy said she could be a flirt."

"Do you know that name of the other man?"

"No."

"Why are you remembering this after all this time?"

Bee paused a long time. "Maybe you think I'm all *lolo,* but since I read the letters, I keep hearing Hillary's voice. Like she's trying to tell me something. I think she wants me to know why she was so scared."

Chapter 5

Annie Moke opened the front page of the Maui Times and took in the headline blaring at her. Just as Jerry had predicted, the discovery of the bones up in the Hilo fern forest was big news.

BONES FOUND OF WOMAN MISSING FOR OVER 70 YEARS

Elisabeth Sparrow Whitehall, the daughter of John and Cathleen Whitehall, disappeared on February 27, 1946 after attending a USO dance and performance at the Naval Air Station. The ensuing month long search, conducted by local police and volunteers, was ended only by the fateful arrival of the tsunami that wiped out most of downtown Hilo. Later, it was speculated that the young woman had eloped due to difficulties at home.

The article went on to describe the discovery of the bones, how Dr. Roger Clark, a forensic anthropologist at UH Manoa, had made the identification and attempted to notify any remaining relatives. Cause of death could not be determined, but damage to the skull and other evidence suggested some violence was involved. Possibly homicide.

"What you got, Annie Oakley?" Annie's police partner, Kimo Fortes, leaned over her cubicle. Of medium stature and lean, he still filled out his pressed Maui Police uniform. A moustache that would challenge Tom Selleck's drooped on either side of his mouth.

"Looks like an interesting case. This the one my father-in-law told me about the other day." Annie turned the newspaper over so Kimo could see the headline.

"Wow. That's an old one. Maybe it should be on the History Channel."

"Or Cold Case." Annie folded up the newspaper and sipped from her coffee. "How's the weather out there?"

"Hot. Boss wants us to go look into a break-in. Some old guy in over in Pa'ia got his place rifled while he was out to dinner last night. Discovered the mess when he got home this morning."

Annie gathered up her notebook, holster and badge and followed Kimo out to their blue-and-white cruiser. "You drive," she said, hopping into the passenger side.

Annie was so happy to be back at work. It wasn't just the routine that she knew would kept her focused on something other than her grief, but she and Kimo worked well together. Kimo was loyal and generous, but just as important, had a slow fuse. Annie was guilty of sometimes jumping in. Impulsive, impatient.

They drove out to the picturesque village of Pa'ia, a sugar mill town started in the 1870s. The last town on the road to Hana, Pa'ia's sandy beaches brought windsurfers and tourists seeking a more subdued Hawaiian experience. When the mill closed in 2000, the old plantation town survived on its natural beauty and all forms of surfing. While Kimo drove, Annie brought up directions and background on the victim on the cruiser's laptop.

"Hmm," Annie said. "Lives in a pretty nice place. Up above the ocean."

"Must have been there a long time. Can't even buy a square inch out there for all the money in the world."

"Or he's a rich *malihini*." Annie looked out at the green countryside passing by. She once read that twenty percent of Maui was now owned by people from the Mainland, some who never setting foot on the land. *How do you get to know the people?* she thought.

"What else you got?"

"Looks like a solid citizen. No record." Annie furrowed her eyebrows and squinted. "Though I wonder what it takes to make it to almost ninety years old."

"Ninety?"

"Eighty-nine. Just about. That's what it says."

They approached Pa'ia, passing Pa'ia Bay and its white sand beach where girls in bikinis carrying surfboards, cars and jeeps loaded with boogie boards and body boards and tourists wearing shorts and sunglasses vied for places to park alongside the busy road. Further on, the famous sign stating. "Welcome to Pa'ia: Maui's Historic Plantation

Town" Underneath were the half-covered words "Please Don't' Feed the Hippies."

"Nice, huh?" Kimo said as they passed old one-story buildings and surf shops, coffee shops, boutiques and eateries on both sides of the busy road.

"Yeah, yeah, though it's really changed from when I used to come here to see my grandparents. So much traffic."

"It's a good place to practice. That's why we call Pa'ia Bay the Baby Bay."

Outside of the town, they continued along the Hana Highway, going past Ho'okipa Beach, Pa'ia's most famous beach, where windsurfing was popular for the most talented in winter. Further on, they went around a tight U-shaped bay. The two-way highway became lush with trees of all sorts: guava, avocados, *kukui*, palms, and Christmas berry sometimes covered with vines. Annie rolled her window down just to breathe the fresh air. It smelled sweet and lusty green.

"The address should be coming up," Annie said. "Look, I see a driveway on the right. Where those lava rock gateposts are. The numbers look right."

"See it." Kimo slowed down. The gate was open, exposing a driveway made of crushed lava rock lined with a mix of kukui nut and ironwood trees. He turned the cruiser in and powered up the lumpy lane. Open fields where some cattle and a lone horse grazed came into view. At the end of the road stood a large plantation-style house – the kind Annie loved with its wide veranda, red tin roof and porch windows that looked out to the ocean. A Subaru station wagon and a Jeep were parked off to the side under a circle of kukui nut trees. As Annie and Kimo got out of the car, a thirty-something woman Annie's age came out on the porch. She wore a short, pink and orchid colored muumuu and sandals. Her lightly tanned face spoke of some mixed island heritage, though her eyes were a sea blue green.

"Morning," Annie said, taking the lead. "We're from the Maui Police Department answering a call about a break-in." Annie showed the woman her badge. "This is my partner Detective Kimo Fortes. And you are?"

"Ginger Cameron."

"May we come in?"

"Yeah, sure. My grandfather has been waiting."

"I understand that no one was at the house last night," Annie said as they stepped into the cool house.

"That's right. We went over to Kihei for dinner and to spend the night."

"Who is we?"

"My mom, my brother and some friends of Papa Joe's." Ginger smiled. "That's what I call my grandfather."

"So you didn't know about a break in? No alarm went off?"

"Oh, Papa Joe. He doesn't believe in that stuff. Says the place was blessed three times years ago: *kahuna*, Shinto priest, and a minister from over in Makawao. And is open to anyone. Never been any trouble. He leads a quiet life since Grandma died."

The house was cool inside with air conditioning running somewhere. The old-style home had a hallway that led to the back and as they followed Ginger through the house, Annie felt a sense of richness and appreciation for family and art. On the white painted wood walls were silkscreen prints depicting Hawaiian gods and stories as well as pictures of what she suspected were family.

Ginger eventually led them out into a large room, a modern addition in all aspects. It sported a high cathedral ceiling, many windows and a rock fireplace. Large paintings and prints adorned what wall space there was. Annie could see Kimo's eyes widen. "Those are Pegge Hopper paintings," Kimo whispered to Annie. "Expensive."

Overall, the room would have been a place of peace if it wasn't in such a state of chaos. Furniture was tossed on its side. Cabinets made of koa wood on either side of the fireplace were rifled of their books, small wooden sculptures were smashed and framed photographs scattered as if someone was searching for a particular item. Standing in the center of the largest pile was a tall elderly white man, wiry as a game cock and leaning on a koa wood cane almost more for effect than need. He had the grace of someone who once had been a physical man, his blue eyes hawk sharp, yet a hint of kindness in the crow's feet that lay on his cheeks.

"My grandfather," Ginger said. "Joe Cameron."

***

Tawnie Takahashi was back in Honolulu when the news about Bessie Whitehall broke out in the city newspaper. Her first reaction was, "*Damn. I should have had this,*" but professional envy quickly turned to concern for Auntie Bee. How did she feel about this? Bessie and Hillary were best friends since first grade. Had Hillary known something about her friend's disappearance?

Tawnie worried the story could hurt Bee in some way, maybe trigger more hidden memories of the worst kind about the tsunami. Grandfather had told her years ago that Bee was found clinging to a door knob on their parent's bedroom door. The door had carried her through roiling waves to rest on top of what was left of several buildings. Her left leg had been so badly broken that it required several surgeries.

Tawnie tapped her polished nails on the desk, then nearly jumped when her KWAI-5 News manager, Dennis Kane, stuck his head into her office. "Aloha, Tawnie. Glad to see you back."

"Thanks, Denny. Working on the last interview footage for the six o'clock."

"Looking forward to it." He cleared his throat. "See the news? Hilo?"

"Yeah, I did. Makes me angry I didn't catch this on the scanner."

"Well, go down there and see if you can get an angle on it."

For a moment, Tawnie was uncharacteristically speechless. "You want me to drop everything and go to Hilo?" All Tawnie could see was the pile of work she had in front of her. Not just news, but her weekly posting on the TV channel's blog and her seven tweets a day she was required to send out.

Dennis smiled. "It's gotta be a good story there. End of the war, world moving on. News account says that this young lady went missing before the big tsunami. Don't you have family there?"

"A great-auntie."

"Good. Get the local opinion. " Kane cocked his head at Tawnie and gave her a chin lift. "Hey, what's going on? You look like you've seen a ghost. Or is the work getting to you? I can always assign the story to someone else"

Tawnie stood up. "No worries. I can handle the load. You know me, but I've got to be honest with you, Denny. While I was down on Maui, my auntie contacted me. By coincidence, she was remembering something that happened a long time ago. Turns out my auntie knew this Bessie Whitehall."

"No kidding. There you go. A great start."

"No, it's going to be tricky. I think you forgot, but I lost most of my family in that tsunami. My great-auntie survived it."

Kane flushed. "Oh. So sorry." He looked truly shamed. His reddened face almost matched the red KWAI-News aloha shirt he wore.

"But I'll go. First, I want to get the six o'clock done. Jim has it in editing. And then I'll catch a two o'clock flight if I can. Have a favor to ask, though."

"Yes?"

"I have a couple of personal leave days I haven't used. I'm worried about my auntie. I'd like to extend my assignment to include some of those days. I promise to report timely."

Kane seemed to have restored his composure. "As you always do. Well, proceed as best you can."

"Can I get Jim, too?"

"He can go down tomorrow."

"*Mahalo*. I'll get you the best story possible."

"I'm counting on it. Tell you what. Finish up and I'll take you to the airport   personally."

As soon as Joe Cameron made his statement to Annie about the break-in at his house, she knew he was no ordinary senior citizen. Joe reminded her of the Pearl Harbor survivor she met while visiting the Arizona Memorial. The old man was bent, but there was a quality about him that struck Annie at the time. *What was the word? Resilient.* A quality Annie was beginning to appreciate in herself. Joe Cameron was resilient, too, but she wondered what he had overcome.

Kimo took the lead asking questions about when Joe got home from Kihei, who else was with him, had he touched anything?

"Was there anything of value taken?" Kimo asked as he wrote down notes in his notebook.

"Broke one of my carvings, but didn't take any artwork. Mostly rifled some of my photo albums." Joe nodded to a brass frame with the glass broken out. "Took a picture out of it and—" Joe frowned, his white eyebrows knitting together. "Can't recall where I placed it, but I think an old album of mine is missing."

"Was it important?"

"It was to me."

Annie jumped in. "Can you describe it?"

Joe laughed. "You young folks probably think it belongs in a museum, but it's a souvenir photo album from the old Mokuola USO Recreation Center in Hilo. Some call the place Coconut Island."

Immediately, Annie perked up. "That was during World War II, wasn't it?"

"Yeah, yeah. You know the island?"

"Swam around there a few years back. Heard the buildings got wiped out in the big tsunami of 1946."

"That's right." Joe's gray eyes got distant. He sucked his lips in. "That's right, he repeated."

"Mr. Cameron," Kimo said. "We'd like to take some pictures of the damage, get you and your granddaughter's statements. When you can, submit a complete list of items to the local police station in Haiku. For now, we'll take notes on what you believe is missing so far."

"I'll see to that, Papa Joe," Ginger Cameron said. "Could you help me upright this big lounge chair, Officer?" Ginger looked at Kimo's name on his uniform. "Ah, Officer Fortes. I think my grandfather should sit for a while. It's been upsetting."

"Pff," Joe said. "You'd think I was one helpless *keiki.*" As Kimo pulled the upholstered chair up, Joe took hold of one of its arms and together they righted the chair. "There," he said, then eased down in the cushions.

"I'll get you some water, Grandpa." Ginger excused herself and went back to the kitchen.

While Kimo took pictures, Annie found a wood chair and set it next to Joe.

"Have you lived up here for a long time?" she asked as she sat down.

"Fifty years. Property's been in the family for a hundred more."

"You're a *kama'aina.* Lived here a long time."

"Born and raised. Fifth generation. I could say I was a *keiki o ka 'aina,* but I respect my Hawaiian ohana. It's them to say."

As Annie listened to Joe talk, she found herself liking him very much. He was not some *haole* from the Mainland who bought up a bunch of property and did what he pleased with it, but someone who understood the Hawaiian Islands and its culture. "What did you do before you retired?"

"Retired?" Joe chuckled. "I don't think I ever retired. Too busy. But, well, I ran a number of sugar mills like my father and his father before me. In the 1980s, I got into coffee. Have a thriving plantation on the Big Island. A new one up on Oahu is doing well. Tourists like cafes with Hawaii- grown coffee. I also started a small brewery. I like being current."

"Like Big Swell IPA?" That was one of Annie's favorites.

Joe grinned. "My competition."

"Anything else?" Annie started taking notes in her notebook.

"I have ranch land that is part conservancy. Like seeing what happens with that. Too many invasive species coming here and hurting our islands."

Annie shifted on the hard, wooden seat. "Mind if I ask what Hilo was like back then? Were you stationed there during the war?"

"I was stationed with the Army. Worked with the Hawaii National Guard there."

"And this USO center, that was a special place? I remember Coconut Island is just off Liliuokalani Park. Pretty place to picnic. Has a tower kids liked to jump into the bay from."

Joe smiled. "We used that for teaching military personnel to jump from a ship into the water and swim with full combat packs." He sighed. "The Mokuola USO Center got started while I was still in high school— 1942, as I recall. We couldn't go there, of course. Off limits to civilians. But after I enlisted in the Army, I ended up back in Hilo. Then I could go. They built a pontoon bridge over to the island. Had a guard on duty at the front. Certain days of the week, a fellow could bring his friends."

"What could you do there?"

"Well, swim and dive. Then there was volleyball, horseshoes. There was a canteen, too, that sold beer, sandwiches and soft drinks. Sometimes there were dances."

"Must have been a nice time, despite the war."

"Well, I never saw action in the Pacific like some of my friends. Hellholes those places were." He paused and looked at her. *Is he looking at my eyes, my Japanese eyes?* Annie wondered. "But that was times past."

Annie brought her queries back to the present situation. "What was in the missing picture?"

Joe looked thoughtful, almost hurt. "Oh, a group of high school friends I knew back in Hilo. Good friends. Still hard to accept that six months later half would be lost in that damn tsunami."

"Mr. Cameron, did you know a Bessie Whitehall?"

The old man opened his mouth like someone had thumped him on the back, then snapped it shut. He nodded, then swallowed. "Why do you ask?"

"Because this morning, the Hilo Police Department announced that bones found up behind the town have been identified as hers. Looks like foul play."

Annie watched Joe react to this news. His gray eyes grew hard and darted, his breathing slowed. He seemed to be thinking, reaching for the right answer. Finally, he said, "Poor girl. That was a long time ago."

"Did you know she went missing back then?"

"Whole town knew. Then the waves came."

Bee was in back tending to her orchids when Asami began yapping up a storm and running around in circles.

"Who's that Asami-san?"

She brushed down her long muumuu and followed her dog around to the front of the house. Standing on the concrete steps was a middle-aged man in Bermuda shorts and aloha shirt. His straight brown hair had bits of gray in it. His face seemed familiar to Bee and she wondered if he was one of her fourth-grade students returning grown up. They sometimes appeared at her door when they came home to Hilo to visit.

"Yes? Can I help you?"

"You Beatrice Takahashi?" The man looked at a card in his hand, then back at her.

"I am. What you want?"

"Oh, I'm from the museum in town. I'm told you have some letters that might fit the story we're working on."

Bee was not normally wary, but Asami continued to yap at the man. "I don't know what you're talking about. What *kine* letters?" She picked up her dog and hushed her.

The stranger came down off the steps. He smiled at her. *And really,* she thought, *it wasn't a bad smile,* but there was something off-putting about him. His posture and caramel brown eyes were a little too intense.

"We're doing a story on life in Hilo during and after the war. I'm told you might have letters about that time."

"Young man, I have nothing from that time. All gone in the tsunami."

"Oh, these letters recently came from the Mainland."

"I'm sorry. I can't help you. You might try…" Bee almost said "Maile Horner, her neighbor," but she clammed up.

"Are you sure?" The man advanced. "They're very important."

Bee tried not to show it, but this man was scaring her. She thought of putting Asami down and let her go at the man's ankles, but just as she was figuring out the next step, a Jeep pulled up at her sidewalk and the morning's newspaper flew through the air over her hibiscus hedge and landed on her lawn.

"Morning Mrs. Takahashi," a voice called.

"Morning, Koa. Come get your tip. I have some macadamia nut cookies for you." Bee looked straight at the stranger. He glared at her, then left, brushing by a college-aged young man as he passed. Bee couldn't see the stranger's vehicle until after he drove off. A silver Ford truck.

"Huh," she said. She smiled when Koa came up to her, putting on a good show of being calm and in control. Koa picked up her newspaper and gave it to her.

"Who was that?" he asked.

Bee put Asami down. "I don't know. One nasty man, I think. I thought he might be an old student of mine."

"Not behind in your bills, auntie?"

Bee swatted his arm. "He was no bill collector." Bee bit her lip. She checked again to make sure the stranger was gone. "So sorry, Koa. I really don't have cookies. I just wanted him gone."

"You want I should call the police?"

Bee shook her head. "No. You get back to your route. I'll be fine, though if you like, I do have some malasadas I got at the bakery the other day. Come around to the kitchen. Won't take a minute." She slid the newspaper out of its plastic sleeve and opened it up as she walked.

BONES OF WOMAN MISSING OVER FOR 70 YEARS AGO FOUND

"Oh," Bee said when she read the next line. Her head started to spin. The sounds of rushing waves roared through her ears, the ground tipped. Her bungalow home seemed to rise up before she hit her head and then blacked out.

"Mrs. Takahashi!" a frantic female voice called from what seemed a distant place. Something cool was laid on Bee's head.

"Auntie Bee?" A male voice asked. "Do you think we should call 911?"

"I did, already" the female voice answered.

Bee opened her eyes. She was lying on the ground with a concerned Koa and her neighbor, Maile Horner, on their knees next to her.

"For shame, I'm fine," Bee said.

"Let those handsome young men decide," Maile said. "Why don't you try sitting up?" Maile put a hand behind Bee's shoulders and with Koa's help got her sitting up. "Anything ache? Hurt?"

"I'm fine. Just got one dizzy spell."

"Someone was here," Koa said to Maile. "I think he upset her."

"Who was that?" Maile asked. The girl was a ginger head with a spray of light brown freckles on her arms that were turning into a tan. Bee had liked her the first time she came over to say hello. With her looking so worried, Bee liked her more.

Bee frowned. "He said he was from a museum in town doing some show on Hilo during the war."

"Hmm. Not to my knowledge," Maile said. "Just had a meeting with all the other historians in town. Nothing remotely planned like that."

Bee started to get up. "Now wait," Maile said. "Your head is bleeding."

"Oh?"

From off in the distance came the sound of a siren. The sound was comforting to most people, but it only made Bee anxious. She looked at the newspaper strewn across the lawn. Bessie Whitehall had been found after all these years. The thought made her shiver.

"Are you cold, Auntie Bee?"

Bee didn't think she was. *Maybe I'm scared.* The fire truck sounded really close now. Now, that was good. "That man was asking about the letters you showed me."

"The letters? The ones being considered for acquisition?"

"I think so. Said they were important."

"That's weird. I haven't looked at everything. I just showed you the ones with your family name in them. There are pictures too."

"Enough of that," Koa said. "They're here."

Before Bee knew what was happening, she was surrounded by three handsome, fit young men and an equally fit young woman. Bee had taught half of them over the years.

"Jason Chee," Bee said to the young man checking her head wound. "When did you get back?"

"I transferred down from Kahului a couple of months ago. Now let my partner take your blood pressure. How did this happen?"

Before she could answer, Koa told the EMT that someone had been here. "Then this." He pointed to the newspaper.

"You know anything about this, Auntie?" Jason asked. "It's quite the sensation down at the station."

"First time I hear about it. Oh, that stuff stings so hard."

Maile said, "I think you're going to need stitches, Mrs. Takahashi. Better let them check your head."

"My head just fine."

"Just as a precaution, Auntie. Concussion." Jason nodded to the blood on the edge of sidewalk. "I think you clipped it. What's her reading?"

"146 over 90," the female EMT said. "Pulse a bit fast."

"What you 'pect?" Bee shook her head, a grin forming on her lips. "All this attention."

"You deserve it." Jason nodded for them to bring over the gurney.

"Can I go along?" Maile asked. "Someone should be with her."

"You'll have to drive yourself. Meet her in emergency. I'll make sure you're going in as friend of the family."

"You better, Jason Chee," Bee said. "She like daughter to me."

Maile blushed. "You're too kind."

Bee took Maile's hand. "You should call me Auntie Bee like everyone else."

They eased Bee onto the gurney and rolled her to the ambulance. "Koa, I'm alright," Bee said as she was transferred into the vehicle. "You go to work now."

Jason chuckled. "You better do it," he said to Koa. "You don't want to get a failing grade from Auntie Bee Takahashi.

Tawnie, dressed in a short sleeved top, designer jeans, and KEEN hiking boots, stood off a game trail near the upper edge of the Hilo Forest Reserve. Holding a microphone with the KWAI-5 News logo on it in her hand, she marveled at the scene around her. *Ohia lehua* trees and their red blossoms poked above the thick collection of *hapuu* tree ferns. Native mint and orchids grew throughout, unimpeded by invasive species often found in other parts of the reserve. Not far off, a stream trickled through a lava rock bed. A picture-perfect native Hawaiian forest. Only this was a decades-old dumping ground for a murdered young woman.

Jim with his video camera on his shoulder waited in front of her. They were recording for their news channel later tonight. Just after Tawnie got the go-ahead to fly to Hilo to investigate the story, she called around to the various hunting stores in Hilo and got the name of one of the hunters who had found Bessie Whitehall's remains. By the time she and Jim left for the Honolulu Airport, she had both hunters agreeing to meet them and take her and Jim in to where they found the remains.

Jim raised his fingers and counted down from five to zero. Go!

"This is Tawnie Takahashi coming to you from the site of the recent discovery of the remains of Bessie Whitehall, the daughter of a well-known sugar cane mill owner. It was late February, 1946. The war was over, servicemen were leaving the island for the Mainland, and Hilo was trying to return to normal. Then Bessie Whitehall went missing. I'm here to find out more."

Tawnie turned to two men dressed in camo hunting gear. Both of them stood a head above her petite frame. "I have with me Kelly Nagel of Mountain View and Jerad Chung of Hilo, the two hunters who found the body. Tell me, Mr. Nagel, what led you to this discovery?"

"Jerad stuck the pig with his arrow, so we were carefully following the blood trail to this stand of fern trees, when we heard it stop squealing. We thought it was going to attack, cuz they're smart like that, but instead, it just keeled over."

Chung added his own description of the story which could have gone on for quite a while, but Tawnie didn't want the interview to turn into a travelogue on the best place to hunt pig on the Big Island. She wasn't even sure if it was legal here.

"How long ago was this?"

"Funny you should ask. About two weeks ago. The cops told us to say nothing until they went public."

"Then what happened next?"

Chung looked surprised. "Found the bones on accident. We took the guts out of the pig to make it lighter fo' take back to town. Kelly here, put on his gloves and tossed the guts over there." Chung pointed to a large lava rock pocketed like the craters of the moon squeezed between two fifteen-foot tall *hapuu* ferns.

In front of the rock, Tawnie could tell that a rude pathway had been made, machetes cutting away the big fronds of neighboring *hapuu* and brush to widen the access. A piece of yellow crime tape swayed gently in the breeze.

"What did you see, Mr. Nagel?"

"Something smooth on the other side of the rock," Tawnie invited the men to go in ahead of her. She followed, stepping gingerly on a lava-rock path barely covered by soil. She was glad Jim told her to bring hiking boots before they left. As she looked behind the rock, she could see the area was cleared. She listened to the men describe how the poncho was placed and its condition.

"It must have been a shock to find a skull and some bones in it."

Nagel admitted that it was. "Thought it was old hunting gear, but Jerad here said the poncho looked much older, maybe military issue from the Vietnam period. We was surprised it dates back to WW II. "

"Anything particular stand out?"

"Not too much left, but one curious thing. There was some wire around the neck bones."

"We wrapped the poncho back immediately, marked the area with my bandana and hightailed it out to the road to get better phone service."

"Well, thank you gentlemen for showing me the site." Tawnie faced the camera, her microphone close to her chin. "I'll be investigating this story further and report later on it later this evening. In the meantime, this is Tawnie Takahashi, saying, Aloha from the Big Island of Hawaii."

Tawnie didn't get back into Hilo until two hours later. After she dropped Jim off at a hotel down on Banyon Drive, she drove her rental car up to her great-aunt Bee's place.

When Tawnie arrived, no one was home except for Bee's dog who was working up a storm of defense. *My fault*, Tawnie thought. *I should have followed up when she didn't answer my phone message earlier.* Tawnie walked around to the back of the house. It had a large backyard crowned by a *ulu* or breadfruit tree over twenty feet tall. She regretted putting her high heels back on. They sank into the rough grass as she walked over to the bench with the orchids. Further back there was a lime tree, two guava trees and a little green house.

"Auntie Bee?" No one answered, except the dog. Tawnie sighed. Now what? She looked up at the sky. It looked like one of the clouds was going to open up for a splash of Hawaiian sunshine.

"Can I help you?"

Tawnie turned around. On the other side of the line of ti plants that served as a fence between Bee's house and her next door neighbor, was a tall, young woman in a teal tank top and running shorts. Golden freckles covered her lightly tanned shoulders.

"Have you seen Bee Takahashi around?"

"Oh, you didn't hear. She had an accident this morning. She's in the hospital. They want to keep her overnight."

Tawnie's heart made a hard thump. "What happened?"

"We think she fainted or fell and hit her head. I found her over there and called 911 immediately. I stayed with her at the hospital while they checked her out." Suddenly, the woman put her hands over her mouth.

"Oh, my gosh. You're Tawnie Takahashi. On TV. I watch you all the time! I love how you sign off, 'This is Tawnie Takahashi saying, Aloha.'"

"And you are?"

"I'm Maile Horner. I'm Bee's neighbor." Maile stepped through the row of ti plants and walked over.

"I know your name," Tawnie said. "You're the historian my aunt told me about."

"Bee's your aunt? Oh, she's the loveliest person. I'm so sorry about what happened."

"Thank you. And thank you for going with her to the hospital." Tawnie clutched the strap on her hand bag. Her heels continued to sink into the grass. This was so unexpected, she wasn't sure what to do. "You don't happen to have a key to the house, do you?"

"Yes, I do. Shall I get it for you? You're welcome to come over while I get it." Maile looked over at the front sidewalk where Tawnie had dropped her luggage. "Can I get you something to drink?"

"That's very nice, but first I'm going to get out of these heels. They're killing me. Think the dog will be OK for a bit more? I hope she remembers me."

"Asami's always on duty, but she's really sweet. She'll be fine. I just fed her."

A few minutes later, Maile and Tawnie, wearing a pair of slippers borrowed from Bee's back porch, walked into Maile's kitchen. It reminded Tawnie immediately of Bee's plantation-style house and had probably been built in the early 1900s too, except Maile's kitchen was modern. It was full of light, and filled with the heavenly smell of wild ginger in a vase. High up on the ceiling, a gecko chirped his greeting.

"That's Fred, my house gecko," Maile said. "And this is one of my favorite places in the house."

"It's very nice." Tawnie looked around. In front of Maile's island counter, was the open space of her living room. Simply furnished with a rattan sofa, two chairs and coffee table, the 1930s fabric pattern of red hibiscus and palm leaves on the cushions further brightened the white room. Prints on the wall and family pictures on a tall rattan bookshelf completed the decorating efforts. "I don't think my Auntie Bee has changed anything in her place since she moved into the house in the 1960s,"

Maile laughed, "My grandmother was the same way."

"You have family here?"

"Oh, yes. My great-grandparents came here in 1908." She sighed. "But I grew up on the Mainland." Maile went to her refrigerator and poured out two glasses of filtered water. Back at the counter, she cut a lime and put a slice into each of the drinks. "Oh, here's the key." She slid it over, then raised her glass to Tawnie. "This is so cool. Never thought I'd have a celebrity in my kitchen. Would you like to sit at the counter for a minute or do you want to get into Bee's house? I'm sure you want to go see her right away."

Tawnie blushed at the compliment. *What's the matter with me?* No chance of acting haughty here. The *haole* girl was a fan, but underneath her gushing, there was something else Tawnie couldn't put her finger on. "I'll sit. It was a bumpy flight. I was just on Maui the other day."

"I saw that interview with Mrs. Yamamura. What a fascinating life."

"You liked it?" Now Tawnie was warming up to her. "We're running the third one on Hana tonight."

Maile sat down on one of the cushioned stools. "I love talking to seniors, learning about their experiences and how they dealt with life. It's a shame people put them in old folks' homes. Assisted living! More like, take-my-money living. I have always loved how Hawaii honors their elders. And that's one of the reasons I love history. There is so much in the past to teach us about today."

Suddenly Tawnie recognized the thing she couldn't put her finger on. This girl knew how to warm someone up for an interview. Was that a historian's skill, too? Tawnie chuckled, then grew serious as she sat down next to her.

"My auntie emailed me a couple of days ago about some letters you had. They talk about her sister Hillary."

"Oh, yes. The whole collection is being considered for acquisition, but funny you should mention them. Something strange happened around Bee's accident."

Tawnie's reporter instincts kicked in. She leaned in, wishing she had her Olympus recorder at hand. "What? What happened?"

"Just before she fell, some guy came to her door. Wanted to see those letters. When she said she had nothing, he pressed her. Bee told me at the hospital that the guy was getting too friendly for her comfort. Fortunately, her newspaper boy showed up."

"Then what happened?"

"The guy left."

"That's all?"

"Well, there was the headline on the local paper. Police identified some old bones found up above Hilo."

Tawnie nodded. "Bessie Whitehall. I read about it in the paper." *And why I'm here to make up for lost lead time for KWAI-5 News.* "What did Auntie Bee do?"

"Koa Makani— that's the newspaper guy's name— said she read the headline and started to wobble right away. Then she went down like a stone."

Tawnie rubbed her arms, feeling a chill coming on. Something wasn't right here. *Why would letters from 70 years ago be of interest to anyone?* "When you first showed my aunt these letters, did she mention her sister who was lost in the 1946 tsunami?"

"She did several times. Again yesterday afternoon as a matter of fact. Said she was thinking a lot about that time. The letters seemed to open up some things she hadn't thought about in years."

"She told me the same, too. Did my aunt say anything about a Joe Cameron?"

"Joe Cameron... Yes, she did. She also talked about another man. She was trying to recall his name. I have pictures of the USO Center on Coconut Island among the materials in that collection. That could help her recall. Just haven't shown her those yet."

"Where are the letters?" Tawnie didn't mean to be abrupt, but she had such an uneasy feeling about the stranger at Bee's door. She had done enough crime reporting to know that things just didn't happen. There was possibly a dangerous story here. A cover up?

"Don't worry. Part of the collection is at the museum. The rest are here at my house, and after this morning's excitement, I've hidden them away."

"Good. Don't talk about the collection to anyone. After I come back from visiting my aunt, I want to see them. Now I'd like to get into the house, calm Asami, and go. We can talk when I get back. I'll bring you something from town. You like plate lunch?"

"Love it."

"Well, then. We have a plan." Tawnie finished off her water. "*Mahalo nui loa* for looking after my auntie. I mean it."

"So, what's your take?" Kimo asked Annie as they left the Cameron residence. Annie was driving this time, keeping her speed low so the lava cinders on the private road didn't bang around under the cruiser's chassis.

"Long time *kamaina*. Lots of money, but not flashy." Annie lifted her chin at the pasture and trees as they passed them. "Knows how to pick a place."

Kimo took a swig of his bottled water. "Didn't you think it odd that the artwork wasn't taken? Those Pegge Hoppers are originals. Seen them in major shows, art books."

Annie smiled. "I wondered, too, but the thief was definitely focused on something particular." Annie slowed down as they came to the gate and prepared to enter the Hana Highway. "But why an album of pictures from long ago?"

"The picture in the frame, too."

Annie tapped the steering wheel. "Hmmm, while you were taking pictures, I talked to Mr. Cameron. He told me some stories about Hilo during WWII. He was stationed with the Army there. I asked him if he'd heard the news about the remains that were found in Hilo. When I said they had been identified as Bessie Whitehall, I thought he was shocked, but a little slow to answer. Said everyone had known about her going missing."

"Maybe it's time to take a closer look at this Joe Cameron." Kimo put his sunglasses on top of his head, then opened up the laptop. He searched for Joe— Joseph Camera—Maui— "Here's one. Joseph (Joe) Cameron of Pai'ia honored at the annual gathering of VFW in Honolulu. Though he served stateside in Hilo during World War II, Cameron was instrumental in training soldiers how to jump fully equipped into the water. Cameron, a native of Hilo and a strong swimmer, instructed soldiers preparing for action in the South Pacific using the well-known tower on Coconut Island. When asked about those days..." Kimo stopped. "It keeps going on."

"I remember that diving tower," Annie said. "Dived off it a few times myself." She gave the car some gas and headed back toward the little town of Pa'ia where she hoped they could take their lunch break. She was getting hungry.

Kimo found another article. "This looks interesting. The headline reads, 'Town turns somber as survivors remember the 1946 tsunami.'" Kimo continued. "Sixty-five years ago today, the little post-war town of Hilo was hit by a series of tidal waves that destroyed the buildings on the waterfront and wiped out the community of Shinmachi. Attending the ceremony was retired businessman Joseph Cameron of Pa'ia, Maui. When asked about that terrible day, Cameron said he was coming into town when the first wave hit. Recognizing it as a tsunami, he turned his car around and headed upland, warning others as he went. By the time he got uphill, his car was loaded. From there, they watched in horror as the second and third waves arrived. Later Cameron was part of the recovery efforts. When asked if he had lost someone he knew, he answered that he knew all of them. 'They were my neighbors and my friends,' he said. 'It's something you don't ever forget, but one especially broke my heart.'" Kimo stopped reading. "Article says Cameron didn't elaborate."

"Wonder what he was referring to?" Annie kept thinking about the look on Cameron's face when she mentioned Bessie Whitehall's name. "I'm positive he knew the Whitehall girl."

Kimo looked up. "But she couldn't have died in the tsunami. She was already dead. Newspapers accounts point to that."

"When we get back to the station, I'm going to call my father-in-law again."

***

Tawnie Takahashi put the photograph down and stared out the window. Her normally clear thinking while on the trail of a story was addled. It had been sixteen hours since she had flown into Hilo and discovered her Aunt Bee was in the hospital. Now after a rough night of tossing and turning in her aunt's guest room, Tawnie was going through the box of letters and pictures Maile Horner wanted her to see. She was sitting at Maile's kitchen counter where the contents of the cardboard box were laid out.

"Is that your aunt Hillary?" Maile asked. She put her finished plate lunch into the garbage and washed her hands at the sink.

"Yeah, yeah, though I never see her in a bathing suit or doing anything with family or friends. My grandfather told me all the family effects were lost in the tsunami. Pictures, heirlooms all washed away. Like the clock started all over again. All he had of his sister Hillary was her high school picture."

"She was pretty."

"Yes, she was." In the black-and-white photo, Hillary Takahashi was sitting on a lava rock wall. Tawnie immediately recognized it from Coconut Island. Her aunt wore a one piece bathing suit. Her hands rested on the wall as she leaned back. Her legs were crossed at the ankles. Pretty as a pin-up. She was laughing at whomever was taking the picture.

Tawnie turned the picture over. "USO Center, Hilo, 1945" was printed on the back.

"I don't know anything about this place," Tawnie said. For just a brief moment, a wave of sadness fell over her. *Auntie Hillary.* So young. Gone too soon. Was she in danger even then as Auntie Bee remembered?

"I can look into that." Maile dried her hands off and sat down next to Tawnie. "The Historical Society has pretty extensive material on the island. You know, I've only been with the Society for a few months. Before that, I lived in Edmonds, Washington, but I'm catching up." Maile picked out some more pictures. "She's in all of these."

"Who is this guy who sent you this material?" Tawnie spread the photographs out.

"Bradley Haines. His father, Eddie Haines, was stationed in Hilo during the war."

Tawnie tapped on her I-Pad. "I'm going to take notes."

The next photo showed Hillary with a group of friends standing at the entrance to a bridge. A large, half-moon sign over the entrance announced the name of the place beyond: the Mokuola USO. Underneath was the warning: "For servicemen only." A young man in an Army uniform stood at ease to the left with a rifle in hand. The group in the photo was a mix of girls and servicemen. One was a curly blonde. Tawnie turned the picture over and was relieved to see the names in written order. The blonde was Bessie Whitehall.

"The girl in the newspaper," Tawnie murmured.

"Definitely." Maile put a news clipping of the recent discovery of the bones next to the photo.

Tawnie squinted at the handwriting on the back of the photograph. Above the names were the words, "Having a great time at Hilo Bay." Another was hand printed "August 1945." She counted seven people in the group.

"Let's see. " Tawnie read out loud, "We have Eddie Haines, my aunt Hillary, Susanne Lee, Bessie Whitehall, Joe Cameron, Lily Palani, and Freddie Maiwela." Tawnie wrote the names down.

For the next few minutes, Tawnie and Maile went through each picture, many with scenes of places on Hilo Bay, the USO Commissary at Coconut Island and a volleyball court that Tawnie guessed was also at this USO place. Sometimes the photographs included servicemen about the town with no females accompanying them while others showed the same crowd of friends. After examining each photograph, Tawnie took a picture. In the last photograph in the collection, the friends were grouped into couples. The one couple Tawnie studied the most was Bessie Whitehall who appeared with someone who hadn't shown up in the pictures before. The young man was handsome with dark hair. He was bare-chested in a boxer-short swimming suit which showed off his lean, muscular physique. Around his neck he wore a medal. He had his arm around Bessie.

Tawnie immediately turned the picture over, grateful someone had taken the time to write the names down. So often, people forgot, leaving nameless faces to anyone's guess.

"My last day in Paradise, Nov 1945," it said, then named everyone in the group. The name of the stranger said "Hick, the old duffer."

Tawnie wondered what that meant. She made a note. "Anything else?"

"Well, there are the letters. The son who sent them for consideration seems to have done a nice job of selecting the ones that might be relevant to the war time period. They have good descriptions of life here in Hilo, the town, Haine's daily activities in the Army. Very little redacted."

"But you pulled out the ones for my Aunt Bee with the Takahashi family name."

"That's right," Maile picked up a folder and handed it over to Tawnie. "There are five. Apparently, Eddie Haines was good friends with that Joe Cameron in the pictures. It's odd, now that I think about it, Bessie Whitehall is mentioned in at least two of the letters."

"And my Auntie Hillary?"

"Yes. I—"

Tawnie's cellphone on the counter vibrated. "Excuse me." She listened and then said, "I'll be there right away." She tapped off. "That was the nurse's station at the hospital. Auntie Bee is being released. I've got to go pick her up. Hold down the fort, will you?"

Annie and Kimo got back to the Kahului Police Station and checked in with their boss, Captain K.J. Honeywell. Before she became the commanding officer of the Maui Island Police Department, Honeywell had served ten years with the military police on Oahu and another ten as a civilian police officer on Maui. A slight woman of Portuguese descent, her stature belied her strength of character and command. She wore her brown hair pulled back in a tight bun.

"Learn anything?" Honeywell asked as she sat at her desk. Stacks of files surrounded her computer.

"Victim's sending us a list of items that were stolen. Place was ransacked in the main room and an office, but according to him, nothing of value was taken."

"The old man had plenty valuable paintings and artwork," Kimo added "but the thief just left them there."

"No one hurt, yeah?" Honeywell asked. With a wave of her hand, she invited them to sit down.

"No. Nobody home at the time." Kimo eased onto one of the chairs facing Honeywell. Annie followed. Sitting at attention, she opened her notebook.

"Glad to hear." Honeywell pushed away from her desk. "Mr. Cameron is one good man."

"You know him?" Annie was surprised that Honeywell had never said anything about that before.

"Yeah, yeah. Tell me what you found. Think there was more than one intruder?"

"Not what we could tell," Annie said. "But we'll see. After Kimo took pictures, we dusted for prints. We just sent the evidence to processing."

From there, Annie and Kimo went on to describe the scene, with Annie noting one curious thing about the Cameron house. In the large family room, there was a window that looked back toward the ocean. All the other windows in the room looked away.

Honeywell stood up. She didn't seem surprised. "He's a tsunami survivor in his own way. Let me know about any follow up."

Kimo took off, but Annie stayed by the door to Honeywell's office. Since coming back from bereavement leave, she had spoken to Honeywell only once.

"How're you doing, Officer Moke?" Honeywell went over to the window and watered one of her plants.

"I'm fine. Glad to be back on duty, sir. Gives me something to focus on and now with David—gone—I need the work. Kid's camp fees and all that."

Honeywell looked up. "How are Kaylie and Evan doing?"

"They want to be around me all the time. Kaylie jumps when she hears a helicopter." Annie sighed. "I know it will take time."

"David was a good officer when he was on the force, but I thought he was equally fine when he started to work at the national park."

Annie ran a finger down the door frame. "He was and so happy. Even though, he grew up in Hilo, he said he fell in love with Haleakala, Kaupo Gap and the silver swords. I suppose—"

Honeywell came over to her. "It was a terrible accident. We all miss him terribly."

Annie cleared her throat. "Thank you, sir. If I may, I'll get on to my report."

"I appreciate that."

Report. Annie felt like she might fail on that point with the Cameron case. Her latest idea about him might be complicated if Honeywell knew the man personally. Annie decided to speak up anyway.

"There is one other thing," Annie said. "Did you see the news this morning about the seventy-year-old remains found in Hilo?"

Honeywell studied Annie. "The *haole* girl. Someone say she was from an old sugar cane family on the Big Island."

"I think our break-in victim knew her, but was trying to hide it."

"Why you think that?"

Annie shrugged. "He seemed shocked about the news, but evasive."

"What do you want to do, Detective? Mind you, Mr. Cameron is an important man."

Annie stood her ground. "Important men can do bad things like everyone else."

Honeywell went back to her desk and brushed down her police uniform jacket. "Again, what do you to want to do?"

"I'd like to contact my father-in-law, Captain Jerry Moke at the Hilo Police Department. Get more information on the discovery and see where Joe Cameron fits in. He was stationed in Hilo during the war. See if he is connected to the woman they found."

"Alright. Keep me posted. In the meantime, get that list of stolen items in."

"Thank you, sir. I'll log it in as soon as possible as well as anything else I find." Annie thanked Honeywell again and slipped out.

On the way back to her cubicle, she caught up with Kimo drinking coffee in the station's little kitchen. "Honeywell says we can look into that Hilo case as long as it relates to our vic in Pa'ia."

"Girl, why are you in such a hurry? Why don't you like the guy?"

"I never said that. Joe Cameron probably is a nice guy." Annie rubbed her arms. "I just don't like hearing about some girl being dumped out in the wild like a piece of garbage. I don't care how many years ago it happened." She adjusted the clip holding her hair back and smiled. "Better get the report logged in. Honeywell wants to see it."

"I wouldn't worry about today. She's going to be over on the coast with her golf pro brother."

"What's up with that? Thought she stay Kahului side."

"It's opening day. Redesigned golf course at the Hale Kawai Hotel. They're having one big luau."

"Just what Maui needs." Annie wrinkled her nose.

"A luau?"

Annie batted Kimo's arm. "No. Another golf course."

"I know, but I got friends who like play over there. Told me this company makes golf courses all over the world. Got endorsements of the PGA and US Open. Attracts big names to tournaments. They're excited about the new design."

"Well, while Honeywell's gone, we better stay busy. I'll check out any details Jerry has about the Whitehall case in Hilo. See if the Cameron name comes up in any of the investigation they are doing."

"And I'll check and see if any new cases have been assigned to us. You going to be OK this evening with the kids gone?"

"Uh-huh."

"I take that like one maybe. Why don't you come over tonight? I don't blame you going back to an empty house. Ronnie's making bean soup."

"Mahalo, Kimo. That would be very nice, though I'm not sure what sort of company I'd make."

"What are friends for? You're my partner and the Fortes family is your *ohana*."

***

"Auntie Bee's still resting," the voice whispered. "Could you call back later?" There was a click, then the creak of a floorboard.

Instantly, Bee Takahashi opened her eyes and sat up in her bed. The move made her head hurt, but she could see out into her kitchen where she caught her great-niece Tawnie moving back and forth like a caged tiger. *When you get so grown up, Tawnie -san?*

It seemed only yesterday Tawnie was a student at the Hongwanji Mission School up in Honolulu. Now she was an important reporter on Honolulu's KWAI-5 News channel.

Taking time to help her auntie. Bee felt both pride and the comforting warmth of love spread through her. Asami must have wanted some of that as she paw-crawled her way to Bee's lap, her feathery tail wagging. Bee leaned down for the dog's kiss, then blinked away the slight dizziness she felt. She hope the headache would go away soon.

"That you, auntie?" Tawnie seemed to get to the open door faster than Bee expected.

"You like some ice tea?"

"Yeah, yeah." Bee carefully scooted to the edge of the bed and put on her glasses. Bracing her arms as she was taught at the senior center a few years back, she swung her legs over. She felt for her slippers on the floor. "What time is it?"

"Noon. You sure you want to get up? The doctor at the hospital said you should rest at least one more day."

Bee patted the air with her hands. "I'm fine." She grabbed the edge of her night table and stood up. Asami jumped down and faced her with her head cocked. "OK, OK, I'll go sit in the kitchen." Bee felt the gauzy bandage that covered the stitches on her head. "Oh, my hair is so bad. How many?"

"Doctor said, 'Four.' I told him you had a hard head. He agreed."

"Hmmph. That Doctor Greene. He was one of my best math students in class." Bee sighed then waved Tawnie off as she made her way into the kitchen and to the aluminum-edged kitchen table. A garage sale rescue years ago, Bee always liked it as it reminded her of the red linoleum-topped one Mama had in the family apartment before the tsunami.

"Now what else can I get you?" Tawnie said once Bee was sitting down. She brought Bee a chilled glass of ice tea, then sat down herself.

"You've done enough already. *Mahalo* for coming down."

"I'm glad I did. What is going on, auntie? You were still pretty groggy last night when I saw you at the hospital. Who was this guy that scared you?"

"Wasn't scared. Just wanted him to go away." Bee kept her face composed. She didn't want Tawnie -san to see that she *was* scared.

"But did you ever see him before?"

Bee shrugged making her sleeveless muumuu slip off her bony shoulder. "At first, I thought I did," she said as she pulled the muumuu back on, "but then I don't know for sure. The paper scared me though."

"Why's that?" Tawnie leaned over and put her hand on Bee's.

Bee gripped it and sighed. Her head ached around the stitches. She felt so old and tired. "So long ago, but like I told you, I'm remembering things. Like Bessie. They found Bessie?"

"That's what they say. I haven't talked to the police yet, but I intend to find out more." Tawnie let go of Bee's hands. "Your neighbor, Maile, said the man was asking about some letters. He meant the letters that she had, right?"

"Yeah, yeah. Though I tell him I didn't know what he was talking about."

"I read one of the letters. But mostly, I looked at the pictures that she had." Tawnie got up and went into the living room. She came back with a large envelope. After sitting down, she pulled out photographs.

Bee's mouth went dry. "Oh, that's my sister, Hillary." Bee's hands balled into fists as she put them over her mouth. Sudden tears flowed over them.

Tawnie rubbed Bee on her back. "Do you recognize where she is?"

"That old USO place on Coconut Island."

"Did you actually go there?"

"Couple of times. Maybe more. I think they had special days when soldiers could bring lady friends. I remember one time I went with Hillary and Bessie."

Tawnie pulled out the group picture with Hillary and Bessie. "That Joe? The one you said was arguing with Hillary?"

Bee nodded slowly. She had forgotten how handsome Joe Cameron was. As fit as a fireman. An image of him diving off the tower on Coconut Island flashed before her. Bee smiled remembering how she had thought he was like Tarzan in the picture shows. He was a strong swimmer, lean with a deep chest. He seemed to look out of the group photo at her, but she didn't fear him. He was always so kind to her. There had to be a reason he and Hillary were fighting. Yet, was that why she was scared? *Don't tell Mama you saw us together.* No, my sister was not scared. She was terrified.

"Auntie, do you remember who this guy is with Bessie?" Tawnie tapped the stranger in the photograph dubbed "Hick, the duffer."

Bee stared at the man in the picture. An image drifted down to her. She must have been around ten. She was at the counter at the concession stand at the USO Mokuloa Club on Coconut Island. The building had once been the house of the island's caretaker. Hillary had just bought her a soda and they were stepping away to join some of Hillary's friends on the wooden boardwalk that went around the house. Next to the stand were some low-growing palms, their fronds swaying in the slight breeze. Behind them was a tall man with dark hair. He was with Bessie, holding her hand. The palms moved back and forth, sometimes hiding the couple like the flickering images in a flip book. But Bee saw him put his hands on Bessie's waist and pull her in. He tried to kiss her. Bessie leaned back, turned her head away. Next time Bee saw clearly, Bessie had twisted away.

"Joe!" Bessie called and ran up to the boardwalk where Joe Cameron was standing with some other soldiers with towels draped over their bare shoulders. She put her hand on his arm as if for protection.

"Why Hillary, you brought little Beatrice," Bessie said.

Bee looked back into the palms. The man was seething, but he came up to the group with a smile on his face.

"Auntie Bee?" Tawnie-san's hand on her shoulder brought Bee back. "Do you remember the name Hick? That's the name written on the back.

Bee shook off the memory and lifting her eyes glasses to see close, picked up the photograph. They all looked so happy. "Yeah, yeah. He was friends with Bessie and Joe."

"But do you remember his full name?"

Bee shook her head. "One time I heard someone say Hickerson. That's all."

"Hick Hickerson?"

"Tawnie   -san,   I   don't   remember."

"OK, Annie," Jerry Moke said. Over Annie's cellphone his voice sounded tinny. "This is what we know from Dr. Clark's investigation of the remains found up in the Hilo Forest."

"Just a second." *Dr. Clark, the UH forensic anthropologist*, Annie reminded herself. She sat down at her kitchen table and took out her notebook. "Ready. How was he able to identify her?"

"Dental records. Started with local dentists. Dr. Mason Fong was one of two dentists from the 1940s still practicing up to ten years ago— his grandson took over after that— so there were records. That match came up pretty easily. Just wasn't prepared for the significance."

"How's that?"

"Well, for one, she was one famous missing person case. Very rare back then. But what I didn't know is that Bessie Whitehall was friends with my grandmother, Lily Palani Moke. Tutu passed three years ago. I'd love to know what she knew about the disappearance, how she felt."

"Any idea of how Whitehall died?"

"She was murdered. That's what the forensic guy said. Funny, what is left behind when someone dies. Clark says the WWII Army poncho she was found wrapped in was perfect for preserving a good deal of her skeleton. The soil helped too. Good drainage, low accumulation of biological matter— think he means plant stuff."

Annie shifted in her chair. "So how do you think was she murdered?"

"Telephone wire. There were fragments around her neck. Clark thinks it came from a military type used for communication back then— guess he should know as he's worked all over the Pacific identifying WWII G.I. remains — he says copper preserves extremely well. The rubber coating over the copper wire had rotted, exposing it to the body. The neck bones around it were intact. He could see damage to them. After all this time."

"That's pretty cool work."

"Clark's the best. I think the thing that really sealed her identity was strands of blonde hair found next to the skull. Turns out copper preserves hair too."

"Does the vic still have family in the area?"

"There are a couple great nephews over on the Kona-Kailua side. We've been in touch with them, but they don't know a lot. They're looking through what family mementos they have, but don't expect much. Said that branch of Whitehall family was troubled. Father abusive. Sugar mill destroyed in the tsunami. Mother committed suicide a year after their daughter went missing. Bessie Whitehall was their only child."

"Oh, so sorry for the family." Annie jotted the information down. "Yesterday, I interviewed a man over in Pa'ia. He was stationed in Hilo during the war. Grew up there. I think he knew the Whitehall girl. Just acted funny when I mentioned the discovery of the remains."

"Really? What's his name?"

"Joe Cameron. Joseph Cameron."

Over the phone, Annie could hear her father-in-law suck his breath in. "No kidding? I haven't heard that name since Tutu died. She used to tell me stories about him and her *ohana* of high school friends that hung together during the war."

"She knew Cameron?"

"Yeah, yeah. Whenever he was in the news, she say, that's my boy Joe. She say he's doing really good but that you'd nevah know the tsunami just about wiped him out. Went to the Mainland for a few years. Went to school, came back. But rarely came back to Hilo."

"Sure his leaving wasn't about the disappearance of the Whitehall girl?"

"I'll look into that, but it's funny you're asking all this. I think Bessie Whitehall might have been a part of Tutu's group of friends too."

"That would put Cameron in with Bessie. Are any of your grandmother's other *ohana* friends still alive?" Annie wrote the names down as Moke spoke.

"Suzie Fong is still going. Played bridge with Tutu all the time. Back then she was Suzie Lee. Freddie Maiwela was another, but he's in hospice. Could be gone by now. Oh, there was another girl in the group, but she died in the big tsunami."

"Do you remember her name?"

"I do. Hillary Takahashi. Get this. She's related to Tawnie Takahashi, that KWAI-5 News reporter."

"Seriously?" Annie put her pencil down. "How did you find that out, Perry?"

"Easy. She called me. I'm meeting with her this afternoon. She's looking into the Bessie Whitehall case, too. Says she has an angle on it."

"She's in Hilo already?"

"Yeah, yeah. She told me she has a great aunt here."

"Wonder what her aunty knows?"

"Hard to say. For sure, we stay busy with this cold case cuz people all of a sudden are asking questions when we don't have answers. A lot of emotion."

Annie and Perry talked for a bit longer, then said goodbye. Annie stood up and stretched, then padded barefoot out to her back porch, coffee in hand. LaBaie trotted out beside her. She laid down next to her with a thump and groan when Annie paused to drink her brew at the porch rail.

Annie chuckled. "I'll take you for a walk in bit, girl. Just need to collect myself." She leaned against the rail and put her cup on the wide top. She closed her eyes and let the scent of *pikake* growing in the back calm her. *I wore it in my hair when I got married.*

Her home in Sprecklesville was set on a tight lot. Her grandparents bought the property in the early 1950s. When Hawaii was a territory. A simple plantation style home, today it was surrounded by homes of wealthy residents, some longtime locals, others *malihini*. Here, memories of life with her grandparents, stories of her mother and uncles growing up here and for the last nine years memories with David, this little place was far richer. The morning throbbed with the calls of mynah birds in the tall ohia tree at the back and a lone dove cooing endlessly as it bobbed around in the dry grass in search for food.

Annie touched the diamond ring on her finger and made a circle around its beveled edges. *Shall I go or stay, David? People say don't do anything for a year. But your father offered. Give me sign.*

When her cell phone rang just inside the door, Annie wasn't sure if that was David answering or just Kimo calling her to work.

"So what exactly are these letters?" Captain Jerry Moke asked. His voice wasn't very friendly.

Must have seen my interview with the hunters, Tawnie Takahashi thought as she sat in Moke's office, door closed. Tawnie noted the mix of family and professional pictures and certificates on the wall. *Grandkids? Golf trophy?* She made a mental note to look into the history of the Hilo Police Station and see if it had a recovery role in the aftermath of the 1946 tsunami. She responded to Moke in her crisp reporter's voice.

"They're letters written by a *malihini* who was stationed here in Hilo during WWII. They have some nice details about life during that time along with some pictures. But there is something else. This serviceman who wrote the letters, Eddie Haines, was part of a group of friends. Bessie Whitehall, your murder victim, was one of them."

When Moke leaned in, Tawnie thought, *Good. Maybe he'll forgive me,* but Moke kept his police captain tone of voice and asked if Bessie Whitehall was mentioned.

"Numerous times," Tawnie said. "And there are pictures of her, too."

"Where are these letters and pictures now?"

"They are in the process of being acquired by the Big Island Historical Society."

"You say there are pictures of Whitehall in this group? Who identified her?"

"My Auntie Bee. Beatrice Takahashi."

"Bee Takahashi? I know your aunt. Taught school at Waiakea Elementary for years. Always hear nice things about her."

"Thank you. I think you ought to know that there are pictures of a woman named Lily Palani in the package too. My historian contact did a search and said her married name was Moke. Thought you might be related."

Moke tilted back in his office chair. "Huh. My *tutu*." Moke frowned. He seemed to Tawnie far away in thought. She brought him back with snap.

"Someone came to my auntie's house yesterday in search of the letters. Thought she had them and scared her."

Moke sat upright again. "He asked specifically for them?"

"Seemed to know that they existed."

"Get any description of the person?"

"Auntie Bee said he looked familiar, but wasn't sure if he was a former student. He was a middle-aged man with brown hair with bits of gray in it. Medium height."

"Local? *Haole?*"

"Hmm, local. Bee said she was too busy looking for a way out and didn't pay much more attention to him. I had to work hard to get her to recall details."

"I wonder if I should bring the collection in as evidence."

"Any reason why?" Tawnie felt herself bristling. It was *her* story and she wanted to be the one who followed all the details.

Moke looked point blank at her. "That's why you're here or do you have something you want to share?"

Tawnie knew she sounded defensive, but her whole purpose for coming here felt like it was being hijacked. "If you're asking about my interview with the hunters, I thought the public should know. And I'll continue to report on the case, but I thought you should be aware of the letters. That's sharing."

"But you want this story."

"Of course. It's big news in more ways than you know because there is something else." Tawnie went on to tell him about why she had come down to Hilo in the first place. Not just the breaking news story 70 years in the making, but because of her aunt's re-awakened memories of the days before the tsunami. Tawnie talked about how the local historian, Maile Horner, had contacted Bee, wondering if she was related to the Hillary Takahashi in the letters and pictures. Then she described how after checking on Bee in the hospital yesterday, she'd met up with Maile yesterday to go over the pictures.

"The friends all seemed to hang out at the USO Center on Coconut Island before it closed at the end of the war," Tawnie said.

"How is your aunt?"

"She's home now."

"So sorry for what happened. Good to know she's OK." Moke seemed to relax. "Want some coffee? Should have asked earlier."

"That would be nice." *Though I could go for a beer at the end of the day if this keeps up.*

Moke got up and made her a cup of Kona coffee with what looked like a shiny new K-cup coffee machine and brought it to her. "Now since we are sharing," he said. "This group of friends my *tutu* was in. Was there a Joe Cameron in it?"

Tawnie kept her face still. *How would he know about that?* "As a matter of fact, there was. My aunt was a little girl then, but remembers him."

"Really?"

"My aunt Hillary was part of that group, too." Tawnie paused. "She died in the tsunami."

Moke grew silent. Finally, he spoke. "Tutu talked about that terrible day. Lost many of her friends. For a while, the details of the events of that time seemed to have been forgotten. The people just moved on. Rebuilt. The 1946 tsunami doesn't begin to match the thousands of people lost in the 2005 Asian tsunami, but it did wipe out the waterfront with many lives lost. Biggest tsunami of the 20th century."

"But you wanted to know about Joe Cameron."

"Yeah, yeah. He might be a suspect in Whitehall's murder."

"Can you tell me why?"

"Ms. Takahashi, we have no working relationship."

"But maybe we do. People we love were in Bessie's *ohana*. We're like family." Tawnie knew she was pushing this, but she wanted in. "Look," she continued. "The Bessie Whitehall story is newsworthy. My boss would be thrilled, but there is something going on that is more important to me. The letters, photos, and identification of Whitehall's remains have stirred my aunt's memories. She believes her sister didn't die in the tsunami. She thinks she was dead already."

"What gives her that idea?"

"She says that after Whitehall went missing, Hillary acted scared. Now someone wants those papers really bad."

"Do you have a list of the names of people in that group?"

"Better yet, I have a photo." Tawnie laid a photocopy of the group picture on the desk. "That's my aunt Hillary. That's Bessie Whitehall and Joe Cameron."

"And my *tutu*. Humph. She never say how cute she was. Who's that with Bessie?"

"Uh, Bee says she can't remember," Tawnie lied. Well, a half lie. Bee really didn't remember much. This is something she wanted to pursuit on her own.

Moke turned the photocopy over in his hands. "Thanks for the information. May I keep it?"

"Please."

"Anything else?"

Tawnie paused. "There is one thing I'd like to know. I wouldn't have the heart to ask in my aunt's presence— she's been through enough already— I need to know what happened to the bodies of the tsunami victims. Was that a police matter? Could there be pictures?"

"Since we're working on a professional relationship here, what is your reason?"

"It's a theory, but what if there were two murders? What if my great aunt was killed because she saw something or knew something about Bessie Whitehall's disappearance?"

"What evidence do you have?"

"Only that Bee says that a few weeks before the tsunami came she was worried about her sister acting so spooky. She started following her around." Tawnie went on to describe how Hillary and Joe Cameron met secretly. "Yet two days before the tsunami, Bee said she saw Hillary and Joe Cameron arguing down by Coconut Island. Later, back at their home, Hillary told Bee not to tell their mother she had been seen with him."

"Did she say why they were arguing?"

"No. But when Bee saw her, she was crying."

Moke seemed to absorb this information. The room got quiet while he mulled it over. *A little too dramatic*, Tawnie thought. Somewhere else in the small building, she could hear a police scanner squawk. It reminded her that she'd better send something to her boss Denny at the TV station and post her tweets for the day.

Finally, Moke spoke. "I think we can work together, Ms. Takahashi. But first, I want you to promise not to release any more information that will hurt my investigation of the Whitehall murder. It's now a cold case gone active. I can give you some new details about the case that could be newsworthy and I think that it would be OK if you report on her connection to that USO Center."

Tawnie was irritated at the restraints he was applying on her own investigation, but agreed. "Alright, what details do you have?"

"Well, you already know about the phone wire around her neck, but among Whitehall's remains, our ME found a small round brass tag, the kind used back in the day at clubhouses—maybe used when someone checked out a towel at that USO Center. On it was stamped 'USO' and the name 'Cameron.' I'd like you to keep that private until we get the evidence we need."

"You going to arrest Joe Cameron?"

"No, just would like to talk to him. I'm working with the Maui Police on that."

"And where do I find records about the victims of the tsunami?"

"The Dodo Funeral Home did a lot of the work for that. Might be in their records from the funerals they did. But for starters, there is someone you can talk to in person."

"Who's that?"

"Marty Chee. He's been retired from the Fire Department for years, but he was new in the department the spring the tsunami came. Credited for rescuing many survivors caught in the debris field as well as pulling victims out and arranging for collection. Oh, sorry. Didn't mean to sound crass. Do you know where they found your auntie?"

"Just south of Coconut Island. My grandfather said Hillary was caught in the debris field. Not swept out like so many of the others." Tawnie turned away and blinked back unexpected tears.

"Think that's where Marty did a lot of his rescue work."

"Would your local ME have pictures?"

"Possibly. We do try to hold records for as long as possible." Moke wrote down a name and phone number on a sticky note and handed it to Tawnie. "Good luck."

Tawnie put it into her notebook. "*Mahalo*, Captain Moke." Knowing the interview was over she stood up. "Oh, here's my card in case you get any new information."

"And here's mine." Moke scribbled something on the back of his. "My direct line. I'm sure you'll share what you find."

"Of course."

"Where are you off to now?"

"Thought I might do a half round of golf," Tawnie lied. "My grandfather used to talk about your municipal golf course here. Then I'll see how my Auntie Bee is doing." At least that part was true. She would check out the golf course and see if she could get a member list.

"Well, if you are into golf and have the time, you should try see the Hale Ke'aloha Golf Course on the Kahala side. At least look at it. Has one fancy layout done by the Hickerson Design Corps a couple of years ago. Tough and spectacular at the same time."

Tawnie's heart jumped about four times. "Hickerson Design Corps. What's that?"

"Surprised you don't know. One of the top companies designing golf courses in the world. Just opened a new one on Maui."

"Guess I didn't pay attention. *Mahalo* again for your help." Tawnie offered her hand to Moke. When he shook it, she prayed he couldn't feel her   excitement   in   it.

Chapter 13

"Are you sure you should be doing this Bee?" Maile Horner said as they drove down toward town. "I thought you were supposed to rest."

Bee tapped the passenger side window in time to the soft, slack-key music on the car radio. "I'm fine. Thanks for taking me to see Suzie. Wasn't ready to drive myself."

"No problem, but I am worried about you."

"I'm fine."

"Is it OK to ask if Mrs. Fong lost family in the tsunami, too?"

"No, they got out, but their restaurant on Kamehameha Avenue was destroyed. They rebuilt right after, but it got wiped out in the 1960 tsunami. Gratefully no one was lost either time. Those 1960 waves came all the way from Chile. Oh, there's the street we want."

Maile turned off the main road and headed up a quiet lane from which several roads led off to homes built in the early 1970s. High grass, lime and papaya trees dotted the sides of the lane, but down the roads, Bee knew the yards were neat.

"There. Turn there, please," Bee said. Her heart pumped as she remembered the time when this development had opened up. Her dear George had been one of the builders. At one time, they thought of living here, but both liked their old style plantation home and their back acreage. They remained in the house she lived in now. *Over 50 years.*

"Which address, auntie?"

Bee smiled when Maile said that. The girl was coming around. "8-0-2 Uilani."

"I see it. There's a car in the driveway."

"Park on the side. No traffic 'cept for that mongoose over there." They both watched the slender brown animal slink down into the grass near the house next door. "Sneaky."

When they came up the concrete walkway, Bee said not to bother at the front door. Suzie liked to be in her kitchen in the back where she could look out on her flowers and trees. "She'll be at her kitchen table. She does Sudoku to start her day."

"If she's one of Hillary's friends, she must be ninety or something. How old is she?"

"Ninety-one. Still lives at home. Drives. Daughter comes by once a day to check, but Suzie stay busy with all her clubs."

They went around the side of the ranch-style house following a path of lava cinder lined with ti plants. A plumeria tree full of pink flowers beckoned at the back. They were nearly to the corner when they heard shuffling and then a crash and a sharp cry. Bee picked up her pace, annoyed that her leg was more temperamental since her fall at her house. She arrived at the lanai and the sliding door to the kitchen just in time to see a man down on his knees next to the prone body of Suzie Lee Fong on the floor. He appeared to be slapping her cheeks as if to revive her, but Bee could see blood slowly spreading around the elderly woman's head and neck.

"Oh," Bee said. Maile screamed.

The man looked up, his face white with shock. He stared at Bee, then scrambled to his feet and ran out the front door. Bee swayed, then steadied. It was the same man who had come to her house.

"Oh, Maile-san, please help me get into the house."

Maile jumped up on the lanai and pulled at the door. It gave way after a couple of tugs. "I'm calling 911. Go see if you can help her."

With some effort, Bee knelt down to see if Suzie was still breathing. Her eyes were open and she tracked Bee's face. "Bee. Little sista—" Suzie tried to say more, but began to cough. Bee was relieved when Maile joined her and pressed a kitchen towel against the wound on the back of Suzie's head.

"The paramedics are coming," Maile said. "What do you think he was looking for?"

Suzie stared at the counter on the kitchen island.

"Here, Auntie, you hold the towel," Maile said. "I'll look." The young woman got up and spread out the papers on top of the counter. "I see the morning paper, her Sudoku page, and a shopping list— Hold on, there's a file under here." She picked it up and showed it to Bee. It was marked WAR TIME FRIENDS with a black felt pen, but it was empty. "This what he came for?" Maile asked.

Suzie didn't answer. She lay still on the floor and gripped Bee's hand. Looking down, Bee was startled by how frail her old friend was, how her bony shoulders stuck out of her gray, mama-san patterned dress and how the blue veins in her hands throbbed unsteadily beneath her paper-thin skin. But now the grip was weakening.

Bee knew then that Suzie was dying and there was nothing she could do but hold her hand. Just like Suzie and all of Hillary's friends had held her hand after the tsunami. Bee had been in the hospital for months and they had come every day to the hospital to cheer a little girl who had lost schoolmates and family. Bee's eyes teared up and her heart jammed up in her throat so she couldn't speak.

"Thank God. I think the ambulance is here," Maile said, but Bee didn't hear her. The tsunami was coming again to tear away the life of another. *I should be grateful that Suzie lived a long, good life after the tsunami,* Bee thought. *But you were Hillary's friend and all I've had to help me cling to her memory.* Bee's tears dropped onto the elderly woman's face and mingled with hers. Suzie was gone by the time the EMTs were at the back door.

***

Tawnie Takahashi sat in her rental car in the Hilo Police Station parking lot and punched "Hickerson Design Corps" into her smartphone. Immediately, several choices came up, the most recent being an article about the opening of the new golf course on Maui. But Tawnie wanted to know about the organization and went to the company's website. A brightly-colored page appeared with a banner showing a golf course in some exotic location place. South Africa? The company's headquarters was listed in California. Tawnie looked at the sidebar and saw a picture of a man in his early fifties. She squinted at the name underneath. Sammy Braga, not Hickerson. Disappointed, she clicked on the tab that said HISTORY and found what she wanted.

As she scrolled through the article, a story emerged. The company had been formed in 1952 in Los Angeles by semi-pro golfer Thomas G. Hickerson after a dismal round of golf at a private course. A graduate in landscape architecture, Hickerson set out to design a course that would be challenging and beautiful. Tawnie skipped the rest of the article which sounded more like a windy brag fest, but she did discover that Hickerson had designed several golf courses in Hawaii. One at Princeville on Kauai, two on Maui, and one on the Big Island. Useful information for further investigation, but most important, Tawnie was sure she had found "The Duffer." Still, she needed more for confirmation.

She searched the website for a picture of Hickerson, but found mostly photos of golf courses. Some featured famous golfers at various golf courses designed by the company— Arnie Palmer, Jack Nicholson and others— all of them winners of the Masters and the PGA. There was one picture of Hickerson with Bob Hope, holding some sort of trophy, but from his hairstyle and the cut of his clothes, it appeared to have been taken in the 1990s. *How old was Hickerson now?* Tawnie wondered. She took a screenshot and saved it for later comparison.

She went back to a general search of his name on the Web and came up with several articles. For the first time, she found a reference to the nickname, "Hick." Thomas G. Hickerson had to be the man in the old group photograph and the man Bee remembered seeing with Bessie Whitehall.

"Drat," she said out loud. To get this right, she needed one more thing. Hickerson's service record. She couldn't access the New Generation Identification (NGI) program developed by the FBI, but she had a friend in the Honolulu Police Department who could. She punched in his phone number and got an answer right away.

"Honolulu Police, Officer Ishikawa speaking. How may I help you?"

"Hi Mel, this is Tawnie."

"Tawnie Takahashi, fearless reporter. Howzit? Or shouldn't I ask?"

"You can ask. I'm on assignment on the Big Island looking into the Whitehall case. You know the one. Gone girl— 70 years ago."

"Yeah, yeah. Anything to share?"

"Well, I just spent the last forty minutes with Captain Moke of the Hilo Police trying to learn more. It's definitely murder. "

"I know Jerry Moke," Mel said. "How did they determine that?"

"Special forensic anthropologist from UH Manoa studied the remains at the site and later at the ME's office. Said she was strangled with phone wire. There's a military connection somehow."

"So what you want from me?"

Tawnie could hear Ishikawa's office chair creak as he leaned back. He had a special one made for him out of koa. The wood was heavy, he said, but the chair was good for his spine.

"I need to have you look up a military record on your NGI."

"What's the name? "

Tawnie hesitated, then said, "Thomas Hickerson. There's a 'G' for the middle initial." She held her breath wondering if he knew the name. Apparently not. "Think he was in the Naval Air Reserve or something."

"Give me about 15 minutes and I'll get back to you."

"Thanks, Mel. When I get back on island, I'll meet you at that Thai place you like so much."

"No gifts. Remember. Though I do like Swimming Rama."

They hung up at the same time. Tawnie punched in a saved number and immediately had her boss Denny at KWAI-5 News on the phone.

"Hey girl, got something for me?"

"Well, there are some new details about Whitehall's background during WWII. I've got Jim shooting video down at an island near Liliuokalani Park. There was a USO club there for servicemen. Whitehall and her friends went there often. Putting together some names."

"When's the next time you can post?"

"I'm going to meet him later today down at Coconut Island. I've got one picture of the old USO place for the news story. Gonna explore what it looks like today. Have a few interviews lined up."

"How's your auntie?"

Hmmm. Tawnie wasn't sure what to tell him without giving away any of the active police investigation. "She's fine. Giving me some good details."

"Well, get it out as soon as you can. Live report tonight?"

"Sure. I'll have enough for the short one. I'll be in touch."

Tawnie leaned back in her car's seat. Moke's coffee wasn't quite enough to wake her up. Sudden activity in the police parking lot did though. Several cars pulled out and took off down the street with lights flashing and sirens screaming full blast.

A police officer tapped on her window. It was Captain Moke. Tawnie quickly lowered the window.

"What's going on?" she asked.

Moke put his hands on the windowsill and leaned in. "There's been a homicide. Sad to say, one of my favorite ladies, widow of one of our past mayors, Mrs. Susan Fong. I think you know her as one of the names on that photograph you showed me. Suzie Lee." Moke frowned. "There isn't something you're holding back from me, is there?"

"No," Tawnie said with confidence.

"Well, I'm going to assign a police officer to Mr. Maiwela, the remaining member of the group."

"What about Joe Cameron?"

"A team from the Maui Police Department plans to question him, but someone has to be working with him. He can't be on two islands at the same time." Moke cleared his throat. "If things worsen, I may assign someone to your auntie. She was one of two who discovered Mrs. Fong."

"Auntie Bee? She was there? She's supposed to be at home."

"Looks like a Ms. Horner drove her there."

Tawnie's normally cool facade slipped. "Please tell me Bee's alright."

"Shaken. Very upset. But she's doing as well as can be expected."

"Can I go see her?"

Moke nodded to a cruiser loading up with a couple of policemen. "Officer Greene is going up there now."

"Do they know who did it?"

"We have a description. Looks like the same guy who came to your aunt's house the other day. Stole some pictures this time."

"Let me call my cameraman. He's down at Liliuokalani Park."

"Think he's already on his way up there." Moke patted the door sill and stepped away. He nodded at the officer getting into the car.

Tawnie quickly closed the window and had started the car when her cell rang. It was Mel at the Honolulu Police Department. "Got a hit," he said. "I'm sending it to you now. What's that I hear, sirens?"

"There's been a major crime tied to the Whitehall murder. I always thought Hilo was a sleepy place. Gotta go."

Chapter 14

Annie Moke stood at the entrance to Joe Cameron's house and swore under her breath. The day was already hot and she was in no mood for complications. "Say again when you think your grandfather left."

"Well," Ginger Cameron said as she held the door open wide, "I talked to Papa Joe around ten last night. He said good night and that was it."

"He never said if he was going somewhere?"

"No."

"*Can* he go somewhere?" Kimo asked. His voice sounded frustrated to Annie.

"My granddad's pretty spry for his age. Swims every day in the ocean. Up to a year ago, he paddle-boarded."

"What happened?"

"Slipped and fell during a hike up at the crater. Just can't get up on the board anymore."

Kimo raised his eyebrows in admiration. Annie thought that proved the old guy could still get around.

She tapped her notebook. "Where would he go? Pa'ia? Kahului?"

"Sometimes he goes to the VFW Center in Kahului. Has friends there."

Kimo stepped back onto the circular driveway. "And what car did he take?"

Ginger frowned. "The Jeep Cherokee."

"What color? Year?"

"'98, I think. Blue. Is my grandfather in trouble?"

"We'd just like to talk to him again," Annie said.

Ginger put both hands over her mouth. She took them away long enough to ask, "What for?"

"We can't say at this time. We'd appreciate your cooperation."

"Can I call my mom?"

"Could we talk to you first?" Annie said "May we come in?" Annie nodded to Kimo. He walked away to call dispatch and order a search for the Jeep.

Back in the room where they first talked to Cameron about the break-in, Annie interviewed Ginger. Neither sat. The woman hugged her arms the whole time.

"What has my grandfather done?"

"Again, I can't say. Just have some questions to ask. When did you last see your grandfather?"

"Last night. I came over for dinner."

"How did your granddad sound? Upset? Nervous?"

"The break-in two days ago upset him, but after Mom and I helped him get the room straightened up, he seemed OK. I came over yesterday to help him clean out the garage. Stayed most of the day, then went home."

"As I recall, that's in Kahului." Annie took notes as she listened. She noticed that the bookshelves were neat and orderly. She supposed that those were new framed pictures put up on the shelves.

"Yes. Near the park." Ginger started to give Annie her address and phone number, but Annie thanked her. Annie had it in her notebook from their earlier visit.

"While you were here, did he watch TV? Watch anything on the news?"

"Are you talking about those WWII old bones on the Big Island?"

Annie nodded.

"Come to think about it, there was something on the evening news. Papa Joe listened to it for a bit, then asked me to switch to a cooking show, though I know he doesn't really watch them."

"So again, when you talked to him last night, how did he sound?"

Ginger frowned. "Sad, maybe a little angry."

Annie closed up her notebook. "Why don't you call your mom now? See if he's there. We just want to talk."

Ginger picked up the phone on the kitchen counter and punched in some numbers, then stopped. "He did say the strangest thing though. Said love doesn't die. That it was stronger than war and all the tsunamis in the world."

"What do you think he meant by that?"

"I'm not sure. He sounded so sad, almost wistful."

"But angry?"

"Yes, there was that too."

Kimo came back in the house. "Got the call out to dispatch. Report on the scanner says they have found a blue Cherokee Jeep in the Costco parking lot. They're checking the registration right now."

Annie put her hand up, motioning Kimo to wait. Ginger was on the phone.

"Mom? Have you seen Papa Joe?"

Annie heard a Charlie Brown wah-wah voice answering.

"No, Mom. The police are here. No, they just want to talk to him again." Ginger was silent as her mother responded. "So he didn't call? OK. I love you. Yes, I'll let you know." Ginger put the phone back in its cradle. "My mom hasn't seen or heard from him since she was over here cleaning up the mess." Ginger frowned. "It's not like him not to answer when we call."

"Maybe we're looking the wrong way," Kimo said. "Maybe he's the one who needs help."

Annie waved Ginger to come back over. "When we interviewed him last time, he told me that he was familiar with the Bessie Whitehall case. Obviously, if he was upset over the news report, he knows something. Did he ever mention the name Hillary Takahashi?"

Ginger looked to the bookcase on the wall. "That photograph taken in the robbery. It had all his high school friends in it as well of a couple of war-time friends. I used to ask him about them. He said they were such fun. Some of his happiest days. They all survived the war and tsunami except for one. Hillary Takahashi. He seemed to care for her a lot."

"How about Bessie Whitehall? She one of the high school friends?"

"Yes."

Annie leaned in. "Don't you think it odd he said only one died in the tsunami?"

"I suppose. But then didn't everyone think she had gone off with some serviceman to the Mainland? Grandpa Joe did. Told me once that people sometimes used war to cover up things, to start over."

"Hmph," Kimo said.

"Thank you, Miss Cameron. We'll be in touch."

"You won't hurt my grandfather, will you?"

"No. Just need to ask him some questions."

***

When Tawnie Takahashi pulled up at Suzie Fong's house behind Officer Greene, uniformed men were loading the coroner's van. She jumped out and ran to the first detective she saw standing on the ranch-style house's red cinder "lawn."

"Where's my aunt? Bee Takahashi?" she asked. She pulled her press permit lanyard out and showed it to him.

He read her name. "Tawnie Takahashi. Moke's been talking about you."

"Captain Moke said my aunt was alright. Can I see her?"

"She's inside," the man answered.

Officer Greene got out of his cruiser and nodded to another police officer standing at the front door.

"Hey, boss, I'm here." Tawnie turned around to face her cameraman. Jim was loaded down with his video equipment. "Heard the names over the scanner," he said. "Decided to hightail it up here, just in case. Got some footage of them bringing out the body."

"Get any info from the cops?"

Jim nodded at the police and EMTs moving around in the yard and along the side of the house. Some were taking pictures, others searching the ground. "Just that there was a forced entry robbery that led to homicide. Seem like they knew the victim. They've been all broken up— and relieved about your Aunt Bee. I got the impression they are very fond of both ladies."

Tawnie thanked him, then went into the house after the police officer opened the door for her.

Bee sat on a chair back in the kitchen. Her eyes were puffy from crying. Maile Horner was outside a big sliding door talking to Captain Moke who must have just arrived. Suzie Fong was part of an important political family on the island. One of her sons had been a state representative with a good record on schools and the environment. Though the room was an active crime scene, it appeared that they were allowing Bee to sit nearby for the moment.

"Oh, Bee," Tawnie said as she gave her aunt a big hug. "I'm so sorry." She kissed Bee on the forehead, and then holding her hand, sat down next to her. "The officer told me you heard a crash and saw the intruder. So glad he didn't hurt you."

Bee sighed and looked up, barely appearing to hear Tawnie. "Suzie was one of Hillary's friends," Bee said in voice thick with sorrow. "And mine since the tsunami took away my home and my sister and brother. Always so kind and supportive. Did you know that Hillary's group of friends put together a fund so I could go to college at the University in Honolulu? Got my teaching degree there. Later, I got my masters on the Mainland. They helped then, too. 'Little Sista,' they called me. I was glad to be theirs." She sniffed and squared her shoulders. "Now we have some bizness to take care of and catch this guy."

"Oh, I think you should go home, Auntie. Maile will drive you. Get some rest. I'll take you out tonight for dinner. How's that?"

Bee seemed resigned to Tawnie's suggestion. "Have you learned anything?"

Tawnie leaned in and whispered in Bee's ear so the officer in the door wouldn't hear, "I think I know who Hick Hickerson is. But right now I don't know who this murderer is. He's got to be younger."

The door slid open and Captain Moke came in. "Mrs. Takahashi, when you are feeling better, I'd like you to come down to police headquarters and look at some pictures."

"I—" Bee started to say.

Tawnie stepped in. "Not now, Captain Moke. She's still recovering from her fall and the shock of this. Maybe later. Her neighbor is going to take her home and stay with her for a while."

"Alright. You going to be OK?" Moke asked Bee.

"Yeah, yeah."

Moke nodded to Tawnie to follow him outside to the orchid bench. "Thought you'd like to know that Jason Chee, the grandson of that firefighter I told you about is here out in front. Maybe he can set you up to meet his grandfather."

"*Mahalo*. When I find something, I'll let you know."

"How about the pictures that Miss Horner has?"

"She says they are in safe place."

"I'm beginning to wonder if I should put police details at both houses."

"I'll be with Bee tonight. Might have my cameraman sleep there too. Thanks again, Captain Moke." Tawnie poked her head back into the kitchen and waved at Bee. "I'll see you later tonight. I love you." She put a hand on her heart. "Auntie Bee-san."

Chapter 15

Tawnie looked at the pictures laid out on the old man's dining room table. Mel Ishikawa had told her once that people often kept the strangest things. Pictures of car accidents, plane crashes, murder victims. Tawnie's stomach churned. She was sure that she was looking at a murder victim. All part of Marty Chee's file of pictures of the victims of the 1946 tsunami he had brought in for identification so many years ago. Lying in debris, Hillary Takahashi was still recognizable, though her naked body was battered and her eyes slightly bulging. Coiled around her neck was the same telephone wire described to Tawnie by the hunters who found Bessie Whitehall. Tawnie had to swallow hard to collect herself and keep the nasty bile down. Her reporter composure had evaporated. *Auntie Hillary!*

"So sorry for those two pictures," the retired Hilo fireman said. He snapped his fingers. "The waves whipped off people's clothes just like that. I covered her up as soon as possible. But I felt it was my job to record what I found." The lines on his light brown face etched deep around his mouth and under his jet black eyes. "Haven't looked at these for some time. So sad. She was a sweet girl."

"You knew her personally?"

"Well, I knew the family. Mr. and Mrs. Takahashi ran a flower shop on Kamehameha Street. Very nice man. I know that Hillary volunteered for the USO during the war. I went to some of the dances myself."

"Ever go to the Mokuola USO place on Coconut Island?"

"Yeah, yeah. During the war, if you had a friend in the military, civilians could go over." He frowned. "That's where I found your auntie. Not far from there."

"Oh." Tawnie asked if she could look at some more of the pictures. In the next one, Hillary was covered up to the neck. In the final one, she was wrapped in some sort of shroud. "Were all the victims found with debris around them? I noticed that wire around my auntie's neck."

Tawnie pointed to the dead girl carefully, not wanting to make him suspicious about her interest.

"Sometimes, but mostly the bodies were just tossed around and resting in the big debris field the waves left. Rest of the victims were swept out to sea and found days later. About forty never found."

"That must have been hard finding people you knew. How old were you at the time?"

"Twenty-one. Got the job with the fire department just after the war ended."

"You've seen a lot in ninety years. I can't imagine." Tawnie cleared her throat. "How long after the tsunami did you find Hillary?"

"Just a couple of hours later. All the buildings on the island and the bridge were washed away. Some of the homes down where the hotels on Banyan Drive are today were wiped out as well as Shinmachi. I found her just *makai* of the bridge to Coconut Island in the little cove there." He paused. "I've always wondered why she was down at the island. There was a USO performance at the Naval Air Station that night. She could have been helping there, then went home late. There was—"

"There was what?"

"There was a young man. I heard she was seeing him quietly."

"Do you know his name?"

"Don't recall." Marty Chee's face suddenly looked his ninety years. Tawnie's interview with him stirred up bad memories.

"Is there a picture of you in here?"

Marty blushed. "Don't know why, but here it is." He pulled a small photographer from the file.

"Oh, you were one good looking guy."

"Yeah, yeah." His picture looked like a police mugshot, but he was in his fireman's uniform and despite its formality, Marty was handsome with hair shaved short around his ears. "You're kind to say that, Ms. Takahashi."

His hand trembled when he put the picture back into the file, disturbing some photographs underneath. The pictures were of dozens of bodies lined up outside of the Dodo Funeral Home.

"This is where Hillary and the others went?" Tawnie said in a shocked whisper. She had to ask hard questions, but this was about family and the danger this case imposed on it.

"Yeah," Marty said.

"May I see these?" Tawnie pulled out four photographs. Three showed bodies lined up in front of the Dodo Funeral Home and people standing near them, some weeping. The fourth scared her. "What is this?"

Marty put his hand over it. "You don't want to see this one."

"Please. I have to. It's for my story as much as about my aunt." In the photograph, bodies were piled up in stacks. Row after row in some building. "Where is this?"

Marty's shoulders slumped. His mouth trembled. "The ice house. It was so hot and so many dead— over 90 bodies— that we had to put them in the ice house." His voice shrank to a whisper. "Later, when they began the funerals, some of the bodies were stuck together." He made a little sob in his voice.

Tawnie took his thin hand and held it. "*Mahalo nui loa*, Mr. Chee, for your care and courage in this terrible time." Tell me, do you remember what they did for my auntie?"

"I know a Buddhist memorial was held for her and the rest of the Takahashi family."

"Oh." Tawnie had been lax in the faith she had been brought up in. Didn't even have a house shrine in her place like Bee did. Tawnie closed her eyes and wept softly, her tears hot. Together Tawnie and Marty were silent for a long time, holding hands.

Finally Tawnie cleared her throat and said. "My grandfather was Jimmy Takahashi, Hillary's big brother."

"I know him. A very fine man. A war hero."

"My Auntie Bee Takahashi is Hillary and Jimmy's little sister. She is the only one left in her immediate family. I wanted to find out the details of Hillary's death." Tawnie stopped, then decided to tell him all. "You heard about Suzie Wong's death? I think Bee is in danger. Someone doesn't want people to know about this time. "

"Why?"

"I think the discovery of Bessie's remains and some letters about the group of friends Hillary knew are tied together. Looking at those photographs of my Auntie Hillary makes me very sure she was murdered."

Marty's mouth opened in astonishment, showing a gold tooth and pink gums where another tooth was missing on the bottom. "How?"

"They both had phone wire around their necks." When Tawnie said that, she had to force down the building wave of grief inside her. She was a reporter first. She picked through the 5 x 3 black-and-white photos until she had the first one of Hilary on top. "Wouldn't you say that is phone wire? Even military-issued?"

Marty peered at it closely and put it down. "Phone wire was down all over."

"Look at her eyes. They are bulging. I've seen enough dead bodies to recognize that. She was strangled. Phone wire didn't have to be in the water. Someone carried it."

"Oh, this is terrible."

"Do you remember the Bessie Whitehall case?"

"Was in on the search for a week or so, then nothing. Very sad about the family."

"Are you surprised about the discovery of the bones?"

"Wasn't what I thought happened to her." Marty frowned. "This is bad, yeah?"

"Yes, it is." Tawnie stood up. "*Mahalo* for your time, Mr. Chee. I really appreciate it."

"I'm sorry for such bad pictures."

Tawnie shook his hand. "No, it had to be done. I never really fathomed what a terrible loss that tsunami inflicted on Hilo. And really, my family. What an amazing people who live here."

Marty gripped her hand. "You be safe."

Outside Marty Chee's ranch style house, the sky was cloudy with a streak of blue to the north. A slight breeze stirred in the lone plumeria tree in the front yard. A rooster crowed at the back of a neighbor's house. *Normal, but why does it feel like the world is spinning?*

Tawnie pulled down on her cotton top to straighten it, then took a deep breath to clear her mind. She needed to get some balance back. The images of Hillary disturbed her on a visceral level. Did Bee have to identify her? Bee's teen-age brother and sister drowned when the apartment was ripped apart and swept away. Did Bee identify them too? Tawnie felt gratitude when she remembered that Bee couldn't have because she was in the hospital. Tawnie's grandfather probably was the one who did the identification along with her great-grandfather, Toshi. Such a tragedy. Tawnie felt shame that she couldn't remember the name of Bee's mother who would have been in the hospital too. Tawnie wiped a tear from her cheek, then checked for text messages on her phone as she walked down to her rental car.

There were several, but Tawnie immediately selected the one from Detective Ishikawa at the Honolulu Police Headquarters. She quickly read through Mel's text messages.

Found the military records you wanted. Thomas G. Hickerson entered the Navy as a lieutenant in February 12, 1942. Assigned to the Naval Station in Hilo September, 1943. Discharged April 25, 1946.

April 25, 1946. Bessie went missing at the end of the month of February. Tawnie calculated what this meant. To kill Hillary, Hickerson had to have been on the Big Island until after the tsunami. When you were discharged from the Navy back then, did you get your discharge papers right away or did you have to go back to the Mainland? Honolulu? Would he go back on a troop ship?

Tawnie got into her rental car and closed the door. Still lost in thought, she didn't start the engine right away. Hickerson could have put in for his papers in February, but didn't receive them until early April. Maybe it would take a couple of weeks by ship to get back to the Mainland.

Look at the other side, her reporter voice said. What about Joe Cameron? That swim tag that was found with Bessie Whitehall's remains. How did that get there? If Moke was going to bring Cameron in for questioning, he must have hard evidence. All this gave Tawnie a headache. She needed a police contact over on Maui to follow the Hickerson lead.

Tawnie tapped the steering wheel. Who did she did know on Maui? Peter Hillard, for one, but he was a newspaper man. And yet, he was also an old college chum. Tawnie sat up. His cousin was with the Maui Police Department. Tawnie reached for her phone. Maybe if she was able to reach her and mention Captain Moke's name, she might be able to get more information on Hickerson. Tawnie punched the search button, then   called.

Chapter 16

Annie was writing down last minute instructions to her neighbor about watching the house and LaBaie when her phone rang. She didn't recognize the number and wondered if it was another call from a business offering financial support or offers to sell the house for her. The Widow's List, a friend called it, gleaned from obituaries. *And somehow got my private number.* She was about to delete it, then thought better of it.

"Moke residence. Who's calling?"

There was a brief pause on the other end but no click so the call was not canned.

"So sorry, but this is Tawnie Takahashi calling from KWAI-5 News. Your cousin, Peter Hillard gave me your number. We're old college friends." Another pause. "First, I want to say that I have been working with Captain Moke of the Hilo Police. I'm developing a story on the Betty Whitehall murder."

Tawnie Takahashi. She had a reputation of being tough on crime reporting and sometimes giving digs to law enforcement. "OK." Annie kept her voice flat.

"He told me that you questioned a Joe Cameron there on Maui."

"That's right. Go on." While Annie listened to Takahashi, she put water in LaBaie's bowl.

"Cameron was part of an *'ohana* of friends here in Hilo during WWII. My great aunt Hillary Takahashi was in that group. She died in the big Hilo tsunami just after the war." Takahashi cleared her throat. "I have reason to believe that she was murdered by the same person who killed Bessie Whitehall."

Annie stood up sharp, her foot jostling the water bowl. "What evidence do you have?"

Takhashi went on. "I just came out from a retired fireman's house. He was on duty during the tsunami. Helped with survivors. Took pictures of the victims he pulled out of the water and building rubble. Auntie Hillary was one of them. He had several photographs of her body." Takahashi paused. "There was phone wire around her neck. Just like Bessie Whitehall."

"Have you told Captain Moke?"

"Not yet."

"Why not? Are you waiting for your six o'clock report? He's my father-in-law, you know, and he's by the book."

"No. I plan to tell him as soon as I can figure out the Maui part of this story. I'm sure you know about Suzie Lee Fong, the widow of the former mayor. She was killed in a robbery at her house."

Annie acknowledged that she knew about it.

"Well, she was a member of this *ohana*. There's something else I've been following." Takahashi went on to tell Annie about the letters and pictures. "There was another guy in that group. Thomas Hickerson. He was dating Bessie. He left the islands after the tsunami."

"Are you thinking he was behind the murder of Whitehall?"

"Yes. My Auntie Bee's a tsunami survivor. She was just a little girl, but tagged along with her big sister Hillary. She remembers Joe Cameron being with Hillary, but lately she has been recalling this Hickerson guy. And they are not good memories."

"What do you know about him?"

"I've been researching Hickerson. Just got information on his discharge papers *and* his history since then. Did you ever hear of the Hickerson Design Corporation?"

"No."

"It's an international company that designs golf courses. They have several here in the islands—the Big Island, Kaui and Maui. In fact, they just dedicated a re-designed golf course on Maui."

Now Annie was paying attention. Honeywell just went to that opening. "Who is this guy? If he's still alive, he must be a million years old."

"Ninety-one."

"And you suspect him, why?"

"Auntie Bee recognized him in one of those old photographs. She recalled him being called 'Hick.' But get this, he was also identified on the back of one of the photos as 'The Duffer.' Totally a golf reference. On the company website, I found one reference to Thomas 'Hick' Hickerson. Bee remembers him pestering Bessie and her being afraid of him."

"Interesting," Annie said and meant it. "So want do you want from me?"

"I can't do it, but I wonder if you could look up any addresses, police records. I'm finding that I can't get the information fast enough."

"For your evening news report? You busted some rules when you interviewed those hunters."

"No. I'm doing it for my Auntie Bee. I think she is in danger."

"From a ninety-one-year old who also might be dead?"

"I don't know what the motivation is. There is someone a lot younger doing all the break-ins. Maybe he's connected with this company."

Annie thought for a moment before answering. Should she say anything about finding out that Cameron had taken a private plane down to the Big Island? That the swim tag was an important clue to the murder of Bessie Whitehall? "Tell you what, I'm coming down to the Big Island in an hour from now. We could meet up later. Maybe talk to your aunt together."

"But you'll look into Hickerson?"

"Yeah, yeah. I can do that."

***

Bee sat on her sofa with Asami's head on her lap. The shades had been drawn though it was early evening and the sun was still lingering. A fan blew a breeze across the room, its hum as soothing as rain on the roof.

George always liked the rain, Bee thought. "Hilo rain beats snow and sleet in Boston," he'd say and give her a hug that enfolded her deep in his arms and tall frame. She wanted that hug more than anything else in the world right now, but George was gone. Bee stroked Asami's soft head and leaning back against the cushions, wept silently. She never thought of herself as a widow — it sounded so pathetic — but she did feel pathetically alone. The kids were all off island — Honolulu, Seattle and Germany. After today, she wondered if she could go on. She ached all over, physically and spiritually. Maybe Tawnie could take her down to the temple. Quiet prayer might settle her unquiet mind. Creaky bones were just old age setting in.

She looked at the picture on the bookshelf of George in his Army Reserve uniform and thought of the good times they'd had hiking, fishing and camping together. Playing golf up at Volcano. Their boys and Janice. Fifty-seven years of marriage. Good memories, but Bee kept seeing Suzie Lee Fong on the floor.

Asami lifted her head with start and growled. Bee was instantly upright. Tawnie had called an hour ago and said that she would be delayed — she was working on a story — but if Bee needed anything be sure to call her. If she felt in any way threatened, call 911, then Maile.

Bee listened, but only heard a car going by. Asami gave one more, deep "wuf," then put her head down.

"Silly," Bee said. She sat back and reached for the TV remote.

Suddenly, Asami was down and scrambling across the wood floor, her toenails clicking like the keys on an old typewriter. She barked at the door, her little head craning up.

"Who's there?" Bee stood up and limping slightly, grabbed the closest thing she could find —a three iron of George's she used to reach items dropped on the floor.

There was a muffled sound. Someone knocked, then clicked on the door handle.

Stupid. I thought I locked the door!

The door opened halfway to reveal an elderly gentleman in slacks and a short sleeved Aloha shirt. He ignored Asami growling as she pounced around his feet.

"Bee?" he said. When he saw her, he searched her face. "You are Bee Takahashi, aren't you?"

Seized with fear, Bee shouldered the golf club like she was at bat. "What you want?"

The man stepped through the doorway. "I came down to see if you were alright. Because of Bessie Whitehall being on the news. I'm Joe. Joe Cameron. I know what happened to her. I just want you to be safe." The old man's voice was raspy with age, but there was something familiar.

Asami continued to make a fuss, taking a good bite on Joe's walking shoes before dashing away. Bee froze and started to shake. "Don't come any closer. My neighbor should be here any second."

For the first time, Joe smiled. "That's one good watchdog you have."

Bee gripped the golf club tighter and made a chopping motion with it.

Joe ignored her and came in further. He closed the door. Bee's heart started to pound. She searched her memories of him — the handsome young man who swam like Tarzan; the soldier who was so sweet to her when he should have been annoyed with her tagging along when he wanted to be with Hillary. *He must be nearly ninety*, she thought. All of Hillary's friends lived up to that age. *But he could still hurt me. I saw him arguing with Hillary. Made her cry. Scared her.*

'Suzie Lee died today," Bee blurted out. "What you have to say about that?"

The shock on Joe's face reassured her that maybe he wasn't going to hurt her.

There was a commotion in the kitchen. Asami let go of corralling Joe and dashed to the kitchen doorway. "Auntie Bee? Are you alright?" Maile came through. "Oh," she said. She held her cellphone in her hand. "I'm calling 911, mister."

Joe looked at Bee. "Mind if I sit down?" He nodded to a lounge chair by the window. "It's been a long day eluding everyone."

"Bee?" Maile came in a bit further.

"This is our Joe," Bee said to Maile. "Joe of the letters." She nodded to Joe that he could sit down.

"Are you sure, Auntie? I'm keeping my fingers on the 911 number button," Maile said. Asami barked her approval.

Joe made his way to the chair. Bee noticed the stiffness of old knees, the lines on his face, wrinkles around his thin elbows, and the perpetual tan of someone who has lived in the islands a long time. His hair was white, thin at the crown. Joe eased down into the chair with obvious relief. "Want to introduce me to your friend? And this character?" He looked down at Asami who had taken up guard by his feet.

"This is Maile Horner, my neighbor. She is a historian in town. And that is Asami."

Joe nodded at Maile. "You said 'Joe of the letters'. What letters?"

Maile stepped in. "She's not answering until you explain why you are really here."

Joe sighed and then patted the cushioned arms of his chair. "Alright. I had a break-in at my home on Maui a few days ago. Robber took some pictures from my high school and Army days in Hilo. Then I saw the breaking news about Bessie Whitehall last night." Joe looked at Bee. "More in particular, Tawnie Takahashi's report with the hunters who made the discovery. Your reporter niece. That's why I was concerned. It's what they said about what they found with the remains."

"Do the police know about the break-in?" Maile asked.

"Of course. Told them all I knew and gave them a list of what was taken. " He smiled at Bee." So what are the 'Joe letters'?"

Bee got all formal. "Long time ago letters given for the museum. Miss Horner works there. There are pictures, too. They were written by one Eddie Haines while he was stationed here during WWII."

"Eddie Haines. I haven't talked with him in years, but heard he passed away last year."

"So you were in touch with him?"

"Decades. He lived in Illinois, came out here to visit a couple of times. Then he moved away to a retirement place in Arizona. I lost contact." Joe cocked his head at the women. "There's more to this then."

"He talks about his life while stationed here," Bee said. "He talks about you and Hillary."

"Hillary?" Joe frowned.

Bee got to the point, still gripping the golf club. "Says he saw you arguing with her down at Coconut Island the night of the tsunami."

"Where'd he get that? I wasn't even in town."

"I saw you fighting with her there, too," Bee said. "After that she was very scared."

Joe gasped. "When was that?"

"A couple of days before the tsunami."

"And you think she was afraid of me?"

Bee nodded slowly. "Though I don't want to think that."

Maile came over and stood beside Bee. She held her cellphone out like a threat.

Joe's eyes filled with tears. He swallowed hard and when he spoke, his voice was thick. "I would never hurt Hillary. I loved her. I wanted to marry her. When I lost her..." He sighed. "We were having a disagreement, Bee, not fighting. I wanted to get married right away, elope, because your mother was opposed to us. Hillary wanted to wait until your father and your brother Jimmy got back into town. Tell them. Felt they would understand. That was all."

Joe continued to appeal to her. "I loved her. I have always loved her. Can you imagine an old man like me with all of life's successes still feeling hollow because he lost the most precious thing in the world?" He swallowed again. "I never forgot you or your family, you know. You probably don't remember, but I went to the hospital several times to see you while you were there. Have always blamed that damn tsunami. Now..."

Bee blinked. Looked at the picture of George. A tear rolled down her flat cheek. "Yes, I can understand feeling hollow." She lowered the golf club and used it as a cane. "You left the island."

"I did. Went to the Mainland. Took on the G.I. Bill."

Maile seemed not willing to let Joe's intrusion go. "If you weren't down at Coconut Island, who did Eddie Baines see?"

Joe looked sad. "The same person who killed poor Bessie. That's why I think Hillary was afraid. He must have thought she saw something. Before Hillary and I argued, she had been upset over Bessie's disappearance. She never explained anything more than that. I wish she had." He continued. "I saw something on that interview your great niece did with the hunters, Bee. I don't think you knew, but I was with the recovery crew that discovered Hillary after the tsunami. I was so broken up after that and all these years I forgot an important detail. There was phone wire wrapped —" Joe choked on his words "— around her neck. Just like Bessie. Fire department just chalked it up to debris."

Bee felt for her sofa's arm and worked her way down to its cushioned seat. "Oh." She bit her lip, but she couldn't stop the slow roll of tears down her cheek.

"She loved you very much, Bee." Joe said softly. "You were her special pet. You must have cared so much for her, too— following us around." He smiled when Bee blushed. "But then you were ten."

Bee looked down at her hands. "I did see you kiss her."

"Then you know I loved her. One way or another, we would have married." Joe looked away.

The room was getting dim. The sun was almost down. Bee could see in her mind's eye the sun's last gasp on the watery horizon, the flash of the green before it drowned in the ocean. She wondered why she thought of the sun drowning. So many drowned back then. She looked up at Joe, his face etched in shadow, but she saw once again the young man she remembered. *We are both survivors*, she thought.

Maile broke the reverie. "You said you knew what happened to Bessie Whitehall. It wasn't you, was it?"

"Maile," Bee reprimanded.

Maile still clenched the cellphone. "No, I think he should say."

Suddenly, there was a loud banging on the front door that sent Asami off into a loud round of barking as she ran in frantic circles between Bee and the door.

"Ms. Takahashi. Hilo Police."

All three of them froze. Bee nodded at Maile. "Would you go?"

Maile went to the door and opened it. On the steps was Jerry Moke. Behind him were detectives Annie Moke and Kimo Fortes.

"Is Bee here?" Jerry Moke asked. "Just coming personally to check on her. May we come in?"

Bee nodded to Maile that it was alright, but she wasn't sure if she was sad or relieved when the room filled with blue uniforms and a startled Jerry said, "Joe Cameron, you're just the man we want to see."

After the police left with Joe Cameron, Bee sat on her sofa with Asami by her side. It wasn't how she imagined meeting him would be. It didn't feel right.

"Can I get you anything else, Bee?" Maile asked. She carried a small bamboo tray with two glasses of guava juice mixed with soda water on it and set it down on a side table.

Bee shook her head.

Maile gave Bee her glass. "You should eat."

"I'm not hungry."

"I can understand. It's been a shock, but think about it." Maile pulled over a wooden chair and sat down. "There's some sushi in the refrigerator. Salad."

"Joe didn't kill Bessie Whitehall."

"Well, the police did say they wanted to talk to him. He went willingly. Maybe they have evidence from her grave site." Maile said the word "grave site" so distastefully that Bee looked up.

"You don't believe it either."

Maile smiled softly. "No, I don't." She sipped her drink and urged Bee to do so, too. "Funny, you read about someone," Maile went on, "and see all the photos, listen to people's memories of the times and then— boom— that someone is here. It changes everything. Historians always wonder what the person they are researching was like. We always play the game, 'Who in history would you like to have dinner with?' What would you ask that person?" Maile smiled at Bee. "He seemed like a genuinely nice man. Maybe Mr. Cameron just has to tell his side of the story."

"He loved my sister. Aloha was so strong in him." Bee frowned. "But what *kine* person goes around hurting and killing old people just to get stuff?"

"You're not old..."

"Seventy-nine feels plenty old." Bee patted the sofa cushion to invite Asami to come closer. She wouldn't admit to Maile that she still ached from her fall. *I'm so creaky.*

"Let's see what the police have to say. If they hold him longer, do you want to go down and see him?"

"Yeah, yeah." Bee sagged deeper into the sofa's soft back cushion. She closed her eyes.

"Hmm, mind if I turn on the TV?" Maile asked.

Bee waved her on. She was too tired to say otherwise.

The news had come on, but they'd just missed Tawnie's update about the Suzie Fong tragedy. KWAI-5 News went to ads. One made Bee perk up.

"Aloha," a man's voice soothed. "Here at Hale Kawai Hotel and Golf Course you can have the stay of a lifetime. See whales off the coast in the morning, golf on one of the most breathtaking courses in the world, sunsets at night. All the best of Maui." There were short scenes of tourists body surfing, sunbathing on the beach, living the life with wine and local beer in hand at sundown, silhouettes of lanky palms against a pink and orange sky. And then, standing on a balcony overlooking a sandy beach front, there was a man in an Aloha shirt. He was medium height with a slight breeze ruffling his straight brown with bits of gray in it. He turned to the camera. Bee saw the same tanned face, the same caramel-colored brown eyes she had seen both times she had encountered him.

"Oh," Bee said. She felt suddenly lightheaded. "Did you see that man?"

"I did. Sammy Braga, Vice President. Hickerson Design Corporation."

Bee shrunk deeper into the sofa. "He's the one who killed my friend Suzie."

***

"OK, Mr. Cameron, tell us one more time about Bessie Whitehall. How did you know her?" Jerry Moke sat on the other side of the metal interrogation table. A small recorder was set in front of him. Annie sat to the side with Kimo, waiting to get in on the questioning. A lawyer, Amy Tapang, had been hastily called in for Joe at his insistence. Annie thought the petite Fillipina looked fresh out of law school. Though Cameron had come to the police station voluntarily, the questioning had turned sharp.

Joe Cameron folded his hands in front of him. "I told you. I knew her since we all entered first grade. Went all the way through high school with her."

"Were you ever romantic with her?"

"Do you mean did I ever take her to the senior prom? The war was on. Ours was canceled. No, she was just a friend."

"But she hung out with you." Moke said.

"Sure. I never expected the Army would assign me to my hometown, but there I was. Nice to have old friends to visit on leave time."

Moke leaned in. "Did you know Lily Palani?"

"Yeah," Joe answered. "We were all friends."

"She was my *tutu*."

"Really? Of course Captain Moke." Joe nodded at the captain's name badge on his shirt pocket. "I sent flowers when she got married."

"You couldn't go the wedding?"

"I was in school on the Mainland. Commercial air flights were rare and expensive back then."

Annie was getting impatient. "May I ask a question, sir?" she asked Moke.

"Yeah, sure."

"Mr. Cameron, can you explain why that swim tag was found on Bessie Whitehall's body?"

Joe's face whitened. "It was found with her?"

"Yeah, roughly where a pocket might be."

Annie slid over a picture of Whitehall's remains as they were found. She made a tapping motion in the air above it so not to touch the photo.

Joe swallowed. He looked genuinely sick. When Joe looked up, there were tears in his eyes. "I gave it to her."

"Why?" Moke asked.

"Bessie had a rough family life. Father was an alcoholic and a wife beater. I don't think he was ever that way with Bessie, but I know she suffered. Bessie coped through friends at school and found a family in the Takahashis."

"You didn't say why she had your swim tag from that USO place," Kimo asked. "You go swimming with her?"

"Sure, we all did. At the USO place she felt safe. After it closed in late 1945, I gave the tag to her. It was kind of a good luck charm for her."

"Uh-huh." Moke folded his arms and switched topics. "How about Hillary Takahashi? What was your relationship with her?"

Joe's eyes looked haunted. "What does that have to do with this?"

Though Annie had only heard the details a couple of hours earlier from Tawnie Takahashi, she now understood Moke's line of questioning. "Just answer, Mr. Cameron," Annie said.

"I loved her. Would have married her if she hadn't died."

"You didn't you kill her?" Kimo slid another picture across the table. It was a blowup of one of Marty Chee's photographs. Joe took only a glance at the picture, then looked away.

At that point, Joe's lawyer spoke up. "You don't have to answer that, Mr. Cameron," Amy Tapang said.

Joe suddenly got up, his thin arms shaking as he braced himself on the table. "Hell yes, I'll answer. I didn't kill her." He shrugged off the police officer who jumped in to restrain him. "And if you're implying I killed Bessie Whitehall, you're dead wrong."

An alarmed Tapang protested the policeman's action while putting out a hand out to soothe her client.

"Calm down, Mr. Cameron," Moke said. "It was only one question." He nodded to the police officer to back away. Moke folded his big arms. The Hawaiian put on his "good cop" face. "You have any idea who did?" He picked up the photograph and put it back in the file. "And if you do, how come you didn't go to the police, say a few decades ago?"

Annie watched Joe slowly sag back onto his plastic chair. He looked every bit his eighty-nine years. She felt a pang of sympathy for him. Not a good way to treat an elder.

Joe rubbed a brown-spotted hand over his mouth, then folded his hands again. When he spoke, his voice was gravelly with age. "You young folks, you just don't get what war or a trauma like a tsunami does to people. WW II is like some picture show to you. You can watch it 24/7 on a dozen channels. But it had a purpose of a sort. But a tsunami — it has no purpose. Just nature doing her thing." He swallowed. "That killer arrived here on the bay in under five hours — it came all the way from the Aleutians— and it took us all by surprise." He paused. "I've always admired the folks of Shinmachi who said '*Shikata ga na*' — 'It can't be helped.' But some of us just can't get those waves out of our head. The things it took away."

Joe looked up. "All of us thought Bessie had gone away with one of the servicemen she knew. If it seemed secretive, she had good reasons to be because of her father. At least that is what I have hoped all these years. But these last days…" He clasped his hands and pumped them up and down to each word he said. He nodded at the file of photographs. "Knowing how Bessie died makes me reconsider everything, including how Hillary died." He swallowed. "Yeah, I'm pretty damn sure who killed Bessie—and my sweet Hillary, too."

Moke cocked his head at Cameron. "Care to share?"

"Sure. You can find him in the news. Thomas G. Hickerson. Founder of a big corporation that designs golf courses. Has a number of them here in the islands."

"He still alive?"

"Don't know."

Annie studied Joe's face when he said that. She wasn't sure if he was lying, but he was hiding something. His brow had beads of sweat on it. Off to the side, Kimo picked up his smartphone and began a search.

"Who was he back then?"

"He was a lieutenant with the Navy. Stationed right there at the Naval Air Station here in town. Like the rest of the military he could go out to Coconut Island to the USO Center there."

"And Bessie?" Annie asked.

"They went together for a while. She was smitten, but I never liked the guy. Too much like her damn father. Charming but manipulative. In the end, I think she was afraid of him. Another reason to leave secretly."

"But you gave her the swim tag some time before that?"

"Yeah, like I said. Some luck." Joe swept the table in front of him with the flat of his hand.

"Yet he was part of your *'ohana* of friends." Annie tapped her notebook with her pencil.

"Yeah, he was. Bessie invited him in."

"Why do you think Hillary is linked to Hickerson?" Moke asked.

"When I saw that interview with those hunters up in the forest reserve, I knew he did it." Joe sniffed. "I was in the recovery group after the tsunami. I found Hillary —" he swallowed. "—with telephone wire around her neck, the kind used in the military. Worst day of my life." Joe's head shot up. "I hope you get the bastard if he's still around."

Annie reached for one of the bottles of water on the table. The room was getting hot and clammy, but she didn't think it was a faulty air conditioner. The space was thick with the hubris of grief and memory. She understood that feeling now personally since she lost David. She offered a bottle to Joe.

"Why do you think he killed them?" she asked.

Joe shrugged. "Whatever his reasons for killing Bessie, Hillary had to be an afterthought. Maybe she suspected something."

"One of our sources said that Hillary was afraid."

"I wish that she had told me." Joe tried to twist open his bottle, but his hands shook. He gave it to Amy Tapang. "Thanks," he mumbled to her when she gave it back. He took a sip.

"And you don't know why she was down at Coconut Island?"

"No." His answer was heavy with sadness. "I was hoping that we could meet up again after her brother and father came back."

"When was the last time you saw Hickerson?" Kimo asked.

"Hmm. Maybe a couple of weeks after the tsunami. Kinda vague about that. I was done with him long before Bessie went missing. Think I heard he got the go-ahead on his discharged papers. He was lucky and got a boat ride back to the Mainland."

"What did he do during that time? If he killed those women, he's a cold-blooded snake." Kimo made a spitting gesture to the side.

Joe slid his hand up and down the water bottle, lost in thought. Finally, he said, "The commander and his men at the Naval Air Station were heroes, in my opinion. The barracks and the mess hall, meant to feed 200, became a gathering place for thousands of survivors. All the grocery stores and bakeries were destroyed, you see. The injured were cared for there, too. Hickerson had no choice but to be there until he had permission to leave."

Moke leaned back on his chair to stretch. Annie was getting stiff too, sitting on the uncomfortable chairs. She couldn't wait to get out of her police uniform and take a shower.

"Thanks for your willingness to talk, Mr. Cameron. There's still a problem with all this. Who is going around breaking in and robbing your place and other members of the 'ohana and kill someone?"

"Maybe it's to keep this information from getting out. Could ruin the company name," Kimo said, then went back to his search on his phone.

"If Hickerson is alive, how old is he?" Annie asked. Joe

"Ninety-one. He was older than I am."

"You're unusually spry, aren't you? But—"

"Sir," Kimo interrupted. He turned around his phone that showed the Hickerson Design Corporation page. "The firm's headquarters are in California."

"But they had a big opening at a golf course on Maui," Annie said. "The Hale Kawai, I think it was called. Our boss Captain Honeywell went there."

"Well, check that out." Moke rapped the table to indicate that he was done for now. "Thank you, Mr. Cameron," he said. "Will you and Ms. Tapang wait here for a moment?" He signaled for Annie and Kimo to join him. Once outside in the hall, they conferred.

"I'm glad he volunteered about Hickerson," Annie said. "Confirms what Tawnie Takahashi told me and more."

"Do we hold him, sir?" Kimo asked Moke.

Moke looked back into the room through the one-way window. "No. He can go on the condition that he doesn't leave the island just yet. There's a murderer running around." He looked at Annie. "Think he has money to stay overnight?"

"We can notify his daughter." Annie looked at her watch. "It's late, but I think he can still get a room at one of the hotels."

"Alright. We'll let him go." He nodded at Annie and Kimo. "Well done, you two. You're one good team. Miss you down here."

Chapter 18

Tawnie Takahashi was waiting in the parking lot of the Hilo Police Station when Joe Cameron was finally released. It was nearly 11 o'clock at night. Dark came hard in the tropics, but the night still held the heat despite the slight breeze rattling unseen palm fronds in the parking lot. Only the station had a few lights on. When she saw a taxi pull up in front of him, she scrambled out. "Mr. Cameron. Joe Cameron, wait."

The old man turned. An overhead light in the entryway illuminated a worn face. His clothes looked rumpled. He stared, then recognized her.

"Can I talk to you?" Tawnie asked as she sprinted up to him in sandals with low heels. She still wore the same clothes from her long morning. "Auntie Bee sent me." As she came up to the station's entrance, she noticed for the first time Annie Moke standing in the doorway. Tawnie nodded to her. "I'll see he gets settled. My Auntie's orders."

"You do that. He's to stay in Hilo." Annie went back inside.

Joe sized Tawnie up. "You're the reporter. One who interviewed the hunters. Bee wants this, you say?"

"Yes, she does. Bee told me her *aloha* heart said you loved Hillary and wouldn't have hurt her.' If you don't know already, you should always listen to Auntie Bee. For you, I'll take you anywhere you want to go. Just not the airport."

Joe's eyes brightened. "I know just the place."

Tawnie guided him back to her car where she introduced her cameraman Jim to him. Joe moved stiffly and bent his shoulders like the world weighed down heavy on him. Jim moved to the backseat while Tawnie helped Joe into the rented Subaru's passenger seat. "Where to?" she asked Joe.

"North."

"OK, North."

"Just the place" was not what Tawnie had anticipated, but when Joe said they were going out to see Thomas Hickerson himself, her reporter's curiosity and passion for getting the story overruled the wisdom of driving along Route 19 so late. With the headlights as their only guide under a moonless sky, the road twisted and turned through the darkest dark. They crossed high bridges over deep gorges, passed waterfalls unseen in the dark and large groves of macadamia nut trees where sugar cane once grew. Sometimes, tall stands of *koa* and *ohia lehua* jumped out at them as they followed the old Māmalahoa Highway which mostly morphed into the newer Hawaii Belt Road. The Subaru station wagon was the only car on it.

"Laupahoehoe is down there," Joe remarked once as they passed a marker lit by their lights. "Lost some good people there in the tsunami. Twenty-four, I think. Only happy story is that one of the teachers found drifting out to sea married her rescuer." He punched something into his phone then put it away in his pants pocket.

He has a smartphone, she thought. *Not so ancient as I thought.* "I didn't know that. So sad," Tawnie said. She took her eyes off the road to look at Joe. "How come you didn't say anything about Hickerson being on the Big Island to Captain Moke or Detective Annie Moke? Or your lawyer, for that matter."

"I just want to have words with the bastard."

Jim leaned over the front seat. "Hickerson has always lived out here?"

"He's been here since late last year. Poor health. I think he has a live-in nurse."

"Why here?"

"Scene of the crime, maybe?" Joe said with a sour voice.

"You kept tabs on him all these years?"

"Well, I'm a businessman and he's a businessman. We sometime crossed each other's paths when he came out here from California. Stayed most of the time over there. I never cared one fig for him."

"But you don't think he had anything to do with the break-ins?"

"No. Too ill. Wouldn't keep him from orchestrating it though."

"Bee says she saw the guy who came to her house and killed Suzie Fong on a TV ad. Said he was with the Hickerson Corporation."

"She see the name?"

"Sammy Braga."

"Really?" Joe scratched his stubbled cheek. "That Hick's grandson."

"What do you know about Braga?" Tawnie slowed down as a fat rat scurried across the road. She flicked her eyes back to her rear view mirror and she noticed headlights far in the distance.

"Not much," Joe said. "Like I said, I didn't pay much attention to Hickerson, unless when the corporation bought up island land through some nasty acquisition. I think Braga took over the running of the firm about eight years ago." Joe rubbed his arms. He was still wearing only his Aloha shirt.

"Jim," Tawnie said. "Isn't your sweatshirt in the back? Could you give it to him?"

"Thanks," Joe said as he pulled on the large sweatshirt with a green UH Warrior logo on the front. He folded his arms and settled back into his seat.

The Hamakua Coast was wild in the daytime. At night it was shifty. A light fog drifted across the road briefly obscuring Tawnie's vision for a half a mile until it suddenly lifted. They drove several more miles in silence.

"The next milepost you see," Joe said, "we have only a little way more."

"I thought you were never in touch with Hickerson," Jim said.

"Think I'm too old for Google Maps and Map Quest?"

"No sir," Jim slumped back in his seat.

"It's alright, son. Didn't mean to snap." Joe chuckled. "My granddaughter Ginger keeps me up-to-date."

A short while later, Joe sat up and peered out the windshield. "There's the milepost. Now a little further. There, on the left. That eucalyptus tree. There's a road going up."

Tawnie slowed down and eased onto a narrow road leading up through a thick dark forest of what seemed to be mostly eucalyptus trees judging by their distinctive trunks when beams from the headlights hit them. "What is this place?"

"You'll see," Joe said.

"You weren't planning on coming up by yourself in that taxi, were you?" Tawnie put the car in lower gear as they entered the private road. To the south from where they came, the highway was still empty though far off she thought she saw a prick of light.

"I had a mind to."

Tawnie turned on the car's bright lights as tension grew inside her. She was glad Jim had come along for the ride. As the car pressed on, rolling from side to side on the primitive road, she regretted not letting anyone at KWAI-5 News know where they were going. What kind of loose cannon was Hickerson? Or Joe Cameron for that matter? As trees loomed over them, she couldn't help but think that this location was not what she expected from a wealthy entrepreneur. There must be something else going on.

The heavily forested road continued on for what seemed an eternity to Tawnie. Climbing higher at each turn, every spooky ghost story her grandfather told her as a girl came back. Once she saw a dozen yellow eyes peering out from the underbrush. Wild pigs? A boar could take out a car if she hit one. Another time she saw the remains of white wooden fencing. Eventually, to her relief, the road broke into a large clearing illuminated overhead by a canopy of a billion stars so bright that once her eyes adjusted, she could make out a mowed field, some macadamia trees, and a fence-lined driveway coming in from another direction. At the end was a large two-story house that opened to the sea. Had they come in a back way?

"If you don't mind," Joe said, "could you please turn off your lights? I think you can see the way in."

Tawnie turned the lights off and put on the brake. "You never said what you planned to do, Mr. Cameron. This could be dangerous, not that I haven't been in tight spots before."

"I only mean to talk to him. I don't think he can hurt anyone anymore. After that the police can do what they want with him."

Jim leaned over. "What about Braga? He's the one who is dangerous. He killed that old woman."

"Watch who you call old." Joe scratched his cheek. "I don't think Braga's the killer type."

They all looked across the field. There was only one light on in the house and a low porch light. Inside a TV set flickered. A single car was parked in front.

"Didn't you say there was a nurse on duty? Could be her car," Jim said.

"From what I know." Joe grew quiet.

"It's late. Almost midnight. Everyone should be in bed." Tawnie nervously tapped the steering wheel.

"Maybe that's the nurse who is up."

"What will you say to him?" Tawnie asked. If there ever was a juicy human-interest story of love lost and justice for the six o'clock news, this was it, but Tawnie, for the first time in her professional life, had mixed feelings about it all. This was Hillary's story, Tawnie's own flesh and blood. What would her Auntie Hillary think?

Joe put his hands on the dashboard. "Personally, I'd like to kill him, but that wouldn't be justice. It's seventy years too late. But I'd gladly see that empire he built with not one iota of conscience take a hit." Joe's voice softened. "I just want to ask him, why? Why Hillary?"

Tawnie took off the brake and rolled the car forward. As they crept toward the house, she powered down the window to listen to the night sounds. Jim did the same thing.

"There are no dogs," Jim said.

"Noticed that, too."

"Listen." Joe put a hand on his ear. "That yelling?"

Tawnie sped up, trying hard to keep the crunching sound of lava rock gravel down to a minimum. She parked the car where the driveway turned into a landscaped roundabout. The house was newer than she thought with a ridiculous Southern California facade right down to a tile roof. The commotion came from a second-story window. A woman screamed.

"We should call the police," Tawnie said.

"Do it then." Joe struggle to get out of his seat. He worked his way alongside the car and ran haltingly for the double front door.

Tawnie jumped out while Jim called 911. "Joe!" she hissed at the old man. "Wait."

The yelling above continued, but she could hear it clearly now through the upstairs screen window.

"You idiot," an old raspy voice said. "What the fuck were you thinking?"

"It was an accident," a younger voice said. "I was only protecting the firm."

Someone on the other side of the front door jiggled the handle and a local woman dressed in a pink nurse's uniform flung it open. "*Ai-jesus,*" she said, then threw herself into Tawnie's arms almost knocking her over. "Are you the police?"

"No, I'm Tawnie Takahashi from KWAI-5 News. What is going on?" Tawnie looked beyond the woman into a half-lit foyer.

"Oh, they're having one terrible fight. Mr. Braga threw me out of da room. It is very bad."

Joe gently pushed her away and started in. "Where are they?"

"Upstairs to the right."

"We called the police." Tawnie assured the woman by pointing to their car. "You can wait in there. Joe, you hold on. You're not Hawaii 5-0."

Together they stepped into a large foyer with a polished tile floor. A grand staircase led up to a balcony that opened to rooms on all sides. A couple of lights on the walls lit the way. Joe grabbed the railing and started up. Tawnie ran ahead to the top of the stairs.

"You can't keep me here," the old voice barked.

"You know damn well why you're here. The guy I loved and admired all my life is a goddam, cold-blooded murderer. You killed that woman. Thought you got clean away with it until those hunters found her bones. How can you look at yourself in the morning? Did Mom and Dad know?"

Tawnie cautiously went around the balcony. For the first time she could hear some sort of medical devices pumping and beeping low. She was relieved when Jim silently joined her.

"Got through to 911," he whispered.

"Good." Tawnie wasn't sure what to do next. Her heart pounded like a drum at a Tahitian dance. Cautiously, she turned her cellphone on to record.

"No," the old voice went on. Tawnie assumed it was Hickerson's. "When did you find out?"

"Last year, when we were renovating the old headquarters after Dad died. I found an envelope with a key in some of your private papers. Maybe you forgot all about it. Took a month but my research led me to a safe deposit box in a little bank in the wine country."

"Huh." A machine beeped. "So?"

"I found it full of newspaper clippings about a missing woman. *Hilo Tribune*, even some Mainland accounts. There were several pictures of you with her and— a bunch of friends from your war years here. Maybe most damning, a notecard from her asking you to stay away. Then I got wind of a collection of letters and pictures coming to the museum in Hilo."

"So you stupidly thought that by getting your hands on these letters and anything else from the others, you could keep this quiet. Well, look what you've done! The company is ruined for sure."

"You already ruined it. Why did you do it?"

There was a long silence. Tawnie could hear someone moving around in the room and for a moment she thought of getting out until the police came. If they came. Her heart pounded so hard that she thought the men in the room could hear it. Still, she angled the cellphone for the best chance to get a good recording.

Finally Hickerson spoke. "Despite asking me to stay away, she changed her mind when she found out she was pregnant. Wanted to get married. The whore."

"God, Granddad. You're disgusting."

"What are you going to do about it?"

Braga's voice hardened. "I'm going to turn myself and you in. Maybe they'll go soft on me. I didn't mean to kill the old lady. But you— I hope you rot in hell."

"I won't let you do that." Hickerson's voice rose to gravelly scratch.

"You know, I could just unplug you," Braga hissed.

"Jim," Tawnie whispered, "What are we doing here? We should go."

"Justice, that's what." Joe came alongside them. "You heard them. He's admitted to killing Bessie. Now to get him to admit killing Hillary."

"Joe." Tawnie put out a hand to stop him when there was a sharp cry and explosion of a gun going off. Someone crashed to the floor in the room.

"I'm on it," Jim said as he rushed past Tawnie and Joe. Joe quickly followed as fast as he could go.

Jim stepped into the room.

"Who the hell are you?"

Before Jim could answer, to Tawnie's horror, a second shot rang out. Jim yowled in pain and fell further inside the room.

"Jim." Without a care for her own safety, Tawnie rushed into the room. On the opposite side of the room, an elderly man wizened from illness, sat propped up in a hospital bed. Attached to him were a variety of machines. He held a pistol in both his hands. Behind the bed, Tawnie could see the legs of Braga. He was not moving. Jim was. He grimaced as he held onto his shoulder. Blood seeped through his fingers. Tawnie knelt down beside him.

For a moment Hickerson seemed stunned, a strange pallor on his skeleton face. The machine pumped harder.

Joe came further into the room. "Not what you expected, Hick, did you? Wasting away."

"Joe Cameron. Hero to the rescue." Hickerson seemed almost delighted to see Joe there.

"Let Ms. Takahashi take her friend out. Then it'll be just you and me."

"Ah, now I recognize you. Tawnie Takahashi. That chipmunk of a woman who calls herself a reporter."

"Hillary's great niece," Joe nodded at Tawnie. "I think she'd be proud of her."

Tawnie looked up at Joe. Tears and anger left her choked up. It was not like her to be so emotional. Suddenly she was afraid for the old man.

"Hillary Takahashi. Haven't heard the name in a long time."

"The police have. Know all about you. There's a living witness who remembers those days too. And she's not all dried up like you are. It's over." Joe stepped past Tawnie and Jim. "Why don't you get him out?" he said to Tawnie. "Maybe the nurse can help him."

Tawnie gently helped Jim to sit up, but she kept her eyes on Hickerson who held the gun with sinking strength.

"Why Hillary?" Joe went on. "Why did you kill her weeks after Bessie? Oh, I know how you strangled them both with phone wire. Remember, I was in on the recovery after the tsunami. Didn't make the connection until Bessie was found." Joe swallowed hard. "How did you do it? Did you lure her down?"

"Ha." Hickerson's brittle laugh unnerved Tawnie. This old man was *lolo*. "You really want to know? Well, I'll tell you. She saw me with Bessie, that's what. Bessie kept asking me to do the right thing. She was afraid of her father. I got mad. I hit her hard, then pushed her into my car. Realized later, Hillary was probably watching the whole thing.

"So you killed Hillary?" Joe's voice shook.

"You want a confession?" Hickerson waggled the pistol at Joe. "Saw her at the USO show at the Naval Station. When it was over, I told one of the other girls to tell her that you wanted to see her. To make up. It was very late. She drove her parent's car down to the island and walked over the old pontoon bridge to meet you." Hickerson waggled the gun at Joe and for a moment straight at Tawnie as she got Jim to his feet. "It didn't take much, but not before we had some time together. Several hours in fact."

"You sick bastard," Joe choked.

With Jim safely on his feet, Tawnie helped her cameraman to a chair outside the room. She was so focused that she didn't hear someone coming up the stairs. When she stepped back into the doorway, Hickerson sat upright, tubes and wire straining from their machines. His hospital gown had slipped off his bony shoulders. "I didn't know what to do with her body, so I threw her into the bay. Then I saw the water pull back. Hightailed it after that." Hickerson grinned as he pointed the gun straight at Joe. "As they say, '*Sayonara*,' pal."

"Joe!" Tawnie leaped at Joe and pulled the old man down to the floor.

A gun fired, but it wasn't Hickerson's. A neat hole appeared in his forehead. His thin mouth opened in amazement as he was flung back, wires tearing from his arms. His body hung head down off the bed by the dark window.

"You OK, Takahashi?" Annie Moke said as she stepped into the room. She put her Glock back into its holster.

"Officer Moke." Tawnie could barely get the word out. "Are you OK, Joe?"

"I'd appreciate a hand up," Joe said as he lay crumpled on the floor.

Annie stooped down to check on Joe. "You know what, I don't think you should move. I'll have an EMT check you out. Should be coming soon." She picked up a blanket draped over a chair and tucked it around the old man.

"Is the bastard dead?" Joe asked her in a soft voice.

"Yes, I'm pretty sure."

"Good. And Braga?"

Kimo went through to check. "Breathing," he said.

The house exploded with activity as more police arrived. Tawnie started to shiver. Annie noticed and put her police jacket over her.

"Mahalo," Tawnie said. "That was close. Never so glad to see you." Out in the hall a police officer and Hickerson's nurse tended to Jim. "You were so fast getting here." Then it dawned on Tawnie that a local police station should be the one responding.

Annie nodded at Joe. "You can thank Mr. Cameron. He texted me a while back. Told me where he was going."

"Texted?" Tawnie looked at Joe in growing admiration.

"Always have back up," he said hoarsely. "You young people."

Ending

Two days later, Joe Cameron, pushed in a wheelchair by Tawnie, made the trip over the long pedestrian bridge to Coconut Island. Auntie Bee walked beside him, holding his hand. Jerry and Annie Moke, Kimo Fortes and Maile Horner followed behind with stacks of leis draped over their arms.

It had been an exhausting, emotional forty-eight hours, but Tawnie had been able to put together three live news reports: one from the crime scene at Hickerson's house, another outside of Hilo Hospital where Jim and Sammy Braga were recovering from their wounds, and a third one when Joe was released after a night's stay. Tawnie was relieved that except for a bruised hip, Joe had suffered no serious damage after she pulled him down to safety. The thought still made tears prick at her eyes. She had grown to love the old man. Auntie Hillary's true love.

Now they had come for a final farewell.

As they walked across the bridge, Joe talked about the old pontoon bridge with its sentry and limited access to the public. This new bridge, designed to take tsunami action, stood on strong concrete pillars and had metal railings and a concrete surface, but the island in front of them remained the same as Joe remembered: the tall, lanky palm trees, a few ironwood trees with their tiny prickly cones, and the large grassy field. Off to the right, Tawnie could make out the tower Joe had talked about jumping off as a trainer during WWII. Now a collection of local kids and a few tourists lined up to jump into the deep water nearby. Joe pointed out where he remembered the concession stand had stood and the location of the old caretaker's house. "Many fine memories there," he said.

"Where do you want to go, Joe?" Bee asked. "Over there?" She pointed to the picnic shelters on the far side that looked back toward the green hills behind downtown Hilo. She had kept her face blank, but Tawnie could see that her lips tremble from time to time. *Still afraid of the water? Or was it the emotion?*

"No, let's go out to the tower. We can throw the leis out from there."

"Alright," Tawnie said. "But I'm still driving." She knew why he wanted to go there. It was on the side of the island where Hillary had been found in the debris not pulled out to sea. They hit the pavement at the end of the bridge and headed over.

Moku Ola. That was the ancient Hawaiian name for the little island. It meant "island of life." Long ago there was a temple here dedicated to healing. *How appropriate*, Tawnie thought. She prayed especially that Joe and Bee would be healed. *Me, too.*

Of course, nothing really could take away the sting of what happened here on the island so long ago. Thomas Hickerson was dead and would never be tried for the murders. Sammy Braga was talking like a myna bird from his hospital bed. He probably would serve time for breaking and entering, and the accidental death of Suzie Fong, but he was co-operating, putting together the evidence against his own grandfather and that might heal him in the end. The Hickerson Design Company was another matter. It had taken a hit on the stock market and while there was a frantic campaign to save its good name, it very well might not heal from the fallout. Tawnie could care less.

"There's a tree on the island they say survived three tsunamis," Jerry Moke said. "My family went through all of them. My mom and aunt have stories handed down."

Joe looked over his shoulder. "I'd like to meet them."

Jerry nodded and said that he'd be happy to arrange that. "I want to hear the stories again, too." He smiled at Annie. "You too. And bring my grandchildren."

They followed the concrete path out to the tower made of dark, irregular lava blocks and rising fifteen feet above the water. Thick mortar held it together. The island itself was rugged with lava rock edges occasionally broken up by sandy beaches. On the *makai* side of the island, Tawnie could see the sea wall that protected Hilo. All under a blue sky dotted with clouds. A gentle breeze tugged at their casual clothes. They made a turn off the path to the tower. At the end of the walk, Joe indicated he wanted to stand up.

"You sure?" Tawnie asked.

"Yeah, yeah. I can manage with all you lovely young *wahines* here." He limped as he got going.

Annie and Kimo walked ahead of him carrying their leis. Maile stopped and put two orchid ones over Joe's and Bee's shoulders. "You too, Tawnie," Maile said as she followed Annie and Kimo to the steps.

The scene suddenly quieted as swimmers and picnickers realized something was happening. Maile went out on the first deck of the tower. Kimo and Annie climbed to the highest one.

"Will you say something?" Bee asked Perry as she walked slowly with Joe.

Perry nodded. He began to chant in Hawaiian. Tawnie closed her eyes, tears welling up. *Damn. Lost my reporter's objectivity again.*

When Perry was finished, they threw the leis out onto the water. Maile helped Joe up on the lower deck and gave him a lei to throw. He walked haltingly to the edge. Bee came up beside him.

"*Aloha nui loa*, Hillary," he said. "See you someday soon." He composed himself, then threw his lei into the water.

Two young swimmers gathered some of the leis and carried them further away from the tower where the flowers floated and rode on the water. Joe's lei was caught by a wave and swept near the spot where Joe said Hillary was found after the tsunami.

"Oh, look, Joe," Bee said, clasping her hands. "I see Honu right out there."

Tawnie could swear the large green turtle raised its leathery head toward Bee and bowed.

The April Fool's Day tsunami that hit Hilo, Hawaii in 1946, was the worst tsunami of the 20th century. It arrived from the Aleutian Island in Alaska in under five hours, killing 96 people in Hilo alone.

I first heard the story of the tsunami that wiped out Hilo when I moved down to Hilo in 1974 from Honolulu. I just didn't know the impact of that event until a woman in a class I was teaching told me the tale of being trapped in her bedroom with only so much air in the corner of the ceiling. She lost classmates that day.

The other piece to the story of Coconut Island is the USO Center on the island. This part of the story came from my husband's uncle. When we were married in Liliuokalani Park, in Hilo, Uncle Ken came over from the Mainland. One of the first things he wanted to see was the island. He said there was a club there during WW II. It had been wiped out in the 1946 tsunami. He told me that there were lights at night and bridge that went over to it. I discovered that it was a USO Club for servicemen.

Many thanks to the wonderful librarians, including Mary Louise Haraguchi, Interlibrary Loan Department, UH Hilo, who ran down sources for this novella.

To learn more about the 1946 tsunami go to the following website:

*Pacific Tsunami Museum, Hilo Hawaiiwww.tsunami.org

*Center for Oral History, UH Manoa

http://www.oralhistory.hawaii.edu/pages/historical/tsunami.html

Some YouTube videos worth watching"

*Center for the Study of Active Volcanoes made this great comparison of now and then (1946) https://www.youtube.com/watch?v=hqleDCrv7EI

*Silent footage of the actual 1946 tsunami

https://www.youtube.com/watch?v=w9jo7v0ys6U

Volcano House

Priceless Manuscript ~ Ancient Curse

By J. L. Oakley

Chapter 1

Kilauea, Hawaii, 1889

The lava lake glowed, its light reaching up into the deep night sky like a living thing. As the volcano belched, coughed and hissed, its light created wavering red and gold images on the *'ohi'a* trees and giant *hapu'u* tree ferns that dared to grow so close. From the crater's belly, a tall column of cloud rose to the stars.

Almanzo Almeida stood on the long veranda of Volcano House and watched the party of twenty guests and their guides depart for Little Beggar on Pele's Throat a half mile away. It would be a good night to descend onto the floor of Kilauea Crater. Their candle-lit lanterns twinkled in the dark like little fairy lights in counter march to the heavens above. Some of the guests, he suspected, wouldn't want to go all the way across to the far lake, but might stop to pull out some thin glass threads of Pele's Hair.

From outside the long ranch-style hotel, Almeida could hear the late night guests chatting around the great stone fireplace inside. At this elevation, nights at Kilauea could be chilly, even cold. The fireplace was always the focal point of the establishment overseen by the superb hospitality of Colonel and Mrs. Malby. Almeida patted his stomach. The food was outstanding, too, something that always amazed visitors, including Mark Twain, who came some years back. No matter if you came up the new carriage road from Hilo or came from Punalu'u by tram and horseback, Volcano House stood out as a first class hotel next to a volcano on a tropical island in the middle of nowhere: a jewel in the Royal Hawaiian Kingdom's crown.

Out in the dark, a horse nickered down by the stables. Almeida pulled out his chain watch. Under the soft glow of a lantern he checked the time, then looked down in the direction of the stables. Shortly, a light appeared and began to swing back and forth. So Casper DeMello was back. Almeida put on his jacket. Moments later he was heading down across open ground, his only light a candle in his lantern.

Down by the low shed that served as a waiting station for guests, a shadow emerged.

"What did you get this time? Anything good?" Almeida asked.

"Yeah, yeah. They nevah gonna miss it. Stupid tourists." The young Portuguese man set his lantern up on a wide stump. When Almeida added his, the area bloomed with light.

DeMello pulled out of a satchel a bag of gold coins, a lady's watch and chain and a silver comb. He set them on the stump. Other items of value were added, all of them sparkling in the candle light.

"Were you careful?" Almeida asked as he handled one of the gold chains, weighing it back and forth through his fingers.

"Course I'm careful. It's all stuff dropped on the steamer and the tram. The rest I just nipped. I was plenty careful."

"Hmph." Almeida grunted. It wasn't easy getting up to the hotel. Tourists who came by a steamer to Punalu'u went from tram to road cart to horseback. It took hours. Almeida opened the bag of coins and counting them all out on the stump, he gave half to DeMello. "Once again, you did good." Almeida gathered up the stolen items and put them back into the satchel. "When do you go back?"

"Tomorrow. I'll catch the W.G. Hall going back to Honolulu."

"Good. Got to keep these things irregular."

A burst of laughter from inside Volcano House sliced the thin night air. Both men froze and looked blindly in that direction. Almeida shielded his eyes from the lanterns to see more clearly. As his eyes adjusted to the dark beyond the corral, he saw no movement on the veranda. He began to relax.

"I betta go," DeMello said. He shouldered a haversack and picked up a walking staff leaning against the corral rail.

Almeida pointed to the haversack. "What's in that?"

"Nuthin'. Just paper."

"Let me see."

DeMello scowled. "What'd you think? I'm cheating you?"

"Just curious. That's nice leather. Nice silver clasp. That a—a thistle?"

DeMello shrugged. He unlocked the clasp then flipped open the flap. "See? Papers." He pulled a packet of papers wrapped with a heavy cotton cord half-way out. The mouth of the haversack sagged wider.

Behind the packet Almeida could see another packet and a *Scribner's Magazine*. "Where'd you get this stuff?"

"Ho'okena."

Almeida's eyes grew sharp and wary.

DeMello pulled the packet out further. A title was neatly handwritten on the front page, but all Almeida could read were the words, "Bottle Imp."

"See? Papers." DeMello grasped the straps tighter. He jammed the packet back in, but when it wouldn't go in straight, Almeida grew suspicious and jerked the haversack out of DeMello's hands.

"Hey!"

"What is this?" Almeida lifted out a long, sharp letter opener. The jewels in the silver handle sparkled in the lantern light—green, white and ruby. At the top was a thistle. "Cheating me, were you?"

"Cheating? You forget we both thieves, only I take all the risks."

"But we must share." Almeida hung the straps of the haversack on his shoulder. He turned the letter opener around in his hands. "I'll keep it. Once I sell it, I'll split the money."

"No! It's mine. I found it. Give it back—"

DeMello's words ended in a cry as Almeida grabbed DeMello's walking stick and slammed it on his head. DeMello staggered back, his hands pressed to his head. Blood began to flow between his fingers. His vision blurred. The last thing DeMello saw was Almeida's sneering face and the letter opener raised high..

Chapter 2

Present day, Big Island, Hawaii

Beatrice "Auntie Bee" Takahashi put the box of books into her car's trunk and shut it. She walked with a slight limp to the driver's side of her Nissan Rogue.

"Is that the last one, Beatrice?" Eleanor Kane asked as she came out of the library with a plastic container of cookies.

"Yeah, yeah. That's what's left from the book sale. Just two boxes. We did plenty good. Made 500 dollars. Now the friends of the library can buy new books for the *keiki*."

"Well, this is the last of the cookies. Kitchen is cleaned up, tables put away. Sylvia Ramone is locking up. I'm ready to go whenever you want." Eleanor put the container on the car roof and brushed down her blue muumuu dotted with bright blue hibiscus.

"I'm ready." Auntie Bee looked back at the library where Eleanor and she had spent the day helping with the book sale. The wood frame building with a brick-red tin roof was set off the highway next to the remains of a tiny patch of sugar cane, the only green spot on the *makai* side of the road. Behind it, broken black lava rocks, some worn down to the size of ping pong balls, stretched down to the aqua sea. On the *mauka* side of the highway, it was green up to the gray blue flanks of 13,500 foot Mauna Loa. A few ti plants and banana trees rustling in the sea breeze made up the landscaping in the parking lot. Once a bank that had gone out of business, the little library was the pride of the surrounding community.

Auntie Bee clipped her shades over her wire-rimmed glasses and eased into the driver's seat. When she winced, Eleanor asked if her leg was hurting today.

"Just reminding me that I'm not sixteen anymore."

Eleanor laughed as she got into the car. "Who'd want that? I heard about Icky Sammy Ito with his kisses from my cousin."

"Legend." Auntie Bee pretended to shiver at the thought. She appreciated her friend changing the subject with humor. Auntie Bee limped ever since her leg had been badly broken in a tsunami long ago. It was just something she had to bear.

Eleanor put on her seat belt and slapped a book onto her lap. "Found this on the dollar table. *Leaving Paradise.* Says on the back a lot of Hawaii folks left for the Mainland two centuries ago." She turned it back to the front cover. "Maybe we should read it for our book club's non-fiction pick."

"Long as it's not depressing. People leaving all the time now or stay stuck in Hawaii. Too expensive to live here."

Eleanor gave the hardbound book a pat. "Well, I'll read it and let you know. Spreading *aloha* around the world not so bad. If the book's good, I'll use it as my pick when we have our picnic to decide on next year's readings. In meantime, we have a birthday to celebrate. Eighty years young, girl."

"Now you make me feel like one old lady."

"Is Tawnie coming?"

"Yeah, yeah. She promised. My kids say they're coming down, too. I'm hoping for Kiro, too."

"Then it will be a birthday to remember."

***

Standing on the wide sandy beach, the slight breeze rustling her sleek bobbed hair, the reporter looked into the camera lens and said, "This is Tawnie Takahashi saying Aloha from Ho'okena Beach." She nodded to her unseen audience and waited until her cameraman signaled they were done.

When Jim said, "That's a wrap," a small crowd of sea kayakers and snorklers standing behind Tawnie broke into applause. Tawnie turned to acknowledge them and while Jim put away the microphone and the rest of KWAI-5 News gear into his hard pack containers, she signed some autographs.

"Ms. Takahashi?"

Tawnie turned to face an aging surfer with sun-streaked blonde hair and a permanent sun tan. In his fifties, she guessed, but very fit.

"Mr. Fowler. We're almost done here."

"Great. Come up to the pavilion when you're ready. Got some cold ones in the cooler." He pointed to the picnic structure perched above the sand. Its wavy turquoise roof imitated the rolling surf in the bay.

Tawnie smiled. "*Mahalo*. I could use a beer." She gave the pen back to the last fan and tugging at her purple linen suit stepped back to give Jim a hand. Her gangly cameraman was the best around, but better yet he seemed to tolerate her sometimes sharp tongue. He'd been with her several years now.

For the past few days, Tawnie and Jim had been exploring the area for an interest story on Ho'okena. The beach and the ruins of its old village was on the west side of the Big Island and out of the way for many tourists visiting the Kailua-Kona area to the north, but it had once been a thriving community both culturally and economically. A local group was working on bringing that back.

"Jim, are you taking this gear to our car? Why don't you just bring it up to the pavilion? I heard there've been break-ins."

"I heard that, too, but I also heard the group that takes care of this place does a really great job. Cut down on the tension between locals and tourists. People coming together."

Jim scanned the dark-gray coral and lava sand beach with its crystal clear, calm waters. "Pretty spectacular place, yeah? I'd like to come back here on my own and do some snorkeling."

"You should." Tawnie chin-pointed to the left of the beach where a number of snorkeling enthusiasts clad in skimpy bikinis or surfer shorts gathered. Not far off were the remains of a wharf. "Well, let's get this gear up to that beer. After that we can find out where we can upload the interviews."

"We're still going Hilo side, right? For your auntie's birthday?"

"Yeah, yeah. Wouldn't miss that for the world."

As Tawnie walked up to the pavilion, her sandals sank into the sand. She wondered if she should resent the Ho'okena assignment or be happy to have the occasional break to do a soft story. She was Honolulu-based KWAI-5's leading crime reporter, but her boss, Denny Kane, had grown concerned after Tawnie's investigation into a 70-year-old murder case came to a violent end with Jim shot and Tawnie nearly killed, herself. "A little too close for my comfort," Denny had said. Then he told her to take some time off. "I'm putting Jim on medical leave for six weeks. We'll reassess when the doctor clears him for work."

Tawnie and Jim had been back to work for ten months now, but Denny still insisted they take on some lighter assignments.

Up at the pavilion, Ackerson welcomed Tawnie and Jim to a concrete picnic table set out with snacks and paper plates.

"Help yourself." Fowler said. He opened a red cooler to display a variety of bottled beer and soda packed with ice. Jim helped himself to a Kona brew, Tawnie took a Longboard Lager. It was cool under the pavilion and the view back to the water worth every effort to get down to Ho'okena.

Tawnie took off her jacket and laid it on the picnic table. She straightened her cotton tank top with its lacy bottom edge, wishing she could get out of her hose. She took great care on how she looked on camera, but there were days when she wished she could put on a muumuu and be done with it. Especially since the old Whitehall matter. Sometimes, she didn't feel so driven to get to the story ahead of everyone else. For the first time in her career, her few friends and family mattered more. She sat down next to Jim who had found a bag of chips.

"Did you get what you wanted here, Ms. Takahashi?" Fowler asked.

"*Mahalo.* I did, though I have a few more questions. And please, call me Tawnie. Can I call you Mark?"

Fowler beamed at that.

Tawnie took the cap off her beer and sipped. "How long have you been park host, Mark?"

"Two years and counting. When I got wind of what they were planning to do, I had to be on the board. My grandparents settled in Kailua-Kona back before World War II. I came down to this beach every summer growing up. Becoming a park host was just a natural next step."

"I appreciate you taking us up to see remains of the old village earlier today. I had no idea of Ho'okena's history." Tawnie looked out to the remains of the wharf. "I can't imagine steamers coming here so early and dropping tourists off."

Fowler helped himself to a beer and settled on the edge of the picnic table next to Tawnie. "Crazy, yeah? Some came all the way here from the Mainland. This was a thriving place."

"But in the 1870s and 1880s? I never knew."

"Well, most were coming to go up and see the volcano at Kilauea. They might stop here at Ho'okena for a bit, but most of the travelers continued on the boat to Punalu'u. Go to Kilauea from there and stay overnight."

"Where?"

"Volcano House. It was a first rate hotel even back then, though much simpler. Here in Ho'okena, the wharf is all that is left of that time."

Tawnie shook her head. "That's amazing." She nodded out to the wharf. "How did people get ashore?"

"Whaleboat."

"Wow," Jim said. "That must have been rough."

"You think? People were adventuresome then. No TSA, no complaining, like today when your ten-story liner gets caught in a hurricane or having to wait out a blizzard on the floor of an airport cuz it's too dangerous to fly. You just took things in stride."

Between the crunch of potato chips, Jim asked if it was true that the famous author, Robert Louis Stevenson, had come to Ho'okena for a spell. "Something like 1889."

"You heard about that?" Fowler looked impressed.

"Something I read. I've been fan of his since I was a kid. You know, *Treasure Island, Kidnapped, Dr. Jekell and Mr. Hyde*. There was a really spooky one, *The Bottle Imp*."

"Ha!" Fowler smiled. "Think I read that one in a *Classic Illustrated* comic book my dad had. Supposed to be set around here."

Now Tawnie was curious. "Where would someone like Stevenson stay in Ho'okena?"

"Probably with the judge. Nahinu, I think. We're trying to put together tours about life in Ho'okena Village back then. Robert Louis Stevenson's certainly one of the most important people from the Mainland to ever come here to Ho'okena. Friend of King Kalakaua, his royal court and all that."

"Wow," Jim said again. He rubbed his scratchy face, the hair stubble on it golden against his tanned skin.

Tawnie was going to ask another question when there was a commotion up the hill behind the pavilion. A couple of locals came rushing down. "Hey, Mark," one of them said. "Call 911."

"What's up, Buzzie?"

"Found someone beat up in the parking lot. Hurt plenty bad."

"Gotta go," Fowler said to Tawnie. "Help yourself to the snacks." He slapped a cell phone to his ear as he ran, the big Hawaiian leading the way.

"I don't think so," Tawnie mouthed to Jim. She grabbed her messenger pack that carried her notebook, camera and water bottle. "Gotta be a story there. Bring what you think you need, Jim. I can record from my little camera for now." Tawnie took off, sprinting after the men through keawe trees and shrub brush.

Up in the dusty parking lot partially filled with cars and SUVs with kayaks and surf boards on top, Tawnie saw Fowler, Buzzie and two others gathered around a Jeep Cherokee. As she got closer, she saw someone slumped back against the driver's seat.

"How long has he been here?" Tawnie heard Fowler ask Buzzie.

"No idea. Blood's almost dry on his head. Good thing the window was rolled down. With this heat, he'd be fried."

"Is he alive?" Tawnie asked as she came beside the Jeep.

"He's breathing. Can't tell if there are any other injuries." Fowler looked at Buzzie. "Get Milton to go out on the road and flag down any medic ambulance you see. Na'alehu or Captain Cook fire stations could be responding."

"How can I help?" Tawnie looked at the man. His mouth was slack, his eyes fluttering. His sun burned neck and face said that he was probably a visitor.

"Do you have any water?"

"Have a water bottle."

Fowler reached over and loosened up the man's bloody shirt. "Mind if I borrow it? He needs it."

"Sure." Tawnie handed over her water bottle. "Anything else I can do?"

"Could you look in his glove compartment and see if there's any ID? I couldn't find his wallet."

Tawnie went around to the passenger side and got in.

Inside the unlocked glove compartment, she found a manual and a rental car receipt. "Found a name. Says Harold Boyd. San Francisco. Car rental from Hilo." Tawnie put the receipt in front of the steering wheel for Fowler to see.

"That's a start." Fowler drizzled some water on the man's lips. Tawnie and Mark were both surprised when he swallowed it, then spoke through blistered lips.

"My car—I was robbed..."

"Shh. Try not to talk. Help is coming," Tawnie soothed.

"No wait," Fowler said. "Did it happen in this parking lot?"

The man shook his head slowly. "No. The old village…"

Fowler picked up the rental receipt. "You Harold Boyd??

"Yes...Har-ry."

"OK, that's enough. You rest." Fowler nodded for Tawnie to stay with Boyd. "Going to check on that help. Could you stay with him? Don't want to move him." He handed her water bottle back. "See if he'll take some more. Just dribbles. I'm keeping the driver side door open for ventilation. I suggest you do it on your side. "

"Found his window sunscreen. I'll put it up."

Tawnie lifted a sunscreen with dolphins and Dory on its cover from the car floor. After setting it against the windshield, she settled back into the bucket seat of the Jeep. Outside, a small group of curious onlookers talked to Buzzie.

Boyd opened his eyes with a jerk. "My papers. Did he take my papers?"

"What papers?"

Boyd swallowed hard. "They're... in... a... box."

"Do you want me to look?"

"Yes. Please. Important," Boyd whispered.

Tawnie twisted around and looked in the backseat. Whoever the thief was had seriously messed it up. Items were tossed everywhere: a suitcase with clothes pulled out, a day pack, a couple of bundled papers and books.

Boyd groaned making Tawnie jump and remember her duty. *Keep him hydrated.* She wet a bandanna from her messenger bag and dripped water on his lips. Tawnie carefully dabbed his bloody forehead. Boyd stirred slightly and opened his eyes. He turned his face toward her. "Thanks. Will you look?"

"Sure." By now Tawnie's reporter's curiosity was kicking in. A random robbery at a park or something more intriguing? *Might as well investigate.*

In the back Tawnie picked through the clutter of thrown items, wondering if she should be doing this. The police would want to look for evidence. She avoided the suitcase and looked at the bundles of papers she had spied earlier. Picking up one collection held together with a large clip, she read the title to what appeared to be a research paper. *Comparison of Mark Twain's and RLS's Writing Experiences in Old Hawaii.* Some of the books looked to be his, but two were checked out from the Hilo Library. But there was no box of any size.

"What are you doing?"

Tawnie stood up so sharply, she banged her head on the door frame. Rubbing her head, she turned to face a tall burly man in a loud aloha shirt and Oakley sunglasses. When the Hawaiian flashed his Hilo Police Department badge, she immediately recognized the policeman as Captain Jerry Moke.

"Just trying to find out more about the victim. That's why looking." She hoped the police captain would remember her kindly as Auntie Bee Takahashi's great niece. Her auntie had been friends with his grandmother back in the day. More importantly, on a professional level, Tawnie had given Moke an important tip in solving the Whitehall case.

"Tawnie Takahashi. Always on the hunt for a good news story." Moke's voice was not unkind.

Tawnie stepped away from the car and closed the side door. "And you? That's the new Hilo Police uniform?"

Moke guffawed. "I'm on vacation with the grandkids." He looked around. "Looks like it's over for now. I'll take over from here. I hear the ambulance."

And it's time I make my exit. Jim was already in the parking lot with his gear. And her jacket.

"So glad to hear. Any idea where they will take him?" Tawnie asked Moke.

"KWAI-5 wants to know?"

"Justice should be served."

"Kona Hospital. Hilo if his injuries are worse." Moke gave her a "We're done here" look, then added, "Say Happy Birthday to Auntie Bee."

Tawnie said she would, but first she had a story to unravel.

Chapter 3

Maui detective Annie Moke opened the small envelope and pulled out a handmade card covered with embossed hibiscus flowers on ivory scrapbook paper. Inside she read:

"In honor of our beloved Aunt Beatrice Takahashi Peterson you are invited to the celebration of her 80th birthday at Volcano House on—"

Annie looked at the young woman standing on the other side of the Kahalui Police Station information desk. She was a pretty redhead in her late twenties with cinnamon freckles that served as a tan on her nose and sleeveless shoulders. "Maile Horner. You said you were Bee Takahashi's neighbor in Hilo."

"Yes."

Annie tapped the card on her hand. "Nice to have an invitation hand delivered. Is this what brought you to Maui?"

"No, not completely. I'm an historian with Big Island Historical Society in Hilo. I've been doing research at the museum in Lahaina." Maile nodded to the card. "Auntie Bee wanted to be sure that you got this. She wants to say *Mahalo nui loa* for helping her last year."

"Well, I'll certainly try to come. She's very sweet."

Annie made motions to leave, but Maile blurted out. "You know, I've always wanted to meet you. I was hoping that we would eventually." Maile cleared her throat. "You see, I knew your father, John Hillard."

"My father? On the Mainland or in the islands?"

"Both."

A voice squawked on Annie's shoulder. Some tourist with ankle injury in Kepuolani Park. Annie turned the radio off. "Let's go sit in the lobby over there. Would you like some coffee?"

Maile nodded yes.

Paper cups of coffee in hand, Annie and Maile sat down in the corner by the window where a large anthurium plant with its waxy, red flowers and long white spadix provided the only decoration in the stark public space.

"Say again how you knew my father?' Annie asked.

Maile took a big breath. "He and my father were in the same unit in Vietnam. I grew up hearing stories about him. A couple of years ago there was a Vietnam Vets reunion in Seattle. That's where I got to meet him."

"You said you met him in the islands, too."

"Yes, though I grew up on the Mainland, I was born here in Hawaii. My family came to the Big Island in 1908. Sugar cane."

"Really? That's cool." Annie relaxed. "Family still around? Sugar cane all gone except for the wild stuff."

"Sad, yeah?" Maile sighed. "I have an uncle in Pahala, but with the mills closed down, he's renting out some of the company homes. Spruced up the main house for a B and B." Maile smiled. "When I was a kid, I visited the Big Island several times. I think your dad and my father went deep sea fishing off Kona-Kailua while I was at my grandparents. That's how I met him here."

"Oh, that's nice."

"I have something for you," Maile said. She took out small package wrapped in rice paper.

Annie opened it up. Inside was a framed 5 x 8 photo of four young soldiers in uniform lifting beer mugs in front of a painted jungle scene. "Why, that's my father," Annie said.

"It is. The night before they shipped out to Vietnam. That's my dad on the right with his helmet all cock-eyed. Looks a bit high."

Annie chucked, then bit her lips. "This is so kind of you."

"Well, I had to give away a lot of things before I moved back to the islands, but I couldn't leave the Mainland without this picture. I thought you might like a copy too. I treasure mine."

"*Mahalo*." Annie briefly squeezed Maile's hand. "Are you staying long?"

"No, I'm done. Catching a flight at three back to Hilo. We're putting up a show about the *Treasure Island* author, RLS, in the islands at our museum in Hilo.

"RLS?"

"Robert Louis Stevenson for short. Really fun stuff. I have an appointment to meet an expert on Stevenson tomorrow at Volcano House."

"Well,   have   a   good   time   with   that."

The way back to Hilo where Auntie Bee lived, passed through Volcanoes National Park. There, Kilauea, the world's only drive-in volcano, was presently spouting steam and making small earthquakes while further down its flanks the lava from Puʻu ʻŌʻōʻs crater was going full tilt down to the sea. In its path the lava torched, then swallowed up, forest and fern, leaving behind loopy black *pahoehoe*. As Bee got closer to the headquarters of the park, she kept the windows rolled up. A library patron at the book sale said that the sulfur smell was strong today.

As the two-lane Hawaii Belt Road passed through a forest of tall ʻohiʻa, *hapuʻu* tree ferns with their giant fronds, and wild ginger, a sign announcing the Crater Rim Drive came up. When Eleanor saw it, she asked Bee if she wouldn't mind if they stopped by the Volcano Art Center Gallery.

"I need to pick up a print for my daughter's office. If you like, we can go get ice mocha at Volcano House before we head down. Check it out for your party. I can drive us home, if you're too tired."

"Yeah, sure. I'm not tired. Maybe get something more than ice mocha." Despite the plate lunch offered to the volunteers at the book sale, Bee was hungry.

Bee made the turn onto Crater Rim Drive, chatted with the park attendant at the entrance station—the granddaughter of one of her former students—then drove down past the Kilauea Visitor Center to the lane that led to the art center. As they pulled up to it, Bee felt a sense of pride. Set in an open area, the little one-story ranch house sported bright banners announcing the latest art show and classes, but there was a time years ago, when the building had been a neglected, nearly forgotten piece of history. In the mid-1800s, it had been the second manifestation of Volcano House. In the 1970s Bee, along with other volunteers, had been part of the group that saved the building and made it into the art center that it was today.

As they climbed the short stairs to the porch, Bee stopped to give her leg a rest and reflect. Her late husband, George Peterson, was part of the crew that cleaned the building out. A contractor who cared for historic structures, George knew the ins and outs of preservation and repurposing buildings. She could hear his voice with its Boston accent—despite years living in the islands—as he helped to restore this very porch.

Bee smiled at the muumuu-clad woman sitting on a wicker chair next to the door making hat bands using dried flowers and ferns. This what she and George had hoped for—bringing the best of island contemporary artists to the center as well as supporting traditional Hawaiian crafts. When she stepped into the main room with its rafters and beams exposed, memories wafted over her. Above the soft slack key music playing on a CD, she recalled the sounds of scrapers, hammers and drills. Where there were now display cases of jewelry, pedestals for blown glass, pottery, and wood bowls, paintings and prints over the old brick fireplace, Bee saw an empty room stripped down to bare wood floors and dust. George's husky laugh as he worked at one of the window sashes.

How come so emotional? she thought. *George gone almost two years.*

"Bee?" Eleanor held a large silkscreen print of ancient hula dancers under her chin. "Think this will work in Millie's reception room?"

"Oh, Dietrich Varez. Yeah, yeah. Very nice. Like his stuff." Bee picked up a package of notecards with Varez prints. "Think I'll get something, too." She looked around the room rich in amber light, then followed Eleanor to the cash register. They headed outside when they were done.

"Hey!" a voice shouted. "What are you doing? Get out of there."

All heads turned to the parking lot. A tourist in a loud aloha shirt was struggling with a skinny local kid with dreads. Bee froze when she saw that it was all happening at the back of her car. The two strangers wrestled back and forth, but eventually, the kid broke loose and ran across the parking lot and down through the trees to Crater Rim Road.

Eleanor stepped down ahead of Bee and went to the car. The tourist was brushing off his arms. "Are you alright?" Bee heard Eleanor ask him.

"I'm OK," the tourist said. "Just my adrenaline spiking. The punk kid was prowling the cars. Caught him in mine." The man nodded at his rental Jeep where a woman in a matching muumuu stood by the passenger side. "Scared my wife. Didn't know they had crime up here."

"Always good to lock the car," Bee said as she came up. "You nevah know." Her heart was pounding, too. She studied her little Rogue. Nothing seemed out of order. Which was a good thing. *She* had forgotten to click the lock closed.

She thanked the tourist for his help in stopping the thief, answered his questions on sights to see in the national park, and then nodded goodbye. As Eleanor got into the front, Bee put her purchase in the lowered back seat half-filled with boxes and started to close the door when she noticed something under the car. "Omph," she said reaching down for it. *So stiff today. Getting creaky.* She picked up a wallet. "Oh."

"What's that?" Eleanor asked

"Somebody lost their wallet." Auntie Bee looked around, but the tourist and his wife were gone. She opened it up. If there had been any credit cards, they were gone. But there was a California driver's license. Auntie Bee pulled it out. It read: Harrison Boyd.

"I can take it in," Eleanor said. "Then let's go for that iced mocha."

"Hope they find the owner. Don't like folks going home thinking we're not the Aloha State."

A short time later, Auntie Bee and Eleanor found a table by the window of the Volcano House Restaurant. Though the building had recently gone through renovations, the view from the long set of the rustic building's windows hadn't changed. It continued to take Auntie Bee's breath away even though she had come here a thousand times over the years. Outside, beyond the old stone wall and the keawe and ohia trees on the crater's edge, she could see down into the maw of Kilauea. On any given day, it was mysterious, but today the steam rising high above the rim reminded her that there had been a recent eruption.

"What you want, Bee?" Eleanor asked when the waitress approached.

"Iced latte. And those fruit skewers."

"And I'll have an iced mocha. My treat." Eleanor clasped her hands in front of her. "So thrilled about the books for the *keikis* at the library. I found some other books for our book club."

"Still working this month's already." Auntie Bee grinned. "Teasing. Finished it last night. *Honolulu* is a plenty good read." She sighed. "Some history never gets told except when it's in a novel."

"Speaking of history when does your neighbor get home?"

"Maile? Tonight. Went to some library on Maui. Working on a show for the Hilo history museum in town. I'm watching her cat."

They talked for a bit longer over their drinks and food, then on the way out, checked on the arrangements for Bee's party. It was an open secret that Bee's book club, The U'ilani Book Lovers Club, was putting her 80th birthday party on here at Volcano House. Beyond that, Bee didn't know much more about the plans except that her daughter, Janice, would bring her up here on the appointed day. The rest *was* secret. Bee wished that all of her family would attend, but her youngest son Kiro Peterson was stationed in Germany with a medical unit. That was a long way from home.

Back at the car, Bee opened the side door and checked on her packages. For the first time, she noticed that the boxes of books were slightly skewed. "Hmph," she said. She went to the back and lifted up the door. Most of the boxes were upright and in order except for a couple that had shifted off to the right on their sides. One of them was a new-looking US postal box, its flaps held down by a bungee cord.

"Need help?" Eleanor said.

"Yeah, sure."

Together, they quickly put the boxes to rights.

"Phew. Heavy," Eleanor said.

"But not this one. I don't remember putting this one into the car. Maybe Sylvia did at the library." Bee plucked on the box's bungee cord, then on an impulse, started to pull the hooks apart. It was harder to do than she thought and let Eleanor take over. It wasn't easy admitting her hands weren't as strong as they used to be.

Inside the box, Bee found a stack of typed papers. She moved them aside to see what was underneath and was surprised to find a package loosely wrapped in brown paper. When she opened it up, Eleanor gasped.

"What is that?" she said.

"Someone at the book sale got all fancy." Bee adjusted her glasses to stare at the leather haversack. It must have been very old. The leather was a deep brown with worn patches the color of amber. The strap was cracked though recently oiled. And in its center, was a tarnished silver clasp in the shape of a thistle. Bee undid it. A musty smell of old paper hit her nose. She carefully pulled out an old magazine, worn by the ages.

"Oh, Maile should see this one. 1887. That's the year the first Takahashis came to the Big Island." Auntie Bee gently put the magazine back in and closed up the box. "First, gotta get home."

"Think he's going to be OK?" Tawnie asked Mark Fowler as the ambulance pulled away, its siren blaring.

The park host nodded at the departing vehicle. "Officer Moke says his signs are good. Dehydrated for sure with a possible concussion. They'll check that out in Kona."

"He was going on about a box of papers he had in the back seat. I didn't see anything like he was talking about, but I did find one manuscript for some research paper. It was all about RLS and Mark Twain in the Hawaiian Islands. Is RLS Robert Louis Stevenson?"

"It is."

"Interesting," Tawnie said. She felt her reporter instinct for story gear up. Lots of questions shot at her. Like what was in the box that had Boyd so fired up? "Didn't you say earlier Stevenson stayed there for a spell, in what 1880s?"

"That's what the records say. Hmm. Boyd said he was robbed out by the old village. Wonder what he was looking for? Kinda hard to figure out without a guide or help from the historical society in Kailua- Kona."

"What was it like?"

"Ho'okena? Well, back then, it was an old-time Hawaiian community. Some say Stevenson wanted to stay there to get away from the noise of Honolulu, though Ho'okena was thriving enough to have a schoolhouse, two churches, a courthouse, and some nice homes. Second largest place on the island after Kona."

"What happened to it?"

"Tsunamis and economics over time killed it."

Jim waved to Tawnie across the parking lot, the afternoon sun glancing orange off his sunglasses. *Time to go. He must have heard something on our scanner.* Tawnie signaled that she was coming, then turned to thank Fowler. "You've been great. Thanks so much for showing us around. I'll let you know when the story goes up. Got some editing to do, but we should be ready no later than tomorrow night's news.

Fowler shook Tawnie's hand. "And thanks for helping out here." He walked her back to her car. Jim was already at the wheel which meant he had something for her.

"*Mahalo* again, Mark," she said as she slid into the passenger seat. "We'll be in touch." She closed the door and immediately shivered from the blast of the air conditioner. "Ooh, so cold." Tawnie rubbed her arms. She waved to Fowler as Jim backed the car out, then searched for her jacket.

"What you got?" She nodded to the Bearcat scanner plugged into the car's cigarette lighter.

"Someone just reported a car prowl up at Kilauea a half hour ago. Volcano Art Center Gallery. Got a hunch and called them. Gal who answered the phone was sweet. Said park police were still assessing but since I was with KWAI-5 News, did I know someone named Harrison Boyd?"

"No. He was up there?

"His wallet was. Someone found it and turned it in. Had to have been from the robbery down here."

"The thief sure moved fast." Tawnie wondered if he was part of some sort of ring that preyed on unsuspecting tourists.

Jim tapped the steering wheel. "Where do you want to go now?"

"Let's go back to Kona. You can work on getting our Ho'okena story together. I'll see if we can go and talk to Mr. Boyd."

"It's just a local story. What would the boss think?"

"Well, I'll make it an extension of our report from here. A RLS angle which our audience might find interesting. There was a tea house in Manoa on Oahu that was supposed to have been used by Stevenson. Went there a couple of times as a girl."

"Oh, that was a replica of his shack in Waikiki where he lived and wrote."

"Hmm."

"Stevenson was a friend of the Cleghorns, the parents of Princess Ka'iulani. Belonged to some Scottish society. Thistle something."

"You must be a fan."

Jim laughed. "You bet. The Hawaii angle to Stevenson's stories have always fascinated me. Love how he said he engaged with the ink bottle darkly."

"Maybe Boyd was onto something. Researching this author's past here on the Big Island might just work as an angle."

Jim and Tawnie didn't get back on Boyd's whereabouts for a couple of hours. An accident on the highway around Captain Cook kept the traffic backed up a mile for nearly an hour and though Tawnie had the historian's location via their police scanner, any information on his condition took some sleuthing. By the time, they got to the hospital, she learned that he had been released. *To where?* Tawnie decided that they should check back into their hotel so Jim could work on their report. She would call her boss, but first some investigating.

Sitting on her bed, Tawnie opened up her laptop and began an online search. First, she logged in and looked for Boyd on LinkedIn and found some bios and recommendations on his background. Boyd, for one, was from San Bruno, California and taught at a local college. He had published a couple of works on Mark Twain and the background to Twain's stories in *Roughing It*, which Tawnie was surprised to learn also included a trip to Kilauea and Volcano House in the 1860s. *Volcano House!* Boyd had also published a long article about Stevenson's time in San Francisco. There was a mention of a book-length work in progress. Tawnie wondered if that was the manuscript she saw in the back seat of his car. Tawnie wrote down some contact information and then sent a request to be linked to him. She found no twitter account, but Boyd had a Facebook author page. Tawnie liked the page and sent a request to friend him.

Jim looked up from his computer. "Find anything?"

"A bit, but no contact information. Oh, wait. Didn't see an email listed. Maybe he answers when he travels."

Tawnie quickly composed an email, requesting to meet him, adding that the park host at Ho'okena had mentioned his name. She made no reference to Boyd's beating, saying instead that she was doing a story on the place and thought some mention about RLS would add to her story. When she was done, she closed down the computer and answered the J-pop ring tone on her phone.

"Tawnie Takahashi here. Oh, Auntie. How are you?"

***

Even before Auntie Bee parked her car, her shih tzu, Asami, was barking to welcome her.

"Asami-san, I'm coming," she laughed as she unlocked the front door. As soon as it opened, the little dog rushed out, like a silky spotted dust mop in a flurry. It leaped up and down. "What you want, silly? You miss me?" Bee picked up her wiggling dog and took Asami's kiss with a laugh before putting her down. "Gotta get something from the car. You like?" Asami scooted down the stairs and dashed to the car parked to the side of the house.

Bee shook her head. That pup had so much energy, though in dog years, Asami was no teenager. Bee stopped to pick a plumeria blossom from the small tree in front of her bungalow and smelled it. The day was fading into evening and getting quiet. Where she lived there were only two lights on: one, a street light coming to life at the entrance to the main road and the other, her neighbor's to the right of her. *Maile's home,* she thought. The rest of the street was quiet. She knew her other neighbors, the Chins, were visiting grandkids on the Mainland. There were no other houses. Just fields of grass, scattered papaya trees bristling with fruit, and cane growing wild on both sides of a hill sloping down toward town. One lone avocado tree and rocks and grass at the back end of the dead end street stood guard. A sliver of Hilo Bay glittered to the east.

Bee opened the car back and placed the box with the mysterious haversack on the gravel driveway. Asami took a sniff and sneezed abruptly. "Dusty, yeah, Asami?" She locked the car up and took the box inside.

On her kitchen counter, she turned her water kettle on, then went to her living room where she kept a small Buddhist shrine. She made a bow to it and then again to the framed picture on the TV set. It was taken five years ago when all her grown children were together in Hilo. *So hard sometime.* Jason-Clarence, named for her brother lost in the 1946 tsunami, lived on Maui. Her daughter Janice, named for her sister lost in that same tsunami, was married and worked as a nurse in California. Kiro, her youngest, was a medic with the US Army in Germany. Bee's wish was that they could all be here for her 80th birthday.

Bee sighed. *Such a silly thing to wish for.* She went back to the kitchen and sat down on a stool. Her slippers left at the front door, she wiggled her toes in her soft slippers and stretched her back. It had been a long day. She hated to admit it, but she was tired. She took off her glasses and wiped her eyes. On the other side of the counter, the box sat like one of her fourth grade students. Quiet, but ready for mischief. She decided to open it. She gave her arthritic hands a squeeze, then went to work.

Removing the brown paper wrapping from the package inside the box, she settled back on her stool and studied the leather haversack. It was definitely old. She ran her fingers over the deep brown leather. She marveled that it had survived mold and damp if it had been in Hawaii for a long time. Adjusting her glasses on her nose, she examined the silver clasp. It was a thistle alright. The thistle design immediately made Bee think of Scotland, kilts and that series of books set in the Highlands her granddaughters were crazy about. She undid the clasp and was hit again with the musty smell of old paper. Carefully, she pulled out the magazine she had seen earlier. *Scribners Magazine*, 1887. Underneath were two other magazines. She lifted them out and placed the three magazines by the side of the box. All that was left were two packages recently unwrapped as the cotton twine on each was undone. She pulled both out and was about to open the first when there was a knock at her back door.

Immediately, Asami was on duty, barking at a prospective intruder, but in just as swift a response, her tail began to wag and wiggle.

"Bee?" A voice said on the other side. "It's me. Maile."

"Oh,   my.   You're   just   in   time."

Chapter 6

The sun was setting when Tawnie and Jim finally took a break and went out to dinner. Sitting on the second floor balcony of Chuckie's Brew House, Tawnie stabbed chopsticks at her pub plate of teriyaki chicken skewers and rice cooked in coconut milk while Jim checked his camera settings. A light breeze tickled the fronds of the tall palms across the street. Out on the waters of Kailua Bay, the dying sun splashed the slow rolling surf with fuchsia, lavender, and gold bands of color. With Kilauea Volcano active on the other side of the Big Island, sunsets these days were often spectacular. Below the balcony, the murmurs of loudly clad tourists speaking in various foreign languages and local pidgin cut through the noise of the light traffic on the street. Jim turned around and took a picture.

Tawnie closed her eyes. Blocking out the street chatter, she let the cool evening breeze take away the heat of the afternoon at Ho'okena. This was paradise. She took a cleansing breath and let it go. She relaxed further on the hard teak chair.

"Phone's buzzing," Jim said.

Tawnie snapped her eyes open and sat up straight, slightly disoriented. She picked up the vibrating cell phone from the table. It said KWAI-5 News. Her boss, Denny, was calling. Tawnie waved to Jim to keep on doing what he was doing.

"Hey, Denny. Howzit?"

For next couple of minutes, Tawnie summed up their work so far in Ho'okena and the story they were sending later tonight. Then she told him about her discovery of Robert Louis Stevenson on the Big Island, his connection to the royal family and his stories inspired by his time at Ho'okena. She hoped Denny would give them the go-ahead on the Stevenson story and his connection to Ho'okena. Her selling point to her boss was that she had booked an interview with an expert on the author who happened to be visiting.

If I can find Boyd, Tawnie thought. *Alive.*

Silence.

Then Tawnie heard Denny tap his pen on his desk. "You know what?" he said. "Folks like to go to Maui all the time. They just think the Big Island's all one big volcano on one side and golf courses and Captain Cook on the other side. There's plenty history on the Big Island. You like the place so much, I'm giving your special report two more days on condition you take two days' vacation in addition. Report often. Besides, you have one sweet auntie. Tell her 'Happy Birthday' for me."

"*Mahalo.* I appreciate it."

"Four days. That's it."

Tawnie said goodbye and set the phone on the table. She was about to turn it off, when it buzzed again. She leaned over and looked at the number on the phone's screen. It wasn't anyone she knew. Tawnie hesitated, then answered.

"Aloha. Tawnie Takahashi KWAI-5 News here. May I help you?"

On the other end of phone with what sounded like someone calling from underwater, a male voice answered, "Please."

"May I ask who this is?"

"Harry Boyd. You were kind enough to help me earlier today."

"Oh, yes, Mr. Boyd. How are you feeling? I've been worried about you all day." Tawnie pretended that she didn't know that Boyd had been released.

"I won't say I'm fine, but I am out of the hospital. I-I was wondering if you knew anyone on the police force—any police force—that might know something more about my things."

"As a matter of fact, I did learn something. Your wallet was found up at Volcano a few hours ago. It's at the Art Center, though the thief was chased off during a car prowl. Could be with the Hilo Police by now. Does that help?"

Boyd sighed. Tawnie wondered if he was really around water because she thought she could hear bubbles. "Would you mind telling me where you are?"

Boyd gave her the name of a hotel that wasn't far from where she and Jim sat.

"Uh, may I ask how you found me? Knew how to call?"

"Saw you on TV in the hospital."

"Oh. Have you eaten?" Tawnie felt immediately stupid because he was most likely not in the mood for eating.

"I wouldn't mind a bowl of miso soup."

"I can do that. Maybe then you could tell me more about the box you were worried about if you'd like me to help you. I saw you're writing something about Mark Twain and Robert Louis Stevenson. Are you missing notes?"

Boyd didn't answer for a moment. The bubbly sound went away. Tawnie realized that Boyd might have been in a hot tub. There was a rustling sound, then something like steps on concrete. Then he murmured, "Something more valuable." Boyd paused again. "Soup would be nice, but would you mind not staying too long? I asked them to release me early, but maybe it wasn't such a good idea"

Tawnie asked for his room number, said she'd bring some soup and anything else he needed, and hung up.

"That Boyd?" Jim asked.

"Yeah, yeah. Do you mind if I go alone? I'll see if we can talk to him later together."

Jim shrugged. "Nice to just sit here and watch the sunset. I think I'll go up to my room early. It's been a long day."

A half-hour later, Tawnie arrived at the door to Harry Boyd's room carrying a heavy paper bag with a container of hot miso soup and small container of rice. It was an old family-run hotel surviving from the 1970s with all the doors on the outside. By now the sun was almost gone and a cool breeze spread the rich, sweet scent of plumeria and pikake through the dark silhouette of palm trees across the small parking lot. Standing on the upper deck, she took a deep breath and knocked. She was shocked when the door slowly gave way.

"Mr. Boyd? Are you there?"

There was muffled sound coming from across the dark room. She put down the food, and reached into her messenger bag for her pepper spray. Cautiously, she pushed the door open. The room was dark but something glowed from behind what she could see was the dim outline of a bed. A lamp? Her heart pounding, she stepped in further, ready to spray if she should be attacked.

"Harry?" For a moment Tawnie regretted that Jim hadn't come along. He did know where she was, but he would be on foot.

"Here," a weak voice said.

Comfortable he was alone, Tawnie felt for the light. As soon as she turned it on, the large hotel lamps by the queen beds revealed a room in shambles: papers strewn across one of the beds, suitcase on the floor with clothing pulled out. At the bed by the curtained window closed up tight, she saw two feet sticking out. Immediately, she was at Boyd's side.

Harry Boyd lay on his back, dressed in bathrobe over a t-shirt and swimsuit. His face was bruised and one eye swollen from his earlier encounter with the thief at Ho'okena. A bandage wrapped around his head was at an angle any self-respecting nurse would object to. As soon as he saw Tawnie, he grabbed her hand. "Thank God."

"What happened? Did you fall?" Tawnie followed his eyes up to the mess on the bed. "Don't tell me you were robbed again?"

Boyd nodded "yes" weakly, then attempted to sit up.

"Maybe you should just stay there. I'm going to call the front desk. Get some help for you."

Boyd shook his head. "No, wait. Just help me up. I've got to tell you something right now. You may be the only one I can trust."

"Alright." First Tawnie put the lamp back up on the side table, then, very gently, Tawnie helped get him up on the edge of the bed and scoot back against the pillows she stacked on the headboard. He was heavier than he looked, making her forehead break out into a light sweat in the unconditioned air. "OK. I'll give you just a few minutes, then I'm calling. Quickly. What happened?"

"I was just settling in after you called, when there was a knock on the door. My head must be muddy, but I thought it was you. I opened the door and some local character rushed in."

"Not the one who beat you up at Ho'okena?"

"No, this was an older guy. Local, maybe Portuguese."

"Did he attack you then?"

"No, but he just wanted my box."

"The one stolen from your car?"

"When I told him I didn't know what he was talking about, he got physical, roughed me up. Pushed me down on the floor. He took off when he didn't find anything." Boyd swallowed hard. His face looked ashen, making the bruising around his eyes and mouth stand out like dark splotches on a Halloween skull. Tawnie looked over at the phone on the other side of the bed then back.

"What's in that box that's so important?"

Boyd leaned deep into the pillows and sighed. "Some very rare papers that belonged to Robert Louis Stevenson. One's an early manuscript of *The Bottle Imp*. The other, a partial chapter of *Master of Ballantrae*. There's a couple of magazines with his published writings."

"Don't know them. Just *Treasure Island. Doctor Jekyll and Mr. Hyde*." Tawnie pulled a chair over. "This a part of your research for that paper I saw in the back of your car?"

"Yes—I found the manuscripts on eBay about a week ago. That's why I'm here. I came over to the Big Island just to pick them up. Stevenson wrote those stories here in the islands." Boyd shifted carefully on his pillows. "I've only had them for a couple of days. Truly amazing collection." He swallowed.

"And this person specifically knew you had them?"

"I guess so. Kept threatening me about them."

"Who did you get them from off eBay?"

172 · J.L. OAKLEY

"From a man named Almeida. Freddy, I think. In my wallet. Oh, lost my wallet." He faltered. He seemed to sink into the pillows.

"I'm getting help right now." Tawnie went for the hotel phone and got the front desk.

"I'm calling 911 right away," the woman at the desk said, her voice in a panic. "I'll be up as soon as possible."

When Tawnie came back, Boyd had his eyes closed. "Harry?"

Boyd's eyes fluttered open. He gave her a half smile, but Tawnie's heart was starting to pick a hard beat. Something was wrong with him.

"Is there anything else I should know? Can you describe this man? Or the person who gave you the box? Do you think someone didn't want to have the box put on eBay?"

"It was a girl who met me. Just outside of Laupahoehoe. A young woman. College age, Portuguese, again. Pretty. That's all, though I might have contact information somewhere. That damn wallet."

"And the one who just attacked you here?"

"Dark hair. Tall. Olive complexion. Tha's all I remember." Boyd seemed to be slurring his words. Tawnie was glad when the hotel manager, a middle aged woman in a flowing *muumuu* and fake red hibiscus in her hair, came to the open door.

"Aide car's on its way," the manager said. "Called the police, too. This your food?" She held up the bag with the miso soup and cocked her head at Tawnie. "You look familiar. You know this guy?"

"We met earlier today. He asked me over about an hour ago. I'm…"

"You're the TV reporter. Tawnie Takahashi. Awesome." She gave Tawnie the thumbs up. She brought the bag over and stared at Boyd. "You OK?

Boyd half raised his hand.

"Well, help is coming. If you don't mind staying with him, Ms. Takahashi, I'll wait downstairs for the medics and the cops. Whoever gets here first."

"Good." Tawnie patted Boyd's hand. "How are you feeling?"

Boyd sighed. "Not so hot. Guess I should've stayed in the hospital. Got a headache."

"Want a sip of soup?" Tawnie opened the bag and set the soup container on the lamp table. Prying off the lid, she gave him a small taste. He seemed to appreciate the hot broth, nodded for more. "Anything else you want me to know about these items in the box?" she asked.

Boyd frowned. "I only looked at them briefly, but I can tell you the manuscript's an original, written in RLS's own hand."

"Really? You know that?"

"Seen enough of his handwriting to recognize it."

"That's really something. When you're feeling better, I'd like to talk to you more about your author and Ho'okena. First, I hope the police can find the thief."

Boyd didn't answer right away. He seemed to drift a bit then focused back on her. "There was something odd about the manuscripts and magazines."

"What was that?"

"There were some faded brown spots on them and not from age which the papers certainly have. I honestly think the spots are blood. That's when I got the idea that I should come over and look at Ho'okena."

"Blood? Whose blood?"

"Think it was Stevenson's. He was often sick with some lung problem—" Boyd stopped there as the sound of wailing sirens pierced the evening air as an ambulance and police both arrived in the parking lot.

"Do you hear that?" Tawnie asked Boyd when she turned back to him. Then her heart sank. Harry Boyd, she feared, was beyond any medical   care.

Chapter 7

"Maile-san, you're home," Auntie Bee said as her young neighbor, Maile Horner, slipped through the door and swooped up Asami before the little dog got outside. "Sit, sit. Have some tea and tell me all about your trip to Maui." She nodded to the cupboard where she kept her tea cups.

"Love to. It went very well, but the plane hit some turbulence coming back. Ugh." Maile tightened her auburn hair in its ponytail, then sat down on the stool next to Bee with tea cup in hand. "How was the book sale?"

"Oh, we made good money. Plenty for the keiki in Kaʻū. We just had a few books left. Going to give them to Goodwill." Bee pushed her can of tea bags toward Maile.

"Aren't you having any?"

"After you."

"*Mahalo*, auntie." Maile picked a ginger lemon tea bag and pushed the can back. "What is that, Bee?" She nodded toward the haversack and papers on the counter as she poured hot water into her cup.

"I was hoping you tell me. It just showed up in the back of my car." Bee frowned. "Funny thing, there was someone prowling the cars up at the Art Center in Volcano. Found a wallet but what *kine* person puts this stuff in a car? "

"Hmm. Could I look?"

"Yeah, sure. They look old. I know you like that *kine* stuff." She beamed a smile at Maile, then started to push the box and the papers over to Maile. "Omph. Heavy." Bee squeezed her knobby hands together.

"Here, let me do that." Maile came around Bee and picked up the haversack and the rest of the contents of the box. "Anything else?"

"Don't think so."

"Well, let's look. Go ahead and fix your tea while I take a peek."

Once settled back on her stool, Maile separated out the items. "How interesting. Scribner's. 1887. And what's this? Oh, my gosh."

"What?"

"I've always wanted to see one of these." Maile picked up the worn paper magazine. "Beadle's Half Dime Library."

"What's that?"

"Some old magazine that told sensational tales, mostly of the West. Deadwood Dick, Dashing Kate were some of the famous characters in those magazines..."

"Think I saw one movie called Deadwood Dick at the Hilo Theater back in the 1940s."

"Dashing Kate is fun. One of the first female detectives in stories."

"Hmph. Might need one female detective to figure this out."

"Annie Moke?" Maile smiled. "I'm sure she's good, but I don't think we have a crime here yet."

"There's that kid up at Volcano Art Center Gallery."

"What was that?"

Bee went on to tell Maile about the kid doing car prowls in the parking lot at the center and how she discovered the contents of the box not long after.

"Wow. Hope you weren't hurt." Maile gave her tea bag a couple of more dips then put it on her plate.

"I'm OK. Feel sorry for the man who lost his wallet. We turned it into the Art Center."

"Anyone you know?" Bee brushed away the steam rising from her hot tea.

"No. Probably missed it when he got back to his hotel." She nodded to the bundle of wrapped papers. "What's in that? I nevah had time to look."

"Let's see." Maile carefully opened up the brown paper wrapping. Inside were some aged papers stacked and loosely tied with string. The ink in handwritten script had faded to brown, but was still legible. "Hmm. Handwriting looks like something from the nineteenth century." She untied the cotton string and picked up the first page which had no title nor name, just a scribble much like the writer was testing his pen. Underneath, however, a page filled with line after line of a scrawling script, Maile read out loud:

There was a man of the Island of Hawaii, whom I shall call Keawe; for the truth is, he still lives, and his name must be kept secret; but the place of his birth was not far from Honaunau, where the bones of Keawe the Great lie hidden in a cave.

"Honaunau," Bee said. "That's Kona side. Above Ho'okena."

"Oh, my gosh. I think I know what this is." Maile turned the page over, then looked on the next page.

"What is it?"

"It's some copy of *The Bottle Imp*. A very spooky story of RLS." She lifted up more pages, all handwritten. No name, no signature. She lifted the whole thing out and set it on the counter.

"Is it old?"

"Hard to say."

"What's that?" Bee pointed to a newspaper scrap on top of the second stack of papers remaining with the package.

Maile picked it up and showed it to Bee. It was a Christmas ad for the Almeida General Store in Ho'okena. Dated 1921.

"Know that store," Bee said. "Family has one store in Hilo and one up at Kamuela."

"Maybe   it's   an   English   project."

"Mr, Boyd? Harry?"

For one brief moment, Tawnie hesitated. Boyd had sunk onto his left side and didn't seem to be breathing. From the sound of the wailing sirens, the aide car was close, but there might be little time to save him. Grabbing his legs, Tawnie pulled on them and laid him out flat on his back before pulling him by his shoulders down to the floor. Immediately, she began CPR. So concentrated was she on her task, she didn't hear the rattle of boots on the outside stairs, the metal clatter of a gurney. She repeated the CPR steps over and over again. "Breathe," she whispered.

"Ms.Takahashi! What's going on?"

"What?" Without stopping, Tawnie turned and stiffened. It was Officer Jerry Moke, the police officer from the Ho'okena parking lot. Right behind him were three buff EMTs.

"It's Mr. Boyd. He's not breathing." She continued to work on Boyd, until the EMTs took over. She slipped out from the side of the bed and stood over by the TV as the medics pulled out equipment and began to work on Boyd.

Moke joined her. "What are you doing here?" He looked suspicious, his dark eyebrows in a glower. He wasn't in off-duty clothes. He was wearing his police uniform.

Tawnie assumed her reporter stance, straightening her sleeveless fuchsia blouse and squaring her shoulders. "Mr. Boyd called me, maybe forty-five minutes ago and said he wanted to see me. I brought him some soup, but when I got to the door, I found it ajar and Boyd on the floor. He was awake. Wanted to tell me something. "

Moke nodded at the floor where the medics seemed to be getting some good results "So you just talked story? Didn't bother to call the police?"

"Yeah, yeah." Tawnie felt a pulse of impatience. She preferred being the one asking the questions. "He insisted he had to tell me something before I made a call to the front desk. I got him up on the bed. Then he just sort of fainted."

"One, two, three, lift." Boyd was placed on the gurney and strapped in while one of the medics gently pumped air into his lungs

"'Did you get a pulse?" Moke asked the lead on the front of the gurney.

"Weak one. Don't know if it will sustain." The medics immediately headed to the open door where the hotel manager and several gawkers looked on. Once they were gone, Moke turned to Tawnie.

"So why he want talk to you? I thought he was out of it most of the time at the beach."

"Well, as it turned out, he was lucid enough to have me look around in the backseat for something. That's why you found me there going through his car."

"He gave a short statement before he was released from the hospital. Doesn't explain why he wanted to talk to you."

"Maybe cuz I'm a reporter, not the police. Maybe he thought as a reporter, I would help get the word out."

"About what?" Moke didn't look too happy about her comment.

"Some papers he had. He was very concerned about them."

"Did he say what they were?"

Tawnie kept her face still, not wanting to give anything away. Her voice was steady when she answered. "Just some material for a book he's writing. Lots of important notes. Years of work."

"Hmph. Someone turned in his wallet up at the Volcano Art Center Gallery."

"Do they know who the thief is that beat him up?" Tawnie asked.

Moke cocked his head at her. "What you want for? Six o'clock news?"

Are you all bluster or should I be careful around you? "Just wondered if it was the same person who came here. That's why." Tawnie folded her arms, then thought better of it and went over to the nightstand and picked up the half full soup container. She put it into the bag with the unopened rice and threw the package away into the waste can by the bed.

Moke wasn't finished. "He give a description of his attacker here at the hotel?"

Tawnie could feel Moke size her up. She didn't want to give away what Boyd was all hot about, but then it wasn't good to hold back just for a news story when a person could be dead.

Tawnie turned around. "One older guy, local, maybe Portuguese. He was looking for the missing material. Sound like the same person who took his wallet?"

Moke worked his mouth. "No. It was some kid prowling the parking at the center. Had dreads. Hilo police is taking a statement from a tourist couple who saw him best. Might be part of island-wide gang that preys on visitors."

Tawnie picked up her messenger bag still on the other hotel bed. "That's too bad. Want to keep people safe." Tawnie pulled herself up to her five-foot height and faced him. "Can I go now?"

Moke seemed to relent the tough guy stance. He chin-lifted at her. "You staying on the island? Oh, yeah. Your auntie's birthday. Not for a few days."

"Yes, my sweet Auntie Bee." She gave him a soft smile, a genuine smile because when she thought of her great aunt the word "aloha" became real. Strength and aloha. That was Auntie Bee. As a reporter, Tawnie had to be strong, but she sometimes hid her aloha part.

Moke smiled back, then gave Tawnie his card. "In case you wrestle anything up."

Tawnie found herself promising to do that. "And you'll let me know about Mr. Boyd? HIPA privacy rules and all that *kine* stuff." She let go of her reporter words and let some pidgin slip in to show solidarity with Moke.

"Yeah, yeah. As you've been on this one case from the beginning. Now, better go and leave the room to the crime scene techs," Moke said, getting all official again. He nodded to the new police officers entering the room wearing papery Tyvek suits and booties.

"*Mahalo.* I'm really sorry this has happened to him." Tawnie shouldered her messenger bag. "Hope he pulls through. He was interested in Ho'okena history like I am. I gather he's a good writer."

"Hopefully, this wasn't his last bit of writing."

"Hopefully."

Chapter 9

"So, Annie Oakley," Kimo said to Annie as they sat in their cruiser in the Kahului Costco parking lot, "you going down to the Big Island for Auntie Bee's birthday? Saw the invitation on your wall."

Annie looked up from her laptop. "Thinking about it. Only met her that one time when we put the leis into Hilo Bay for her sister. But you, your *tutu* knew the family."

"Uh, huh. That's why I like to go. My family survived that bad tsunami, too."

They were talking about the April Fools' Day tsunami that wiped out Hilo in 1946. The town's layout was changed when it was rebuilt. Today, Hilo was set far back from the bay. Kimo had told Annie that Bee Takahashi was just a little girl when the waves wiped out her parent's' store and apartment overhead. She survived but a sister and brother did not. Another sister thought drowned was later proved to have been murdered just last year.

Annie looked out the window and thought about another body of water. Puget Sound. Seattle. She still couldn't get over the idea that the historian from Hilo who brought her the invitation to the birthday party had known her father. *Is our world that small?* Annie was touched that Maile Horner thought enough of her, a stranger, to give her the photograph of her father on the night before his unit shipped out. Might be interesting to talk to her some more. Annie decided that she would call Maile Horner when she got off duty.

The radio in the car crackled. 10-56. Someone driving drunk in the park. Kimo tapped his responder on his chest and said they were on their way. Duty called.

***

Maile Horner tip-toed over to her kitchen nook and picked up her Siamese cat, Buster. "What you got? Not another gecko? You leave

Adam and Eve alone." She gave her cat a kiss on its head, then shivered. A dead cane spider lay curled up on the bay window sill, legs up. Ever since she moved back to the Big Island, the large, long-legged creatures seemed to pop up everywhere. They were one of the things she had forgotten about life in the islands. *Probably for good reason.* "Eeuw. Thanks for being on patrol."

Buster let out a lusty "Mur—ow" then rubbed his head under Maile's chin.

"Silly." She gave Buster a hug, then put him down on the bench. Outside her little bungalow, a red-crested cardinal called from the edge of her long property where a lime tree and some papaya trees grew. Maile tried to see if the bird was in the avocado tree in the grassy field beyond. A flick of red said closer. She'd have to keep an eye on Buster.

On the kitchen table, the day's *Hilo Tribune* laid rolled up in its plastic wrap. Maile undid it and laid the paper out. Buster jumped up on the table, but before he sat down on the newspaper's edge, the headline to the lead article jumped out at her:

ALMEIDA FAMILY AT ODDS OVER LATE PATRIARCH'S ESTATE.

Almeida. There was that name again. She pushed Buster's tail back to read a long article about how the elder Almeida, Josef, had been born in Hilo in 1925, served in the Navy during the war, and had taken over the daily operations of the mercantile business in the 1950s. Family fortunes increased when the hotel business boomed over at Kailua-Kona. A large tract of land sold for millions for the construction of the iconic Hawaii Ono Hotel, but not before a lawsuit was filed by Anthony DeMello, who claimed the land had been stolen...

Buster, at this point, stretched his sleek body across the entire sheet and blinked his blue eyes up at Maile, his purr a loud rattle.

"Oh, you are such a *kolohei*. How can I get anything done? Guess, it's time for work." Maile glanced at the clock above the French doors. It read 8:30. She had enough time to finish making her lunch, then head down to the museum. The RLS exhibit was six weeks away, but there was a lot to get done: the final mounting of the acquired photographs, loan papers to complete for the ephemera and artifacts which included a pin from the author's time as a member of the Thistle Club in Honolulu, and of course, all the text for labels. Yet, as she thought of the 1921 ad in the pile of copied papers that Bee had, she wondered if they had information on the Almeida family at the museum. For the past ten months, an intern from the UH Hilo history program had been gathering information on old island family businesses. The name Almeida rang a bell.

Maile gave the ruffled lei collar on her short lime green muumuu one last straightening, then blowing a kiss to Buster, grabbed her purse and headed off to work. Ten minutes later she was there.

The Big Island Historical Society's offices were located on a quiet street up on a hill overlooking downtown Hilo. In the past, the museum consisted of a lone turn-of-the-century frame house built by a sugar cane magnate. Twenty years ago, the society added a modern two-story wing in the back to accommodate the growing collection on Big Island life plus two rooms for rotating exhibits. The museum had state of the art methods for preservation and an archives program open to the public twice a week. Maile parked her Subaru station wagon in the back and went into the concrete block building.

"Aloha, Ester," Maile said as she poked her head into the collection's management room that comprised of bookshelves, a scanner and a large table where artifacts could be cleaned and cataloged.

"Howzit!" Ester Ogawa looked up from her seat at the table. Her white gloves gently held a leather bound book entitled, *The Master of Ballantrae.* "Had my coffee," Ester beamed. "Did you get what you wanted in Lahaina? Wasn't here when you brought the stuff in."

"Couple of good things. Did that historian from the Mainland ever call? He didn't show."

Easter shook her head. "No."

"Weird. Well, gonna check my email, then we can talk. Is Carl done with the painting in the main exhibit room?"

"Yeah, yeah."

"Great." Maile waved to Ester, then went upstairs to her office.

"I'm home," Maile said to the fern on her desk as she opened the blinds, letting the morning sun glance off the framed prints and photographs on the bookshelves and file cabinets. Her office faced away from the historic house and into what was the original gardens of the estate. A huge Banyan tree, planted one hundred and ten years ago, dominated the space.

Maile clicked on her computer and sat down to check on the dozens of emails she knew would be waiting. As the society's historian, she fielded questions from all over the island and abroad. Mostly questions about a family, a particular industry or historical event. Maile saw nothing from the historian Harrison Boyd, except an earlier exchange from a few days ago about meeting up. *What happened?* She composed a new email with an invitation to reset the appointment and sent it off to him.

Maile got through a few more emails before she decided to open up her Past Perfect program the museum used to catalog artifacts, photographs and ephemera as well as gift shop sales and docents. Once Maile had it opened, she typed in "Almeida." Instantly, several categories popped up: one in the early industries and businesses on the Big Island showing text and newspaper articles, another in the photograph collection with over 55 entries. A third was artifacts. Maile decided to check out the photographs first. She typed in Josef Almeida, the patriarch of the family who had just passed away. Several entries came up.

Good job, intern.

The computer screen quickly filled with thumbnail pictures. The first two, judging by the clothing, were from the 1930s. A family gathering at Liliuokalani Park. Maile counted twenty people in one, including Josef, aged 11, according to the notes. There were several other photos of the man as a boy: Josef in front of the family store in Hilo, Josef with his sisters and brother on horseback up at Kilauea, and Josef in a baseball uniform. Some pictures included his time in the Navy as a very young seaman. Then the thumbnails jumped to an assortment from the 1950's and 1960s and onto a picture of groundbreaking in Kailua-Kona of the Hawaii Ono Hotel.

A photo entitled "Lava Coffee Stand" caught her eye. She clicked on the thumbnail and its catalog information. The picture showed the coffee stand on the edge of a gas station. Maile knew it was one of the first in the village of Volcano. Maile clicked to another of Josef standing next to Volcano House.

"Hmm," she said out loud. "Supporter of the hotel's recent renovations." She scrolled through the photo entry data and hit the word "Volcano House" to go onto the next page. Suddenly, Maile was looking at an entry from the historical society's digitized newspaper collection. In particular, from the *Pacific Commercial Advertiser*, August 1889.

MISSING SON FOUND DEAD AT KILAUEA. LIFE CLAIMED IN HORRIFYING ACCIDENT. SCALDED TO DEATH IN STEAM VENT.

"What?" Maile looked around behind her. "Menehune at work, I guess. Or the intern didn't encode it right," she muttered. Maile returned to reading about the gruesome accident.

"Casper DeMello, son of the late Frances DeMello, was found in a steam vent near Volcano House. He had been missing for a week. Death comes at a difficult time for the DeMello fortunes. Victim's widowed mother…"

Maile stopped reading. *What did this have to do with Almeida? DeMello. DeMello.* Auntie Bee said one of her book club members was a DeMello. Maile wondered if they were related to Casper DeMello. She searched the newspaper article and came up with one name. Pasco Almeida. From Ho'okena.

"Maile?" a voice called from the hallway. John Hauser, museum director and her boss. "Got a minute?"

"I do. How about coffee in the staff room? Just have to close this out." With that, one click of her mouse and the Almeidas and DeMellos disappeared from Maile's screen, but not before the photo of a handsome young man dressed in a high, starched collar and soulful, dark eyes flickered like a ghost in the machine, then disappeared. It sent a chill down her spine.

I   know   that   face.

Tawnie Takahashi woke from a sleepless night to the buzzing of her cell phone. Opening one eye, she picked it up and stared at the screen. Jim calling. Time to get to work. Only she didn't feel much like it. *What is the matter with me? I've been in hard places before. Why does Harry Boyd bother me?*

Tawnie felt like calling her contact at the hospital, but she was afraid of what the answer might be. *Dead.* Maybe I can help him, she thought. Find those papers. Might mean working with Moke, her only police contact in Hilo.

The phone buzzed again. This time Tawnie answered. "Morning, Jim. Howzit?"

"Was going to ask you that? Crazy day, yeah?"

"Uh-huh."

"You OK? Wanna get breakfast? Free downstairs."

"Yeah, sure. Did you get anything done last night? I couldn't." Tawnie walked barefoot to her messenger bag on the hotel entertainment stand and pulled out a notebook one-handed.

"Got the Ho'okena Beach stuff done, but called Denny and explained what happened to Boyd. The beach story will go out tonight instead."

"Thanks. I mean that. They got cereal down in the breakfast room? I'm treating."

"As long as it's Fruit Loops."

Fifteen minutes later, they were down in the hotel's small breakfast room, one of a few places that did that without charging an arm and a leg. The place was abuzz with tourists getting ready for a day of adventure and sunburn. A family with matching aloha shirts scored a table by the lanai window that looked out to the beach. Tawnie found a place in the corner where they might talk and eat. As soon as they had their trays filled, they sat down.

"So, boss," Jim said as he sat down with a plunk. "What you want to do today? Got those extra days. We could go to the historical society and see what they have on the historic Ho'okena Village."

"Good idea. We do need to be focused on that." Tawnie took a bit of pineapple on her plate. "But, I've been thinking about poor Harry Boyd. He said those papers were real. Valuable. Kinda think we should try to find out what happened to them. I feel a bigger story here than just a mugging."

"Why didn't you tell the police what Boyd said?"

Tawnie shrugged. "I don't know. Always have to get the story first." She smiled at Jim. "Though since we nearly got killed on that last big one, I don't know."

"You're the best crime reporter I know Tawnie. You have good instincts."

"Aren't I about the only one you've worked with?"

Jim chuckled. "Got me there. Did work for the military press when I was in the Army. Saw stuff. You're good. No, you're great. " He took a sip of his coffee, then added more French Vanilla to it. "You saved your Auntie Bee's life and solved a painful, family mystery. *And* got the killer. Not bad work. So, where do we start with Boyd and his missing box?"

Tawnie swallowed. She often gave her gangly associate a hard time, but he was a good sport and excellent cameraman. Lately, she realized what a good friend he was. She patted the table near his plate. "OK, let's start with a name Boyd gave me. Freddy Almeida. We'll search that. We should go to the library and see if they have some of RLS's writings. Want to see that *Bottle Imp*."

Jim lifted up his phone. "Might be on Google Books."

"OK, run that one down. Boyd said that the author was inspired by a trip to the City of Refuge." Tawnie finished up her fruit plate, coffee and bagel, then got up. "How much time do you need to get ready?"

"Fifteen minutes. I can meet you in the lobby if that works for you."

"Great. Sounds like a plan." She put her paper plate into the garbage bin and shouldering her messenger bag, stepped out into the hall next to the stairway going up to a balcony that looked over the lobby dressed up with ti plants in containers. On a stand was the day's newspaper. Tawnie put in some coins and took a newspaper out.

Immediately, the headline about the fight among the Almeida heirs caught her eye. *Did Boyd know about this?* Tawnie quickly scanned the article, making mental notes to take to the library. She flipped to the inside to see if there was more to the story, but found only a mix of local and island-wide hard news. As she started to fold the newspaper up and put into her messenger bag, a story in a column at the bottom of the inside page caught her. "Local man killed in high speed chase with police." Tawnie's eyes widened as she read further. "Unidentified man in his late teens was killed when his car rolled over. Hilo police had been searching for him since yesterday. Wanted for multiple thefts in the Volcanoes National Park."

Tawnie let out a gush of air.

"What's up?"

"Look at this. Wonder if this was the guy that robbed Boyd?"

"Maybe you have to call Moke after all."

Tawnie rolled her eyes. "Not yet. Not until we go to the library first. There's just something weird about all this."

Chapter 11

Auntie Bee put her fruit tray on Eleanor Kane's dining table then set her book on the rattan sofa in the living room before going back to the table full of *pu pu*. Eleanor's house was a modern take on a Hawaiian-style ranch house with skylights and open space between the kitchen and dining area. Prints by local artists graced the white walls. Over the food-laden table, the sun attempted to beat its way through the roman shade that covered the skylight. As the rest of the U'ilani Book Lovers Club gathered for their monthly meeting to discuss their book, some of the women were already buzzing about the book sale and the strange box with the haversack and papers.

"So good sales, yeah?" Tina Gleeson asked as she chose some sushi and carrot sticks for her plate.

Bee nodded. "Very good. So pleased we could help that community library."

"Heard you got some extra literature on the way home."

"Oh, that. Not sure if it came from the book sale or Volcano, but it's plenty fun to look at. My neighbor, Maile Horner, says the magazines are really old. The rest student stuff." Bee got her own plate and started to fill it with hummus, crackers and her fruit salad. When her left hand trembled a bit, she put the salad plate down on the table. *Gotta get back to lifting weights.*

"I'd like to see that," Mari DeMello said as she came up to Bee. She was a slim woman in her early-forties with dark hair and dark eyes. Her face was quiet, not her typical expression.

Bee picked out a sushi roll and some chocolate fudge. "Yeah, sure. I brought part of it today. Maile has the magazines, but I can show you it after our book discussion."

"Is it true there was an ad for the Almeida store in Ho'okena?"

"Uh-uh. Why you worry about that?"

Mari sighed. "You know why, Auntie."

"Hmpf." Bee stopped loading her plate and led Mari by the elbow into the kitchen. When they got over by the window, Bee turned around.

"Are you OK, Auntie?" Mari cocked her head at Bee.

"Hum?"

"You're limping."

"Oh, that. Never mind. Just stiff today. Now," Bee said as she patted Mari on her arm, "you got to stop thinking about things so long ago, Mari-san."

"I can't help it. Not with the Almeida family all over the news. That store in Ho'okena was my great-great-grandmother back in the 1890s. She lost it and property in Kona when her son—my daddy's grandfather—died. Hard times for the family for many years."

"Yet the DeMellos have done plenty good. One doctor, three teachers. You, a scientist, working with the Smithsonian here."

Mari looked down at her hands. "True, that. My grandparents and my folks saw to that."

"There—"

"—still, there has always been a story that the land was stolen. That my great great grandmother was forced to sell." Mari straightened up. "Some even say my ancestor was murdered."

"Mari-san." Bee had always been fond of Mari. Her mother was her long-time teaching partner, Patsy DeMello

Mari sniffed, like she had a cold. "I'm sorry, Bee. Our families have never gotten along. Though, I have to say that the DeMellos have done well in that last fifty years. The Almeidas always seem to have some tragedy happen every so often."

Bee frowned. "I remember the poor Almeida boy—Tommy. He was a student of mine at my first teaching job. Always had an easy smile. Think he fell from the *pali* at Halapē." The memory of his death still choked her up, but the loss of her own family had given her an understanding that helped to comfort her small flock of fourth graders.

"Terrible. Oh, let's go back to the others. I have some questions about the book we read."

Bee slipped her arm through Mari's. "Good idea. I want to talk about Duke Kahanamoku and Waikiki boys."

Annie Moke picked up her desk phone and for just a brief moment, hesitated. Learning that Maile Horner knew her beloved father was a surprise. *Small world, for sure.* She decided that if she did go down for Bee Takahashi's birthday party, she should set up a time to visit with Horner. In the meantime, she was just returning Horner's call from earlier in the day. Annie looked at Horner's business card and punched in the phone number. She immediately got a woman on the line.

"Big Island Historical Museum, Maile Horner speaking."

"Ms. Horner, this is Detective Annie Moke from Kahului Police Department. Got your message that you wanted to talk to me. Something about police archives."

"Oh, thanks so much for calling me back quickly. I just got back from lunch. Do you mind? I have to put something away." Annie heard some rustling of papers and a click on a computer, then Maile sitting down. "I was wondering," Maile continued, "if I wanted to look up old police records, is there a place for that?"

"Depends on the year."

"Well, this happened back in the 1880s."

"That old? You don't have records at the museum?"

"We've got old newspaper accounts, but from what I've been told, police records could be at the state archives in Honolulu. Just wondering if anything would be held local at a police station."

"Meaning the Big Island."

"Yes."

"Well, when I was with Hilo Police Department, we did have an archive of cases. Don't think they went any further back than the 1950s.

Earlier stuff could have been wiped out in the big tsunami. Who are you looking for?"

"A man named Almanzo Almeida."

"Almeida. That the same family I read about in the newspaper? Big family uproar over a will?"

"That's what I'm working on to find out. From what I know, it's complicated."

"Why so far back?"

"I'm just curious. I did a search of our records about early families on the Big Island. The Almeidas have been a very successful family for over a hundred years, especially after they sold land to start the Hawaii Ono Hotel in Kailua-Kona back in the 1970s. But I found something in the notes that said that the DeMello family had protested that they owned the land and were cheated out of it."

"Do you think a crime was involved?" Annie reached for a pen on her desk and wrote the two names down in her opened notebook.

"Well, the spooky thing is that back in 1889—sorry, I get all historian over this stuff—a Casper DeMello was found dead in a steam vent up near Volcano House. I did further research through land grants, etc. and found that the DeMello family did own a store in Ho'okena and property at the present-day site of the hotel."

"And this Almanzo Almeida guy?"

"I found a few newspaper accounts about him. Generally, a good citizen, but also kinda like the black sheep of the family. Suspected of cheating tourists going up to Kilauea to see the "lava lakes" as they called the lava flow in the crater, but never proven. Later, he is running the DeMello store in Ho'okena."

"They had grab and go back even back then?"

Maile laughed. "Appears so"

"What about the DeMellos?"

"Still working on that family."

"Hmm. Why not contact Officer Jerry Moke in Hilo? He's my former boss. He might be able to help." Annie didn't add that he was also her father-in-law.

"Thanks. I'll do that. Actually, you got me thinking. The historical division of the UH library branch here in Hilo might have something, especially court documents. I've only been here for a year, so I'm still learning about resources."

"Well, if you need any further assistance, let me know. By the way, I'm planning to come to Bee's party."

"That's wonderful. The birthday party is at 2:00 at the Volcano House Restaurant. You coming down the same day?"

"Pretty sure, but I plan to stay over."

"Oh, good. Auntie Bee knows about it, we just haven't given her all the details. Friends in our book club are behind it, but we meet outside of our monthly gatherings to plan. Got some surprises."

"Looking forward to it and if you have time, I'd love to hear about your encounters with my father."

Maile said, "I can do that. Mahalo," then signed off.

Annie put her receiver down, visions of her father as a young soldier in   her   head.

Chapter 13

And he opened a lockfast place, and took out a round-bellied bottle with a long neck; the glass of it was white like milk, with changing rainbow colours in the grain. Withinsides something obscurely moved, like a shadow and a fire...

"This is a strange thing," said Keawe. "For by the touch of it, as well as by the look, the bottle should be of glass."

"Of glass it is," replied the man, sighing more heavily than ever; "but the glass of it was tempered in the flames of hell. An imp lives in it, and that is the shadow we behold there moving: or so I suppose. If any man buy this bottle the imp is at his command; all that he desires - love, fame, money, houses like this house, ay, or a city like this city - all are his at the word uttered. Napoleon had this bottle, and by it he grew to be the king of the world; but he sold it at the last, and fell. Captain Cook had this bottle, and by it he found his way to so many islands; but he, too, sold it, and was slain upon Hawaii. For, once it is sold, the power goes and the protection; and unless a man remain content with what he has, ill will befall him."

"And yet you talk of selling it yourself?" Keawe said.

"I have all I wish, and I am growing elderly," replied the man. "There is one thing the imp cannot do - he cannot prolong life; and, it would not be fair to conceal from you, there is a drawback to the bottle; for if a man die before he sells it, he must burn in hell forever."

"What a creepy story," Tawnie whispered to Jim across the library table. "So *lolo.*"

"That's why I've always liked it." Jim grinned, peering around from his laptop and his stack of books. "Stevenson could really tell a great horror story."

"Did you find anything on the Almeida family?"

"Well, the senior Almeida has two sons, Matson and Frederick Almeida. I suppose that could be the Freddy Almeida Boyd mentioned.

Matson has been acting CEO since last year. Frederick is a co-partner of Almeida Ltd., but he also has his own company working on land preservation.

"That almost sounds like a conflict right there. Anything else?"

"Found a history of early families on the Big Island in the genealogy section. Almeida's listed. Came to the island from Portugal in 1870s. Worked in the canefields on the Hamakua coast and Punalu'u. Started a store near Ho'okena to take advantage of the tourist traffic coming to see the City of Refuge."

"Anything else?"

"There was another store in the area. Run by the name of DeMello."

"Hmm." Tawnie hit "save' on the Google book selection of *The Bottle Imp* and opened up a new search for the Ho'okena area. In addition to maps, images and websites, she found a pdf copy of the 1888 *Directory of Hawaii* at the UH Manoa Library. It was full of ads, people's names and addresses on all the islands as well as descriptions of some of the towns. Kohala, Honokaa, Hamakua and Hilo on the Big Island were listed, but Kona was "sparsely populated." She was amazed to read about the "new carriage road" to Kilauea from Hilo and discovered several pages solely devoted to Volcano House. The hotel definitely was a well-known fixture on the island even back then.

Tawnie found ads for the Almeida store and the DeMello store. Out of curiosity, she brought up the 1890 Directory and scrolled to the Big Island section. The Almeida store was listed, but the DeMello store was gone. *Economics*, she thought.

"What about the modern-day family?"

Jim and Tawnie worked for another half hour, then called it quits when one of the library patrons recognized Tawnie and came over to talk. Turned out he was from her high school in Honolulu.

"Hey, Tawnie," he said. "Howzit?"

"Russell Ito. What you doing here?" She shook his hand. They had been friends since ninth grade when they were on their school's Knowledge Bowl team.

"My baby sister's getting married tomorrow. Came down to give her away."

"So sorry about your dad. Cancer's hard, yeah?"

Russell sighed. "But life goes on. So I'm taking his place." He smiled at her. "What are you up to? Tracking down a killer? You get all your leads in one library?"

Tawnie chuckled. "You'd be surprised. Oh, Russell, meet my cameraman, Jim Milstead." Jim rose up and shook Russell's hand. "We're working on a report about the park at Ho'okena. Will air tonight."

Tawnie pulled out a wooden library chair for Russell, then welcomed Jim to stay. Better to have two sets of ears listening in.

"So some big crime story about Ho'okena. What? Surfers and snorkelers get in one big water fight?"

"No. Just the beach park and its surrounding history." Tawnie smiled, tapping her pen on her notebook.

Russell said sat down. He nodded at the books. "That's tame. Haven't been there in years. Usually just stay here in Kailua-Kona or up at Mahukona."

"Didn't your Uncle Ken do construction around Ho'okena in the 1970s? Just before the boom?"

"Captain Cook to be precise."

"But did he ever work on the early hotels up here?"

"Plenty. Big jump in the number then. But he was here before that. Late 60s after he got back from Vietnam."

"What about the Almeida family?"

"The Almeidas. What you want with them?" Russell's voice hardened.

"Uh, they had a place in Ho'okena long time ago." Tawnie studied Russell's frown. "What's wrong? You don't like the Almeidas?"

Russell looked down at his hands and tapped his thumbs together. "Didn't like the way they treated my uncle."

"How's that?"

"How about the Hawaii Ono Hotel? The Almeidas were behind that. My uncle was there right from digging the hole."

"What happened?"

"He was top foreman of the project, but when he submitted his final invoices, a lot of them weren't honored. He eventually took them to court. They settled, but at one big loss to my uncle. That's why hard."

"So sorry." Tawnie could understand how someone's action could change the whole outcome of a family. "Well, I am trying to find out more about the Almeidas. Maybe you can help. Been trying to figure out Almeida history in Ho'okena without having to search a title company. Their name came up in my search."

"You digging into the will controversy? Seems to be in all the papers." Tawnie's silence must have confirmed it to him. Russell shrugged. "Well, I could do that through my real estate company. What would you like me to find out?"

Tawnie took a deep breath and told him just as much about Ho'okena and Boyd as she felt necessary. At the last minute, she mentioned the name Freddy Almeida. "I just ask you to be discreet."

"No worries. I'm on it. Just like cramming for information in our Knowledge Bowl days."

Tawnie chuckled. "Do be careful, though. We don't know who is doing the attacking. Don't want to mess up your sister's wedding."

"You think?" Russell promised that he would be discreet as her best informant.

***

Tawnie went out to their rental car and along with Jim loaded up their gear. Sitting on the passenger side, Tawnie took out Moke's business card and turned it over in her hands. *Probably get all lolo if I call, but I need to know about Boyd. And that kid killed in the police chase. Did he have Boyd's stuff?*

"You gonna call?" Jim asked.

"Yeah, yeah. After talking to my friend, I think I should." Tawnie smiled at Jim, then chuckled. "Just have to know about Boyd."

"You're the boss." Jim grabbed his Nikon D1700 camera and got out of the driver's seat. "There's some nice bougainvillea over there to shoot. Yell if you need help."

"Extra Fruit Loops for you if I do."

"You're on."

Tawnie wiggled her toes in her sandals, noticed the bright red polish was in need of repair, then punched in Moke's number.

"Hilo Police Department, Officer Moke speaking."

Tawnie slipped into her reporter voice. "Officer Moke, this is Tawnie Takahashi of KWAI-5 News."

"Ms. Wata-na-be."

"Wonder if you heard anything about Mr. Boyd?"

There was a pause. "He's alive and holding on. Looks like the strain of the second assault brought on a stroke."

"Oh, the poor thing. Is he conscious?"

"Nurse said he woke about a half hour ago. Nodded to her questions, then drifted off. He's in ICU and probably will there for some time."

"Too much. At least he's in good hands."

Pause. Tawnie waited for Moke to say more, but when he didn't, she just jumped in. "Heard there was a terrible car accident in Hilo. Wondered if it was the thief who stole stuff at Ho'okena."

Moke's silence got even more intense.

"I know about the car prowl up at Volcano Art Center Gallery," Tawnie went on. "Boyd's wallet showing up there. Did you find his papers in the kid's car?"

"Maybe. But first, you tell me what you're holding back from me. What exactly did Boyd tell you? You think I'm stupid, Ms. Takahashi?"

"I do not. I respect the job you are doing. I'm also trying to protect Mr. Boyd. Somehow, he's gotten mixed up with something bigger than a research project, but I promised him I would help get the papers back."

Moke snorted. "You going soft? Thought the news came first."

"Maybe I'm changing," Tawnie muttered.

"What did you say?"

"I said I care about Mr. Boyd." Tawnie took a big breath. "In the interest of helping him, he told me the stolen materials belonged to that *haole* author, Robert Louis Stevenson." Tawnie went on to tell Moke about RLS in Ho'okena in the 1880s. To her surprise, she ended up telling Moke everything she knew except the eBay connection and the purchaser.

Moke whistled. "*Dr. Jekyll and Mr. Hyde.* My daughter likes that kine spooky stuff."

"That's the author. Tell me, was there a box with a haversack in the dead kid's car?"

Pause. Finally, Moke said, "No. That's what's missing? Did he describe it?"

Tawnie told Moke what Boyd had said about it. "It has a silver thistle on the clasp."

Silence. Tawnie could almost hear Moke thinking.

"Ms. Takahashi, this is off the record, OK?"

"Yeah, sure."

"We didn't find any haversack with papers, but in the back seat, we found an old letter opener with a thistle on the handle. Must have gotten tossed around when the car rolled."

"Do you have a name for the thief? Off the record, of course." Despite the kid's sorry end, she couldn't help feel anger at the chaos he had caused.

"Miles Wilson. We're notifying his family right now. Looks like a nice family. The things kids get into. Mother's a local, father's from the Mainland."

"Too bad. You think he's part of a theft ring?"

"If I tell you what I think all the time…"

"I won't talk story. Just say we have an understanding."

"Hmph."

"That letter opener. Wonder if it went with the haversack. Even belonging to Stevenson himself."

"Well, I plan to contact the historical society in Hilo to see if they could identify how old the thing is, but now with this information about Stevenson one more thing to ask. An interesting case, for sure. Trying to find the guy who roughed Boyd up at the hotel."

"I hope no one else gets hurt."

"Why you say that?"

"Cuz, Boyd said one of the papers inside the haversack was an original manuscript of *The Bottle Imp*. You ever read that story? Spooky. Very few end up well. Got one curse. Even the City of Refuge is mentioned."

Moke laughed. "Who believes that *kine* stuff?"

"Don't know. Boyd got hurt. The thief didn't turn out so well. Wonder who else?"

Moke said he had no answer, but since Tawnie had agreed to say nothing until the investigation was winding down, he'd keep in touch with her about Boyd. "Aloha, Ms. Takahashi."

"Mahalo, Officer Moke. I promise to let you know what I find." Tawnie ended the call and put down her phone, wondering what sort of crime Boyd had exposed when he bought the box off of eBay.

The U'ilani Book Lovers Club members were wrapping up their discussion and into another round of wine when Maile finally arrived from the museum. They greeted her with "You're just on time, Maile—Hawaii Time," and a burst of congenial laughter. She sat down on a padded folding chair next to Auntie Bee and crunched on a piece of celery.

"Sorry I'm late," Maile said, "but got hung up with a last minute call. How did everyone like the book?"

Bee tapped her copy. "It's one good story. Everyone talking about their families working sugar cane, coming over as picture brides, starting bizness."

"Did the Takahashis come from Japan to work in the sugarcane fields?"

"Yeah. Yeah. 1889. But plenty soon, my grandfather's father started a small store on Hilo side"

The one that got destroyed in the tsunami or another? Maile thought. "What did Eleanor think about Duke Kahanamoku and the Waikiki Boys? Kinda fun in the story."

"I think he's beautiful. Sexy." Eleanor Kane patted Maile's shoulder. "Glad you could make it."

"Thanks for inviting me, Eleanor. And you, too, Auntie Bee." Maile had always wanted to be in a book club, but never had time on the Mainland. This book club was special, made up of smart, involved-in-the-community women. They had welcomed Maile in when Bee suggested her name as a new member. Maile enjoyed the friendships she continued to make here.

"Oh, have you met Mari DeMello?" Eleanor asked as a slim woman in a short blue patterned muumuu slipped around Bee and Maile and stood in front of them. "She's been wanting to meet you.

"Howzit?" Mari said. She dipped her head at Bee, then held out her hand to Maile. "I'm Mari. Bee told us about the box."

Maile got up and shook Mari's hand. "She showed you the writings?"

"She did," Mari said, smiling at Bee. "Everyone's talking about it. Wondered who wrote it."

"I'm trying to find that out," Maile said.

Bee chuckled. "We turning into one big history class." She nodded to a woman with tips of purple in her short gray hair, talking to another book club member. "Dottie's grandmother taught school in Captain Cook in the 1920s. Always heard stories about the school in Ho'okena."

"And my family owned a store in Ho'okena." Mari picked up a folding chair around and sat down next to Maile.

"DeMello. Do you have family down in Punalu'u?" Maile asked.

"Yes, I do. Cousins."

Maile smiled. "Me, too. The Morrisons. Jenny, Tom, Peter. I came over once when Tom graduated from high school. I met one of his friends who was a DeMello."

"I know Tom. And that would be my cousin Lenny DeMello. They both played defense on the high school basketball team."

"Small world, isn't it?"

"Yeah, yeah."

"So how you find out where the writing comes from?" Eleanor Kane asked.

"Lots of ways," Maile said. "Generally on what was found with it, where it was found. Context for starters. I did do a documents search on that ad found in Bee's box. Got some listings for photographs, text. Strangely, an old newspaper account came up about a Casper DeMello. Do you know who he is?"

Mari's face turned pale. "He's my great-grandfather. His family owned the store I was talking about." Mari swallowed. "It's one old family story."

"Kinda shocking how he died." When Mari frowned, Maile said she was sorry to bring it up.

"It's OK. It was a long time ago."

"He was handsome," Maile said. "That's why I asked if you had cousins, because he looked just like my cousin's classmate in Punalu'u— your Lenny DeMello."

"You think?"

Maile nodded yes. Suddenly, she felt awkward. She stared at her piece of celery and wondered if it would be impolite to finish it.

Bee stirred in her chair. "You two keep talking. Gotta say goodbye to Dottie." She braced herself with her hands on the cushions and slowly stood up with a little help from Maile. She patted Mari on her shoulders as she passed by.

"I didn't mean to get personal," Maile said. "I'm afraid I get wrapped up in my history searches. Always a family story in there."

"I don't think I've seen the newspaper account for years. What did it say again?"

"Talked about where he was found, that his mother was widowed. Think I read that he left a wife and baby."

"My grandfather."

"So sorry. May I ask what happened after that?"

Mari sighed. "Casper's mother was widowed the year before after his father was killed in a wagon accident. Casper was oldest of three kids and the only boy. Some say she just couldn't keep the store going after Casper died, but others say it was the Almeidas, one of the brothers who pressured her. Made up stories about Casper stealing, cooking the books, shoddy produce. I don't know. She finally sold the store and some lands up in Kona."

Maile bit her lips. She didn't know what to say, so she said, "What a terrible story."

"Mari?" Bee called from the front door. "Tony's here."

Mari stood up and sniffed. Her eyes were full of tears. "My son and my ride."

Maile, still stunned by the conversation got up, too. "History hurts" had always been her motto, because sometimes terrible, untold stories were often the result of research. She collected herself to look at Tony DeMello. It was Casper all over again: young, athletic with dark eyes that touched the soul with laughter and sorrow.

After Tawnie finished her call with Moke, she got out of the car and called to Jim. He was snapping close-up pictures of the plants next to the library. "Time for lunch. Research made me hungry. How about you?"

"Oh, I've been thinking I should get back to the hotel. Check in with Denny about our report for tonight. I can catch something back around there."

"You walking?"

"Yeah." He patted his stomach. "Exercise would do me good. Thought I'd walk down to the beach. Go home that way." He cocked his head at Tawnie. "Anything come out of talking to Moke?"

"Well, the good news is that Boyd is still hanging on. Turns out he had a stroke, but he woke up an hour ago. He's in the ICU, so he's getting good care. Because of that, I felt I should share some of the things we knew about Boyd's papers. I didn't tell Moke about the eBay part, but I told him plenty about what was in the box."

"And?"

"Glad I did. Moke's going to share what he's found as long as we don't jump ahead of the criminal case that's developing. The kid who was killed in the police chase was the same one who broke into cars at the Volcano Art Center Gallery. Moke said he didn't find a box and haversack, but they did recover a letter opener. He thought it was pretty old looking. Has a thistle on the handle. Seems to fit with the haversack in the Stevenson collection."

Jim came over shouldering his camera case. "Do you think the kid has a connection to Almeida?"

"I don't think so. Just a random act. But the guy who attacked Boyd, that's another matter."

Jim nodded at Tawnie. "So what are you doing after lunch?"

"I want to look at those newspaper articles again about the Almeida family, particularly, Freddy Almeida. And I hope to hear from my friend Russell about land deeds, grants in the Kailua-Kona and Ho'okena area."

"If you went way back then it would be the Royal Hawaiian Kingdom, right?"

"I guess so. History was nevah my strong point." Tawnie emphasized the pidgin word.

Jim chuckled. He walked over to get his sun hat on the driver's seat. "Check the backseat. I bought today's newspaper. Has an article about the family. It *is* curious about Boyd's box. It's like someone wanted to get rid of it and someone else didn't."

"That's why I like working with you, Jim." Tawnie came around to the front of the car. Her heeled sandals clicked on the sidewalk. "Wouldn't it be weird if this has something to do with the hotels back in the 1970s?"

"What about the girl who handed the box over to Boyd? How does she fit in?"

"I'm going to check the obituary for the senior Almeida. Family members are sure to be listed."

Jim gave Tawnie the keys to the car. "See you in a bit."

After Jim took off, Tawnie drove down to the restaurant and bar where they had dinner the night before. *Seems like a year ago.* So much going on since they wrapped up their news story on Hon'okena Beach. Tawnie wondered how Boyd was doing now. *Awake?*

Her cell phone rang. Tawnie didn't know the name, but answered. "Tawnie Takahashi KWAI-5 News."

"Oh, Tawnie. This is Eleanor Kane. I'm one of your Auntie Bee's book club members. I hope you don't mind me calling you."

"No, not at all. How is she? Big day coming up."

"That's why I called. We just finished our monthly book club meeting. After she left, some of us stayed back to talk about final arrangements for the party at Volcano House. Lots of people coming from all over."

"When should I be there?"

"Party starts at 2:00 but we'd like people to show up no later than 1:15. We've made some throw pillows for friends and family to sign. One has a picture of her dog, Asami. Another has Honu. You know how she loves her sea turtles."

"Yeah, yeah. I can do that. Any word on Kiro? She misses him so much. It would be wonderful if he could make it, but getting leave and flying all the way in from Germany is a bit of stretch."

"Haven't heard. All of her other kids will be there with *their* kids. Plus all Bee's friends. We'll have to hide all the cars."

Tawnie laughed. "Anything else I should know? Anything I can do?"

"I'll let you know, but just being there will mean a lot to her. You're her brother Jimmy's favorite grandchild."

After the call ended, Tawnie ordered a salad. While she waited, she checked for messages on her phone. Finding only one from Denny at the KWAI-5 News station in Honolulu, she quickly read it, responded and then opened up Google to search obits on Josef Almeida. Several came up, one of them was in the *Honolulu Advertiser*. The Almeida name appeared to be well known throughout the Hawaiian Islands. Tawnie read through the accolades and found what she wanted: a list of who was mentioned as survivors. She laid open the newspaper on the chair next to her and reread the Almeida story on the front page. Matson and Frederick (Freddy) Almeida were mentioned in the dispute—"a difference of opinion" was how the newspaper put it. But the story didn't reveal more family members beyond the two brothers.

The obituary, however, was different. It seemed the whole family was listed. *And "Freddy Almeida" is the preferred name,* Tawnie thought. Included in the "survived by" list was Josef's oldest son, Matson, and his two sons and then son, Freddy, his wife Gina Almeida, and their children, David, Victor and Angie Almeida.

Tawnie leaned back in her chair. *Angie. Was this the girl that handed the box over to Boyd? How had he described her? A young woman. College age, Portuguese. Pretty* Tawnie sat up deep in thought. *What was going on here? Why did the family want to get rid of the box? What secret did it hold?*

Officer Jerry Moke was waiting for Maile in the lobby of the museum when she got back to work. It wasn't totally unexpected as they had talked a couple of hours before, but Zita Chin, the volunteer receptionist, must have taken it the wrong way.

"Is he here for the break-in at the dumpster?" she whispered to Maile.

"No. I think we're fine with that. Nothing of value there."

Zita nodded, making the purple eyeglass chain dangling off the ends of her glasses swing. She went back to stacking brochures on the counter.

"Officer Moke," Maile said. "Good to see you." She held out her hand and after he shook it, she directed him to a small room off the lobby. "Did you bring the artifact?"

"Have it right here. Right now it's a part of our investigation in the fatal car crash I told you about." At Maile's invitation, Moke sat down at the koa wood table. He settled his big frame on the chair, then unrolled a plastic police evidence bag. He put on latex gloves and took out a long silver letter opener.

"Beautiful," Maile said.

"Is it old?

Maile put on her own set of gloves. "I think so. May I?"

"Yeah, sure."

Maile held the letter knife in her hands and marveled at its silverwork. A beautiful piece, someone had taken great thought into creating it. The blade and handle were sterling silver. The designer had cast the letter knife as one piece. "Definitely Victorian."

Maile looked for an engraved stamp on the back and found a brand she didn't recognized, but the name was definitely Scots—Ferguson. Maile reached over to a box on a bookcase next to the table and took out a ruler. "Eight and half inches. That's fairly standard length, though I don't think this would be part of a ladies' writing desk." When Moke gave her a quizzical look, she went on explain what a writing desk was. A portable writing desk with everything the writer needed to write a letter in it. Authors used them, too.

Moke face became still for a moment. "Interesting. So a writer could have one like this."

"Yes."

"And that writing desk. I learn something new every day. It just like one laptop today."

Maile laughed. "It is like that in some ways. We always think we have invented something new. Many Victorian ladies put their pens, nibs and a small letter opener in a small pencil box which was then set in the writing desk. The pencil box protected the writing instruments being jostled around when traveling or could be just carried on its own. The letter openers designed for that use tended to be smaller. This could have been a man's, but that's just a guess."

Maile turned over the letter opener. For the first time, she noticed the design on the handle. A Scottish thistle. The design looked familiar, but at first she couldn't remember why. She studied the delicate lines that formed the feathery flower of the thistle. So realistic. Below the flower, the thistle's spiky bulb was represented by cross hatches that reminded Maile of a pineapple. Two jagged leaves encased the bulb. "It really is work of art."

"And you can verify that it is from the 19th century? That it's plenty old?"

"Yes. I can write something up for you if you like."

"That would be very helpful, but you don't need to do it right away."

"Hmm. Did you notice the bulb below the flower? I think there were gems in it."

"Really?" Moke leaned over the table.

"See?" Maile pointed out scattered holes smaller than a sixteenth of an inch throughout the cross hatches with her finger. She reached over to the bookcase again and picked up a long handled magnifying glass. "Some of these holes, though little, are gouged. Like something was lifted out with a tiny tool." She handed the glass over to Moke.

"Funny, you say. I think something was left behind." He gave Maile the glass. "A tiny piece of emerald. I'll have forensics look at the letter opener thoroughly."

"The tip is sharp but something organic has stained it. The color is bit off for the rest of patina on it. I do mind if I take a picture of it?"

Moke stood up and nodded that she could.

Maile took some shots of the letter knife with her phone, honing in on the thistle for a couple photos, and then let Moke put the letter opener away in his evidence bag. He was done, he handed his card.

"*Mahalo* Miss Horner for your help and good eye. You can email me comments on the age of this tomorrow. Or fax it. "

"I will. Is that all you need?"

"For now. 'Preciate your help."

They went back into the lobby. The sounds of hammering came from the exhibit room. "Our next show," Maile explained.

A poster on the wall, next to the room's entrance, announced the exhibit's opening. Moke froze. "Robert Louis Stevenson. That guy is getting around. Been seeing his name all the time lately."

"I hope so." Maile came up to the poster. "A lot of people don't know how popular it was to visit the Big Island in the 19th century, largely due to Kilauea and the accommodations up there. Mark Twain did. You could stay at Volcano House. It's now the art center gallery. RLS didn't get up to Kilauea due to his health, but he did come to the Big Island to write. He visited Ho'okena and went up to the City of Refuge. Wrote *The Bottle Imp* and *The Master of Ballantrae*. 1889."

Moke rubbed his chin. "You don't happen to know a Harold Boyd?"

"I do. I haven't met him, but we've been emailing back and forth for months. He's an expert on the author. From the Mainland. We were supposed to meet here last night, but he didn't show."

Moke cleared his throat. "Because he had an accident yesterday. That's why. He's in an ICU unit in Kailu- Kona."

Maile gasped and put her hands on her mouth. "Oh, no. Is he going to make it?"

"It's an active case right now, so I can't tell you much, but he's stable. I'll let know you if there are changes. Actually, visiting him might help him remember what happened." Moke looked at Maile. "Do you have time to do that?"

"I can make some time. Anything to help him."

"*Mahalo*. When I hear he's awake and the nurse says he can have visitors, I'll call you. And thanks for looking at this." Moke lifted up the evidence bag.

"You're welcome."

Maile saw Moke out the door but on returning to the lobby, she had a sudden thought. The thistle on the letter opener matched the clasp on the old haversack.

Auntie Bee, who in the world put that box in the trunk of your car?

After Auntie Bee dropped off the last of her fellow book club members, she drove down to the local mall to run some errands. The late afternoon was cloudy with hints of "Hawaiian sunshine" in the forecast. The coconut palms in the parking lot stirred as Bee entered the plaza of big box stores and small mom-and-pop franchises. She wondered if her umbrella was still in the back seat. After parking, she hurried in to pick up vitamins for Asami and then came out. For a moment, she stood on the covered sidewalk and watched a rainbow blossom on the green hills that rose back to Mauna Kea's shoulders. Light and shadow playing together as a soft curtain of rain came down. For all the years she lived in Hilo, the sight never bored her. *Makes for one good fourth grade science activity. Teacha, where do rainbows come from?*

The mall parking lot on the other side of the mall road was packed. She was about to cross, when she heard a couple arguing a few doors up.

"Your uncle is never going to let this happen and you know it," the young man said. "Why do you think your parents will?"

The young woman leaned her head into the young man's chest. She clutched his tank top and shuddered. He murmured something Bee couldn't hear, then put his arms around the woman. He kissed her head and rocked her. Suddenly he was looking at Bee. His tanned face turned white. The young woman looked up and froze.

"Don't tell," he mouthed to Bee. Bee put a finger to her lips and shook her head. She wouldn't say a word. *But what* kine *crazy mixed up world we live in?* she thought. Tony DeMello was in love with an Almeida girl.

***

After Tawnie finished her salad, she walked down to busy Ali'i Drive on the waterfront.

A light rain had passed through a while ago, briefly leaving the sidewalks and roofs on the two-story shops and restaurants glistening. The sun was already drying them up.

She crossed over to the concrete wall that lined Kailua Bay and walked toward the Pier. Out in the water, locals and tourists played in the turquoise water. For a moment Tawnie stopped and leaned against the wall to watch. So many memories of beach parties and body surfing down at Ala Moana Park and Waikiki growing up in Honolulu.

I was so content then, she thought. *Am I content now?"* Tawnie pushed back from the wall.

"What a silly thought," she said to herself. Then she remembered the story of *The Bottle Imp.* To save yourself if you owned the imp, you had to be content when you sold it to another. Tawnie thought for a moment. She loved her job as a television crime reporter and where it had taken her so far. *But I'm thirty-three and I can do better.* But did that mean she wasn't content? She always had a driven, competitive side.

Her cell phone rang. "Russell, howzit? Aren't you at the wedding?"

"Tomorrow. I couldn't resist doing some research. You got me thinking about my uncle and the Hawaii Ono Hotel. I found some interesting things."

"What did you find?" Tawnie kept walking to the Pier and made the turn.

"First of all, none of the property in question at Ho'okena or the hotel site is leasehold—nothing connected to Bishop Estate lands. I thought I'd find the Almeidas the first to put in a claim, but DeMellos were there early on. Opened their store in Ho'okena. 1880. That's significant."

"Why is that?" Tawnie looked for a bench along the Pier occupied by small vendors spread along its length.

"The first group of Portuguese came in 1878. Came to work in the cane fields, many of them as managers. The DeMellos moved right into the mercantile business. Had some cattle, too."

"How did you find this stuff?"

"Title companies. But the old business directories list the taxes in the back. Give you a sense of the times."

"I looked through those directories. Saw some ads for the DeMellos and Almeidas in the 1887 one, but in the 1890s, the DeMellos are gone." Tawnie found a bench with a dry spot and sat down. "I also reread Josef's obit and it said that Matson Almeida is acting CEO of Almeida, Ltd. but his brother Frederick Almeida had some land preservation company."

"That's Hawaii Land Hui. Freddy Almeida's on the board. It's eco-friendly and deals with issues like invasive species, land preservation. Almeida Ltd. holds the titles to various properties. This Freddy is listed on most of them. "

"Doesn't sound like someone who'd cheat you."

"Well, he would have been a kid back when the hotel was being built."

They talked for a few more minutes, Tawnie writing down the details he gave on the titles to Ho'okena, Captain Cook, and Kailua- Kona. "Mahalo, Russell," she said when they were done. "Really appreciate it. How can I thank you?"

"Ha. I'm staying on island for a few days after the wedding. Why don't we go for a beer? Catch up."

Tawnie wondered if he was asking her for a date, not just catch up. There was something in his voice. When Tawnie thought about it, Russell Ito had been always close friend back in high school. Good looking, too. After she went off to college, they had kept in touch for a couple of years. *Until I got real busy with the news business.* "Sure. Let's see how this Almeida story pans out. Right now, I'm doing it on my own time."

"Great. Hmm. You wouldn't consider coming to the wedding reception?"

"That's very nice, Russell, but I really am under pressure to get the Ho'okena story done before my auntie's birthday party. There's also a chance I might be asked to help out on some party planning for it, too. A beer will be fine. And *mahalo*, Russell, for asking. It will be nice to talk to you."

After she ended the call, Tawnie turned around on the bench and faced the water. *Am I content?* Maybe a change was in the wind. When her phone buzzed, it seemed like it was. Boyd, Moke texted, was awake and strong enough to talk. He's asking for you.

Chapter 18

After Moke left, Maile went upstairs to her office and closed down her computer. For a moment, she sat at her desk, looking out into the yard where a couple of tourists were reading signage about the different plants and trees in the garden. It was still an hour away to closing time, but Maile had been given permission to go up to Volcano and pick up a print at the art center for the auction that would coincide with the RLS exhibit. She would also run an errand for Eleanor Kane: deliver a complete list of all who were coming to the restaurant for Bee's party. After the private birthday party for family and book club members, there would be a surprise reception for Bee. The Hawaii Teachers Association was giving her a special award for her years of teaching which had influenced leaders in local and state government, education, arts, conservation and preservation and all the children of Hilo. Maile felt blessed that Bee was her neighbor.

Maile stacked the papers and files on her desk. On top was an article on *The Bottle Imp* she had downloaded from the Robert Louis Stevenson Society website in New York. She leaned back in her chair and stretched, thinking about the letter opener and the haversack. They had to go together. The thistle designs were the same. Maile was sure of it. She was also positive that the manuscript, despite the 1921 Almeida store ad found with it, was a genuine, original copy of *The Bottle Imp* story written by Stevenson in *his* own handwriting. She had seen enough of the author's handwriting in the past eight months as she worked on the exhibit to recognize it. What if it was Boyd's? In an email to Maile a week before, Boyd said his main purpose coming to the island was to pick up some material for his next book. What if this kid had a stolen it from Boyd? All Moke said was that Boyd had had an accident and that it was an active case. What if Boyd had been robbed? Maile wondered if there was a way to find out where Boyd and box had last been together. Moke wasn't going to help, but maybe Annie Moke could. *Moke. Were they related?*

A few minutes later, Maile was out the door and on the road to Volcanoes National Park. It would take her about 40 minutes to get there if the traffic wasn't crazy. Once she was out of town and on the

Volcano Highway, she opened the car's sunroof and turned on the local radio channel playing Hawaiian music. Her thoughts drifted. What should she tell Auntie Bee? A better question, should she contact Officer Moke about her suspicions? When she finally arrived in the little village of Volcano, she decided that she would ask about the car prowl at the art center gallery. First, she'd get an iced mocha at the Almeida Store on Old Volcano Road.

As she got in line to the Lava Lady, a drive thru coffee stand built like a grass shack, she got out of the car and stretched. The late afternoon was already turning to shadow as tall trees blocked the sun's descent. The air felt chilly, but then, Volcano was almost 4,000 feet above sea level.

On the other side of her car, Maile noticed an older man with a dark moustache and a wide-brimmed Panama hat come out of the main store. His aloha shirt was neat and his pants ironed. Everything about him was slick and smooth. Not a thing out of place. Maile wondered why she noticed that. Maybe he was a businessman. When he walked over to his red Grand Cherokee, he paused and turned. His dark eyes seemed to drill into her as he stared. Maile didn't know how to respond, but she didn't flinch. He finally got into his SUV and took off in a roar. The car behind her beeped, making Maile jump. She waved gaily back and got into her car, but the man with the Panama hat made her shake. She was still unsettled when she arrived at the Volcano Art Center Gallery. She took a deep breath, then went inside.

The gift shop was getting ready to close for the day, but the print for the auction was wrapped and ready to go. "Thanks, Peggy," Maile said to the Hawaiian woman at the cash register. "The historical society appreciates this donation." They talked story for a bit, but Peggy must have noticed Maile's restlessness. "Something wrong?" she asked.

"No, I'm fine. I did hear there've been car prowls up here lately."

"Yeah, yeah. Been going on for a couple of weeks, but stopped after da kid was killed."

"I read about that. Did you ever see him up here?"

"Think maybe he came into the shop a couple of times. One local kid with dreads." Peggy hit a button on the register to run off the day's receipts. Maile had to talk loud over it.

"Did he take anything from here?"

"Don't think so." Peggy ripped off the long tally strip and folded it. She placed the tally into the register and turned the machine off.

Maile hefted the heavy package. "You know my neighbor, Bee Takahashi. She was up here during the last one."

"Oh, Bee. Something wrong? Is she sick? "

"No, nothing like that. Just that someone put a box into her car. It wasn't leftovers from her book sale. She thinks someone did that up here. I wonder if it was the car prowler."

"Important stuff?"

"Yes. Valuable. It might have been stolen."

"That's *lolo*. Take stuff, then put something back. Wait a minute." Peggy locked the front door and turned the OPEN sign to CLOSED. She motioned for Maile to follow her as she went around the building checking all the windows and turning off lights. "There might have been someone with him. When I went out to see what the fuss in the parking lot was all about, I saw the thief run off down the road. Not long after a car follow him." Peggy jangled her keys. "Maybe the Hilo and national park police will figure it out. We don't want this kine stuff happening up here. Kilauea is sacred."

Maile left a few minutes later. By now she was convinced that the thief had taken the letter opener out of the box because it was valuable and put the rest of the contents in the box into Bee's car. Other than the letter opener, nothing else would have appeared saleable. The kid wouldn't know how valuable the manuscript would be at auction. Thousands.

Maile hopped in her car and started for Volcano House. On the front seat was a basket and the list of birthday party attendees on a clipboard. When she came to the stop at Crater Rim Drive, an SUV came up behind her. No other cars were on the road or in the parking lot. At first Maile thought it might be Peggy taking off for home in Pahala, but when the vehicle came directly alongside her, something warned Maile to be careful. The windows on the SUV were dark. She couldn't make out the driver inside. Maile looked across the drive to the road that led to the Volcano House hotel and restaurant and wondered if she could make it there. She started to go forward, but the mysterious driver blocked her.

Maile's only choice was to go right onto the drive that went around Kilauea's rim. Maile honked at the driver, but the SUV pushed against her car.

Maile turned, then hit the gas and sped away. She hoped she could find an exit to get back out on the main highway, but the driver of the black SUV had no intention of letting her do that. The vehicle sped up behind her. It came close, its chrome grill like a grinning mask. Maile pushed down her rising panic. The drive was worn and narrow and surrounded on both sides with keawe, tall lehua, and tree ferns. Her car bounced and jostled on the worn road. It took all her concentration to drive and keep a distance. She sped up one more time, but it was too dangerous to go any faster. No one was else was on the road ahead, but beyond the trees, the road opened into grassy lava fields. Maybe someone would be at the parking lot for the steam vents. The SUV came after her again.

The car hit a pothole. The basket on the passenger seat bounced, throwing out her cell phone against the cup holder console. Maile grabbed it and opened up the phone app one-handed. She had no clue how to reach the park rangers, but hitting "A," Annie Moke's contact came up. Maile pressed that with her thumb. When Annie answered, Maile yelled "Help me," but it was too late. The SUV came alongside and pushed against her car. Maile couldn't get both hands back on the steering wheel in time. The car swerved and shot off the road, crashing into a ditch. The last thing she remembered before everything went black was the car flipping and airbags exploding around her.

It took three rings for Annie Moke to reach her father-in-law on the Big Island.

"Annie. Howzit?" Jerry said.

"No time fo' talk story. Got the weirdest call from Bee Takahashi's neighbor? Maile—"

"—Horner."

"She was crying for help, then I heard a terrible sound of glass and metal crashing. I think she's in danger."

"Do you know where she was calling from?"

"I have no idea." Annie heard Moke's voice go in and out as he moved about.

"Got one idea," he said. "Just saw her in person more than an hour ago. She said something about going to Volcano to do an errand at the art center." Moke's voice went away, then came back. "I just sent an alert to the park police. Hopefully, they can find her."

"What's going on? Just this morning she asked me how she could get police records from a long time ago. Like a hundred and twenty years ago."

Moke didn't answer.

Annie went on. "Maile Horner told me they were doing an exhibit on the *Treasure Island* author at her museum in Hilo. The stuff she's pulling together must be valuable. Do you think some theft ring is after it?"

Moke cleared his throat. "Alright. That is one case we're following. Robbery and battery of some *haole* writing about Robert Louis Stevenson. And, that *wahine* TV reporter, Tawnie Takahashi, has her nose in it."

Tawnie Takahashi. Sometimes Annie just wanted to groan when she heard the reporter's name because in the past Takahashi had called all police incompetent. Takahashi could be aggressive when doing crime reporting. Yet in the last year, Annie had mellowed toward Takahashi because of Tawnie's great aunt, Bee Takahashi. Annie and Tawnie were almost "let's have a beer" friendly.

Annie let her father-in-law relay all he knew about the Boyd case. "Never thought Horner could be in danger," he said. "All I did was ask her opinion about the letter opener."

Moke's voice went away again, then came back. "They found Horner. They're calling in an ambulance right now. Sounds like a really bad car accident. I better go. Oh, when you coming over?"

"I just might make an excuse to do it now."

"Do that. It will be good to see you."

***

Tawnie Takahashi took a deep breath and stepped out of the hospital elevator. The ICU hall was nearly empty, but from the rooms, floor was alive with the sounds of beating monitors and the murmur of hospital staff attending patients. She showed her reporter's pass to the attendant at the nurse's station. He checked a clipboard and nodded for her to follow him.

Tawnie's heart pounded. She hated hospitals. Her grandfather Jimmy Takahashi, WWII war hero and civil rights lawyer, had ended his days in one. An image of his frail body lying in bed brought tears to her eyes.

"Is Boyd still awake?" she asked. "Officer Moke said he was."

"He was when he was last checked. He's responding to questions, but his speech is slow. Sometimes that clears up. I can't tell you anything more. HIPA." The male nurse looked at her again. "I'm not sure how you got clearance, but if you're on to some big crime news breaking, you'll have to wait."

"I'm just concerned about him. He-- well, he asked me to help him. Even if he can't respond, just wanted to let him know that I'm doing what I promised. Might help him to be calm."

"Alright."

They stopped at UCI unit #4. From inside the room, the sounds of beeping equipment played a sharp counterpoint to a quiet discussion in another room. *Grandfather.* Tawnie just couldn't shake the image. When she stepped into the room and saw Boyd lying propped up in clean, white hospital bed, all she saw there was *Ojiisan. Jiji.* Tawnie almost jumped when the nurse said he'd give her five minutes. No more.

Tawnie pulled a chair over to the bed. Boyd looked like he had aged since she last saw him. His hair had more gray in it and there were dark circles under his eyes. One side of his face seemed to droop. She was relieved when Boyd opened his eyes. He turned his head.

"Mr. Boyd," Tawnie said, "I'm so sorry for what has happened. They tell me you are doing well."

Boyd opened and closed his mouth. His effort to speak seemed to exhaust him.

"You don't have to talk." Tawnie cleared her throat. "I just wanted you to know that the police are actively looking for your box. In fact, they found something that might have come from it. A letter opener. Was there one?"

Boyd smiled, the left side of his mouth drooping down. He patted the bed with the flat of his hand.

"That's a yes. Good. That's very important." She went on to tell him about the thief who had the object. She described the young man as Moke had related to her. "Is he the one who attacked you at Ho'okena and in Kailua-Kona?"

Boyd worked his mouth. "Furz one, yes. N'other—" Boyd waved the word away.

"So there are two different people. I think you told me that at the hotel." Tawnie sighed. "At least, the first attacker has been identified, but whoever did this to you at the hotel is still at large."

Boyd lifted his hand. "Blud."

"Blood?"

Boyd nodded.

"Oh, the manuscript. When it's found, they could do some tests. I think the police are planning to check the letter knife." Tawnie thought for a moment. "This may sound like an odd question, but how much money is this collection worth?"

Boyd made a circle with his hands and expanded them

"Lots." Tawnie was relieved that his hands and arms appeared unaffected by his stroke.

Boyd nodded.

"On the other hand, what if this collection was stolen long ago?" When Boyd frowned, Tawnie went on. "You've concluded that this is an original, handwritten manuscript by Stevenson. How did it stay hidden all these years? Some private collection?"

Boyd gave her a puzzled look, then brightened. He made writing motions with his right hand. Tawnie got her notebook and pen out of her messenger bag. Holding the notebook down with the flat of his hand, Boyd held the pen like he was going to stab the paper.

Maybe the stroke did affect him, Tawnie thought.

When he finished his note, Tawnie read: I haz my sus pigeons.

"Really? You were wondering, too?" Tawnie leaned forward. "Then the question is why did someone put this out on eBay? Did you know that this Freddy Almeida is part of a family dispute over a will?"

Boyd slowly shook his head.

"I did some research and I think the girl that gave you the box is his daughter, Angie Almeida." Tawnie wanted to talk more but she knew that her questions were tiring him. Besides, her five minutes had to be up. Yet, she had to ask. "Somehow, this box contains evidence to an old crime that the family or someone close to the family has tried to hide for a long time. When Stevenson was on the Big Island in Ho'okena, do you think something of his was stolen? He did ever write about his time there?"

Boyd made a mumbling sound and wrote again.

Trivels in Hawai

"Travels in Hawaii?"

Boyd nodded.

"Time's up." The male voice seemed to explode in the room. "You have to go, Ms. Takahashi."

Tawnie straightened her skirt. "*Mahalo* for letting me in," she said to the nurse. She patted Boyd's arm. "I'll be in touch, either in person or through Officer Moke. Take care."

Tawnie walked back down to the elevator, glad to be out of the room and soon the hospital. She punched in the button for the lobby. Her phone rang.

Officer Moke. His message was short. Maile Horner was in a bad accident and was being transported to Hilo. She had reported to a park employee that she had been followed and then run off the road. "Where are you now?" he asked.

"I just left Boyd's room."

"How is he?"

"He's awake. Can't quite talk and he misspells words when he writes, but his color is much better than when I found him at the hotel. He says that the letter knife is a part of his collection."

"Great. Anything else? You didn't shove a microphone under his chin, did you?"

"No! What *kine* person do you think I am? It's not always about news. I can care about someone." Tawnie's voice grew tight. She jackhammered the elevator down button with her finger.

"I'm sorry fo' say that, Ms. Takahashi. Didn't mean to be brusque. Just been upset about Ms. Horner. Police have a caring side, too, you know." He cleared his throat. "I'm going to put a police detail on her at the hospital."

Tawnie sniffed. "I think you should put one on Mr. Boyd, too." Then Tawnie told Moke how Boyd had got the box off eBay from Freddy Almeida, one of the sons in the contested will case in the news. "I think it might have to do with a century-old crime. Perhaps a murder."

Chapter 20

When Maile came to, her car was upright but caught on some vegetation. The air bags had deployed leaving a fine powder everywhere, but along with her seat belt, they had secured her. Not so much everything else in the car. All the contents in her basket, auction print, beach mat, umbrella, and every else not tied down seemed to have joined her on the front seat. As she looked at the damage, she felt lucky she was alive. The front of the car was smashed in like a soda can, the hood half-sheared off. The doors on the driver and the passenger sides were open, laying out like the torn wings of a wounded bird. She pushed the airbag away from her face, then screamed from the pain exploding in her left arm. Whimpering, she closed her eyes and took a big breath. When she opened her eyes, she wondered if she had passed out. Using her right hand, she pushed away the bag and looked to her left. Her bare lower arm was bruised and bloody, but she saw no bone sticking out. When she touched a small wound, though, it stung enough to make her feel sick to her stomach. She leaned forward and undid her seatbelt, then passed out.

She dreamed of surfers on the North Shore.

"Miss. Lady." A male voice that sounded like a young Duke Kahanamoku entered her dream of surfers carving waves. Maile's eyes snapped open when someone touched her shoulder. Not the Duke, but someone just as dreamy as a local lifeguard at Waikiki. The man was tall with wavy, dark hair pulled back into a short, ponytail. His dark eyes showed concern. He wore a fleece vest over a flannel shirt.

"I've called the fire department. I'm not going to move you until they come. Don't smell gas, so I think you're safe."

"*Mahalo.*" Maile stared at his ball cap with a logo of a volcano on it. She felt like she was still in the dream. "Are you a park ranger?"

"Yes, I'm a biologist who works here. Want some water? Just to wet your mouth."

"Uh-huh." Maile's head throbbed, adding additional misery to the increasing pain in her arm. She took a sip, then lowered the water bottle.

"Are you hurt?"

"My arm hurts pretty bad. Everything else just aches."

"What's your name? I'm Liko Hanale."

"Maile Horner." She took another long sip before closing her eyes.

Liko touched her shoulder. Like he wanted her to stay awake. Somehow she didn't mind her handsome rescuer doing that.

"Do you remember what happened?" he asked.

"Someone followed me. Pushed me off the road." She stirred in her seat.

"Did you see the guy?"

"No. Window was dark. Could you find my cell phone?"

"I'll look." Liko straightened up. "I hear a siren. Help is coming soon."

"OK." Maile started to feel cold.

"Hey, look at me," Liko said. A blanket appeared in his hands. *Or had he just stepped away?* He gently tucked a fleece throw around her. "Tell me about yourself. What do you?"

"Museum curator."

"Here in Hilo? That's cool." Liko kept talking to her. Suddenly, she was aware of activity around her as a team of firefighters arrived. One moment she was in the driver's seat, the next on a backboard set into an ambulance. The last thing Maile saw before the doors closed in jerky motions was Liko's concerned face. A distant voice warned. "Be careful. She's   going   into   shock."

Chapter 21

Jim Milstead was in the hotel lounge drinking a beer when Tawnie arrived from the hospital.

"How is Boyd?" he asked.

"As well as can be expected," Tawnie said. She pushed aside a palm frond blocking her way to his chair and sat down on one next to him. "He was able to talk with me—well, communicate. He didn't know about the Almeida court case, but did say the letter opener was with the box. I'm getting worried. My auntie's neighbor—the historian—was run off the road up at Volcano. It looks deliberate. Officer Moke said Maile Horner knew about the letter opener. He had asked her to identify its era and any historical import just an hour before the accident."

"Wow. Is she alright? What's going on? This is crazy."

Tawnie motioned for Jim to share his beer and took a sip from the bottle. "She's spending the night in the hospital in Hilo. Just to observe. I think it's all tied to the Almeida family and the fight over the will. When Freddy Almeida put the box on eBay, he exposed a crime someone wanted to keep secret. The hunt is on to find the rest of the box." Tawnie took another sip and gave the bottle back to Jim. "The neighbor's phone is missing from her car. Someone may want the names on it."

"What do you want to do?"

"Go back to Hilo. I'm worried about my auntie."

"Right now?"

"Yes. What if they think she has something? She lives right next door. Whoever it is does not care if he hurts someone. "

Forty-five minutes later, Tawnie and Jim were on the road going toward Kamuela and Honokaa. They decided that they would not take Saddle Road and its new highway portion due to constant fog issues. At night it was too risky to take the shortcut across the high desert road to Hilo. Instead they would do the Hawaii Belt Road that circled the island. Go up to Kamuela and Honokaa and down through Laupahoehoe. As they cut across the dark, flat lava fields that bordered the highway out of Kailua-Kona, the headlights of their car illuminated ghostly piles of a'a rocks and sparse patches of dry grass.

Too much like the last time we raced for trouble, Tawnie thought. She was glad Jim was at the wheel. Holding her cell phone in her hand, she leaned back against her seat. She was still dressed in the short skirt and sleeveless top she wore all day, but glad she wore her cardigan sweater, too. She turned the car's air conditioner off and turned on the heat. She closed her eyes and pushed away the last two days' drama.

"When was the last time you talked to your aunt?" Jim asked.

Tawnie snapped awake. "Yesterday." She stared out the windshield and wondered where they were. The white picket fences and the cone shaped hills illuminated by the car's headlights suggested Kamuela.

"Sorry," Jim said. "Got about an hour to go. Wondered if you had a plan."

"Kinda late to call Moke again. I'm just going on a hunch."

"You never said anything to him about your aunt and her neighbor?"

"No." Tawnie chewed on her thumbnail. "It's always been about the birthday party."

"Well,   we'll   go   straight   there."

Chapter 22

Asami was at her watchdog best as she scrambled across the koa wood floor to the front door. Once there, the dog pirouetted under the doorknob and barked.

"Coming, Asami." Dressed in capris and a shirt, Bee put a cotton cardigan on her shoulders and slid into her slippers. A soft knock at the door sent Asami into another round of high-pitched barking.

Bee opened the door. Standing on the other side of the screen door was a young man dressed in a t-shirt and surfer pants. The glow of the porch light made his face golden against the last gasp of twilight behind him. "Why Tony DeMello, what you want, making an old lady get up from her sexy book?" She smiled and winked at him. "Come in."

"So sorry, Mrs. Takahashi. I apologize for coming by so late. I had to see you."

"You're just in time for tea. Always get some this time of night."

Bee padded out to the kitchen, her slippers making a flip-flop sound. She turned on her tea kettle and invited Tony to sit on one of the stools while she brought down two cups and her selection of teas. "I always like the chamomile this time of night."

"Thanks." Tony selected a tea, then chose a cup with a picture of the Volcano Art Center Gallery on it and pulled it toward him.

"So, what's going on? You for shame I saw you with your girlfriend? Think I'll tell your mother?"

Tony tapped his cup. "I know you won't tell. And my girlfriend is my fiancée. We want to get married, but it's complicated. I think you know who she is."

"An Almeida girl." Bee tapped her chin. "Angie. She was in Mrs. Chase's fourth grade class, but she came to mine for book club. My last year teaching."

"That's right. I love her, but we don't know what to do with all this mess with her family in the news and my family's history with the Almeidas. No love lost there."

"And your mom doesn't know."

Tony shook his head. "No."

"How did you meet?" Bee lifted up the kettle when it clicked off. Tony grabbed it when it wobbled in her hand. He poured the boiling water into her cup, then did his.

"Well, we've known each other from grade school, but as we grew older, any friendship was discouraged. Then in high school we were thrown into a study group and I liked her right away. We became close friends and fell in love in college. Just didn't tell my mom."

"Your *tutu* was my teaching partner for many years. She nevah showed any animosity toward an Almeida student, but then she just wouldn't. But your mother. I know she has been upset lately."

"That's because she started doing family genealogy on that ancestor website. I guess some of the family stories might be true."

"Your mother was talking about the store in Ho'okena this afternoon. It upsets her every time she tells it to me."

"My mom thinks our ancestor was murdered for the land there and in Kailua-Kona."

"That's one hard thing." Bee put her tea bag on a small plate and took a sip of her tea. "Do you think Angie's parents know about you?"

"Her dad might. Angie said he was going to fix something. Make things right. Just don't know what that means." Tony nodded at the book on *paniolo* cowboys of the Big Island on the edge of the counter. "Is that the sexy book you were reading?" He grinned. "You're so funny, Mrs. Takahashi."

Bee smiled. "I knew some nice looking *paniolos* up in Kamuela long time ago. I like to tease. Why don't you call me Auntie Bee? Everyone does. Not so formal." She took a sip of her tea. "What would you like me to do?"

Tony blushed. "I'd like you to meet Angie. Could I bring her here?"

"Yeah, yeah. But someday, the two of you will have to face your parents."

"Unless, we elope."

Bee sighed. "I know you're hurting, but wait just a little bit more—until the big legal fuss is all *pau*. In meantime, come here any time with Angie. And maybe, I can get your mother over here, too, to meet her. Get used to the idea. You need a family ally."

Tony frowned. "The probate court could take a while."

Bee patted his hand. "I know, but love is strong. When I fell in love with my George, my family wasn't sure about a *haole* from Boston. He knew nothing about the islands except from Bob Hope movies and that sexy scene in *From Here to Eternity*. But he had such *aloha* in his heart for me and the islands. Love won out with my family. We had a good marriage and they adored him." Bee looked away as a sudden burst of grief caught her.

"Auntie." Tony placed a hand next to her. "I'm sorry."

"It's OK. I get sad sometimes—What's that?" Bee pointed to bobbing lights going around Maile's house.

Tony went over to the sliding glass door. "Cops? Looks like cops."

They both watched as three shadows went around to the back of Maile's house. Moments later, lights went on inside. Through the windows at Maile's house they could see two men and a woman move from room to room. Finally, the police officers came out on the porch and seemed to discuss something. Then the house went dark and they left.

"What is going on?" Bee felt a sudden chill in her stomach. It had been hours since she had last seen Maile at the book club. Why were the police at her house?

"I'll see if anything is on TV," Tony said. "Do you want to call your friend?"

"Yeah, yeah." Bee slid off her stool and picked up her line phone by the wall. The phone rang for a long time before the message machine went on. "This is number 808—" Bee put the phone back on its cradle. "She's not there. I'm going to call the museum, though it might be too late to call." Bee picked up the phone again and dialed the museum's phone number. To her surprise, she got an answer.

"Big Island Historical Museum, Ester Ogawa speaking."

"Oh, Ester. This is Bee Takahashi. Is Maile still there/"

"Oh, so sorry fo' say, but she's at Hilo Hospital. She was involved in a terrible car accident this afternoon."

Bee put a hand to her chest. "No. The poor thing. Is she OK?"

"She's in the ER, but our director said that she will most likely be moved to a regular bed later tonight. She's very lucky. Lots of bruises from the airbag, but she has only a broken arm. No head trauma."

"Oh, thank goodness." Bee frowned. "Anything else going on? There were police at her house just a few moments ago. Why is that?"

"I'm not sure. Heard that she was run off the road up at the national park. That's all I know."

Bee closed her eyes. She couldn't imagine. Who would want to hurt Maile-san?

"Auntie Bee?" Ester asked. "Are you still there?"

"Yeah, yeah, I'm here. Just bad news all at once."

"Well, if you like, I can keep you posted. Our director, John Hauser, has permission from the hospital for any updates."

"*Mahalo*. Maile Horner is my neighbor and a sweet girl."

"And a good friend of mine. Well, you take care. Don't you worry. There is plenty *kokua* for her. And for you, Auntie, an early *Hau`oli Lā Hānau.*"

Tony came back into the kitchen. "What happened?"

"My neighbor was in a bad accident up at Volcano." She put the phone back in its cradle.

Her hand shook.

"Do you want to go sit in the living room?"

"I'm OK. Just bad news." Bee waved him way, then swayed. "Alright." She gave him her hand. After she was settled, Tony went back for their tea cups. He set them on the glass top coffee table in front of her.

"I'm sorry about your friend."

"That's why shaky. Don't understand people these days. Always in a hurry, always wanting something." She sipped a bit of her tea, then leaned back against the throw pillows on the sofa.

In front of Bee was the box. The haversack was opened and one of the *Scribner* magazines pulled out.

Tony sat down on an armchair next to her. "What is that?"

"Oh, some old stuff left in my car after the book sale."

"This is cool. Love old magazines. What else is in there?"

"Some old handwritten stuff. Maile says it's a copy of *The Bottle Imp.*"

"Never heard of it."

"By the Treasure Island writer. It takes place here on the Big Island and Oahu." Bee nodded at the box. "There was an ad for the Almeida store in Ho'okena in there, too."

Tony frowned. "Really?"

"Yeah, yeah. 1921."

"We were long gone from there. The haversack is neat. That silver clasp..." He carefully opened the *Scribner Magazine* dated November, 1888. Its thick yellowed pages were still intact, though some were stuck together from moisture and age. He turned the pages slowly. He immediately found a piece by Robert Louis Stevenson: *Master of Ballantrae, I.* "Wow. This is like looking history in the face."

"What did you find?" Bee asked. She needed something to talk about to still her worry over Maile.

"A novel excerpt by that writer." Tony read the first page out loud and gently turned to the next, before going back to the table of contents and finding another piece on engineering by RLS. He lay the magazine face down and went to the article from there. As he tried to open to the page number, he found the pages stuck. He wiggled his finger between two of the pages and they separated.

"Look at this. A letter." Lying between the pages was a sheet of paper folded in thirds. Tony handed it to Bee.

Bee adjusted her glasses and put the document close to her eyes. It smelled of mildew and mystery. "Wonder what it is?" Together, they opened it up.

It was a neat, handwritten letter in blue ink that filled the page, but its words dripped with darkness:

I confess to God that I was responsible for the death of Casper DeMello. I also confess that he and I were stealing from haoles *coming to see the Volcano. I killed him in a fit of jealousy, though he was my friend...*

Tony crossed himself. "Is this what I think it is? All this time the story is true? My great- grandfather was murdered for nothing?"

Bee tapped the box with both hands. "I nevah imagined what secrets this box held, but it's like it wants to talk story. Wants to be known."

Tony read on: *I confess to my sins of greed and avarice, in the pursuit of earthly goods and to the wanton destruction of my friend's family while our own fortunes rose. In confessing, I pray that I can save my children from Hell that is certain for me, but in this life stop the greed and arrogance that festers in them. I wish to God I had been content.*

Almanzo Almeida, 1949.

For a long time Bee and Tony were silent, the only sounds of croaking peepers coming through an open screened window. Finally, Bee took the letter and folded it. "Life is so *lolo*. You nevah know what you're going to get." *Like a tsunami wiping out your family and half the town. Finding true love from an unexpected place.* She slipped the letter into the *Scribner's* and placed the magazine on top of the stack of magazines on the end table next to her. "I think we should show it to the police tomorrow."

She smiled at Tony, but he had his face into his hands. When he shuddered, Bee put a hand on his shoulder. "It will be alright."

He looked up suddenly, tears in his eyes. "How can that be? Angie and I will never be together now."

"How do you think I made it to official *obasan*?" Bee tapped her temple. "Wisdom."

"Auntie Bee—" Tony sniffed and half-smiled.

"It will be alright. I'll do my best to make it so, starting with your mother. You can help, too, Tony-san. Angie will need your *aloha* and *kokua*. I think this will break her family into pieces."

Outside, there were footsteps, then the doorbell rang.

"I'll get it," Tony said. He jumped up and opened the door.

"Well, look who's here," Bee heard a male voice say. "The bastard who's screwing my cousin. Fancy meeting you here." The screen door screeched as it was wrenched open and the intruder was in, a gun aimed at Tony. Tony backed up with his hands up. Asami growled and attacked his the intruder's ankles, but the man shook the dog off.

"Asami!" Bee cried, afraid the man would kick her dog. "*Hele* on." Asami went in for one more bite then scurried out of harm's' way into the kitchen. Bee hoped the dog would remember she was to go next door. Even though Maile wasn't home, she would be safe.

Bee scooted to the edge of the sofa and summoned her stiff legs to stand up. She was relieved when she heard the doggie door click as her *shih tzu* went out. Once standing, she tried to move around the coffee table.

"You stay there." The intruder waggled the gun at Bee, before covering Tony again. "I've come for what is ours." He cautiously walked over to the coffee table. "Put everything into the box, old lady. That haversack, papers."

"David Almeida. What bad *kine* way to talk to your teacher. Where are your manners?"

David looked startled and ashamed when he recognized her, but not for long. "Do it." He waved Bee back, forcing her back down onto the sofa.

"Auntie," Tony shouted. Almeida waved him back with his gun. "Just do it."

Bee rubbed her arms, but obeyed him. She put the haversack into the box, but he didn't seem to know what was originally in the box. She left the *Scribner's* with the confession on her magazine pile. "What do you want with this old stuff?" Bee asked David.

"That's for me to say." he growled.

"I know why," Tony said. "You're hiding something. Like the murder of my great-grandfather. How you stole our lands."

"Shh," Bee warned.

David's eyes narrowed. "What would you know? Has Angie been talking?"

"No. It's in that box you want so much. You ran Bee's neighbor off the road for it, didn't you? Thought she had it."

David sighed. "I think you both know too much." He pointed his gun at Tony. "Get over there. You," he said to Bee, "just stay where you are."

"So what you want? You going to shoot us?" Bee said. "Throw us over a *pali*?" Bee sat up straight and shook her finger at David. "For shame. You were a good student in my class. Had one good science project on all *kine* lava rocks Madame Pele makes. But this...This is bad stuff, Davie Almeida, but you can stop right now. Take the stupid box and go."

"You remember that?"

"I remember all my students. Especially boys trying to be mean when someone is hurting them."

Outside, Asami began to bark. David turned his head. Instantly, Tony's hands were on the gun. While the two men struggled for it, Bee scooted forward on the sofa, armed with a pillow. Once standing, she threw it at David's legs. It was enough to throw him off, giving Tony the chance to push him back against the wall. Bee's bookcase shook. Knickknacks crashed to the floor, but Bee had no time to worry about valued treasures. Her heart pounding, she limped as fast as her bad leg could bear to the kitchen and the phone.

"9-1-1. How can I help you?"

A shot rang out in the living room. Someone yelped and fell to the ground. Bee clutched the phone to her chest and tried to open her sliding door with one hand. She fumbled with the latch when someone grabbed her from behind.

"You're not going anywhere." A strong hand jerked Bee around to face a middle-aged man with a dark moustache. His dark eyes were not friendly. As he loomed over her, Bee beat her fear down. She immediately recognized him from TV ads for the 50th anniversary of the Hawaii Ono Hotel. Matson Almeida. Despite the family squabble, plans were in motion to celebrate. But Bee remembered him from her teaching days. He was the parent who never came to any of the school events, including parent night. Like he couldn't care less.

"Where's Tony? Is he hurt?" Bee tried to shake him off, but he kept a steady grip.

"Shh. No talking. Just listen. You're going to have to take a trip."

It was close to eleven at night when Tawnie and Jim pulled up in front of Bee's bungalow. The lights in the house were off except for the one in the kitchen that her aunt always kept on. Tawnie jumped out of the car and ran up to the front door. She was about to take out the key when she noticed that beyond the screen door, the main door hadn't quite closed. Cautioning Jim that something was amiss, she waved for him to go around to back.

"I'll go in through the front," she whispered.

"Shouldn't we call the police?" Jim's voice was low but it sounded like a rumble.

"It could be a false alarm. She may have forgotten to lock up. She just recently started doing it."

"Doesn't she have a dog?"

"Yes." Tawnie frowned. "Asami is usually on patrol." And that was a big worry. Tawnie's heart started doing drumbeats.

Jim switched on a penlight. "I'll check the back."

Tawnie quietly opened the door and went in, keeping the creaking of the screen door to a minimum. The little entryway opened to stairs going up to the second floor. To her left was the living room. "Auntie Bee? It's Tawnie." Silence. Tawnie stepped in further. The kitchen light spread a soft glow to the edges of the living room. She could make out the sofa beneath the cupboards over the kitchen counter, but most of the room was in darkness. The house was silent. No Asami. No Bee. *Maybe she's at a friend's house. No, she'd be worried about Maile. Thinks of her like a granddaughter. At the hospital?*

Tawnie decided to risk turning on a wall switch connected to a lamp. Tawnie flicked it on and gasped in horror. The bookcase across the room had crashed to the ground narrowly missing Bee's house shrine. Books, picture frames, and knickknacks lay in a jumble. The coffee table was askew, stained with liquid from overturned tea cups telling of some major struggle. But the most unsettling of all were drops of blood on the sea grass rug and the floor. Terrified, Tawnie ran to Bee's bedroom across from the kitchen. To her relief, she found it undisturbed. The bed was still made and everything else in order. But where was she?

"Tawnie," Jim shouted from outside. "I found her."

"My auntie?"

"No, the dog."

Tawnie turned on the outside light and wrenched the sliding door open. Jim stood on the narrow sidewalk. He swung his penlight over to the hibiscus hedge that separated Auntie Bee's yard from Maile's. Underneath the dark foliage, Asami crouched close to the ground and trembled. The coat on her body appeared wet and matted. When Tawnie called, "Asami-san, come," the furry eyebrows above Asami's eyes rose in recognition. The dog bolted out from the hedge into Tawnie's arms.

Tawnie picked her up and hugged her, shocked how tiny the dog's body felt under its fur. Asami licked Tawnie's face over and over again. "Asami-san. Poor baby. Geesh, she's shaky like a motor, Jim." She gave the dog a kiss on its head and went back into the kitchen.

Jim came in behind her. "Call Moke, now?"

"Please."

As if on cue, they heard sirens in the distance. "Could you go see? I'm putting Asami in my auntie's bedroom." Quickly, Tawnie grabbed a kitchen towel and gave the *shih tzu* a good rubdown. When she was done, she put Asami in her dog bed in Bee's bedroom and closed the door.

Out front, blue and red lights twirled in the dark. "Halt!" a women shouted.

Tawnie dashed to the sliding door and stepped onto the sidewalk. At the front of the house, she could make out Jim with his hands raised. Tawnie cautiously went forward. Several police officers appeared. One patted Jim down. "You," an officer yelled to Tawnie. "Stay where you are."

"I'm not moving. My auntie is missing. Her living room is torn up."

The female police officer waved her forward. "And you are? Oh—the TV reporter."

"Tawnie Takahashi. I got worried about my auntie when I learned that her neighbor had been in an accident. Drove over from Kailua-Kona. Just got here. You can ask Officer Moke about me."

"Ms. Taka-ha-shi." Jerry Moke's weary voice cut through the night air "It's alright, Officer Harris." Moke came around to the side swinging a large flashlight.

Is it me? Or the constant contact? Tawnie thought. "Aloha, Officer Moke."

"Oh, call me Jerry. We're becoming a habit. Anyone dead inside?"

Tawnie ignored the sarcasm. *Still skeptical Officer Moke.* "No, but there's blood on the floor. The living room is trashed, my auntie's little dog was hiding outside. Auntie Bee is missing!"

A chill came over Tawnie, a reaction she often suppressed reporting stories at difficult crime scenes. She suddenly felt choked up, frozen in place. Tears were forming in her eyes along with a pounding heart.

Moke nodded for two officers to go into the house, then came down to her. He put a hand on her arm. "You alright?"

Tawnie shook her head, no.

"Someone tried to call 9-1-1 from here," Moke went on, his voice softening, "but the call was cut off. You must have arrived not long after we located the call. I'll get my best people on it. I promise you that." He patted her arm. "Does your auntie keep anything to drink?"

"Some wine, maybe, but I could use a beer."

An hour later, after taking pictures and evidence, the police left. The furniture in the living room was hastily straightened, but someone would come and clean the blood spots from the rug and floor in the morning. Exhausted, Tawnie took Asami to bed in Bee's room, while Jim crept upstairs to one of the guest rooms. They had promised Moke they would let him know if they discovered anything of importance to the break-in that could lead to finding Auntie Bee.

As she lay on the bed fully dressed, Tawnie's mind raced. It was not conducive to sleeping, though she was bone tired. Every ugly, unimaginable crime scene that she had seen in the past five years rolled through her thoughts. The drops of blood on the floor scared her to death. *Was Auntie Bee hurt? Was she dead?* Time was of the essence, critical. And here she was tossing and turning on the bed. Moke said to wait. *But how can I?*

An all-points bulletin was out for Bee, but Tawnie wasn't assured of a quick resolution. Tawnie sensed that Moke had no clue where her aunt was or who had taken her. *But then, what didn't he say out loud?* Tawnie stroked Asami snoring next to her side. *Moke didn't say the break-in at the house was tied to Boyd and Maile Horner's attacks. But I believe it is and so does Moke.*

At some point, Tawnie fell asleep. She woke to Asami growling. Tawnie rolled to her side and looked at the clock on Bee's nightstand. It read 4:10 AM. She sat up sharply when Asami jumped off the bed and raced to the front door.

"Damn!" Tawnie said out loud. *Was Moke back?* She was ready to go out when caution set in. Keeping the light off, she tiptoed into the kitchen and listened. Out in front of the house, Tawnie heard the sound of gravel crunching as a car stopped and parked by the gate. Asami continued to growl.

"Jim?" Tawnie whispered when she heard someone come downstairs.

"I heard it," Jim whispered back as he slipped into the living room. "Someone's car is out there."

"I'm going around," Tawnie said.

"That's crazy."

"I've got Moke on speed dial."

Making sure Asami didn't get out, Tawnie quickly went out the side door, taking a long spatula and her cell phone in her hand. The moon was low in sky, but bright enough to illuminate shapes in the side yard over to the hibiscus hedge and the huge breadfruit tree in Bee's backyard with its curved bench full of orchid plants.

Once her eyes were accustomed to the dim light, Tawnie crept forward to the front. As she peered around the corner, two car doors slammed shut. Tawnie heard loud whispering out on the lane.

"I'm sure Tony came here." *A young woman's voice.* "He was going to talk to Mrs. Takahashi, then come see me later. But he never came. That was hours ago. Oh, Papa."

"If this wasn't so urgent, I never would have come at this hour. But it's my fault. I set this in motion. Never imagined that Boyd would get hurt."

Boyd? Tawnie was alert now.

"Should I go knock? Someone is home. I hear a dog." *The young woman's voice.*

Two ghostly figures walked up the sidewalk. As they got closer, Tawnie made out a pretty twenty-something dressed in a running suit. Her dark hair was tied in a bun on top of her head. A tall lean man in a sweater over an *Aloha* shirt and khakis walked beside her.

Boyd. Boyd of the box? And who was Tony? Suddenly, Tawnie's instincts for a story were beginning to tie things together, make sense. Tawnie straightened her shoulders and stepped out.

"What you want?" Tawnie said.

The young woman gasped and grabbed the older man's arm.

"*Ai-jesus!* Where did you come from?" the man said.

"I'm asking the same of you. This is my auntie's house."

"So sorry. We're looking for my daughter's fiancé, Tony DeMello," the man said. "He was to come here a couple of hours ago. He's missing."

"So's my Auntie Bee. The police were here a few hours ago. And you are?"

"My name is Freddy Almeida. And this is my daughter—"

"Angie Almeida. So glad to finally meet you all. I'm Tawnie Takahashi with KWAI-5 News."

Chapter 24

Annie Moke was just past security at the Kahalui Airport and retrieving her gun when her Kimo texted her.

Kimo: Where you went?

Annie: Taking the early flight to Hilo already.

Kimo: OK. Heads up. Just saw on TV that there was a bad accident up at Volcano. Someone ran a woman off the road. Think you know her. Maile Horner.

Annie quickly left messaging and switched to her phone. "Kimo, what happened? Is she alright?"

"Guy they interviewed was a Liko Hanale—"

"—Why that's David's cousin. He's their biologist up at Volcano. What did he say?"

"He said she had a broken arm and some bruises, but came out better than he hoped for."

Annie shouldered her carry-on and walked down to her gate. "Anything else? Is she at home or in the hospital?"

"Hospital."

"I'll see if I can visit her when I get in. Don't know visiting hours."

Kimo cleared his throat. "Heard something else. Someone broke into Bee Takahashi's house and trashed it. She's missing."

***

Auntie Bee woke up with a bad headache and a stiff neck, wondering where she was. A groan somewhere across the dim room brought her back to hard reality.

"Tony?" Bee used her hands to work her way up to a sitting position on a hard cot. Her head bumped against a window sill. Cabin. Shed. Somewhere up in Volcano Village

"Tony," she called again. Bee rubbed her head, then swung her legs over the cot. She brushed down her capris and then set her wire-rimmed glasses on her nose. As her eyes adjusted, she could make out a form on the floor. She pushed forward into a standing position and went to it. When she touched Tony, he opened his eyes.

"Mrs. Tak—"

"Shh. Auntie Bee. How are you feeling?"

"My arm hurts plenty bad."

"Do you think you can get up?"

"I'll try."

Bee helped Tony stand and led him to her cot. "I'll see if I can find water."

Bee looked around the space. They were in a room stuffed with boxes, shelving and garden tools. They were put in here unceremoniously and locked in after being shoved into a Jeep at her house and brought up to Volcano. Bee thought she knew where they were—close to the old Volcano Highway, back among the older houses in the woods. Some of the homes were built in the 1890s. What she couldn't figure out was why Matson Almeida, a well-known figure on the Big Island, would risk everything, including kidnapping her and Tony, for a box. But of course, she knew. It exposed a deadly family secret.

Odd, though, that the confession was never found before. But then, having worked many years with old books and magazine gathered for the U'ilani Book Lovers Club annual sale for literacy, Bee knew the pages in an antique magazine like *Scribner's Magazine* could easily become stuck, hiding the confession between its pages for decades. Maybe since the writer's death in 1949 or whenever that was. *Did the family know about it?* Bee thought not. But she was sure they did know about getting the DeMello land and business through cheating.

The truth wants to talk story, to be known.

"Ah, found a jug of water." Bee lifted the plastic container off a shelf with two hands and a "oomph."

Tony leaned against the wood plank wall. His face was pale, the makeshift bandage around his upper arm, bloody. Near his head was a window covered with black cloth. A little bit of dim light peeked through a loose edge. Bee put the jug down next to him and stood on tiptoe to pull out a pin. That was far as she could reach without getting on the cot. Still some light got through, exposing an old spider web in the corner of the widow and a thick foggy world outside. She could only guess the hour, but she sensed it was still very early.

Bee found a coffee mug missing a handle. She tried to open the cap on the water jug, but it was too hard for her to turn. She sat down next to Tony and gave him the jug. Gritting his teeth, he twisted the cap off, then sagged against the wall.

Bee poured water into the mug and gave it to him. "Drink," Bee said. "Lots."

"Where do you think they are?"

"I don't know."

"They can't do this to us."

"Someone will come." Bee tapped her chin. "What about Angie? Weren't you going to meet her last night?"

Tony nodded.

"No worries, then." But Bee was worried.

Outside the building, Bee heard voices arguing. As they came closer, she was sure that it was David and his father. Someone rattled a key in the door and flung it open. Matson Almeida, in slacks and a golf shirt with a Volcano Golf Course emblem on the pocket was the first to enter. David, Bee noticed, was a bit reluctant as he followed his father in. He kept his eyes down and wouldn't look at Tony.

Almeida tossed the keys in his hand like it was the most natural thing to kidnap two people and lock them up. "Sorry for the inconvenience. My son was a bit over-dramatic at your place. But he was absolutely correct that the box belongs to our family." Matson pulled over an armchair missing half its back and sat down. "Now, I want to know how that box got into your hands. Did you get it off the Internet?"

Bee sat up straight and folded her arms. An image of her big brother Jimmy Takahashi standing tall in his WW II uniform came to her mind. *The 442nd. Courage.* "What do you think? I never got it off anything. Someone put it in our book sale. That's all."

Matson put his hands on his knees and leaned toward her. He gave her a faint smile. "Something is missing. A letter opener."

"Never saw." Bee looked over her glasses. She decided that Matson Almeida reminded her of one her most recalcitrant students in her fourth grade class, Aaron Fong. Third row, left side by the bookcase. Privileged, didn't take "no" for answer, and a bully. *You think you know a lot. You think you are smart. Be nice.* Eventually, Aaron did turn around. She wasn't so sure about this man. But she would try.

"Miss Horner didn't give it to you?"

Bee shrugged. "I have no idea what you're talking about. The box had only one haversack and papers." Bee looked at Tony who was quiet but listening. The look in his eyes told her he was thinking about the confession, too. "Why are you so worried about things?" Bee put her hands in her lap. "You worry too much."

"Because we have an important event coming up and I want to make sure it goes smoothly. Tell me, did my brother ever talk to you?"

"I don't know who he is."

"Freddy Almeida. Tony would know. He's seeing his daughter, my niece." Matson glared at Tony. "But not for long."

Bee shook her finger at Matson. "Yeah, yeah, especially not for long if a doctor doesn't see him soon."

"As soon as we solve a few things. David said that Tony implied that there was a secret in the box that talked about our troubles with the DeMello family. It's a complete lie that my ancestor did anything to appropriate their lands. Absolute fabrication."

Tony straightened his body against the wall. "Wouldn't you like to know?"

Bee cautioned Tony by clearing her throat. "What else you want to know before we can go home? I'm getting creaky. For shame for keeping us here." She stared at David who had raised his head. His eyes looked haunted.

Matson frowned. "Something is missing here." He pressed his palms together. "What would I like to know? Huh?" He sprang from his chair and grabbed Tony by his ear, nearly knocking Bee over. "Get up." He twisted Tony's ear to make him rise and come over to the chair. Bee pounded on Matson's arms, but she could not stop him. Matson slammed Tony onto the chair. Bee nearly fell off the cot.

David leaped forward. "Dad. That's too much. You're hurting him."

"Shut up. You already hurt him." Matson pushed David back so hard he crashed against some boxes.

"Stop." Bee pushed on her hands to get up and stand. She felt tired and her leg ached, but this had to be done. "You don't have to be mean. Just ask."

Matson opened and closed his mouth.

"I think the box is very old and the things in it have made you all *lolo*."

"And what is she talking about?" Matson pushed on Tony's wounded arm making him cry out.

"A confession," Tony said through clenched teeth.

"By your great-grandfather, Almanzo Almeida," Bee went on. "He killed Casper DeMello, Tony's great-grandfather."

"Confession? I never saw this."

"Because it was hidden." Bee squared her shoulders, stood in her best teacher stance, though her bad leg trembled. "Let us go."

"You saw this?" Matson asked David.

"No, Dad. I didn't."

Matson smiled crookedly at Bee. "Then how will I know it's true?"

"Because for a long time," Bee said, "you've known that through misfortune, your family took what belonged to the DeMellos. Maybe you knew it was by murder. Maybe you didn't. But now there is proof. The police will know soon. So sad what this has done to families."

Matson's face grew dark, his mouth an angry snarl. "Where is it?"

"At my house." Bee continued to stand strong.

"My stupid brother put the box up on eBay. Some guy writing a book bought it and it ends up at your house." Matson jabbed his hand at Bee. "I'm going to kill him."

Tony swayed on the chair. "So that's what Mr. Almeida meant when he said he would make things right. He did it for Angie. And for me. To get rid of the shame." He glared at Matson. "Funny thing, your family kept the evidence all these years. Yet, maybe the dumbest thing you did was not recognizing the papers themselves. If they are old like Auntie Bee thinks they are, then they are priceless. Robert Louis Stevenson, *Treasure Island* writer, writing in Hawaii. Your great-grandfather wrote that he and my ancestor were stealing from tourists way back then. The manuscript is the real thing."

Matson's eyes narrowed. Bee thought they looked like the eyes of a wild boar she had once run into up on Saddle Road. Mean to the bone. *No chance to save Matson. I should have reported him to the principal.*

"So the DeMellos aren't so clean," Matson growled.

"I can accept that," Tony answered. "It's what we became afterwards that I'm proud of."

"Hmph." Matson waved David over. "Watch them. I'm going to make a call. You can keep guard outside. Then I'll decide what to do with them." Matson pushed on his son to go. Seconds later, the door locked behind them.

"Auntie, I feel sick."

Bee helped Tony back to the cot, then got up on it. She took out another pin in the window cover to see where they were. The shed was in a woods of *ohia lehua*, koa and tree ferns, their trunks ghostly shapes in the fog. *Vog?* Madame Pele at Kilauea was so active these days adding her own foggy weather to the system. Further away Bee could make out the edge of a house, but she wasn't sure.

Bee got down slowly, first to her knees on the cot, then feet on the floor. "Tony?"

Tony opened his eyes. "Hum?"

"Drink more water." She filled the mug again and helped him drink. When he was done, Bee sat down on the cot with the mug in her hand. "We have to get out."

"You know how to pick a lock?"

"Never." Bee avoided patting his arm. Instead, she said that she was going to try.

Over on the shelves, she searched for some sort of thin wire. She found a box of jumbo paper clips and pliers. Standing at the door, she closed her eyes, trying to remember the descriptions of lock picking in the many cozy mysteries she read over the years. Housewives, librarians (Miss Zuka was her favorite), book club readers, and quilters—all solving mysteries. She remembered that the inside of the key hole had pins. She needed to straighten out the paperclips, so she could put pressure on the pins. She opened out two bends on the paper clips to make straight lines, using the pliers to bend the end of one paper clip at a 90 degree angle. It would work like some sort of wrench.

"How's it going?" Tony asked. His voice sounded weaker. Bee knew she had to work fast.

"It's coming." *Now what was the next step? Push down on the lower end of the lock with the wrench and turn it gently the direction you would unlock a door.* She turned the clip one way, but felt pressure, so she turned it the other way. When she felt less pressure, she inserted the second paperclip into the back of the lock and pulled it out quickly, continuing to hold her "wrench" in place. Something gave way. Bee thought she heard a click. So far so good. Onto the next pin. She was so intent on getting the next series of pins to move, she didn't heard footsteps coming back to the shed.

"Auntie," Tony whispered hoarsely. "Someone's coming back."

Bee backed away in time as a key was inserted into the lock outside and the door flung open. It was David Almeida, half-hidden in a swirl of fog that would put London to shame.

"Hurry," he said to them. "I'm going to get you out of here."

Chapter 25

Tawnie Takahashi led a startled Freddy Almeida and his daughter into Bee's house. After a quick introduction to Jim, she announced that she would make some coffee, though she wasn't sure where the coffee pot was.

"I'll get it going," Jim said. He had already turned on the lights. Bee's kitchen light over the sink cast a mellow glow on the floor and counters, but the lamplight in the living room revealed a stark scene.

"*Ai-jesus.* What happened here?" Freddy gaped at the room.

"Please. We can go to the kitchen."

"No. What is going on here?"

"Mr. Almeida, I heard you say the name Boyd. For the past two days I've been trying to help him recover a box that was in his possession. He was robbed of it in Ho'okena, later attacked in Kailu-Kona. Do you know about the box? It had materials in it written by a famous author."

"Robert Louis Stevenson." Freddy sighed and cleared his throat. "I'm the one that sold the box to him."

Now we're getting somewhere, Tawnie thought. *Now for the heart of the story.* "What is so dangerous in that box? Did you know my auntie's neighbor, Maile Horner, was run off the road up at Volcano? She had just examined a letter opener in the police custody. It was confirmed to be from the box."

"The one with the thistle, Papa." Angie twisted her hands and looked around the room. Her lips trembled.

"No, I didn't know that connection." Freddy Almeida frowned. "Why would anyone come here and trash this place? What is your auntie's part in this?"

"It might be that she is a friend of Maile. I called some of her book club members and they knew nothing. They're alarmed."

A coffee grinder went off in the kitchen, making Tawnie and the Almeidas jump.

"Mind if I sit down?" Freddy asked.

"Not until you answer my question." Tawnie was getting impatient. She was sure Freddy Almeida held an important key to her investigation into Boyd's box. "What is so dangerous about the box that would make someone attack the buyer? Or an historian from a museum for God's sake? Does this all have to do with your family fight over your father's will?"

Freddy's face paled. Tawnie must have hit a deep sore spot. He pulled Angie close to him and hugged her shoulder. "It does and more. Years ago, really over 120 years ago, my family and the DeMellos were immigrant families starting new lives in the islands. They both opened mercantile stores in Ho'okena. Then there was a falling out. My family ended up with their lands and the store."

"Where does the box come in?"

"I'm not sure. It's been in the family as long as we've been here. My father always said that my great-grandfather, Almanzo Almeida, was always paranoid about the haversack and all the contents in the box. Said never to let it go. My Grandpa Josef acted the same way."

"What about your father? Funny, I've never read about him in the newspaper"

"Because he's dead. Died of a heart attack when I was in my twenties. Just me and my brother Matson."

"So sorry. Didn't know."

Freddy asked if he could sit down on the sofa. Tawnie nodded that Angie was welcomed to do so, too. "How's the coffee coming?" she called to Jim.

"Just about there. I'll bring it out. Did you see the fog out there? Been developing for the past few minutes."

Tawnie looked out Bee's front window. It was still early morning, pre-dawn, but light enough to backlight a dull gray presence outside.

Sitting on the sofa, Freddy leaned over his knees in thought. "I always thought protecting the box and the old stuff in it was stupid, growing up, though I never saw it when I was a kid. Not until I was in my twenties. It was not allowed. I also thought the feud between the DeMellos and my family was stupid, too. I had several friends who were DeMellos."

Freddy squeezed Angie's hand. "Then my beautiful, smart daughter met and fell in love with Tony DeMello. He's the kind of son-in-law any father would want. Loves my daughter, honest worker, funny, and respectful. I thought it high time to get rid of the box. From what I can see, it has poisoned *my* family for a long time."

"Any idea where the rest of the box is?"

"I have no idea."

Jim brought a tray out with coffee cups for all and cream and sugar. As he set it down on the coffee table, Angie shifted down toward the end table where a stack of magazines were piled. She took her turn getting a mugful of coffee and added cream before she leaned back against the sofa in a slump.

Even this early hour gets to a young person, Tawnie thought. *I'm beat. And sick with worry.*

No one spoke. They held their mugs in their hands like they were drawing energy from them. Occasionally, someone took a sip, savoring the hot brew.

"Papa. Look," Angie said. "Isn't this from the box?" She held up an old tattered magazine with a tan cover and wreath motif below the large title.

Everyone turned their heads at the same time. Freddy put his mug down. "*Ai-jesus*. It's one of the *Scribners*."

"What's that?" Tawnie asked.

"Robert Louis Stevenson wrote for the magazine regularly. There were two in the haversack."

Tawnie stood up and stared at Jim. "Oh, my God. The box was here." She looked around the room. "It was *here*. That's why the room was torn up. But how on earth did Auntie Bee get it? And where is she?" She grabbed her cell phone from the coffee table and punched in Jerry Moke's phone number.

Freddy stood up, too. When Angie handed him the magazine, its pages flopped open. A letter floated down to the coffee table.

"For if a man dies before he sells it, he must burn in hell forever."

The words from *The Bottle Imp* came back to Tawnie as she watched the letter land on the table with its three folds opened.

Freddy picked it up. He gasped when he read it and put a hand over his mouth.

"What is it, Papa?"

"The worst, but also the truth." Freddy showed it to Angie.

"Oh. Tony." Angie sank onto the sofa.

"A confession." Freddy handed the letter to Tawnie. "What the DeMellos have said for years. My great-grandfather killed Casper DeMello."

Tawnie's phone played a throbbing J-pop ringtone. She answered immediately. "Tawnie Takahashi. Oh, Officer Moke, so sorry for the early hour, but I had to call. The box was here at my auntie's house. Someone took her for the box."

"Do you have any idea who that might be?" Moke's voice went from sleepy to alert.

Tawnie turned to Freddy. "Who do you think has the box and my auntie?"

Freddy's eyes darted to the letter on the coffee table. "My brother." He swallowed. "I know where to find him.

With David Almeida supporting Tony DeMello, Auntie Bee followed her former student out into the thick forest that surrounded the shed and isolated homes of Volcano Village. Further adding to the isolation was the thick fog that curled around the trees up to their branches, creating an otherworldliness that wandered between muffled sounds and silence. The fog was moist, but had a sting to it. Definitely *vog*.

"Where are we going?" Bee asked. She rubbed her arms as the chill of predawn hit her. Back at her house, Matson Almeida had given her no time to grab a coat to put over her light sweater. Wearing only her slippers, her toes felt cold. Her bad leg ached. *Not going to complain. Been in one big thing worse than this.*

"There's a horse trail just a few yards from here," David answered. "It comes out not far from the park visitor center. So sorry for not bringing anything warm to put on, but we have to move."

Tony leaned on David, his arm around his shoulder. "Why aren't we going down to the main road and the cafes there?"

"Because my father is there. This way takes us directly to help. Even if the visitor center isn't open, there will be people in park housing who can protect us. Oh, good. Here's the trail."

Bee squinted. Her glasses were getting fogged up and her nose itched from the *vog*. It was hard to tell where they were, but as she went forward, the ground became more solid as ancient *a'a* lava rock and soil came together. As they felt their way along the wooded trail and its unseen direction, she looked back. She thought she saw some blurred light moving in the ghostly trees, but it was only the fog shifting around the legs of the wooden water tank Bee had seen earlier from the shed's window.

For several minutes they silently hustled along the path, going as fast as Tony could bear. Bee's thoughts drifted to Hilo where the sky would be welcoming dawn if it weren't foggy. Bee hoped that Asami would be safe. *Maybe my 911 call got some action.*

David stopped. "Did you hear that? Sounded like a car door slamming."

"I nevah hear," Bee said. "How much further?"

"It's still a ways. Break in the forest is just ahead, then more trees, but we'll be coming out on the highway opposite the park. Let's keep moving," David said. "Are you doing alright auntie?"

"Yeah, yeah. You take care of Tony. It's Tony you should worry about."

David turned back. "I'm so sorry. I never meant anything bad to happen. My father—"

"Damn you, David Almeida!" The words were distorted, hanging in the thick air like a disembodied wraith. It was hard for Bee to tell which direction it was coming from, but its meaning was clear. Matson Almeida had discovered them gone and he would have none of it.

"Got to really move now." David hitched Tony's arm higher around his neck and began to trot.

Chapter 27

Tawnie Takahashi peered through the windshield of Freddy Almeida's Subaru and shook her head. Although it usually took forty minutes or less to get to Volcanoes National Park from Hilo, with the dense fog that seemed to rise and fall every two or three mile posts along the two lane highway, the drive was much slower. Sometimes she could only see the metal guard rails and telephone poles on the sides of the road, while other times visibility was good and she could make out a mix of tall trees, coconut palms, wild ginger and false staghorn ferns beyond. Occasionally they would pass houses with their low tin roofs, hints of pastures and roads that led off to communities lost in the murk. As they climbed higher toward Volcano, the vegetation gave way to *hāpu'u* tree ferns and rugged forests that made the road feel even more closed in the fog. A stand of dead *ohia lehua,* killed by a lethal fungus, made the scene even more eerie as their naked, twisted limbs rose into nothingness. Tawnie was relieved when they passed Milepost 24. She knew they were getting close. Clock on the dashboard said 5:55. Almost sunrise. It should start lightening up now. Maybe the fog would break up, too.

"Do you think Officer Moke alerted the park police?" Angie Almeida asked from the back seat.

"Hope so," Tawnie answered. She turned around to Jim sitting behind her. "Do you want to check again?" Tawnie had no idea how Freddy would confront his brother, but blood on the floor at Bee's house made her stomach do back flips. *Auntie Bee.* She brought a fist to her mouth and stared into the gloom.

"Milepost 25," Freddy said. "Almost there."

"Got a text from Moke," Jim said. "He's on his way. Said there was an accident on the highway down by the Volcano Golf Course. Park police answering to that, so are delayed."

Tawnie swallowed. She wanted no repeat of what happened a year ago when she and Jim approached a killer. Jim got shot. "What do you have in mind when we find your brother?" she asked Freddy.

"Make him come to his senses. He's gone too far on this."

"Don't think that's a plan. He has a gun."

"He doesn't like guns. But—*ai-jesus*. My nephew does. Likes to hunt pig."

"Hurting someone with a gun doesn't sound like David," Angie said.

"You think your nephew's with your brother?" Tawnie was not liking the odds for potential violence.

"I have no clue. Poor kid. Matson's picked on him for years."

A sign announcing Old Volcano Road appeared. Freddy quickly turned off the highway and onto the road that led into the community of Volcano Village. They passed a couple of homes tucked into the trees, then a cafe, all popping in and out of the shifting fog. The Lava Lady coffee stand's sign appeared next. It didn't look like it was opened for business yet.

"Think your brother is there?" Tawnie rolled down her window. Cold air mixed with a strong smell of rotten eggs hit her face. She quickly rolled the window back up.

"I'll look." Freddy pulled up alongside the store front. Behind the windows displaying posters for events at the Volcano Art Center and the national park, the store was dark. He turned on the heater, and leaving the car running, got out and went to the store's door. One key turn and he was in. He came out one minute later. "Not here."

"Now what?" Tawnie asked when Freddy was back in the car. She was never one for bad nerves, but not knowing where Bee was undermined Tawnie's general cool.

"We'll go to his house. It's just up the road and back in the woods. A little more isolated than some of the homes there."

Tawnie thought Freddy must have sensed something urgent. He risked going faster.

They passed through what was the center of Volcano Village and past the post office. The fog lifted enough to see about fifty feet in front of them. At the entrance to the last road, Freddy slowed down. Further down, Tawnie knew, the Old Volcano Road ended at the Wedge, the place where the road rejoined Highway 11. As Freddy prepared to turn right on the road to Matson Almeida's house, a white SUV came rushing up from the highway. It turned right in front of them. A green stripe with the brown national park emblem told Tawnie it was a national park police car. The SUV tore off into the fog.

"Maybe Moke got through to them," Freddy said. "They're heading down to my brother's now."

Freddy started to follow the park police when a red Grand Cherokee rolled to the corner. For one brief moment it was opposite them. The driver turned and looked at Freddy and Tawnie, his face full of anger and hate. Then the Jeep turned and sped off toward the Wedge.

"Papa. That's Uncle Matson's SUV."

"I know. I saw him."

Tawnie slammed her hands on the dashboard. "Follow him."

Freddy hit the gas.

As soon as they gave chase, the red taillights of the Grand Cherokee seemed to flee away ahead of them like the eyes of a demon. At the entrance onto the highway, the red eyes sped off to the right.

Tawnie turned back to Jim. "Did you see anyone else in the Jeep?"

Jim leaned in. "Hard to say. The back window was dark." He fell back against his seat when Freddy pressed on the accelerator.

"Sorry. Don't want to lose him." Freddy made the sharp turn onto the highway.

"Where do you think he's going?" Tawnie strained against her seatbelt to find Matson's Jeep. The fog floated above the two lane road like a massive gray canopy with one edge dipping down to the road in front of them. The light beams on Freddy's Subaru bounced back at them.

"Not sure. You can't get back to his house from this side—unless you walk out through the forest. Park's just ahead. Just darn hard to see in this stuff."

"Then don't go so fast, Papa," Angie said.

The devil's eyes appeared again in front of them as Freddy closed the distance to Matson's Cherokee. Then they disappeared. Suddenly, there was the sound of squealing brakes, a loud, explosive thud and a scream. The taillights on Matson's Cherokee swerved then continued on. When Freddy caught up, Tawnie glimpsed someone lying ahead on the shoulder of the road. Freddy didn't slow down and followed his brother into the foggy wall.

"Aren't you going to stop?" Tawnie yelled at Freddy. She rolled down the window and looked back in time to see a woman and a man come out from the *ohia lehua* forest onto the side of the road before the fog enveloped them. *Auntie Bee?*

"No. I have to stop him now. Someone call 911."

Jim called 911.

Tawnie called Moke.

The red lights made a hard left off the highway. Tawnie briefly glimpsed the national park entrance sign and then they were on the same national park road as Matson. Ahead of them, the lava rock park gateway seem to rise out of the fog, its pagoda-shaped roof floating like a hat. As they came closer to it, Tawnie could make out the back of the red jeep as Matson tore through the gate. At this early morning hour, there was no attendant.

Tawnie's phone began its J-pop ringtone. "Tawnie Takahashi."

"Moke, here. Where are you?"

"Oh, Jerry." Tawnie had no idea why she called him by his first name, but having no control of where they were going, she could at least get a handle on outside help. She heard Moke chuckle, then grow serious. "You at Matson Almeida's house? Because the park police are there."

"No, we're following his car."

"Who's we?"

"His brother, Freddy Almeida, his daughter, and my cameraman."

"Let us take care of this. I'm almost there."

Tawnie turned to look at Freddy. There was an odd expression on his face, something between determination and fear. "I'm not driving." She peered through the fog. "We're on Crater Rim Drive heading toward the Visitor Center. At least the sign says so."

Tawnie swallowed. "There was an accident on the highway. Matson Almeida hit someone. Did they find my auntie? Because if they didn't, I think just saw her on the road with the victim."

"Just heard about the hit and run from the 911 dispatcher. The park will send an ambulance though they are still cleaning up after the earlier accident. Fog is really bad."

Moke spoke to someone in his car, then said to Tawnie. "Avoid any confrontation if possible. If you are going to start calling me Jerry, I'm asking politely."

Tawnie looked at Freddy Almeida again and thought that would be hard not to. "I'll call you when I know something. How's that?"

Moke didn't answer. The only sound was the wail of a police siren.

"He's coming?" Jim asked. Tawnie could hear the tension in his voice. *He's thinking the same thing—that confrontation last year. He's afraid of getting hurt again.*

"He's on his way. And I think he's bringing back-up."

They continued to follow Matson's taillights, passing the wide intersection that led off to the Jaeger Museum and the Volcano Art Center Gallery on one side and the present day Volcano House on the other. Tawnie only knew where they were because of the gold lettering on the hotel's large lava rock wall cutting through the gray. After they passed, the road dropped down deeper to thicker murk.

"Where's my brother going?" Freddy muttered. "There's nothing beyond here."

"There are the steam vents, sulphur banks, Papa," Angie said. "Crater Rim Drive goes all around the caldera," she explained to Jim Milstead.

Everyone in the car became quiet. The ferns, trees and low rock walls along the Crater Rim Drive came in and out of the fog like figures in an amusement tunnel ride. Tawnie felt like they were following a ghost, driving blind behind red lights that winked on and off. Tawnie was getting the tin can feeling again when the claustrophobic feeling lifted. The fog was still thick, but she guessed that they had come out onto the treeless plain where the steam vents were. The ground here was so hot that tree roots could not survive. Only grass and plants grew here.

"I see the lights again," Tawnie said. "Is he slowing down?"

"I think he has," Jim said. The red lights disappeared for a moment and then were back, turning to the left.

"He's going into the parking lot for the steam vents," Freddy said. When they arrived at the entrance, Freddy followed his brother in. The Subaru bounced and rocked on the uneven pavement.

Tawnie's phone sang out again with steady beats from her J-pop ringtone. It was Jerry Moke again.

"Where are you now?" He sounded more than a bit exasperated.

"Pulling into the steam vent parking lot. At least, I think that's where we are."

"Stay there."

Tawnie didn't have any time to say that she didn't think so because as soon as Freddy's headlights hit the passenger side of Matson's Cherokee, Freddy put on the brakes and got out.

Like a scene from a bad horror movie, Tawnie stepped out of the car into a fog as thick as one finger poi and so moist that it tapped droplets on her cheeks. At least, visibility wasn't bad within fifteen feet. When she squinted at Matson's Cherokee, she could see the motor was still running. *Was someone in the car?* She stepped in closer. Where Freddy's headlights illuminated the jeep, Tawnie saw for the first time damage to that side of the car. The headlight was smashed. Standing in the one working light's beam was Freddy, arguing with another man.

Two car doors slammed, the sound muffled by the fog. Jim and Angie joined Tawnie.

"What's happening?" Jim whispered. He shouldered his camera.

"Freddy's talking to Matson. I assume it's Matson. Record or write down whatever you hear, Jim," Tawnie said. "I've got to find out where he has Auntie Bee." *Or if that was her on the highway.* With that, Tawnie crept over to the Cherokee and felt her way around its back.

"What were you thinking, Matson? Kidnapping, assaulting people. I don't understand."

"It doesn't matter anymore. I—"

Tawnie peered around the car. Though Matson Almeida was the same height as Freddy, all resemblance ended there. Their choice of clothing, and posture was entirely opposite: Freddy looked down-to earth, his older sibling Matson high-end fashioned and monied, which wouldn't help him here. As Matson turned into the light beam, Tawnie could see blood dripping down the side of his face onto his shoulder. When he swayed, Freddy steadied him on his shoulders. Matson twisted away.

"Matson, you've got to tell me where Bee Takahashi is. Then, turn yourself in."

"The hell you say. You should never have put the box on eBay."

"That stupid box. Do you know what we found? A confession from Papa Almanzo. Did you know he killed Casper DeMello? All this time, our whole family fortune's hung on that."

Matson stumbled back.

"Is Tony DeMello with Mrs. Takahashi?"

Tawnie watched the expression on Matson's face changed from defiance to horror. He nodded and looked away.

Angie gasped as she came up behind Tawnie.

For the first time, Freddy noticed Tawnie standing by the Cherokee. "*Ai-jesus.* They got away, didn't they?" Freddy froze. "Oh, my God. Who did you hit up on the highway?"

Tawnie walked up to the front of the jeep. She saw more damage than she thought. The windshield on the right side had a large, spider web crack in it.

Matson bit his lips. "David." He choked on his words, his eyes darting around. The fog lifted up its skirt as though it was showing him an escape route. It revealed the trail that led out to the crater's rim. *Or was it because the sun had finally risen and was trying to break through?* From far off came the sound of sirens.

"Stay," Freddy said. "Don't do anything stupid, Brother. I'll help you."

"Leave me alone." Matson pulled away from Freddy and limped over to the trail. He instantly disappeared into the fog.

"Stay on the trail. I'm coming." Freddy's voice was frantic. When he saw Angie, he told her to stay with Tawnie.

"No, Angie stay with Jim," Tawnie said. "I'm coming with you, Freddy. The police will be here anytime. Jim, see if you can get any footage of the damage here" Tawnie joined Freddy and together they hurried after Matson.

Tawnie couldn't remember the last time she had been up to the steam vents—years, probably—but she could remember the park ranger's warning to stay on the trail at all costs. Throughout the grassy plain dotted with fern and low-lying scrub trees, there were steam vents. One was enclosed up by the parking lot—to prevent people slipping in—but out on the plain there were active ones known to the park that were to be viewed only from a distance. Unknown vents could open unexpectedly.

The safest way to the rim of the crater and the steaming bluffs was the maintained trail that went out from the parking lot. Other marked trails followed along the crater's rim or came in from further back up the road. With the volcano so active these days, anything was possible. Earthquakes were common in the national park and in Volcano Village where the main worry was damage to pipes connecting to the water tanks every household had or the tanks themselves.

Tawnie walked as fast as they could go in the fog. The trail was wide and well used, but she could see spots where an area might be mistaken for a path. Visibility was improving, but it still hard to see more than twenty feet ahead. Somewhere out there was Matson.

"Your brother has a head wound," Tawnie said as she hiked beside Freddy. "You think he might have a concussion?"

"I don't know. He's been so angry with me lately. Hard to tell."

"Hope the police get here soon. I want to know how my auntie is" Tawnie touched Freddy's arm. "So sorry for your nephew. Let's hope for the best. If that was my auntie with him, then he was doing something good."

"Matson," Freddy called.

"Leave me alone." Matson's voice was thick and sounded close, but Tawnie couldn't tell which direction it came from.

"David's going to be alright" Freddy called out. "Ms. Takahashi said an ambulance was on its way." When Matson didn't answer, Freddy said, "Let's move."

They took off at a trot, trusting in the path's direction to the steaming bluff. There visitors safely could look down into the volcano's caldera. Steam vents were prolific as cracks met water. Tawnie thought she saw signage which meant they were close. Suddenly, the ground began to shake.

"Earthquake. Oh, God. Matson. Stay on the trail." Freddy grabbed onto Tawnie as the trail and grassy plain began to roll under their feet. There was a sound of rocks knocking together and falling. Somewhere ahead a crack opened up not far from the trail, releasing an explosion of hot steam and rubble. As they steadied themselves, Tawnie caught a glimpse of Matson to her right. Though he was not next to the new vent, he seemed to be having difficulty standing. To her horror, she realized that he was in the grass, not on the trail. As the ground continued to roll, behind her she heard sirens and someone honking a car horn. But Tawnie's eyes were on Matson. He was trying to keep his balance, like a beginner on a surfboard.

"Help me," he cried out. He looked straight at her and Freddy, then disappeared from sight. Tawnie wasn't sure if he screamed or if Freddy had screamed but suddenly they were risking everything and moving as fast as they could on the shuddering trail. Two long, pitiful screams came from the grassy field, then there was silence. The ground stopped shaking, the only movement the newly formed vent letting off a tower of white steam and pushing up the fog.

Freddy leaned over and vomited. Tawnie went to help him. Then they just held on until Moke and the park police arrived.

Thinking back on it later that morning in national park headquarters, Tawnie wondered what exactly the meaning of life was. *Get one prize for best crime reporting? Do bad, fall into a steam vent? Where was that in the order of things?* She pulled the wool blanket around her, her hands shaking as she held her coffee cup. She just couldn't get warm.

"Here you go," Jerry Moke said. "Got you some saimin courtesy of the park rangers. Should warm you up." He gently took her coffee cup away and put the ceramic bowl on the table in front of her.

The steam rising from the hot broth and noodles made Tawnie's stomach lurched, but she had to get over all images of that natural force.

Tawnie sighed. "Where's my auntie?"

"She's with Annie Moke in Hilo. I had just picked Annie up at the airport when your cameraman texted me. I brought her along."

Tawnie shook her head. She didn't remember Annie Moke being here.

Moke sat down opposite Tawnie. "Bee's doing fine. Just a little chilled. Annie went with her to the hospital to check her out."

"That was nice of her. Any word on David Almeida?"

"He's in surgery in Hilo. Broken pelvis, ribs, and various wounds, but miraculously, no serious head injury. He's going to have trouble walking for some time, but will recover. He will be facing charges."

"And Tony DeMello? Angie's all worried."

"He's out of surgery. Will spend the night there or two. Lost a lot of blood."

Tawnie opened the package of chopsticks, broke them apart, and knocked away any splinters on them. She took a stab at the *char sui* laying on the noodles.

Moke must have sensed her quiet thoughts. "Nice that historian, Maile Horner, met Annie's father back in Seattle. They're talking story right now, I'm sure. And Annie's looking forward to Bee's birthday party."

Tawnie sipped the broth. Moke was right. The soup warmed her up better than the coffee. She felt so out of sorts. "Sounds like half the people I know are in that hospital."

"Miss Horner's home now." Moke chuckled. "Got a young man interested in her already."

Tawnie didn't ask who. She had so many other questions. How was Freddy Almeida doing? When would they be able to retrieve his brother's body? Boyd. How was he doing?

Tawnie felt exhausted. For once, she let Jim get the story particulars going. Despite the fog still obscuring the site where the tragic event had taken place, they were able to do a report out in the parking lot where the sun had finally burst through. Jim recorded Tawnie's report on his camera then sent it to his smartphone. While Tawnie answered questions from the park police and Moke, Jim went to Volcano House and accessed their wi-fi for the initial report. Thinking ahead, Tawnie then sent him to Matson Almeida's house in Volcano Village—one of several homes he owned, it turned out—and make another report from there. KWAI-5 News again was front and center with a breaking story. At one o'clock, Tawnie and Jim would go back out to the steam vents and broadcast their full story. Her signature, "This is Tawnie Takahashi saying, Until next time," could well be heard not only in the islands, but all over the Mainland and beyond. Any news story involving the volcano at Kilauea stirred national and international attention.

Tawnie ate some noodles, then tapped her chopsticks on her bowl. "Did you recover the box?"

"It's in police custody now, along with the letter opener."

"Good. There's one more thing. A magazine. It's at my auntie's. I don't know if it qualifies as police evidence or has a place in the courts, but there is a written confession in it, dated and signed by Almanzo Almeida. Says he murdered Casper DeMello a long time ago."

Moke dropped his hands on his knees with a loud smack. "*Auwe.* This has been one weird case. Boyd, the Wilson kid, Miss Horner, Matson and David Almeida. Hurt or killed. All for a box. You did say *The Bottle Imp* was one spooky story. I think I'll leave it at that."

"Where will the box go? Back to Harry Boyd?"

"Yeah, yeah. It's legally his. I would assume he would want it all together." Moke stood up. "What are your plans for the rest of the day?"

"Jim and I are going back out to the steam vents to finish our report. Then I'm going back to Hilo to see my Auntie Bee. I'm all *pau.*"

Encased in leis of pikake, orchid, and plumeria up to her ears, Auntie Bee was led into the Volcano House dining room on the arms of Tawnie Takahashi and Maile Horner. As soon as Bee entered, a big "Aloha, Auntie Bee!" filled the room. Someone blew into a harmonica for a pitch and the room was off singing "*Hau`oli Lā Hānau.*" At the end of the birthday song, everyone in the room stood up to clap.

Bee covered her mouth with both hands. Tears came to her eyes. Even though her U'ilani Book Lovers Club friends had made no efforts to hide the planning of this party for weeks, she was not prepared to see her grown children Janice and Jason Clarence and their children, her neighbors, and friends from all over the Big Island all in one place.

"Ah, Auntie Bee," Tawnie said. "No need to cry. We all love you."

The room exploded into words of *aloha* and laughter.

"We do indeed," Maile said. Her left arm was in a sling, so she patted Bee's hand with her right.

"OK, OK," Bee said as she wiped the tears from her cheeks. "Now I'm officially over the hill."

There was more laughter and a few "ahs" from the crowded tables. Bee blew a soft kiss into the room, then limping slightly, followed Tawnie to a large table where Janice and Jason were seated by the long window that looked out over the Kilauea caldera. The day was clear and bright today, the only sign of any cloud, was the steam plume rising far back at the Halemaumau Crater.

"Mom," Janice said as she rose and gave Bee a kiss. "Happy birthday."

Bee fanned her face with her hand. "Oh, I'm going to get all weepy again." Which had been pretty much her state for the past two days.

David Almeida had successfully led her and Tony through the fogbound forest out to the edge of the highway. He had been attentive to both of them. Whenever Tony needed to stop, David waited patiently until he caught his breath. He helped Bee get over downed branches, through rough patches of rocks and fern. All the while, he kept asking for forgiveness. Supporting Tony the whole way, sometimes David looked back and listened through the gray wall that swallowed the trees behind them. Bee could tell that he was afraid.

"You were right, Mrs. Takahashi," David said at one point as they inched through the trees. "I was mean to others in elementary school. Made classmates be afraid of me. But you saw through me. I loved working on that science project. It was the first time I did something for myself." David paused. "My dad hated it. Said I was a sissy."

"So sorry, David."

When they got to the road, visibility was poor. David offered to go up and see where they might safely cross over to the visitor center. Leaving Tony and Bee at the forest's edge, he went up to the narrow shoulder. Bee watched him look both ways and then waved for them to come up. David stepped off the shoulder. Suddenly, out of the fog, a red vehicle came at him and struck him. He was thrown over the top of the jeep and back to the edge of the highway. No one stopped. Not even a second car following. Bee could still hear his screams in her head. *Or was it from a long time ago?*

Bee took her seat at the head of the table. Her son Jason relieved her of some of her leis. "So I can enjoy this *ono* food," she told him. He kissed her head before he sat down to her left. To her right was Janice and her tribe of kids ranging from teenager to post college grad. *My wonderful grand keiki.* Tawnie sat next to Jason and his family. A waitress brought Bee a passion-orange sparkling water drink and wished her a happy birthday. When Bee thanked her, she saw the smiling face of a student from down the years.

Age, she thought, *can slow you down but it also gives you wisdom.* As Bee looked around the dining room festooned with balloons and pink and white anthuriums on the linen-covered tables, she knew how privileged she was to be turning eighty, to have such family and friends. It put things in perspective. It made you grateful.

After she was released from the ER where the doctors had treated her for exposure to the cold, Tawnie had taken her home and spent the night with her. They talked well into the morning.

David Almeida was going to live and so was Tony DeMello. Harry Boyd was being released to a rehab center before going back to the Mainland where he had family. Bee worried about that, never having met him, but Tawnie said that he continued to improve after his stroke.

And the box that caused so much heartache and death?

"Once the police release it, Mr. Boyd's donating it to the Big Island Historical Society Museum," Tawnie told Bee, "with the stipulation that he has free access to it when he is doing better. Wants to finish his book. He believes that all the items in the box should stay together and that Maile Horner is perfect curator to take care of it. It's a Big Island story and should stay where *The Bottle Imp* was inspired."

"What did you say about that story in the box?"

"The bottle imp can grant you wishes, but if you die before you sell it, the Devil will get you. If you sell it—always for less than you paid for it—and you are not content, the Devil will get you, too. In the end, the imp goes away with the last buyer."

"Isn't it bad for the museum to keep the box and everything in it?" Bee wondered.

"It's a story, Auntie. But I think the collection has always wanted to be together. Boyd wants people to know about Robert Louis Stevenson and his love for our islands. To hear how *The Bottle Imp* came to be."

Lunch was served. Tables were filled with all the island staples of Ahi poke, Kalua pork, poi, mahi mahi and other prepared seafood, teriyaki chicken, fruits, and salad vegetables from Puna.

Bee thought of the story. Was she content? *Yeah, yeah, I'm content, except for two things, but one I can accept.* Bee looked out the window beyond the lava rock wall and the trees below it to the steam rising from the far end of the Kilauea caldera and thought of George and the first time they had come up to Volcano House in the 1950s. She felt him close, a hand on her shoulder.

Someone started to play a guitar. A group of men ranging from their twenties to their fifties—all former students—gathered nearby. Bee turned to listen. In a clear tenor voice, one man began to sing, "I remember days..."

Bee put a hand on her heart. Her and George's song, *Ku'u Home O Kahalu'u*. Another voice joined in the harmony. He was wearing a loud *Aloha* shirt with green turtles all over it. His dark moustache looked crooked like it was going to fall off any moment. It got worse as he sang, his eyes full of tears. It was Kiro, her son all the way from Germany, in disguise.

Auntie   Bee   was   content.

When I was student at UH Manoa years ago, I heard of a thatched house at the Waioli Tea Room in Manoa that Robert Louis Stevenson, the author of *Treasure Island,* had lived in for a time. I was never able to go see the house-- a replica of the original house built in Waikiki for the royal family's many visitors in the late 19th century—yet the house's history intrigued the historian in me. (The original house had been moved to Manoa's Salvation Army property in 1926). It was the first time I was aware of famous 19th century authors visiting the Hawaiian Islands. RLS wrote that he "engaged with the ink bottle darkly" in that place.

In 1889, when Robert Louis Stevenson was living with his family in Honolulu as a guest of King Kalakaua, he made a trip to the Big Island. While most travelers went on to see Kilauea, RLS got off in Ho'okena and stayed there for several days. While there, he went up to see the City of Refuge where he was inspired to write *The Bottle Imp.* Place names on the Big Island are named in the story which, by the way, I understand was first published in Samoan. In Samoa, RLS would live out his final years. *In The Eight Islands* he recounts his time in Ho'okena, Honolulu, Molokai, and other islands in the South Seas.

Mark Twain also visited the islands and wrote about his 1860s travels in *Roughing It.* The thing that caught my eye was Twain's account about going up to Volcano House at Kilauea.

During the 1970s, when my husband and I lived in Hilo, we spent one day cleaning out a building up at the Volcano National Park. The only thing we were told was that it was an old tourist cabin. I honestly don't remember what we did that day, but I later found out that the building, which would become the Volcano Art Center Gallery, was the original Volcano House from 1877. In the late 1800s, it was best place on the Big Island for food and comfort to those making the arduous journey to see the lava lakes at Kilauea. This second version of Volcano House was after Twain's time but the same couple Twain complimented in *Roughing*

It, the Malbys, ran it. I taught several weaving classes at the art center in the 1970s.

Thus this story, *Volcano House*. I have many fond memories of going to the present day Volcano House, rebuilt after a fire in the 1940s and recently remodeled. In addition to lunches there with friends, I also had my wedding breakfast there and a last dance and night in the hotel before the birth of my first son. The Volcano National Park has a great website where you can see some registers from 1865 through the 1920s. A remarkable and fascinating resource. How bold were these tourists, traveling   by   ship   or   steamer   to   see   the   lava   lakes. https://home.nps.gov/havo/learn/historyculture/volcano-house-registers.htm The national park also has some postcards on their website. Great   fun   and   a   good   resource. https://www.nps.gov/havo/learn/historyculture/postcards.htm

I hope that in reading *Volcano House* readers will support the Volcano Art Center   Gallery   http://volcanoartcenter.org/--and   Hawaii   Volcanoes National Park, one of the great parks in our national park system. https://www.nps.gov/havo/index.htm

Many thanks to Michelle Senda of AQUA-ASTON HOSPITALITY (Volcano House) for permission to use the wonderful photograph of Volcano House at night. The photo was taken in March 2017. Since then, Kilauea has been very active, reminding us that Madame Pele is still a force on the island.

And again, many thanks to the wonderful librarians at Kailua-Kona Public Library and Hawaii State Public Library for their help.

Hilina Pali

Lies Have Consequences

By J.L. Oakley

Prologue

Volcano, Hawaii 1940.

"What you want, Lolo? Think you can break rock as fast as me? Wait 'til we get back to da machine."

"Everyone breaks rock faster than you. Even the guys in B Squad. All you do is break wind."

"Yeah, yeah." Gary Kaiwiki took a bite of his sandwich, chuckling as he put it back into the tin pail. He took a drink of water from his thermos. "That's why hard being your friend. Always give me stink talk." He elbowed Lolo, then pulled the rim of his canvas hat down over his eyes. Lolo laughed.

Where they were sitting on lunch break, the sun was hot. The wind coming up from below constantly tugged at their tan shirts and dusty dungarees and stirred the stunted trees and grass. It was a wild place, marked by lava rock, low growing shrubs and grassy patches. A lone māmane tree grew nearby.

Gary leaned back on his elbows. The view from here was breathtaking. He never tired of looking down on the lava desert far below and the sparkling turquoise blue ocean beyond. The Hilina Pali ran for twelve miles along the coast, but here you got the best view and the awestruck wonder of a cliff that plunged 2,000 plus feet down to sea level. Though they were working on an irrigation project for the Volcano National Park a little ways back up the road, all the boys in the squads liked to come down here to eat their lunches and rest. At the moment, only Gary and Lolo were eating here. Wimpy and Popeye, their squad mates, sat further back. The other squads were up by the shelter.

"What are you going to do with your five dollars?" Lolo asked. "Payday is this Friday."

"I think I'll take the bus to Hilo, see my *tutu*. She gets the big bucks from the CCC." For which Gary was grateful. Gary's parents had been killed in a fishing accident when he was ten. Twenty-five bucks a month in the Great Depression was a lot of money for a widowed lady raising five grandkids. His being enrolled in the Civilian Conservation Corps made this monthly allotment to his grandmother possible. He worked, learned skills and got a chance for education. His *tutu* got money to make ends meet.

"What about you?" Gary asked. "You going to see that *wahine* again?"

"None of your damn business." Lolo pulled a blade of grass next to him and chewed on it.

"I think she likes Duke mo betta."

"Hey." Lolo pushed hard on Gary causing one of his arms to collapse. Gary righted himself immediately and scrambled back. They were pretty close to the edge of the *pali*.

"I'm sorry fo' saying that."

"Ah, you're just jealous."

"Maybe." Gary picked up his lunch pail and thermos. "Nevah hear back from the girl I met at the last dance." He stood up.

"Cuz you can't dance." Lolo reached over and playfully jiggled one of Gary's legs. It caused the booted foot on his leg to slip.

"Oh." Gary used his lunch pail and thermos to counterbalance, but the grass was spotty, covering the bits of lava rock. They rolled under his boot. He began to pitch forward.

"Gary!" Lolo grabbed onto Gary's boot to keep him from falling further, but it only made Gary twist to his left and fall down. There was an audible sound as his head hit a large rock. Someone rushed down to grab him, but it was too late. The lunch pail spilled open, its contents flying over him and down the slope. Gary rolled with them. The last thing he saw was the look of horror on the faces of his friend and the lone enrollee from B Squad as he slid over the pali's edge. He kept rolling and rolling and then took flight beyond the cliff's face until the earth   smashed   up   and   killed   him.

Chapter 1

Present day, Honolulu, Hawaii

"I love you, Ojiisan," Tawnie Takahashi said softly as she laid a plumeria lei next to the marble marker set in the neatly mowed grass. She wiped a tear from her cheek. "I miss you. Auntie Bee sends her love."

She stood up and looked around the military cemetery grounds nestled in the Punchbowl Crater. Down the twin traffic lanes lined with Chinese banyan trees, she could see the massive white marble memorial rising up at their ends. At its center rose the statue of Columbia. Tawnie couldn't count the number of times she had come here in her early days as a TV reporter. Most often for a Pearl Harbor remembrance or Memorial Day. Recently she was coming for a personal reason. Her beloved grandfather, Jimmy Takahashi, was buried here. An honored WWII vet and hero of the all-Japanese-American "Go For Broke" 442nd Regimental Combat Team, Ojiisan had been everything to her.

"He was one good soldier." Tawnie started and turned to face an elderly man with a brown face and salt and pepper hair under a baseball cap. He leaned on his walker.

"You knew him?"

"Yeah, yeah."

"In the 442nd?"

The old man straightened up. Tawnie noticed he had an old bike horn on one of the walker's handles and a plastic hula girl on the other. "Nevah was in the 442nd. I stay Camp Kilauea."

"Hmm." Tawnie had heard a couple of stories from Ojiisan about being in the Civilian Conservation Corps. A Great Depression program, it had put millions of jobless young men to work all around the country, including the Alaska and Hawaii Territories. Tawnie just didn't remember when her grandfather was in it. "What year was that?"

"1939."

"Ah." Tawnie paused. "And you are?"

"Harry Sato."

"I'm Tawnie Takahashi. Jimmy Takahashi was my grandfather."

"I know, Miz Takahashi. You're the crime reporter at KWAI-5 News. Always catch the bad guys."

Tawnie smiled. "Well, I leave that part to police. Just hate to see people get away with murder." She reached into her messenger bag and handed him her business card. "I'd love to meet you for coffee sometime. Want to hear about my grandfather's time in the CCC." She looked around the nearly empty cemetery. "Do you have a ride?"

Harry gave her slight bow as he took her card, then put it in the little basket in front of his walker. "Don't worry about me. Morning exercise. Gotta keep up with my great-grand *keiki*. Heh, heh."

"Well, *mahalo* for stopping by." Tawnie nodded at the grave stone. "I think he would like this place. So peaceful and with all who served." She said goodbye to Harry and started for her car when something like a circus clown horn went off behind her. She turned around.

Harry squeezed his bike horn one more time. "Heh, heh. Always warns the skateboarders I'm coming."

"Well, you got my attention. Is there something you need?"

The old man turned serious. He cleared his throat. "Do you do old cases? Like the one story you did about those bones from long time ago up in Hilo Rainforest. That was plenty bad."

"It was bad." *Because it involved my own family.* "Not very often, unless there is a public interest or safety issue. Is there something you know?"

Harry nodded at Jimmy Takahashi's marker.

"My grandfather? The 442nd? You know about some crime?"

"Yeah, yeah. But at Camp Kilauea." He puffed his breath out. "Jimmy knew."

Tawnie put on her professional face—calm and steady, but her heart skipped a beat. Her honorable grandfather would never be involved in a crime. "What happened?"

"One of the CCC boys in my squad went over the *pali*. I think he was pushed, but I think they got the wrong guy."

Chapter 2

"Asami-chan. What you want?" Auntie Bee Takahashi wiped her hands on her kitchen towel and walked over the kitchen side door. Her little Shih Tzu was in a tizzy, leaping up and down at the door latch like a box spring. Bee adjusted her wire rimmed glasses and looked out.

"Oh, it's Maile. You want?" Bee asked. Asami barked, then tore out the door when it opened.

Bee chuckled. On the other side of the *ti* plant hedge that divided their property, her neighbor, Maile Horner, was on the front porch of her plantation style house. *Talking to that nice young man, Liko Hanale.* They had met three months ago when someone intentionally pushed Mailes' car off the road up at the Volcanoes National Park. Liko had rescued her. They made a handsome couple: Maile with her auburn hair and freckles; Liko with his black hair, tall and filling out his park uniform. *He must be going to work.* He held Maile's hand. Bee thought for sure he was going to kiss her, but Asami's sudden arrival put an end to any romantic intention.

Bee heard Maile laugh and look in Bee's direction as Liko picked a squirming Asami up. Her dog licked his face. Embarrassed, Bee stepped away from the door. She didn't want to hurt Maile's happiness. She had had a rough recovery from the accident. Her arm was still in a cast and bruises on her left leg evident.

The couple talked a few more moments, then Liko put Asami down. They walked back to his truck and said their goodbyes. After he took off, Maile came over to Bee's side door, Asami leading the way. Bee slid open the door for her.

"Auntie Bee. Howzit? Did you lose Asami?"

Bee put a hand over her mouth. "So sorry for breakin' your talk with that handsome Liko. Asami wanted to see you soo bad." Bee grinned. "You like Liko, Maile-san."

Maile blushed. "Yes, I do."

"Well, come in and tell me everything. You like some tea?"

Maile laughed. "I always like some tea." She flicked off her slippers and came in.

While Bee turned on her electric kettle on the counter, Maile settled on one of the kitchen stools covered with a hibiscus pattern. "Which cup do you want, Bee?" Maile asked. "The pink honu or Honu with the rainbow?"

"Rainbow, please. I could use a rainbow today."

Maile reached for the cup in the cupboard above her. "Oh, is something wrong?"

Bee sighed. "Just thinkin'."

"Oh, Bee. Today's the anniversary of your brother's passing, isn't it? I'm so sorry."

Bee looked down at her knobby hands. "That's why hard. Always get a little choke up."

Maile put the cup on the counter and gave Bee hug. "I would be too. I can't imagine what it's like to lose a brother. Even though I wanted to kill mine when he was little, I'd miss him so much."

Bee chuckled and wiped a tear from her eye. She sniffed and brightened. "He was like one father to me, too. And my only surviving brother after the tsunami."

The tea kettle clicked off. Bee selected her tea. Maile poured the hot water into her cup, then filled her own. Maile raised her tea cup. "Here's to Jimmy Takahashi. May he always be remembered."

"To Jimmy." Bee felt a calm come over her. Things would be alright. She was grateful for Maile's *aloha*.

Ever since Maile moved next door two years ago, she had become like a daughter to Bee. Well, like a granddaughter—Bee's own children were in their early 50s and lived off island. Maile was kind, considerate and smart—*da kine things I like in one girl*. As the historian at the local museum, Maile always brought interesting pieces of Big Island history to their daily visits. Bee wished she had known some of the stories Maile discovered to tell to her fourth grade students when she was teaching. Such rich history!

As for her brother, until he passed, Jimmy Takahashi was the last remaining member of her family. Bee had lost a brother and a sister in the terrible April Fool's Day tsunami of 1946. Jimmy had been just coming back from the war and was off island when the big waves wiped out Hilo. Her father, too, as he had gone to meet Jimmy in Honolulu. Her mother had survived, but was never the same.

"Speaking of Jimmy Takahashi," Maile said, "I just saw his name on a list at the museum. I didn't know he was in CCC. Do you know anything about that?"

Bee tapped her chin. "CCC. The one up at Camp Kilauea?"

"That's it."

"I was one little *keiki* then. Maybe three. Don't remember much. Except one time when Jimmy brought some friends down to Hilo. So many boys in uniform in our living room."

"That was your apartment over the store?"

"Yeah, yeah. Tiny. Mama said she made shoyu chicken and rice for them, but I only remember there weren't enough chopsticks to go around. The one *haole* had to use a fork. Mama felt shame for that." Bee dipped her tea bag a couple of times and put it on a little dish with a Shih Tzu on it. "Why is Jimmy on a list?"

"Oh, that. New exhibit for next fall. We're doing it on Camp Kilauea. If you have anything, let me know."

Not so much. We lost everything in that tsunami. Everything.

"Tom Harleson. Howzit?" Police Captain Jerry Moke asked as he stood at the front desk of the Hilo Police Department building. Moke leaned over to shake Harleson's hand. "Good to see you, soldier."

"Good to see you, too."

Moke shook his head. Harleson had been in his son's, David Moke, squad. Tall, athletic like a runner, Harleson was the model of a first-rate Marine, except for the two prosthetics he stood on. But that was always the second thing Moke noticed. Tom and David had been close after their service and came over immediately when David was killed in a helicopter accident a year ago up on Haleakala on Maui. "What brings you back to Hilo?"

"A little mystery."

Moke chuckled. "Well, I'm plenty good at that. Come on back to my office. Want coffee?"

"*Mahalo*. It's been a long flight."

After they were settled back in Moke's office with coffee mugs in hand, Moke asked Harleson how he had been. "How's your family? Did they come with you or is Mrs. Harleson a little shy of coming over?"

"They're fine. She and my daughter are coming next week. I'm going to run in a half marathon. I came early to do some family history."

"Is this the mystery? The historical society might the best place to do that. I can give you the number. Know the young historian there."

Harleson frowned. "No, I think that this is something that police might want to look into even though it's a really old case." He reached into his courier bag hanging on his chair and took out a mailer envelope addressed to Richard Harleson.

"My mom found this in my grandfather's belongings. He passed away a couple of weeks ago."

"So sorry to hear. What's in the envelope?"

"A couple of photocopies of 1940 *Honolulu Star Bulletin* articles, a small photo of a bunch of guys standing around with picks and shovels, and a one hundred dollar bill." Harleson reached inside the envelope and pulled out a slip of paper. "And this." On the paper in bold typed letters were the words, REMEMBER HILINA PALI. "I don't know what it means, though I know that Gramps was in the CCC here on the Big Island."

Moke picked up the slip of paper. "Hilina Pali is in Volcano National Park. Camp Kilauea is what you're thinking. It's a military camp today. Don't know much about it as a CCC camp. Why should my department be interested in it? You want to know who owned this?"

"Yes. Gramps said while he was working on a CCC project for the park, an enrollee fell off the Hilina Pali. After an investigation, the police labeled his death murder. Someone in another squad was blamed. The kid got kicked out of the CCC and did some time. Gramps was always upset about that. Thought the kid was framed."

Moke grunted. "Is this kid still alive? Gotta be 90 years old."

"I don't know."

"Could I see the articles?"

Harleson pulled them out of the envelope and smoothed them out. "I think these were made not too long ago."

"The newspaper heading is old. I recognize the old Honolulu Star banner." Moke quickly read through the copies. One copy had the entire article about the accident at Hilina Pali, the long columns cut and carefully arranged on the paper. The other had short articles about the sentencing. An appeal to help the victim's family.

Harleson pointed to the one with the long columns. "Read the part about the kid going over. The CCC camps were run by the military, so the boys worked in squads. Article said there were two different squads eating lunch at the *pali* edge."

"Two witnesses. Actually, three."

"Now read about the sentencing. Kid nicknamed "Duke" says he was trying to stop the victim from going over the *pali*. It was an accident. He got framed because he was seeing a girl someone in the other squad liked."

Moke shook his head. "Some things never changed. But it says here that the Hilo Police Department did an investigation and with the three witnesses, their findings look solid. Let me see that picture. You still have the hundred dollar bill?"

"Kept it right in the mailer. From the get-go, I thought the whole thing was weird. Can't tell whether it was threat to my grandfather or a call to action with the money." Harleson took a sip of his coffee. "There are names on the back, but darn it, most of them are nicknames."

Moke laughed. "Popeye and Wimpy. Goosey. One of the kids is circled in the picture."

Harleson leaned over. "Wimpy." He settled back down on his chair and turned over the mailer. "Still doesn't explain why there's money in this. What did the sender want? There's no return address. No special postal rate with the post office."

"Maybe this is why." Moke held up the article reporting on the death of the CCC boy. "Look at the date. If I'm adding it up right, Gary Kaiwiki died seventy-seven years ago this Friday."

"Maybe that's what Gramps was trying to tell me. He got a stroke near the end of his life and had trouble speaking. He got very agitated the day before he died. Kept saying, Duke, Duke. It must have been troubling him. Gramps would be that way. You see, he was an honorable man. He became a judge in district court back in Minnesota. Always looked out for injustice. I think he wanted justice for his friend."

T awnie Takahashi poked her chopsticks into her steaming saimin bowl and speared a piece of *char siu*. She ate it and then laid the chopsticks on the ceramic bowl.

"So tell me more about my grandfather and this CCC camp. I don't know how this squad thing works. It sounds like the military." She waited for Harry Sato to soundlessly slurp his noodles in and finish chewing. They were sitting in an old family-run restaurant near Punchbowl that served all sorts of plate lunch dishes and local favorites. Café curtains in the window next to them blocked part of the view of the parked cars on the street.

The old man lowered his chopsticks for a moment, his eyes growing distant. "It *was* like the Army cuz the camps were run by the military."

"Even on the Mainland?"

Harry nodded, took the last of his noodles out of the bowl and ate them, then wiped his mouth on his paper napkin. He leaned back and thanked her. "The CCC get started in 1933. Hawaii was one territory then. First the CCC stay Haleakala, then plenty soon, a camp was located up in the Volcano National Park."

"Right by the volcano?"

"Nah. Down on the Byron Ledge."

"Wait. Isn't that next to the caldera?"

"Yeah, yeah. Right by Kilauea herself."

"Was Jimmy Takahashi there?"

Harry chuckled. "Heh, heh. He would have been one *keiki*. Jimmy and I were there in 1939-40."

"Oh." Tawnie took a drink of her soda water. She felt totally unprepared for talking about the CCC, a subject she knew nothing about. She usually did some serious research before taking on a story. *Wish I had listened to Ojiisan more.* Maybe because it predated his time in the 442nd. Not that interesting. Now she was all ears. If her grandfather was involved in something bad...

She put her glass down. "What things did you do in the CCC?"

"Built all *kine* things—retaining walls, the Visitor Center, interpretive museum, overlook buildings around the Kilauea Caldera. We widen trails or made new ones, like the Hilina Pali Road. "

"That's pretty impressive. How does the Army fit in?"

"They ran the camp. All 200 of us. Projects were made up by the national park."

"Did you have to salute and all that?"

"Yeah, yeah. Reveille, calisthenics. Line up in uniform for inspection. All military *kine* stuff."

"You were going to explain what CCC squads were. A squad is small unit, like the military today. Was Jimmy in yours?"

"No. That's why hard to figure out what happened." He picked up his chopsticks and turned them over in his hands. "I was in C squad. Me and Tarzan--"

"Tarzan?"

"Yeah, yeah. We all had nicknames. No one wanted to be Gold Brick, though."

"What's a 'Gold Brick?'"

"A slacker." He tapped the chopsticks in his hands, like he was measuring his words or maybe just trying remember details. "Me and Tarzan were the only Nisei in the squad. Rest were Portagee or Chinese-Hawaiian."

"My grandfather was named Tarzan?"

Harry laughed. "No. He stay A Squad. Guys called him Rooster because he got up so early. Before reveille."

Tawnie smiled. Ojiisan always said he liked to hear the birds at the break of dawn. Helped him get through the war and afterwards. "Who was killed?"

"Gary Kaiwiki. He was a local boy from Hilo. Rough life and tough, yet he looked after his *tutu* and his younger siblings."

"How sad." Tawnie leaned in. "What was the name of your friend who was blamed?"

Harry started to open his mouth when Tawnie's cellphone began to throb with the beat of the latest J-pop tune.

"Sorry. Gotta take this. Tawnie Takahashi, here. Oh, Denny. Howzit? No, Jim's off until 3:00." Tawnie put a hand over her phone. "My boss at KWAI-5 News," she whispered to Harry. "Could you write the name down? Please. *Mahalo.*" Tawnie got back on the phone. "Right away. I'm up near Punchbowl. Can get there in ten minutes if the traffic behaves. Aloha." Tawnie stood up and put some money on the table "So sorry, but there's a big fire down at Pearl City. Some people had to jump." She picked up her messenger bag. "Can you get home OK?"

"Yeah, yeah. No worries."

"This should cover everything. You still have my card. We can talk again.   Very   soon,   I   hope."

Chapter 5

After her second cup of tea, Maile looked up at Bee's clock. "Oh, I better go. I've got to get to the museum for our planning meeting."

"You gonna talk about your new exhibit? So sorry I don't have anything."

"Oh, Auntie. Forgive me. I wasn't thinking." Maile gently squeezed Bee's hand. *Stupid,* she thought. *The tsunami.* Suddenly, she had a bright idea. "Auntie, how would you like me to find your brother's records from Camp Kilauea? I can do it. Just say yes."

"At the park?"

"They'll have some things—hopefully pictures—but I can get all of Jimmy Takahashi's records at the National Archives in St. Louis on the Mainland. They have all the CCC official records—his enrollment papers, classes he took, etc. We're highlighting some of the enrollees who were up at Volcano." When Bee's face brightened, Maile felt a sigh of relief.

"Yeah, sure," Bee said. "That would very nice."

"Good. Now you behave. Asami be good, too." She brushed down her short muumuu and slipped into her slippers. "See you."

It took Maile ten minutes to get down to the Big Island Historical Society Museum. It was housed in an old plantation-style mansion on a hill up from Hilo's town center with a contemporary addition. Maile parked in the back near the big banyan tree and went in. Six members of the museum staff were already crammed into a side room they used for meetings. She greeted her boss, John Hauser, the museum director and Ester Ogawa, who was their collections curator with a "Howzit" and waved to the others.

"Howzit, Maile." Junior Bravos, their building manager, which included building exhibits for their shows, raised his hand to her. "Auntie Pearl made malasadas. They're in the kitchen."

"Sounds yummy. Think they'll make it to lunch?" Maile said as she sat down next to him.

Junior weighed his hands. "Maybe." He was Maile's age, a native of Kamuela. His dark eyes and surf-tanned face was offset with a turquoise streak in his hair. He constantly teased her, but he was a true friend. When she was hurt in the car accident up at Volcano, he offered to stay with her on the nights that Bee couldn't. Maile was too sore to look after herself for nearly a week. They never dated, but they did go out for coffee. Maile suspected that he might have a boyfriend elsewhere, but never asked.

"When's the cast coming off?" Patsy asked.

"Tomorrow. Can't wait." Maile looked John Hauser. "I won't miss a beat. I'll be in at my regular time."

"Good. Now let's look at our calendars."

They talked about plans for the exhibit. When all the photographs should be collected and scanned, text developed for the side commentary. If any, models and ephemera. When dates were set, Hauser addressed the photographs and files in the middle of the table.

"Since we got the word out in the newspaper, we've been getting a heavy interest. Patsy, want to tell us what these are?"

"Families are coming by with photographs. This came in this afternoon. I know Maile's getting a lot of email requests for information on family members who might have served. These came from the national park."

Maile put on cotton gloves and reached for one of them. The black and white picture showed a line of young local men dressed in ties and uniforms. A Model A car was parked next to a man who looked like an overhead—a title given to those in the military who ran the camps. She turned over the photograph. 1939 was scribbled on the back along with a couple of names.

"Anyone recognize these names?"

Patsy Omura, who ran the museum shop said she knew two. "I know Toshi Yamamoto. My grandparents knew him. His family ran a store in Shinmachi. They lost everything in the big 1946 tsunami."

That's when Auntie Bee got hurt, Maile thought.

"And that's Sammy Ito. But the other two are nicknames." Patsy turned the photo over. "That's Jimmy Takahashi's face, for sure, on the front. He was so handsome."

Bee's big brother. "Did you ever meet either of them, Patsy?" Maile asked.

"Only Jimmy. Toshi died in the tsunami."

"Oh, so sad. Guess we'll have to figure these two nicknames out."

"Well," John said. "Could you write them down? When these photographs are put into our Past Perfect program, at least the names will show up on our finding aid. Someone's got to know them."

Ester pulled a picture toward her. "Are there any from the late 1930s? My great-uncle was an enrolled there. Think 1939."

"Is he still around?" Maile asked.

"Uncle Harry? Yeah, yeah. He's one tough cookie. He stay Honolulu."

"A lot of them at the camp were tough. Hard times." John nodded to Patsy. "Do you think he'd sit down for an interview?"

"If he'll do a phone interview. I could try Skype."

"Did Harry grow up here on the Big Island?" Maile asked.

Ester said that he did. "Pāhoa."

"That's great. I do want to highlight the Big Island CCC boys. I plan to do something on Jimmy Takahashi."

"The war hero." John wrote something down on a pad. "Well, I think we're on the right track. The exhibit should reflect on how the CCC was formed, who was in it and what were some of the lasting projects they did up there."

"Maybe impact on the community at large." Patsy put the photo back in the center. "There were dances, basketball games with Hilo High School."

"Did any of the boys get in trouble?" John asked.

Ester and Patsy's heads went up at the same time.

Chapter 6

"Hey, Annie. This is Tom Harleson. Howzit?"

"Tom. How's the weather in Minneapolis?"

"Not as nice as Hilo. I'm in Hilo." Standing on the stone *lani* of the Hilo's best restaurant, Banyan Tree with beer in hand, Tom Harleson faced Hilo Bay. A slight breeze stirred the coconut palms that edged the water. Low waves tapped the large rocks placed on the beach for sitting.

"Seriously? What's up?"

Harleson laughed and stepped back and sat down on one of the cafe chairs. "I'm here to run in the Hilo Bay marathon. Checking out the layout of the race."

"What did you enter in?"

"Half-marathon. About my speed. Got new running blades."

Annie Moke chuckled. "You're amazing."

"You can blame David for getting me into it." David Moke, Annie's late husband and Tom Harleson had known each other from their tours of duty in Kuwait years ago. Harleson had been critically wounded on one assignment and ended up losing both lower legs. David saved him then and later when Harleson, suffering from PTSD, had ended up on the streets of L.A. Now, Harelson was happily married with two teenagers. To say that he and David had been close as brothers would be an understatement.

"So what are your plans, Tom, other than scoping out the race course?"

"Following up on a curious package I found at my grandfather's after he passed. Thanks for the card by the way. Appreciate it. Anyway, I just came from seeing your father-in-law at the police station."

"Jerry? What's wrong? You talking about some crime?"

"Possibly. Something fishy." Harleson went on to describe what was in the envelope. "I don't know what to think of the one hundred dollar bill. Don't know what I'm supposed to do with it. Find out who these guys are in the photos?"

"That's crazy," Annie said, "Definitely fishy. What did Jerry say?"

"Moke said that right now other than an odd collection of disparate clues, it wasn't serious enough for a police matter. Said I should talk to people at the local museum and the archivist up at the national park. They might have info on the guys listed on the back of the photograph. If something more concrete came up, I was to let him know."

"Sounds good," Annie said. "Ever see pictures of the Hilina Pali?"

"Looked it up on Google Earth."

"Well, if you want to look around up there, you should get in touch with David's cousin, Liko Hanale. He works for the park and can get you back there. The view is spectacular. I'll text you his contact info in just a sec."

"Thanks. Worst case scenario, mystery never solved, but I learn more about my grandfather's work here in the CCC." Harleson took a swig from his beer bottle. "Never asked how you doing? How are you? The kids?"

"Doing good enough. I stay busy at work. Kids are back in school. They're glad to be with friends again." Harleson heard her move something around. Annie sighed. "To tell the truth, it's hard sometimes. I hate to put David's things away. I sometimes think he'll just walk in the door."

"I know it's not same as losing David, but I understand that feeling."

"I enjoyed meeting parents that time they came to Hawaii. Hey, where did your grandfather grow up?" Annie seemed glad to change the subject.

"Minnesota. Why?"

"How did a *haole* from the Mainland end up with the CCC on the Big Island?"

"It's long story, but just say it has a tramp steamer, no job, and the Great Depression."

Harleson was glad when he heard her laugh.

Auntie Bee was moving one of her orchid plants on her circular bench in the backyard, when Asami tore off to the front of the house. By the time Bee got to her, all Bee could see was Asami on the sidewalk barking her head off at a disappearing red SUV on the other side of her ti plant hedge.

"Asami-chan. Such commotion."

Asami wagged her feathery tail and then spinning around, dashed up the steps to the door. Leaning against it was a padded package. Asami bit down on it, but couldn't pull it away. She grabbed it again and this time swung it around. The mailer went flying over the steps and landed at Bee's feet.

"Good girl." Bee leaned down to pick it up, rescuing it before Asami got her teeth into it again. "Oomph. Getting creaky. Gotta get to chair yoga this week." She turned the mailer over. It was addressed to her, but had no return address. "Hmm."

Bee decided to go check on her mailbox. As she stood on the gravel parking strip in front of her hedge, she could make out the tire tracks laid by the SUV. It had rained lightly an hour ago. *Hawaiian sunshine.* Hilo always had some sort of clouds or sprinkles, but now the sky was blue and the air hot. She waved to her neighbor the next house down and took an assortment of letters and flyers out of her box. "Come, Asami. Let's see what we got."

Back at the bench where Bee kept all her orchids under a large breadfruit tree, she laid out her mail in order: a postcard, four bills, two letters and the mysterious mailer. She tackled her postcard first. It was from her daughter-in-law in Germany where Kiro, Bee's youngest son, worked at a US Army medical unit.

Bee tapped the postcard with her finger and smiled.

Next she read a letter from a friend of Bee's teaching in New Zealand for the summer. The other was asking support for a local candidate. When she was done with mailbox mail, she turned her attention to the mailer. It didn't look like much. Smaller than her laptop, she could have easily fitted it into her cloth bag she used as a purse. She turned it over and pulled the tab to open.

"Oh." One of the first things she pulled out was a clear plastic sandwich bag with a zipper. Inside, were several 3 x 4 black and white pictures with fancy white borders. She recognized her brother Jimmy immediately. Lean and tall, he had been a handsome young man. *My hero.* As she pulled them out and set them carefully on top of the letters, she realized that she had never seen these before, though one looked familiar. Any photographs that her family might have had were lost in the tsunami. Jimmy was in uniform, but it was not an Army outfit. *CCC.* A treasure trove of memories she was too young to remember without aid.

But pictures brought the sound of young men laughing, a hot summer day with all the windows opened in the apartment and eating around the family table. One picture showed a group of young men dressed in work clothes holding or leaning on shovels. A lone *haole* stood next to a CCC boy holding his shovel like a long-necked *ukulele.* Jimmy stood on the other side. Bee turned it over. "B Squad + Rooster" was written on the back in pencil. She turned it back. A faint line had been drawn under Jimmy's feet.

She went through the other photos. Jimmy was in all of them, a couple of group photos listed as "C" or "B."

Bee reached inside the mailer again and pulled out an envelope. Inside was a hundred dollar bill and a strip of type-written paper with the words: REMEMBER HILINA PALI.

Bee had no idea what it all meant. But a memory stirred. Her mother and father standing under the faint light of the overhead kitchen light, talking after midnight about a friend who had lost her son. And her brother's name, "Jimmy." They were whispering about Jimmy.

Chapter 8

"So Ester, what happened up at Camp Kilauea?" John Hauser asked as the museum staff leaned in over their small conference table. All eyes were on Ester and Patsy, waiting for an answer. Maile quietly opened her notebook.

Ester looked at Patsy. "Well, there was the usual *kine* things young men do, like stay drunk in Hilo. Or be lazy for work and sneak away. Steal cigarettes. But my grandfather say that there was one bad time when someone in his squad fell off the Hilina Pali. People say he was pushed, but my grandfather wasn't so sure."

"Who fell?" Maile asked.

"Gary Kaiwiki," Patsy answered. "My grandparents knew his family."

"You said someone was pushed. Was someone arrested for that?" Maile hadn't planned to go into details like this. She wanted the exhibit to be all positive, to celebrate the amazing work of the CCC. She had grown up around CCC projects such as state parks and trails in her home state of Washington.

"Yes." Ester looked sad. "An enrollee—that's what they were called—in another squad was arrested and given jail time. But to this day, my grandfather—"

"—Harry Sato," John said.

"Yes. He thought the enrollee was innocent."

John looked at Maile. "Well, not to get sidetracked, but think this is something you could look up in the newspapers?"

"Sure. I'll check."

"See anything else in these, folks?"

"There's a letter B with a circle around it on this photo. Bunch of guys crushing rock."

"Looks like one big puzzle. Well, let's get this exhibit moving."

After the meeting, Maile went upstairs to her office, turned on her computer and opened the program the museum used to track everything from collections to museum staff and docent schedules. As she waited for the program to load, she looked out her window onto the museum grounds where a banyan tree spread its tangle of massive roots and branches over half the length of the museum property. She never tired of looking at it. Even though an exotic import to the place a hundred years ago, the tree symbolized the grace of old Hawaii to her.

The printer and scanner dinged that they were ready. Maile watered her plants, then made herself comfortable in her office chair and laid out the photos Ester had shown at the meeting. She spent the next hour scanning and entering them into a database with what notes that had been scribbled on the back.

As she carefully put each photo into an archival sleeve to protect them, she was struck by the photo of the young men standing in their uniforms next to the Model A car. Patsy had identified Sammy Ito and Jimmy Takahashi. Bee's older brother, the one she loved so much, certainly was a handsome young man. He was tall for someone of Japanese descent, with hair cut short on the sides, leaving him a mop of dark shiny hair on top. But who were the ones with the nicknames? She laid out the series of pictures on her desk. John said that men worked in squads, like the army. She flipped over the pictures showing groups of young men working in some sort of trench or piling rocks for a wall.

"Here's something," she said out loud. "C Squad." She peered at the list of names and nicknames—she counted eight in the group—strewn across the back of the photo. One of the names was Harry Sato. She studied the position of his name, then flipped back to the front. She guessed the skinny kid with the canvas hat so many of the CCC boys seemed to wear, was him. *So many young guys in a squad.* She decided to make a diagram. On a sheet of computer paper, she drew eight ovals in a circle and put the letter C in the center and began to label each oval. When she was done, she had a partial list, except for the remaining two men in the photo:

Gary Kaiwiki

Wimpy

Popeye

Sammy Ito (Tarzan)

Harry Sato

Lolo

Satisfied she had identified most of the names in in the photograph, Maile put it into a sleeve and went through the rest of the group photographs. By now, she recognized Jimmy Takahashi every time she saw him. Finally, she figured out which squad he was in: A Squad.

Maile leaned back and stretched her fingers. She had been able to type with the cast on, but it was tiring. Fortunately, the break was in the middle of her left arm, not by the wrist. Still, physical therapy was inevitable. She hoped it wouldn't be extensive.

Maile's eyes strayed to the picture of Jimmy with his squad mates. *Oops, I promised Bee I'd get his CCC records.* She got on line and found the form for requesting CCC personnel records at the St. Louis branch of the National Archives. She didn't have a lot to go on except for a stab at the dates he was at Camp Kilauea, but she had at least his parents' names. Whole fields were left blank. She paid the fee with the museum credit card and sent the form in, hoping that something would come.

Since she was searching for his CCC records, Maile decided to do a general search for him in the on-line historic newspapers. She plugged in Jimmy Takahashi and got several articles dating from 1945 to some as recent as four years ago. Curious, she checked the latest article and read an inspiring story of the reunion of the surviving members of the 442nd. Bee's brother was prominent in the local Hawaiian newspaper account.

"Wow," Maile said. She read a few more articles about Jimmy and bookmarked them for later reference. She stacked the photos carefully for placement in the archive's physical files, then on a whim, put in James Takahashi into the search. Although there was one other James listed, she chose the name with the middle initial "T" for Toshiro.

Immediately, several articles came up. To Maile's shock, they were all about the death of the CCC kid at the Hilina Pali. After reading through them, Maile looked out the window, feeling a weight settle on her shoulder. What should she tell Auntie Bee? In each of them, they talked about the sentencing of a CCC boy, Henry Oh, for the death of one Gary Kaiwiki. It had been ruled manslaughter. Cited in the articles were witnesses to the crime Oscar Garcia and Walter Chin and then two enrollees who were also present at the time, Richard Harleson and James Takahashi, reprimanded for some reason.

"Oh, goodness," Maile said. She went back to the little pictures and spread out them, looking for the names mentioned in the article. When she found the photo listing the boys in C Squad with Gary Kaiwiki, she searched for it again in her Past Perfect program and printed it off. Then she called Officer Jerry Moke at the Hilo Police Department.

Tawnie looked into the camera and signed off with her tagline, "This is Tawnie Takahashi saying, Until next time." She hoped she kept her reporter face intact for underneath she was hot, tired and shaken from covering the fire the past three hours. It had taken two lives and a dog was missing. The fire threatened another apartment complex next to it. The firefighters were doing mop-up, their hoses splayed out across the street like the roots of a banyan tree behind the yellow police tape. An ambulance prepared to leave. Smoke probably got the victims. Poor little dog... She didn't want to think of her Auntie Bee's Asami.

Tawnie waited for her cameraman, Jim Milstead to give the signal they were no longer live, then stepped over to him.

"You OK?" he asked. "Those flames were massive. I was getting worried we were getting too close when the wall fell."

Tawnie brushed down her purple linen suit jacket she had thrown on as she rushed over to the fire. For a time, ash had been falling when the wind blew her way. "Fine, but I could use a beer." She handed Jim her microphone, then helped him pack away the rest of the equipment into his bags.

He zipped up one of the bags. "How did your visit go at Punchbowl? I find that place so peaceful. Sometimes I go up there just to sit and get away from work."

"Like you said, always peaceful, but it was a bit harder today. It's the anniversary of my grandfather's passing. Miss him so much."

"From what you've said, he was a wonderful man."

"He was." But what Harry Sato had said was disturbing. *Was he a witness to a crime? Or more?*

Tawnie picked up her messenger bag Jim watched for her and stepped back. Her cameraman was a gangly young man in his early thirties. They had been working together for a couple of years now. A near-death experience on assignment had made them good friends, though she never considered dating him. She liked things on a professional level, though he was certainly a part of her small *ohana* of friends and family. A good friend she had learned to trust.

Tawnie opened her messenger bag and took out a water bottle. "Oh, sorry for not saying, but I met someone up at Punchbowl who knew my grandfather." She took a drink and chuckled. "Said everyone had nicknames. Jimmy's was Rooster."

"Was this Punchbowl guy in the Army?"

"No, CCC. Civilian Conservation Corps."

Jim picked up his bags and started for their SUV with KWAI-5 News decals plastered all over it. "Really? I didn't know they were here. There were a number of CCC camps where I grew up in Michigan. Built a lot of the state's parks."

Tawnie started to answer him when she spotted her contact at Honolulu Police Department standing by his police car. "Just a sec." She waved to Mel Ishikawa and walked over. "Howzit, Mel. This was one bad one."

"Yeah, yeah. You been here the whole time?"

Tawnie nodded yes. "So sorry for the loss of life. Lots of people lost their homes." She paused, then asked the question. "Do you have any names?"

"Now, you know Ms. Takahashi I'm not supposed to say anything." He was frowning, but there was slight smile on his lips.

"Just inquiring. Wondering why the police were here. More than crowd control."

Mel looked around casually as if he was checking on eavesdroppers. "Fire appears to be an accident. Started far away from the victims in another part of the building. Neighbors said they tried to warn them, but no one answered. Neighbors had to hightail it and left it at that. Fire department went in and discovered the bodies in a bedroom and on the living room floor, but they appeared to be dead for at least a day or two." He leaned in. "Looks like murder-suicide."

Tawnie's heart leaped. She was a crime reporter after all, though her boss still gave her human interest stories. "You got names? I won't say a word until the official report."

"You're persistent, aren't you?" Mel looked around again. "There was only smoke and water damage to the unit. Some scorching on the wall connected to the hallway, but the sprinklers in the hallway put the flames out. When I was called in, we made a preliminary search of the apartment. We did find identification. Mr and Mrs. Wally Chin. Elderly couple." He paused.

"What are you holding back, Mel? There's Thai food on the line here."

Mel shrugged. "Place was full of all *kine* family pictures, awards for service in the electric company, stuff like that. Most of it will probably have to be thrown out. Water damage is bad enough, but smoke kills anything that survives a fire. Still, I could see from the bottles on the kitchen counter that one of them was on heavy medication. Possibly, the woman in the bedroom was in hospice."

"Anything special?"

Mel sighed. "Alright. In kitchen drawer not damaged too much by the water, there was one envelope. Had some pictures in it of guys in work clothes. A picture of a pretty young wahine. Looked like the 1930-40s. But weird part was one slip of paper all cut up. Doesn't make sense, but maybe it points to their suicide. When I put the pieces together, it said,   'Remember   Hilina   Pali.'"

After finishing his call with Annie Moke, Tom Harleson sat on the lanai chair and waited for the text to come in with Liko Hanale's contact. He supposed he should check on the course map for the marathon. From his registration materials, he knew the full marathon started at Waianuenue Ave. near the canoe launch and went all the way out to the Hawaii Tropical Botanical Gardens before turning back. He could always take his rental car and just follow with the GPS map. The race brochure promised breathtaking views of the Pacific Ocean along historic roads with lush tropical forests, scenic waterfalls and sugarcane fields. He could do that, but he kept thinking about the contents of the envelope and what they meant. The pictures and newspaper clippings were one thing, but why the $100.00 bill? Was there a point? A message?

Moke said that he should ask at the historical museum in town. He had even given him the name of the historian there before they parted. "Miss Horner should be able to help you. She knows all *kine* stuff."

A dove with its incessant cooing landed at the edge of the lanai and strutted its way toward Harleson, its head bobbing like a pendulum toy. "Nothing here, partner," Harleson said. The bird did a U turn and went back only to come around again, cooing loudly.

Harleson chuckled. *Dumb bird.* Smaller than Mainland pigeons, doves were ever on the hunt for—*what did David Moke say? Kau kau. Food.* He ignored the bird and took a sip of his beer. A slight breeze had picked up, stirring the fronds of the coconut palms. Across the bay, a cloud made its way down the green hills that stretched up through the dark forest toward white-headed Mauna Kea.

He sure liked Hilo. It was rainier on this side of Mauna Kea, but it had a charming old town personality. He had had no time to enjoy it the first time he was here, thus the marathon. *But damn.* He was looking forward to the race, but those bold words, "REMEMBER HILINA PALI" pulled at him. He decided to ditch his plan of following the course and instead go out to the museum and see Miss Horner.

***

Up the hill, Auntie Bee was equally bothered by the words and the memory of her parents' hushed talk. It was such a fragment that Bee couldn't remember why she had wandered into the kitchen at such an hour. It must have been around four. All she recalled was the honey-colored glow of the overhead kitchen light and the worried look on her parents' faces. They were speaking in Japanese, which they rarely did, but she remembered hearing Jimmy's name.

Bee looked at the photo of the young men in work clothes and noticed for the first time a circle made by a ball point pen around one of the young men. He was standing at the end of the row. What was the person who sent the package trying to say? She unfolded the copies of newspaper clippings. The headline on the first sheet jumped out:

HENRY OH SENTENCED TODAY. STILL CLAIMS INNOCENCE

Adjusting her wire-rimmed glasses on her nose, she quickly read through the article, then stopped cold when she read, "A number of the CCC men were held for questioning, including James Takahashi of Hilo and Richard Harleson, Saint Paul, Minnesota. No charges were filed, but they were disciplined."

Was this what her parents were upset about? Her honorable brother in trouble? Bee couldn't believe it. She clutched the paper sheet and sighed out loud. Asami immediately jumped up on the bench and tried to lick her face. "Asami-chan." She folded the little dog into her arms. "I'm OK. Just bad times coming on Jimmy's passing." She gave her dog a kiss and rocked her in her arms.

"Bee? You here?" A voice sailed out from the side of the house. A plump woman with her dark hair piled up on top of her head came down the sidewalk lugging a large plastic container. Her long purple muumuu swayed as she walked. Her slippers slapped the ground.

"Eleanor, what you want?" Bee let Asami jump down and run to her friend.

The woman laughed. "Special delivery. I have the book club kit from the library." She came and sat by Bee with a big omph. "You OK? I know it's a rough day for you."

Bee shrugged her bony shoulders. "Jimmy gone. But this." She held up the sheet of paper with the news story about the sentencing. "That's why hard."

Eleanor Kane was one of Bee's best friends. They had both taught for many years in the Hilo School District, though Eleanor was younger than Bee. They had first met at the U'ilani Book Lovers Book Club, composed of elementary school teachers, eighteen years ago.

"Let me read it," Eleanor said.

Bee held Asami while her friend read all the articles on the sheets. When Eleanor was done, she said, "Hmm."

"Is that a good *kine* "hmm" or bad *kine* "hmm"?" Bee asked. "Do they say anything more about my brother?"

Eleanor put the sheets on her ample lap. "Is this what is upsetting you? It's hard to say what's really happening here. This Harry Oh was charged with manslaughter and was sentenced to jail time."

"Does it have anything to do with this?" When Bee showed Eleanor the slip of paper, her eyes grew wide.

"That's hard. That came with your package?"

Bee nodded yes.

"I don't think I ever heard of this incident. So long ago. But essentially, the newspaper says there was some work being by the CCC on the Hilina Pali Road. Where the shelter and signage is today—where we went for a picnic with our book club."

"I remember. Wind blew so hard we almost lost our paper plates."

Eleanor chuckled. "Anyway, this says they were having a lunch break." Eleanor tapped the sheet. "A local boy named Gary Kaiwiki fell off the *pali* up there. This Henry Oh was accused of causing him to fall. Very sad." Eleanor gave the sheet to Bee. "Thought I knew all the families here, but not this family, Kaiwiki."

"I think I do. There was one family by that name my parents knew, but they moved away after the tsunami. But the paper says Jimmy was questioned and disciplined. I can't imagine him getting into trouble. He

never say." Bee frowned. "Do you think they would take away his medals?"

"Ah, Bee. Let it go already." Eleanor took Bee's hand. "Everything will be just fine."

Bee blinked back tears and sniffed. "Maile says she was going to look up Jimmy's record for me the National Archives."

"There you are. She's an historian. She'll clear things up." Eleanor pointed to the pictures. "What are these?"

"Friends of Jimmy's. Maybe you can help me figure them out."

"And this?" Eleanor picked up the hundred dollar bill.

"Money for something. But I don't think it's for dog food."

"What do you want to do now?" Jim asked when Tawnie rejoined him beside their SUV at the Pearl City fire scene. "Personally," Jim went on, "I'm going to check back in at the station. Prepare footage for tonight's broadcast. Our boss just messaged me and said we didn't need to do remote from here, unless something further comes up. Denny might want us to go to Queen's Hospital to check in on the injured. One's critical after jumping to escape the fire."

Tawnie looked back at Mel Ishikawa as he strolled back over to the burnt out apartment building. The blue light of his police car was still whirling, a reminder that the place was now a crime scene.

Jim snorted. "But by that look in your eyes, something has come up. What did your police contact say?"

Tawnie straightened up her five foot frame, though she felt like taking a nap. "Appears the dead couple inside was already dead. Possible murder-suicide. That's why the coroner showed up." Tawnie sighed. "Do you ever get the feeling that the universe is trying to tell you something?"

"Only when I'm hungry. What's up?"

"I think I might go over and see that old man I met earlier. He was in the same CCC camp as my grandfather over on the Big Island. He wanted me to look into a death that happened a long time ago at the Hilina Pali."

"That's the universe calling? Some granddaddy dot com search?"

Tawnie laughed, then grew serious. "No." She nodded at the apartment building. "It's that couple. Mel found an envelope in their kitchen with pictures and a note that pointed to the Hilina Pali incident. I think the universe wants me to investigate."

Not long after saying goodbye to Jim, Tawnie was on H-1 going back toward Punchbowl and the residential area slightly *makau* of it. She took the Pali Highway exit and after a mile turned right. She had taken down Harry's address when they first sat down in the cafe. Now she hope the GPS in her car would get her to the right street. The neighborhood was made up of old-style houses painted white with dark-colored pitched roofs and set off the ground. Plumeria trees, boxwood and hibiscus serving as hedges and spare lawns marked the narrow street Tawnie turned onto. Here the lots looked big, some with short driveways and hints of deeper yards in the back. She listened to the voice on GPS telling her in an Australian accent that they were close, but her heart sank when she noticed red and yellow lights flashing on the back of a white ambulance parked in front of what she realized was Harry Sato's address. She pulled up immediately behind the small group of neighbors standing in the driveway one house over. Grabbing her messenger bag, she got out.

"What happened?"

"Oh, poor Mr. Sato had one heart attack," said a small Chinese woman with a short haircut and graying bangs.

Tawnie craned her neck to see a group of EMT personnel coming out of the house with someone on a stretcher. "Is he OK?"

"His daughter was with him when it happen," another woman said. "I think, she did CPR or something. Got him in time."

"Where are they taking him?" Tawnie asked, keeping an eye on the ambulance as they loaded the stretcher.

"You a friend?"

"Yeah, yeah. I just had lunch with him three hours ago. He knew my grandfather." Tawnie hoped that she could remain inconspicuous, but in this aloha-wearing crowd, some were taking a second look. "He was fine then," she added, her voice trailing off. She wanted to use her reporter voice, but it didn't come. She felt like she was a little girl in danger of losing a friend, a connection to the past her grandfather didn't often talk about."

"Queen's Medical Center."

A middle aged woman came out on the porch talking to one of the EMT's. The worried look on her face told all. Tawnie decided to take a chance and going around the small group, passed the ambulance parked on the street and went quickly up the driveway to the awning-covered porch. "Ms. Sato."

"Mrs. Ogawa. Julie Ogawa." The woman's dark eyes widened when she recognized Tawnie. "Tawnie Takahashi. We just saw you on TV an hour ago. Terrible fire. My father said he had a nice time talking to—" She choked on her words and put a hand over her mouth. "So sorry."

"I'm the one who is so sorry. We'd been talking about his time in the CCC and stories about my grandfather. He was fine then. You were with your father when he had his heart attack?"

"Yeah, yeah. I'll be along as soon as I can," she called out to the EMTs getting into the ambulance. She turned to Tawnie. "He was fine, too. Then something came in the mail and he got all upset. I was in the kitchen when I heard him collapse. Thank God they got here plenty fast."

"May I ask what was in the package?"

Julie shrugged. "I found some old pictures on the floor around him, but I nevah looked in the envelope. Too busy trying to save him." Julie Ogawa's eyes followed the ambulance as its sirens sounded and drove off. "I should go."

"Please, may I see? Maybe I can help you find out who sent it. What upset him. I promise you, this will remain private."

Julie hesitated for a moment, then said, "Alright." She opened her screen door and led Tawnie into living room with rattan chairs and sofa and a paper screen separating a small office area in the corner. Large pictures on the white walls held doll-size kimonos of various styles and fabric. All very clean lined and direct interior decorating except for the commotion on the floor where the EMTs had tended to Harry. Laying on the floor against the sofa was Harry's walker, the plastic hula girl trapped under the handle.

"Is this the envelope?" Tawnie reached down to the floor and picked up the mailer. She noticed right away it had no return address, but there was a cancellation date and a location in the upper right hand corner. The mailer had been sent two days ago from the Big Island. She showed it to Julie. "May I check it out?"

Julie nodded yes and invited Tawnie to sit on the sofa and lay out whatever contents on the coffee table. There wasn't much inside, except for some copies of newspaper clippings, but she was beginning to think this package was similar to the one Mel had described at the fire. When she pulled out a crisp one hundred dollar bill, she felt she had to be right. The envelopes were connected. She was disappointed when she didn't see any a slip of paper with the words Mel had quoted.

"What does it mean?" Julie asked. "Why did it cause my father to have a heartache?"

Tawnie tapped the newspaper. "I think it has to do something with his time at the CCC camp on the Big Island. You don't happen to know someone by the name of Wally or Walter Chin?"

"I don't think so. After the war, my father stay Hilo, then moved to Honolulu in 1950 to work for the Hawaii Power."

"I shouldn't tell you, but this Wally Chin was the one of the two people who died in the fire. Apparently, he was in the CCC the same time as your father."

"Oh. That's why hard."

Tawnie looked at the photos on the floor. "May I look at them?"

"Yeah, yeah." Julie joined Tawnie on the floor and helped to arrange them on the table. "Oh, that's my father. So young."

"Do you recognize any of them?"

"Hmm. There's the *haole*."

"Who?"

"That one. He kept in touch with my father all these years. I think his name is Harleson. Dick Harleson."

The enrollee's face didn't ring a bell with Tawnie, but she was touched when a photo of him and her grandfather appeared together. They were sitting at table filled with other young men dressed in uniforms.

"Do you mind if I borrow everything from the package? Again, I'll be discreet."

"Alright. I have to go now."

The women stood up at the same time. Tawnie put the photographs, newspapers and money back into the mailer, then grabbed her messenger bag. As she stepped out, she up righted the walker. "I'm sure your grandfather will be needing this." The hula girl sailed up unscathed. Underneath the edge of the sofa was a slip of paper. Tawnie reached down, her heart pounding.

It was as Mel had told her. REMEMBER HILINA PALI

Jerry Moke listened for one more minute, then said, "Yes, Miss Horner, it is possible to search old police records. Is there a particular date?" On the other end, Maile gave him two dates, both in the year 1940. Moke wrote them down on a pad by his phone. "Anything for Auntie Bee." He tapped his pen on the desk. "Is there a reason you're asking?"

"I promised Bee that would look up her brother's CCC records at the National Archives. Since I was on the subject, I was just curious about any newspaper coverage about Jimmy Takahashi—the 442nd for sure and came across—well, it was a bit of a shock, but did you know that he not only served up at Camp Kilauea, but got in trouble for some reason? Got a reprimand along with another guy. It was during the trial of a CCC boy accused of killing another enrollee."

Moke sat up straight. "Say, again." He heard Maile rustling some papers around. "Bee's brother was disciplined, though I don't know what for. A guy by the name Gary—"

"—Kaiwiki."

"You know this story?"

"Not until today. Who was the other enrollee?"

"A Richard Harleson was disciplined."

Moke muttered under his breath. "Well, Miss Horner. This is one good thing you called. I might need *your* help. A man by the name of Tom Harleson came in today—he's a friend of my son and daughter-in-law—his grandfather was up at Camp Kilauea, too. He was also looking for information. Apparently, his grandfather knew Gary Kaiwiki."

"The one who went over the *pali*,"

"Yeah, yeah. Did you know that the anniversary of his death is in two days?"

"I didn't realize that. I've been focused on the names."

Maile went on to explain the exhibit the museum was working on and the flood of material from the public about the topic. The batch of pictures from the national park had been interesting. It had led to a staff discussion about the incident. "So many nicknames, but I figured out who was in Gary's squad. That's why I wonder what police records might reveal."

"You have names?"

"For C Squad. That's the one Gary was in. And for Auntie Bee, I figured out what squad Jimmy was in. A Squad."

"What about Richard Harleson?"

"I haven't figured it out, but he could have been friends with the kid who got sentenced."

"What was his name?"

"Henry Oh."

"Hmm. Nevah heard of him, but Tom Harleson said something that I've been thinking about. He said his grandfather was upset about how this kid was treated. Possible false accusations."

There was silence on the other end. Finally, Maile said, "Can you look him up on your police program? See what happened to him? I don't want to alarm Auntie Bee if there is some issue about Jimmy Takahashi. It could hurt his reputation. He was a civil rights lawyer, after all, with such public admiration. I suppose I can go to the archives for old court records."

"I'll see what I can do. In the meantime, could you send that list of names, I'd appreciate it. "

"Of course. I'll send the picture too. *Mahalo* for speaking with me. I'll be in touch."

Moke got off the phone and then called the front desk. "Who's getting plate lunch today?"

"Officer Santos."

Moke put in his order, then went back to work on police reports. He was about to put the files away, then his phone rang. "Line two," the receptionist said. "It's that TV reporter."

Moke sighed and took off his steel-rimmed readers. Tawnie Takahashi had always bothered him like a pesky mosquito. Over the years, she had poked her face into stories that seemed to be hyper-sensationalized with a subtle disdain for the police, but he had noticed a change recently. After the last incident he was involved with her over a rare stolen manuscript, Takahashi's fierce love for her Auntie Bee seemed to soften her and perhaps make her a little vulnerable. Under her powerhouse persona, there was a sensitive woman.

Let it go already. You get stressed out.

He picked up the phone. "Tawnie Taka- hashi. What brings you to call? Where you stay?"

"I'm in Honolulu, but I'm seriously thinking of flying down to Hilo."

"Got some big news story for the TV? Plenty quiet here."

"It's my grandfather, Jimmy Takahashi. Something strange is going on. Something dangerous."

Officer Santos came to the door and raised a paper bag of take out. Mokes' lunch. Moke pantomimed where to put it, then mouthed, "Close the door."

"Alright. What you got?" Moke took the plate lunch box and a pair of chopsticks out of the bag and put them in front of him.

"Did you get a chance to see the fire in Pearl City?"

"Sorry, for say, but I've been working. Haven't seen the news. I suppose you were there."

"I was. It was terrible. A couple of people died and many are now homeless. But that's just one of the reasons why I called. Today's the first anniversary of my grandfather's passing, so I went up to Punchbowl to pay my respects. While I was there, I met a man who knew him down at Volcano. Harry Sato. He was in the CCC."

Moke was in mid-action of banging the wood spurs off his chopsticks. "What year?"

"1939-40."

"Wait." Moke was all attention now. "Did he know anything about incident involving a man going over the Hilina Pali."

"Yeah, yeah, but that's isn't all." Tawnie went on in a hurried voice to tell about the mailers the Chins and Harry had received and the words "REMEMBER HILINA PALI."

"*Auwē*. Where is Sato now?"

"Queen's Hospital. He had some heart issue."

Moke let out a rush of air. "*Lolo*. Crazy."

"Why do you say that?"

"Because someone is going around dropping off packages with similar pictures and news articles and those very same words."

"You got one?" Tawnie sounded intrigued, but more like, what aren't you telling me.

"No, the grandfather of a friend of my son's did. He was up there, too."

"I only have a quote from my contact Mel Ishikawa here in Honolulu Police Department," Tawnie went on, "but both packages came from somewhere on the Big Island and they all point to an injustice."

"Humph," Moke said. "Something is going on. In two days, it looks like it will be the seventy-seventh anniversary of the death of Gary Kaiwiki. Did both packages have a hundred dollar bill?"

"No mention of one in the Chin mailer, but oddly, the words were all cut up in his. Who was the friend?"

"Tom Harleson's grandfather."

Tawnie gasped. "Richard Harleson. Harry's daughter said they kept in touch all these years."

Moke groaned. "Ms.Takahashi. Is there anything you're not telling me?"

"No, I've told you all I know. But I do want your help. To work with you this. This is a story worthy of news, but it's also about my grandfather." To Moke's surprise, the formidable Tawnie Takahashi choked on her last words.

"Why don't you come down as soon as you can? We can quietly work on this together, but first I want you to talk with Miss Horner at the museum. She is working on an exhibit on CCC up at Volcano and has identified some of the names involved in this Hilina Pali incident."

"*Mahalo nui loa,*" Tawnie said.

Moke   thought   she   meant   it.

After Eleanor left, Auntie Bee took the mailer and its contents back inside and set them on the counter. She laid the latest book club pick on top. While Asami dashed to her water bowl, Bee filled a glass of filtered water from her refrigerator. She was still getting used to the new setup. The double-sided refrigerator with ice cube and water dispenser had been a birthday gift from her grown children. *So fancy.* At least it didn't talk like book club member Dottie's refrigerator did. She got enough talk story from Asami.

Taking her glass of water, she limped into her living room on the other side of the kitchen wall and bowed to her house shrine. Next to it on a shelf were pictures of George Peterson, her late husband, and their children. Grandchildren filled out the rest of the space. George came over in the 1950s from Boston and never left. He was a tall man of Scandinavian stock and she was short. Maybe that made them the odd couple, but he had been the love of her life. Said no worries when she asked to keep her last name cuz many in her family had been lost in the tsunami. They had been married 57 years. "So what you think, George? If you got a hundred dollar bill and other stuff, what would you do with it?"

Asami seemed to have come up with an answer as she tore to the front door and barked. Bee went to the window to see. At first, she thought it was Maile's cat, Buster, on the hunt for lizards by her hedge, but as she looked, she saw the tip of a red SUV roof over the top of the hedge. Had the driver come back? Bee's heart began to pound.

Bee stayed where she was, but no movement came from the car. Asami barked again. "Shh, Asami. Come" Bee backed away from the window and went back to the kitchen. She picked up her mobile phone from its cradle and quietly slid open her side door. "Stay." Bee slipped outside and closed the door, her finger near the 911 button.

As she went down alongside the house, she listened for the sound of any car door closing or someone coming to her front door. All she could hear was the chatter of the myna birds on Maile's roof next door. Bee swallowed, but continued her way to the front, hoping her hedge would hide her most of the way across her short lawn. When she reached the corner of the hedge, she took a big breath and stepped out onto the gravel parking space on the other side. There she came face to face with a battered red Jeep Cherokee with mud splashed on its running board. The windshield was dark, but she thought she could see the figure of a young woman through the passenger side.

"Can I help you?" Bee kept calm, like the time when she was closing up her fourth grade classroom at night and she thought there was an intruder in the school hallway. She had picked up one of the softball bats the boys kept in the room for recess and ventured out. Down the long dark hall, she could hear clicking and metallic clanging noises on the linoleum floor. When the sound came closer, she raised the bat only to confront someone's pet goat, its rubber collar covering the chain around its neck. The rest of the chain and a metal stake dragged behind it. She had laughed her tension away.

Bee continued talking as she came closer. "Did you know my grandfather? That's why you gave me the package?" Bee motioned for the person to roll the window down. "I like you to say something." Bee thought she saw the window crack open a bit, but it stopped when Asami came tearing out onto the road, barking her head off. Bee had forgotten to lock the pet door.

"Asami!" But it was too late, the Jeep's engine roared to life. The SUV backed up at high speed throwing gravel in all directions. A stone hit the little dog causing her to yelp. The driver turned the car around and sped off, leaving Bee stunned and outraged. But not before she saw that the driver was young, with light brown hair streaked with a raspberry highlight and a sticker on the back bumper with the black and red logo of "Vulcans University of Hawai'i Hilo."

***

After Maile got off the phone with Jerry Moke, she sat quietly for a moment with her eyes closed. She had so many thoughts running around in her head, mostly about the way the Hilina Pali incident was starting to take priority over the general search for CCC history up there, but occasionally an image of Liko Hanale flashed in. Liko surfing at Banyans over on the Kona side. Liko hiking up around Volcano. Liko filling out his park uniform. In the few months after he came to her aid after she was violently pushed off the road up at Volcanoes National Park, he had become more than a close friend. He took her everywhere, reacquainting her with the places where her family had settled in the early 1900s and showing her the places he loved. He even got her back on a surfboard, her cast heavily wrapped in plastic. *I'm falling in love with him.* Every time she was with him, his presence was almost overwhelming. Surely he sensed her feelings when he dropped by to see her this morning. If Asami hadn't shown up, he would have kissed her. *I would have lost it then.*

Maile opened her eyes and cleared her throat. "I better get cracking," she said to her plants. "Priorities, priorities." She went back to work.

After talking to Moke, her curiosity about Henry Oh continued to grow. She decided to start there. Who was he? Moke would do a police records search. She could start with a general search in the newspapers. Try the librarians at the state archives. She typed in the name Henry Oh. Several references came up on LinkedIn, but they all seemed young and current. She tried the newspaper site and this time printed off the articles about his sentencing. As she read over them, she noticed the mention of two names at the court's sentencing. A Mildred Oh and Joan Oh. After closely reading further, it appeared Mildred was the name of Henry Oh's mother. Was Joan a sister?

Maile jotted down the names in a notebook full of names and notes about the CCC. She liked being old school like that, referring important information to the computer for final draft. The notes would stay in a file when all was done. She grabbed a telephone book, somewhat outdated in these times of technology, but still useful. There were a dozen on one page. They all seemed to be up north of town where sugar cane factories used to be just a couple of decades ago. Maile decided she'd ask her colleagues if they knew any of the names as she had as she had only been here for a year.

She tapped her finger on the keyboard. Henry Oh. She looked at the photo in the newspaper print out. The mixed race kid looked so young, his dark eyes sorrowful as he looked into the camera. She wondered not only what became of him but his family. As she recalled, an enrollee in the CCC got thirty dollars a month, twenty-five of that going directly to the enrollee's family. That was around one hundred dollars in today's money according to the Inflation Calculator program she used. One hundred dollars a month was a lot of money for people in the Great Depression. What happened when an enrollee died? What happened to Henry's family when he was dishonorably discharged?

Maile leaned back, causing her computer chair to creak. Moke said that Tom Harleson's grandfather was upset about Henry's sentencing.

Could there have been a false accusation? She didn't know why she thought that. She read the articles again, making notes of who were witnesses, then went onto Facebook and located a group she had joined that shared stories about the CCC all around the country. She typed in:

Hello, Hive. I have a question for you. Two really. What happened to the family of an enrollee who died during his enrollment in the CCC? Was there an insurance policy? Also want to know if an enrollee was dishonorably discharged, what happened to that family's monthly allotment? Mahalo.

Maile stood up and stretched. Outside, a misty rain fell, the sun cutting through it creating a prism of rainbows. Maile smiled. A typical Hilo day. The cardinals in the parking lot didn't seem to mind it, only to fly off onto the lawn near the Banyan tree when a car pulled into the parking lot.

A tall, athletic man got out and headed for the front entrance of the museum back on the street walking on prosthetics limbs. *With running shoes*, she thought. He disappeared around the corner, out of her line of sight. The birds flew back into the parking lot by his car looking for something that might have fallen out, only to startle and fly away when Ester Ogawe suddenly came running out of the building and climbed into her car. She drove off in uncharacteristic speed. Maile craned her neck to see where she was going.

The phone peeped, louder than normal.

"Maile, here."

"Oh, this is Zita. You have a visitor. Can you come down?"

"Yeah, yeah. I'll be right down. I just saw Ester rushing off. Is something wrong?"

"It's Ester's grandfather. He had a heart attack. She going to catch the first flight out to Honolulu."

All   Maile   thought   was,   C   Squad.

Tom Harleson pulled on the handle to the ornate koa wood double door and stepped into the lobby of the Big Island Historical Museum. It felt more like the foyer of an old plantation owner's home, which in fact it had been. Colorful banners in tropical aqua blues and tan and figures from the City of Refuge announcing the current show about Robert Louis Stevenson's time on the Big Island, brightened the wood walls. A woman with short black hair and kukui nut lei worn over her *muu muu* stepped out from a counter to greet him.

"Aloha and welcome to our museum. Are you interested in a tour?" She kept a smile on her face but he knew she had just noticed his prosthetic legs.

"Actually, I was hoping I could talk to the historian, Ms. Horner. Is she free? I'm visiting from the Mainland."

"I believe she is. May I ask your name?"

Tom gave her his name and why his interest in talking to her.

"You know about the CCC up at Volcano?"

"Learning more every day. My grandfather was up there."

"Wonderful. Did you know we are putting together an exhibit of the very topic?"

Tom said he didn't.

Zita Chin made the call. "She'll be down right away." She jumped when there was the sound of a door slamming from the back of the house." She pushed her purple glasses up on her nose. "So sorry. One of our staff got some bad news about a relative. He stay Honolulu so she's going right away. Please, you're welcome to look around the gift shop while you wait."

The wait wasn't long. He wasn't expecting someone so young as a museum historian. Pretty too with her auburn hair and freckles that could almost be a tan. Thoughtful brown eyes. They shook hands, then she invited him into a side room off the lobby.

Tom eased down on to a chair at a round koa wood table. "Thank you for taking the time to see me."

"Strangely, you are someone I wanted to meet."

"Really? Did Office Moke mention me?"

"He did." Maile moved an empty coffee cup off to the side and set her cell phone down. "Said you were looking for information about your grandfather when he was in the CCC."

"Yes. In particular, an incident that led to criminal charges for an enrollee. I believe that my grandfather wanted it looked into before he died." He took out the envelope and pulled out some of the contents. He laid out the photographs. "Do you know any of these guys?"

"I do." Maile pointed to all the names she had figured out so far.

Tom was impressed.

Maile smiled. "I started out wanting to know as much I can about the CCC and the projects they did up at Kilauea, but lately it looks like I've stumbled onto a homicide investigation."

"Someone was framed. That's what my grandfather thought."

Maile pointed to Henry Oh in the newspaper account. "Have you ever seen a picture of him before?"

"There's something familiar about him."

"He's the one who was charged with manslaughter for the death of Gary Kaiwiki."

"Hmm. I wonder what happened to him."

"I've been asking that myself. The article says he was given a two year sentence. I've made an enquiry to a national CCC group as to what the real cost was. But beyond that, I don't know. Working on that."

"Maybe he got swept up in the war."

"Perhaps. Officer Moke said your grandfather knew Gary Kaiwiki. I know what squad he was in. C Squad. One of our staff members father was in that one. I've been trying, however, to figure out which squad Henry Oh was in."

"I think I know. B Squad." When Maile looked curious how he knew, Tom said that before he came over, his wife had called. She had found some letters scattered in a box up in the attic. They had been mixed up with WWII memorabilia. "Henry Oh was in B Squad with my grandfather." Tom opened his wallet and took out a little cellophane package. It contained a brass medal the size of a silver dollar. "This wasn't part of the envelope, but it was something that my grandfather kept in a box on his dresser. You'll see that the name, Henry Oh, is written on it."

"May I?" Maile tuned the medal over in her hands. "I've seen these on the Internet, but never a real one. Very nice." On the front of it was a scene with two barracks surrounded by pine trees. Smoke rose from a chimney.

Harleson pointed to the medal. "Look at the words around the border."

Maile read out loud, "Loyalty. Character. Service."

"It's an honor award. Do you think someone awarded one of these would kill?"

"I suppose not."

Tom took the medal back, holding it in the palm of his hand. "My wife Sarah is scanning those letters I mentioned and will send them to me as soon as possible. She found several references to Henry Oh. Apparently, my grandfather has been in touch with some of his friends from CCC days. Jimmy Takahashi, for one and Harry Sato."

"Harry Sato? That's my colleague's grandfather. He's at Queen's Hospital. He had a heart attack."

"Really? He OK?"

"We hope so." Maile nodded to the envelope on the table. "When Ester asked her mother what happened, she said that he got upset after something arrived in the mail. It sounded like a package like this one."

"Is Ester still here?"

"Catching first flight she can get for home."

Ping

Maile looked at her cell phone. Some had answered on the Friends of CCC Facebook page. "Just a minute. Let me see if they answered my question." Maile swiped her phone a couple of times and got to the group's page. The message made her sad:

In answer to your question, the family of an enrollee who died while enrolled would receive the young man's last paycheck. Embalming, transportation, and burial expenses of a deceased enrollee were paid regardless of the cause and place of death. An enrollee who was dishonorably discharged had all forthcoming pay and allotments forfeited.

Maile showed it to Tom. "This is really terrible. Obviously, Gary Kaiwiki's family suffered financial loss when he was killed. I think the newspaper account said he was sending his money to his *tutu* and his four siblings she was raising."

Tom frowned. "But what about this Henry Oh and *his* family? Maybe this is the injustice that my grandfather was talking about. "Before he died, he kept saying, Duke, Duke. Now I believe that Duke is Henry Oh. If he was dishonorably discharged under false accusations, his family suffered too. It was still the Great Depression, after all." Tom pulled out the last two items in the envelope: the one hundred dollar bill and the strip of paper.

"I wonder if Mr. Takahashi had the same things in his envelope. I think it's a call to action, though I don't know what the money means."

"Maybe that's what five dollars in today's money would roughly be."

Tom unfolded the strip of paper with REMEMBER HILINA PALI on it.

Maile's eyes widened. "That was in the envelope?"

"Yes. We need to find out what happened to "Duke." Moke says it will be seventy-seven years since the Kaiwiki's death. Someone wants us to remember and do something about it."

Snuggling Asami in her arms, as soon as the red Jeep made the turn at the end of her lane, Bee went back into the house and grabbed her purse and the car keys to her Nissen Rogue. "Come, Asami. We're going for a ride."

The Jeep had turned left to get out to the main road that ran parallel to Hilo Bay far down below. Based on the Vulcans sticker on its bumper, Bee hoped it would return to the campus at UH Hilo. Either the young lady was a fan or better yet, on some sports team. Bee was hoping for a sports team as there could be a poster. As she drove down to the college, she checked to make sure Asami was clipped into her new doggie booster seat. Asami seemed to be enjoying her ride. Bee made sure the air conditioner was on blast.

At the campus edge, its brick red metal roofs glistening from a light rain that had passed through a few moments before, Bee drove to the parking lot closest to the library and parked. She put up her parking pass and rolled the windows down. "I'll be right back."

Outside, the air was warm, a slight breeze tickling the tall palms. She walked as fast as she could, but her bad leg could only do so much. She had to slow down to a rolling limp. Once under the huge roof that covered the library's brick lanai, she entered the lobby through the glass doors. As she had hoped, on a free-standing board near the front checkout desk, there were several team posters showing the current season of members. The Vulcan women's basketball team attracted Bee's attention. She adjusted her glasses to look closer. "Ah," she said out loud. "There you are."

"There you are, who?" a male voice said beside her.

Bee straighten up immediately and smiled at the tall man wearing an Aloha shirt and surfer shorts. He was, after all, one of her all-time favorite students "Jason Chee. What you want? You playing hooky?"

"My forty-eight hours off. I'm taking some classes."

"Ah." She was so proud of him working as an EMT for the Hilo Fire Department. He had even helped her once.

"Didn't know you liked basketball that much." Jason smiled at the poster. "It's a great team this year."

"I like watch the girls' volleyball team. Feisty. I remember when the international volleyball tournament was here with a team from China." Bee pointed to the girl with a raspberry highlight. "Do you know her?"

"Sure do. She's one of the top scorers. Kelcie Shephard. Want her autograph?"

Bee batted his arm. "I'd like to give her one teaching."

"How come?"

Bee told him how come. When she was done, he looked speechless, his mouth slack. Kinda funny, Bee thought for someone who was the EMT calendar pick for March. But then again, she could still see where he sat in her fourth grade classroom. He made a lot of faces then.

"Have you called the police?" Jason now looked worried.

"She hasn't done anything wrong. Just passing news along." Bee sighed and nodded at the front desk. "I can't stay long. Asami's in the car, but I did want to see if Stephanie Hillard was around. I like want to do a search for someone named Henry Oh."

"Henry Oh? I haven't heard that name in a while.

"How come you know his name?"

"Because, long time ago, when I was in high school, I did a project on local men who served in WWII. Though he didn't live here after the war, Henry Oh did grow up here. In Mountain View where my dad lives now. Turns out, Henry Oh was a hero. Saved a number of men under heavy artillery fire on a beach in the Pacific, but lost his arm as a result. Got a medal for it."

"I'm happy to know that. People can have troubles, then change." She recalled the news story in the newspaper and Henry Oh claiming innocence. The strip of paper that shouted out to her: REMEMBER HILINA PALI. She hadn't told Jason that.

"Auntie Bee? You look lost."

"Thinkin," she answered. "Thinkin' is one thing about getting old. You remember lots of stuff to think about, but sometimes you forget where you put it, so you got to think some more." She chuckled. "No worries. I'm not *that* old."

"You said people can have troubles, then change. Were you talking about Henry Oh? "

"Yeah, yeah. Does the family still live there?"

"No. The family moved to Kaui before the war."

Bee sighed. "Too bad. I need to sit down."

"Of course."

They sat on a bench near the door. "That envelope Kelcie dropped off," Bee said, "had all *kine* stuff, but mostly it was about a death up at the Hilina Pali. You ever go there?"

"I like to hike up there. Pretty spectacular view. Have you been?"

"A few times with George, my husband and the kids. My book club did a picnic there once. From the newspapers and pictures I learned that my brother Jimmy worked on the Hilina Pali Road. I was too little to recall anything about that time when the CCC were there." She went on to tell Jason what the news articles said and the slip of paper asking to remember what had happened there. She was pleased that after listening patiently, he asked good questions, helping her to figure out what it meant.

"Henry Oh said he was innocent," Bee said. "Maybe I'm supposed to look for the truth. Do you think he still might be alive? Maybe that's why he had the package dropped off?"

"He'd be getting up there in age. He could be gone."

"I know. But I think this one thing has to be solved. Then I won't worry about Jimmy so much anymore."

"Because he got a reprimand."

"Yeah, yeah."

"Auntie Bee, from what my great-grandfather shared about his experiences in WWII, the military accepted all sorts of men into the ranks. Maybe that's why I never heard about this. Just know Henry Oh turned out to be a hero."

"But someone got hurt. Someone told a lie." Bee frowned at him. "Didn't you learn that in my class? Lies have consequences."

After changing up her clothes at her apartment, Tawnie made it back to KWAI-5 News headquarters in downtown Honolulu in time to catch her boss Denny Kane on his way to a late afternoon luncheon. She waved to him in the hall outside of the main news room where machines pinged and clattered. He gave her a shaka sign for a job well done on the fire report.

"But where you went after that?" he asked.

"I did a follow up to an earlier interview." Tawnie was careful to frame the information Mel had told her and the envelopes the Chins and Harry had received. She cleared her throat. "I've discovered something at the fire. I think it's going to be an important case that curiously the Hilo Police Department is also working on. Officer Moke has invited me down to see firsthand how they work."

"You already know how they work. Not the first time you've worked with them or shall we say, ahead of them on a breaking story."

"This is important. There's a possible crime in progress. I promise you, our followers on Twitter and Facebook will want to know."

Denny gave her a what-are-you-up-to look. "I suppose you want Jim to go too."

"He's the best cameraman around."

"Don't get him shot."

Tawnie took that as a go. "*Mahalo*, Denny. You won't regret it."

"Keep track of expenses. And... oh, never mind. Say "Aloha" to your auntie."

Tawnie passed through the open space of the newsroom to her office. She quickly checked the bank of monitors that hung from the ceiling. Here news from around the country and the world was displayed.

Tawnie noticed that their channel was already running footage of her reporting of the fire. In her office, she messaged Jim to see her. They were going on assignment as soon as they could book a flight to Hilo. She would let him in what it was all about. After greeting a colleague, Tawnie went into her small, but private office and closed the door. Taking a deep breath, she called Mel on his direct line at the Honolulu Police Department.

"Mel, howzit?"

"Calling so soon? I barely got back." Tawnie could hear his chair creak in the background.

"Just wanted to know if you knew anything more about the fire victims."

"The Chins. Coroner has the bodies, now. He'll do due diligence."

"What happened to the package?"

"You mean the envelope. That's gone to evidence."

"What about the pictures? You said there were pictures of guys in work clothes and a single one of a young wahine. Were any of them underlined?"

"What you want with that?"

"When you described what was in that envelope, I went immediately over to see an elderly man who knew my grandfather on Big Island. Both were in the Civilian Conservation Corps in the late 1930s. I got there too late. He had a heart attack."

"So sorry for hear. What does it have to do with the Chins?"

"I was able to talk to Harry Sato's daughter before she went to the hospital. I found the same envelope with similar items—photos, newspaper accounts of the sentencing of a CCC boy and—the words you found torn up in the envelope, REMEMBER HILINA PALI, on a strip of paper. Someone mailed it to him. Walter Chin has to have been up there the same time as Harry."

"Hmm."

Tawnie was glad he sounded interested. "That isn't all. I spoke to Jerry Moke in Hilo about another matter and he said that a *haole* from the Mainland came into the police station this morning with a similar envelope. All with the same words."

Mel's chair creaked again as he apparently sat up. "This is a story you're working on?"

"Yes, something is going on, pointing to the death of Gary Kaiwiki back in 1940. Someone wants to have it investigated and the kid who was sentenced absolved. I don't know if anyone is in danger, but Moke said there is a time factor here. In less than two days, it will be the day that Gary died. I'm flying down to Hilo tonight. A historian at the local museum has been working on matching names to faces. I have permission from Mrs. Ogawa, Harry's daughter, to take the envelope and its contents with me. It would be great if you could speed up the analysis of the Chin's materials."

"I'll see what I can do. Get them scanned and sent to Moke. He can decide if he wants to share." Mel paused. "What got you on this?"

"I was up at Punchbowl this morning, saying my respects to my grandfather. It's been a year to the day that my grandfather passed away. Harry was there and said he knew him. They were in the CCC at the same time. Said they got the wrong guy."

"And now, he's in the hospital. Where you stay?"

"My auntie's."

"Keep   me   posted."

"What do you want to do now, Auntie?" Jason Chee asked as he sat with Bee on the bench inside the UH Hilo Library.

Bee leaned over to get up. "I need to get Asami out of the car. Then I like take her home." She planted her feet like she practiced in her chair yoga class and stood up. She picked up her cloth bag and brushed her short *muu muu* down. "There."

Jason shot up, embarrassment on his face that he hadn't helped her. "Uh, Auntie, could you use some assistance working on this—mystery?"

"Yeah, yeah. That would be nice. I'm going to ask my book club if anyone knew the Oh family and maybe the Kaiwiki's."

"I'll ask at the station too. Do you have any of those pictures with you?"

"Just one. It has Jimmy in it."

"May I see?"

Bee took the small photograph out of the plastic student homework folder she always carried with her. Jimmy standing with a group of young men. "That's Jimmy," Bee said proudly.

"Smart looking. That's the uniform they wore? Looks so military."

"My neighbor says the CCC camps were run by the military."

"All locals except for that lone *haole*. Let me take a picture." Jason took out his phone and snapped a picture. "I'll show this around. In meantime, let me walk you to your car."

Back home, Asami dashed around to the back of house, while Bee stopped to pick some plumeria flowers from her tree. She looked to see if Maile might be home for lunch, but there was no green Subaru parked in front. *Maybe I should call her. Tell her about the package.* Bee decided not to bother her. Instead, she'd do some researching of her own.

Inside, she poured herself a glass of water from her refrigerator and took it into the living room. She plugged in her old laptop on the coffee table and while waiting for it to load, sat on the sofa to think. A small pad from an end table drawer helped along with the process.

What do I need to know? She used to ask her students to consider that when they started on their projects. *What do I know? What did I find? Make a Venn graph.* Bee decided she needed to know about the two families, the Ohs and the Kaiwikis. So far, she didn't know much except both of families had lost a son one way or another.

What did she need to know? She needed to know what happened to Henry Oh. How long did he serve time in prison before he went to war? What happened to him after the war? And where was his family today?

Ever since Maile moved in next door over a year ago, she had been showing Bee some interesting websites for doing genealogy, researching Hawaiian and Nisei history, and following groups that protected turtles around the world, one of Bee's great interests. Last month, Maile had shown her where to find old directories on-line at the University of Hawaii Manoa as well as censuses and old newspapers. Bee decided to look at the 1940 Hawaii Territorial census. She took a sip of her water. Asami joined her at her side on the sofa.

For the next hour Bee searched and read, making notes on her pad. When she was done, she felt she had learned a lot. It made her sad too.

The 1940 Territorial Census revealed that Gary Kaiwiki's *tutu* had been head of the household. In addition to Gary, there were four other children, two girls and two boys ranging from age eight to fifteen. No parents. Bee worried about what happened to the children with Gary dead. She understood that boys in the CCC sent money home. Would his family have lost it? The Great Depression still held its grip on many parts of the country in 1940.

Checking the census list for Henry Oh brought equal stress. His father was a disabled cane worker living in Mountain View, his mother a housewife. Henry Oh was their only child. Bee supposed that the Oh family lost their monthly check and took home instead the shame Henry brought when he was sent to prison. Bee picked up Asami and hugged her. As a teacher, she had seen poverty over her many years in the schools. Many hard stories. But this story was affecting her differently. If someone told a lie and sent Henry to prison, there was surely consequences for his family. Bee put Asami aside for her laptop and did a quick research of the Oh family on Kaui in 1950, but she found nothing. Henry Oh and his family had disappeared.

She did one more search in the Territorial Census. Her family in 1940. As she looked at the names of her parents, Alfred and Riko Takahashi and her siblings, Janice, Clarence and James, they seemed to shimmer before her eyes. Three of them would be gone in the 1950 census. Now they were all gone. Yet her brother Jimmy was alive as ever. She needed to know the truth.

After saying good-bye to Maile at the museum, Tom Harleson headed back to his hotel down on Banyan Drive. He had received a text from Sarah back home saying she had sent him the first of several letters she had scanned. Tom promised Maile he would let her know if they was anything pertinent to the Henry Oh story. He was hoping that the correspondence between any of Gramp's CCC friends might have some clues.

At his hotel, the staff, wearing the hotel's uniform of blue Aloha shirt or muu muu and a black *kukui* nut lei, greeted him. Tom picked up the local newspaper and chatted with the young man manning the desk. They talked about local sports teams at UH Hilo and fishing. Tom got a recommendation on next week's deep fishing excursion his family could go on.

Upstairs, he turned on his laptop, then took off his prosthetic legs and their silicon liners. He flopped back on the bed and putting his hands behind his head stared at the ceiling. He was feeling the jet lag of four hours' time difference plus the ten hour flight. His eyes threatened to close, but his head was full of images and questions. *Coffee. I need coffee.* He slid off the bed and walked over the coffee pot on his bare stumps. While he waited, he looked out the window onto a park. Liliuokalani Park, the front desk said. Later, he'd check it out.

Coffee in hand, Tom maneuvered himself back on the bed, grateful that he kept up working on his upper body strengthening. He remembered how weak he was when he first started physical therapy—before he got his prosthetic legs. He took a sip of the coffee and set it on the side table, then made himself comfortable. He opened the laptop and looked at his emails.

There were several, including one from his oldest daughter, Megan. He chuckled at the meme she sent and her growing excitement about coming to the islands. It would be a first for all of his family. There was an email from the IAVA veteran's organization of which he was a member and then four emails from Sarah. He went to those and read her greeting peppered with some sexy hot words on what she planned to do with him when she got there. *Did you book the room for the kids? Just checking. Smiley face.* Then he opened the next one with attachments. Here Sarah wrote that she thought these were the most important letters he should read. There were some older ones she would send later in the day. He took another sip of coffee, grabbed a hotel note pad and pen and downloaded the attachments.

The first letter dated just a year ago to the day, was a letter from Harry Sato. There was a banal greeting and an update on a family news, then Harry got down to brass tacks.

Been thinking about Camp Kilauea again. There was talk of having a reunion, but I don't think the few of us who are left are up for it. We got off to such a great start in '39, but that prick Wally Chin messed everything up. Poor Duke. I know he was only trying to help, but then Lolo blamed him when the Hilo cops came. Honestly, I thought when it came to the trial, Lolo was going to take it back--that it was really an awful accident, but Wally Chin just pushed the knife deeper into Duke. Damn dance. I wish we'd never gone. All this over a wahine. *If you want to go ahead with our plan let me know.*

Tom stopped reading. He rolled over and grabbed a canvas file folder off the chair next to his bed. He took out some papers Maile had given him at the museum. One was a diagram of the three different squads mentioned in the newspaper articles and copies of some group pictures. Maile had identified most of the people in C squad, Harry, and the dead kid, Gary Kaiwiki. Wally Chin's picture was labeled, "Popeye." Tom smiled when he saw his grandfather in two of the group photos. The only one not identified was Lolo. What was his real name?

Tom finished the letter, then opened the second letter. The letter was out of order, having been written a few months before, but gave more insight into life in the CCC camp. Harry reminisced about the main camp at Kilauea: pool games in the recreation hall, the barracks that got cold enough to warrant a stove for heat, the food in the mess hall. It once held 200 enrollees but when they were there in 1939-40, the population was down. Some of the boys got regular jobs with the national park as fee collectors and guides. The description of a boxing match caught Tom's eye.

Didn't think Duke would take Wimpy's challenge to a boxing match, but he did it. Thrashed him good. I always thought Wimpy was a mean drunk when we went into town on leave, but I finally figured out he was mean when he was sober. That thrashing he took from Duke and then Duke dating Alice Kapuna just made him meaner. Only don't think he realized that Lolo was on the trail for her too. Wish we could do something for Duke. Just wasn't fair what happened to his family. Just about the nicest people I ever met and the poorest.

Tom stopped reading and savored his coffee. In other parts of both letters, he felt a real affection between the two men. He could appreciate the fact his grandfather stayed in touch with friends from his CCC days. After all, the army ran the camps and Gramps and Harry were old comrades. Working together in squads building walls and roads, restoring plants and trees around Kipuka Puaulu, putting in telephone all the way up to Mauna Loa was essentially the kind of teamwork Tom relied on when he was in the military. He opened one more letter, deciding he'd save the fourth for later. He really needed to lie down after this.

The third one was back in timeline order. Written a few weeks after the first letter he read. There was a funny anecdote about a goat eradication program where squads were sent out to drive the goats into pens. Goats were destroying native plants even back in the 1930s. Tom had the opportunity to see some herds in action up on the Saddle Road a few months back. The black goats poured over the lava rocks like liquid molasses. Tom could imagine the damage that they did to plants in the park, but the roundup sounded fairly comical.

There was another paragraph about a new great-grandchild. Harry's handwriting was a bit shaky and the words seemed to wander, but eventually, the subject turned back to Duke, the unfortunate Henry Oh.

Duke's in poor health. Heard from his daughter that he had a second stroke. Thinking on that, I asked her if she ever got his CCC records from the National Archives in St. Louis. She said that she did. They had come a few days ago. She said that it was sorrowful to see the number of awards and certificates he had received, then his dishonorable discharged paper. She didn't understand. She didn't show that file to him. Thought it would be upsetting.

Well, old friend, another anniversary of Gary's death passed. I think we should go ahead with our plan before we're all gone. Wish Jimmy was here. Rooster would be waking the universe up again.

PS When you are going to learn how to do email? My granddaughter taught me.

Tom chuckled at that. Gramps was old school. Didn't like all those devices and even asked Megan and Sean to park their cell phones when they came to visit their grandfather at his home.

Tom looked again at the date of the scanned letter. Written about eleven months ago. What did it mean "go ahead with our plan?" What were the old codgers up to? He pictured the two elderly men sitting at a small table with a light overhead. No, that wasn't right. He had no clue if they ever met in recent years.

He leaned back on the pillows stacked against the headboard. Was the envelope part of the plan? And why the hundred dollar bill? Tom never finished his train of thought. Jet lag finally overtook him as his head   sagged   deep   into   the   pillows.

Tawnie stood at the airline counter and took a big breath. "So the flight is canceled?"

"So sorry, for say," the young woman with a pink hibiscus in her dark hair said, "but the airplane had an engine trouble. We can book you for the first flight in the morning."

"There's no standby?" Tawnie motioned for Jim to start checking on his smartphone to see if all other flights to Hilo were full. He stepped away and began searching.

"No, so sorry."

So much for inter-island travel. Tawnie tried to think of anyone with a private plane she could contact, but the hour was late. They were getting out later than planned, but she had to do a follow-up with Julie Ogawa and see how her father was doing. The good news was that Harry had responded very well. He had been whisked into the emergency room and discovered that he didn't have a heart attack, but heart arrhythmia caused by stress. He was awake and talking. Tawnie told Julie that she was thinking of him and was on the trail of who sent the envelope. She didn't add to the woman's anxiety that other members of the CCC squads had received envelopes.

Tawnie turned to Jim, then seeing she was holding up the line, she told the agent politely that she would be happy if they were booked on the first morning flight.

"Be here at 4:30 AM," the agent said as she gave Tawnie her ticket. She gulped. "And *mahalo* for understanding, Ms. Takahashi."

"No worries." Tawnie gave her a big smile and stepped away with her carry-on. "What did you find, Jim?"

He looked up with start. "Nothing. All flights are filled. No chance of standby."

"Well, we're on the first flight out. Question is, what to do now?"

"Let your auntie know?"

"Yeah, yeah, I could do that." Tawnie looked outside through the large glass windows. Night always came early in the tropics. The coconut palms next to the terminal under spotlights stirred gently in the breeze. Beyond them the sunset was gone. "Guess I'll go home. Get up before the mynah birds." Tawnie brightened. "In the meantime, let's get a beer, but not here. Where's that new brewery tap room you're always talking about?"

"Queen Street, back in town."

"Let's go. We can strategize. I'll show you what I brought from the Takahashi home."

***

Auntie Bee put away the dishes in her small dishwasher, then sat down at the small rattan rocking chair by the sliding doors to drink her tea. She was disappointed that Tawnie couldn't get in until tomorrow morning. She had wanted her to show pictures of Jimmy and the newspapers articles. Maybe, help her research an answer to Jimmy's "discipline." She would sleep better. But she understood that Tawnie-chan would probably stay busy working on some investigation. Only come over to sleep. Bee sighed. One year anniversaries were fine for a keiki, but not the passing of a beloved brother.

Outside, night had fallen. There were no lights on in Maile's house, except the front porch light that went on automatically. Maile was staying out. Maybe with Liko. She smiled and took a sip. Asami came over and flopped down at her feet. Bee wasn't settled in long when the phone on the counter rang. It was Eleanor Kane.

"Eleanor, why aren't you watching your show?"

"I should be reading our book club pick, but I've been calling around to see if anyone remembers Henry Oh or Gary Kaiwiki.

"Oh?"

"Not much luck, but some remembered grandparents talking about the dances in Hilo. They were big before the war. Lots of young people went there to hear the bands and dance. I asked if anyone knew any stories of CCC boys at these dances and a friend at the library said she knew several families whose grandmothers met their future husbands there. There was one *wahine*, named Alice Kapuna. Her folks stay Paukaa, but she had an auntie in Hilo and would come down on the bus for the dances. She was only a girl, maybe sixteen-seventeen, but men were always fighting over her. She was beautiful and had plenty spirit. Maybe a little too wild. Ran off with someone from the camp before the war. I'm sorry. Not sure that's what you were looking for."

"Well, thanks for asking."

"You OK?"

"I'm fine." Bee drummed her fingers on her lap.

"You don't sound fine."

"OK, I think I found out who dropped off the envelope."

"Already? Who is it?"

"Kelcie Shephard. She plays basketball at UH Hilo."

"How did you find that out?"

"She showed up again at my house," Bee said. "When she took off, I followed her."

"Oh, Bee. What could she be up to? She's a good girl. I know her mother."

"Officer Moke, sir, there's someone out in the lobby wanting to see the head officer."

Moke looked at the clock on the wall. "It's 5:30. Station is closing."

"I told him that. He's making one big stink. It sounds like this." She obviously was holding the phone out because he could hear a male voice ranting and swearing.

"Get him calmed down, but ask for backup if it gets worse. I'll be right out."

Moke strapped on his utility belt with its taser and other gear. He smoothed his hair down in the mirror by the closet door and hurried down the hall. Before he reached the lobby, he squared his shoulders and slowed down. The person making the racket was not slowing down. Moke wondered what drug he was on.

"You damn right you gonna do something," the tinny voice said. "Where is he? What do I pay my taxes for?"

"Aloha, what you want?" Moke was surprised to see the troublemaker was an elderly man of Portuguese descent. "What can I help you with?" Moke came over to the desk, nodding that was OK for her to slip away.

"This," the man growled. The thin white mustache on his lip quivered with rage. He threw an envelope onto the counter. "I like you stop this."

Moke's heart took on a couple of thumping beats. *The same envelope.* "And you are?"

"Alvin Olveria. Someone is threatening me."

"Where you stay?" Moke asked calmly.

"Kamuela. I don't have a lot of time."

"Why don't we sit over there and you can tell me what's going on. Who's threatening you?"

Olveria grumbled, grabbed the envelope and then shuffled over to the corner to a small table. Moke offered him coffee, but the old man declined.

Moke sat down with a pen and pad. "So what's this about?" He could hardly contain himself. Olveria was one of the names Miss Horner had identified in the photos. C Squad. Wimpy. That was his nickname. Moke wondered if it was because he liked hamburgers.

"This. Someone like want me to get trouble." Olveria pulled photographs from the mailer. Moke recognized most of them, except one. Newspaper articles came next.

"May I see?" Moke asked.

Olveria pushed the items toward Moke with the flick of his hands.

There were three photocopies. The first one was a small entry about the death of a CCC boy up at Camp Kilauea, the second, the headline of Henry Oh's sentencing. The third article stopped Moke. It was an obituary dated June 6, 1944 for Delbert Oh. *Henry Oh's father?* Passed away in Princeville, Kaui. Preceded in death by his wife, Delores Oh. Survived by son Henry Oh serving in the Pacific region. That was all.

Moke cleared his throat. "Why do you feel you are being threatened? Are these pictures of old Army friends? They look so young. "

"Not Army, CCC. Civilian Conservation Corps. We were plenty young. Worked up at the national park."

Moke strung Olveria along, the information that Tawnie Takahashi had uncovered just a few hours ago disturbing and haunting. He waited for Olveria to say something about the incident at Hilina Pali. They were both distracted when a middle-aged man came into the lobby. "We're closed now," Moke said in a not too friendly voice.

"I'm with him. I'm his son."

"You are?"

"Bento Olveria. I drove him here."

Moke motioned him to sit on a bench away from where he was interviewing Alvin, then went and locked the door. "Now where were we, Mr. Olveria? What are these articles about?"

Olveria frowned. "Long time ago *kine* stuff. Not important."

"They must be important to you. Who do you want to stop? What do the pictures mean to you?"

"It's that *malihini,* Harleson."

"Ah." Moke picked up one of the pictures. "Wouldn't happen to be this man?"

"Yeah, yeah. That's him. The *haole*. Still getting me in trouble."

"What trouble was that?"

Olveria sighed, his tanned face from years out in the Hawaiian sun wrinkling at the brow. "It was a long time ago. We worked on the Hilini Pali and a shelter. Sometimes, we take lunch break at the shelter. Someone from my squad fell—got pushed over the *pali*."

Moke acknowledged how terrible that must have been. "This the one who did it, Henry Oh?"

For a slight moment, Olveria hesitated. "Yeah, yeah."

Why? Moke thought. *Why hesitate? Unless it's one big lie.*

"And Harleson. What was his name?"

Olveria's age began to show. By his face, he was searching for the name. "Dick. We called him Haole, but I don't think he knew what it meant. Dumb Haole."

"Why would he be sending this package to you? I see no harm."

"He called me one liar. We had one big fight. I was afraid I'd get kicked out of the CCC. It was bad back then. All my money went to my parents."

Over on the bench, Bento Olveria leaned in, listening. Moke caught his eye, wondering if he had heard this story before.

Moke picked up the article about Henry's sentencing. "You testified?"

Olveria's voice grew soft. His shoulders slumped. "Yeah, yeah."

"With someone else. Would it happen to be Walter Chin and someone named Lolo?"

Olveria's mouth opened wide in surprise.

"Was it the truth?"

Bento Olveria gasped. Moke paid no attention to him. "I asked, was your testimony the truth?"

Olveria didn't answer.

***

Blocks away from the Hilo Police Station, Tom Harleson woke with a start, still foggy from a dream that mingled walking in a far off desert in the freezing cold and a rugged road that followed the edge of the Hilina Pali. At the Hilina road's end, a full moon lit a lava flat two thousand feet below and the ocean beyond. Someone had called his name.

Outside his hotel window, the sun had gone down, but the night life seemed to have bloomed. Strains of Hawaiian music and voices came up from the lanai. Spotlights illuminated the palm trees. He rubbed the back of his neck and sat up. "Damn," he said when he saw the time. 7:30. He didn't have time to sit around.

He swung off the bed, taking his liners with him. In one of his carry-on bags, he took out a long travel kit, then dragged a chair along with his liners kit to the bathroom. He spent the next few minutes sitting on the chair. He inverted the silicon liners and cleaned them with Dial soap and a micro washcloth. When he was done rinsing them, he set them on folding liner drying stands he brought from home. Cleanliness was more than next to Godliness. It was a health issue of the highest importance for an amputee. Sitting on the chair, he looked at his white bare stumps that came to weird, folded ends. He needed to get a tan.

Back at the bed, he put on a clean t-shirt and shorts, fresh liners and his prosthetics. He checked the time again, read the trifold with info on the hotel's bistro, and decided that he had enough time to look at the last letter posted four months ago. He fired up his laptop and read. He soon discovered this:

I got my records from the National Archives in St. Louis today. Highly entertaining to read all the certificates I got there. Certainly helped me get a job with the Electric Company after the war. Saw I had one demerit for drinking in Hilo. I did a pretty good job staying out of trouble. How about you? Always felt bad that you and Jimmy got busted by the police for fighting in the courtroom, but Popeye and Wimpy had it coming for lying like that. It burns me that you two had to spend a night in jail. Lucky for you, you only got demerits on your record and CCC overheads didn't throw you out of the 3 Cs. Still, I don't understand why Alice Kapuna lied too.

I'm putting in this postcard of the Hilina Pali my grandson picked up a couple of weeks ago at Volcanoes National Parks. It's sometimes hard to believe that we were there. He asked about some of the structures we built and got a list from the park. Many are still there, including our walls. But that day when we were taking our lunch break, I swear I saw Lolo jiggle Gary's foot and cause him to lose his balance. Just horsing around. When he fell down and started to slide, Duke was one of the first to reach him. I saw him grab Gary by the shirt, but it tore away. By the time our mates from C Squad got there, Gary was gone. I can still hear his screams. And Lolo. I never heard such pain and grief. So, I'm asking if we are going ahead with our plan. I just can't stand it anymore.

Tom closed down the computer. What the heck was the plan? And who was Alice Kapuna? The sound of voices and music on the lanai seemed to have increased. Tom's stomach growled. It was time to go down, but first, Tom was going to make a call to Liko Hanale.

Chapter 21

Back at the Hilo Police station, Moke was getting irritated. Old man Olveria was giving him the runaround.

"Well, I'll take your silence on your testimony as a yes. You lied. What about Jimmy Takahashi? He was there according to the article. Got disciplined. Reprimanded by the CCC overhead. What was that for?"

"Fightin.' Same as Haole." Olveria's voice was almost a whisper.

"Well, I have plenty good news for you, Mr. Olveria. You probably know Jimmy Takahashi passed a year ago. But Dick Harleson and Wally Chin are also dead."

"Dead? Wally's dead? When?" The tan on Olveria's face drained to the color of ash. "When did Wally die?"

"Dead in the fire in Honolulu this afternoon. You ever talk to him all these years?"

"Three days ago. We're longtime friends."

Good to know, Moke thought.

"He was in that fire on TV?"

"Yeah, yeah."

"Is—Mrs. Chin OK?"

"No, she's dead too."

Olveria made a moaning sound in his voice. One of sorrow. He shook his head in disbelief. "Alice Kapuna… she was one beautiful girl. Everyone wanted to go out with her."

"Really. Where did you meet her?" Moke leaned his elbows on the table, his Hawaiian frame looming over Olveria. Bad cop pose.

"The dances. There were dances in Hilo we went down for on leave." Olveria's eyes got a distant look in them.

"Who wanted to go out with her? Gary Kaiwiki? Henry Oh?"

"We all did."

"But Wally Chin married her. Did she date Henry Oh?"

Olveria choked a sob back. "Yeah..."

"And Lolo?"

"Yeah, yeah." He waved Moke away.

"Poppa." Bento got up and started to come over.

"Stay where you are," Moke barked and turned his attention back to Alvin Olveria. "Who made you falsely testify? Lolo? Or someone else."

Olveria's eyes filled with tears. He sighed. "I don't think Lolo thought it would go so far as to arrest Duke. Days before he fell, Gary accused Duke of stealing his cigarettes, but I found out later Wally was doing that. Alice testified, too at the trial. Said Duke was being fresh with her."

"And Duke is…?"

"Henry Oh."

"Were you threatened to testify?"

Olveria shrugged. "We were all afraid of being dishonorably discharged. If we were, our families would lose their allotment."

"Who made the point of that? Lolo? Or Chin?"

"Wally. It was Wally. How come you know all this?"

"Because you are not only one who received envelopes such as this. Harleson and Chin received envelopes with various pictures and news articles. By the way, was there a hundred dollar bill in your mailer?"

"No. Just a slip of paper."

"Did it say, Remember Hilina Pali?" Olveria's eyes widened. That was enough for Moke. "Did you ever wonder what happened to Henry Oh?"

Olveria shook his head. "Nevah."

"Do you think he's still alive?"

"I don't know."

Moke pushed away from the table. "Did you know it will the anniversary of Gary Kaiwiki's death very soon?"

Olveria said he forgot.

"Well, maybe you should remember, Mr. Olveria. It's long time past for any legal action, but there's no limit on shame. Dick Harleson's grandson was here this morning. Come all the way from Wisconsin. He showed me a medal that Henry Oh owned. Must have given it to Dick Harleson before the trial. An honor award. Do you remember what it says? Well, I'll tell you." Moke could feel his chest filling with a rage he couldn't explain, but he was thinking of Tom Harleson on his prosthetic legs and sweet Auntie Bee with her worries about her honorable brother. "It says Loyalty, Character, Service." Moke stood up, causing Olveria pull back in his chair. "I think you forgot it all. And over a damn *wahine*."

Moke nodded to Bento. "I want you to help your father write out a statement. It can't change anything, but it might bring a closure to all this. We still don't know who is sending out the envelopes, but I think the message is clear: Remember Hilina Pali. If it's Henry Oh—should he still be alive—then there could be some danger to you and the remaining enrollees   from   that   day   long   ago."

Auntie Bee Takahashi rose early and for a few moments did yoga stretching exercises on the edge of her bed. When she was done, she padded barefooted out to the kitchen to make coffee. It was still dim out, though she could see her orchids on the bench under breadfruit tree. She turned on her tea kettle, fed Asami and then when the water was hot, made coffee in her French press. She opened the sliding door a crack to listen to the birds outside and sat down on her rocking chair with cup in hand. *My morning routine. Need to do something different. Like go swim.*

But she didn't feel like doing anything different. This is how she and George started their mornings after retirement. The calm before they went off to do something together or a separate interest, always coming back for lunch or a walk. He'd go golf or to build a project for Habitat for Humanity; she to volunteer in the classroom or the library or raise money for her beloved Honu.

As the sky brightened and the first pink flush of sunrise rose, she felt a presence in the kitchen, soft and comforting. Not George, who was everywhere. Her eyes strayed to the envelope up on the counter. Photos lay on top.

What you want, Jimmy? You want me to go up there? Take something for your goodbye? She got up to retrieve the stack of items from the counter, when Asami got up and growled. Bee limped to the door. Through the glass, she could see that Maile's front porch light had turned off, but she saw no car. She slid open the door part way, then decided to put Asami in her halter before stepping out. She stepped into her slippers. They went together, Asami gruffing, her ears going back and forth as she strained against her leash.

"Asami, be good."

As Bee came around to the front, she saw once again the red top of the Jeep she had seen twice before. The motor ran a loud purr. This time, she did not hesitate and went straight up to the driver's side. She tapped on the window, startling the young woman inside.

"Kelcie Shephard, you like to come inside?" For a moment, Bee thought she would drive off, but instead, Kelsie turned off the motor. She rolled down the window. Up close, Bee thought how young she looked—maybe nineteen? Her dark brown hair with its raspberry streak and deep brown eyes contrasted her fair complexion. *She has tears in her eyes.*

"How do you know my name?"

"I saw your face on a poster at UH. Number One scorer on the Vulcan team. You want to come in? Tell me why you dropped off that envelope?"

"You followed me?"

"Yeah, yeah."

"Oh." Kelcie bit her lip.

"I'm not going to bite you," Bee said. "I just want to know why you gave me the envelope with all *kine* stuff in it. About something bad that happened a long time ago and my brother was somehow involved. Or, someone just wants to make everything right, yeah?"

Kelcie slowly nodded her head. A tear rolled down her cheek.

Bee sighed. "I read up what happened to the Oh and Kaiwiki families. They lost their sons and they lost the money they needed to survive during hard times." Bee put a hand on her heart. "Poor Henry's family. Mother died while he was fighting in the Pacific, then his father. Couldn't help them while he was in prison. Hard labor, I bet. Then home wounded from the war. But he didn't come home, did he?"

Kelcie shook her head. She sniffed. "I'm sorry. You must hate me. You won't tell my coach, will you?"

"Why would I hate you, Kelcie-chan?"

"Because...Oh, will you help me, please? Tutu-vo always said that you would be kind, have integ-grity. Like your brother."

"For dropping off photographs? You're not in trouble for that."

"No, not for me. For my Tutu-vo. I worried that he's going to do something stupid."

"What would that be?"

"I think he's going to jump off the Hilina Pali."

Bee's voice became loud. "Why would he do that?"

"Because he's the one who started it all, making trouble for Henry Oh, but he wants to make amends. He's my great-grandfather, Oscar Garcia, but folks have always called him Lolo."

Chapter 23

As soon as Tawnie landed in Hilo, her cell phone fired up with a message from Mel at the Honolulu Police Department. *Got more info on the Chins. Give me a call.* While Jim grabbed his gear and headed to the rental car desk, Tawnie found a quiet corner and called Mel.

"Aloha, Mel. What's up?"

"Where are you now?"

"Hilo. Just got in."

"Ah. On a story hunt." There was a pause. "You asked for more information on the couple in the fire."

"Yeah, yeah." Tawnie looked around to see if anyone was listening in, but passengers coming off the plane were busy gathering luggage, being greeted with leis or heading out to awaiting cars at the pickup curb or landscaped parking lots beyond. Further back, the green hills behind Hilo were covered with mist, yet she could feel the heat of the developing morning. "What did you find?"

"I asked for fast results on the Chins. They're well known in the swap meet world and I wondered if there was some connection. Preliminary on Mrs. Chin is that she died of an overdose of her own painkiller. Medical records revealed she was dying of lung cancer."

"That's hard," Tawnie had to admit. "And Mr. Chin?"

"Self-inflicted gunshot."

"You never say before."

"That's because I have standards." Mel's voice sounded a bit irritated.

"What about the envelope?"

"Looks like some stuff related to Volcanoes National Park. Civilian Conservation Corps. Nevah knew they were here."

"I've heard stories that part of Schofield Barracks in Wahiawa on O'ahu are CCC buildings."

"Humph."

Through the glass wall, Jim signaled to Tawnie that he had the car. She gave him the thumbs up. "What about that torn up strip with Hilina Pali on it?"

"Seems tied into some articles in old newspapers and the pictures. Not sure if it was a threat."

"What about the picture of the woman? Did you find out about her name?"

"Mrs. Chin when she was a young woman. Very pretty, I might add."

"Her maiden name?"

"Alice Kapuna."

"*Mahalo,* Mel. For everything."

"You know I like Swimming Rama the best. And green curry, level three hot. I'll be expecting a full report of your findings."

"Didn't I say you would? You'll get all the notes on whatever I uncover."

"So, where are you going now?" he asked.

"To see my auntie, then I'm going up to the Hilina Pali to see for myself. Oh, by the way, did you find the missing dog?"

"Safe and sound. OK, we're all *pau* here." Mel hung up. At least, he didn't sound that upset.

Tawnie dropped Jim off at police headquarters and headed up to Auntie Bee's house. The street was still when she arrived. The only life stirring was a chorus of myna birds challenging a cat running back to Maile Horner's house and a mongoose slipping into the field of tall grass and sugar cane opposite Bee's plantation style bungalow. Tawnie was happy to see Bee's Rogue in her carport. Tawnie looked at car's clock. It read 8:30. Bee would be up.

As she got out of the car, she heard Asami barking inside. The little dog made Tawnie grin. Always protecting the house, under that small facade of terror, there was a sweetheart. Tawnie went around to the back, because Bee seldom went through the front. She expected the dog to come running out, but when she got to the sliding door, she saw that the pet door was locked. Asami was on the other side of the glass. "Where's Bee? Go get Bee."

Asami cocked her head, but stood her ground and kept barking. Tawnie tried the handle on the door, but it was locked. Tawnie cupped her hands on the door and peered in, worried that perhaps Bee had fallen. "Bee?" she called. "Auntie Bee-san." Asami kept barking.

Tawnie turned and ran to the orchid bench. She searched for the hidey key in a green ceramic turtle in one of the large pots. Dashing back to the door, she got inside and called again. Asami leaped up and down to get attention, than ran into the living room. Tawnie followed her, but not before checking the bedroom and the bathroom. "Bee?"

Tawnie had traveled in capris and sleeveless blouse and sandals. She bounded the steps to the upper rooms. *Where are you?* Bee knew she was coming down this morning. Tawnie hadn't see Maile's car next door so Bee couldn't be visiting with her. Back downstairs, Asami ran back into the kitchen. Tawnie sat on a stool to think. Then she saw a notepad. Tawnie picked it up.

Tawnie-chan. Make yourself at home. Don't worry. Taking a friend up to Volcano to see the sights. Be back at noon.

Tawnie shrugged. Not to worry. She checked the cupboard for Bee's coffee tin, then boiled water for some French press coffee. While it brewed, she wrote a note back to Bee, telling her where she'd be if she wanted to do lunch.

The house was quiet. Asami at her feet. It brought memories of Ojiisan's house back in Mānoa Valley before the traffic and development took hold. Pink and white plumeria trees, papaya and lime trees. Lava rock fence with two tiers of breeze blocks. The house with its pagoda shaped roof and polished wood floors. The blue green of the valley and the rainforest at the feet of the Ko'olau Mountains. The trail to Mānoa Falls. A simple life.

With all the reporting on the fire and then Harry's heart scare yesterday, she had no time to process the first anniversary of her grandfather's passing. She poured the coffee and grabbed creamer out of the refrigerator. Coming back to the counter, she noticed a pile of papers on Bee's rocking chair. She stepped closer and froze.

In a black and white photograph, Jimmy Takahashi smiled out at her, his arms draped over Harry Sato's shoulders on one side and Henry Oh's on the other. Henry had his arm on the shoulders of Dick Harleson on the end. They were wearing their work clothes and boots, their faces dirty and sweaty, but Tawnie could see genuine comradeship. They were a team. She bent over to pick it up, then realized where the photograph came from. An envelope mailer. *Auntie Bee got an envelope!*

Immediately, she called Maile on her direct line at the museum. Tawnie wasted no words and asked if she had seen Bee.

"No. Isn't she home? Her car's still there. Why?"

Tawnie told her why. "I just got in from Honolulu."

"She never said anything about getting an envelope," Maile said.

"She left a note. Said she was going up to Volcano. Could she mean Hilina Pali? It's unlike her. We were to meet up when I got in." Tawnie started shifting through the newspaper copies and photos. Some of the articles were the same that she had seen in Harry's envelope and what Mel had described to her at the Chin's apartment. Some pictures were circled. When Tawnie dug into the envelope, there was a hundred dollar bill. "Maile, did you figure out all the names in the different squads?"

"Pretty much."

"What about the guy named Lolo? I never got a chance to talk to Harry Sato about him."

"C Squad. Same as his and Gary Kaiwiki's. Just a minute." Tawnie heard Maile clicked on her keyboard. "Here it is. Oscar Garcia. Turns out he still lives on the Big Island." Maile voice grew concerned. "I don't know why Bee didn't tell me. But then I didn't come home until late last night."

"Do you know where Garcia lives?"

"Up near Kurtistown. He lives with his daughter and great-granddaughter."

"What are their names?"

"Rebecca and Kelcie Shephard. What are you going to do?"

"I'm going to call Officer Moke. Go pick up my cameraman and go up to the national park. I'm worried that Bee might not be going on her own. Tomorrow is the anniversary of Gary Kaiwiki's death."

"Let me help. Liko's on duty today. I can call him to be on the lookout for Auntie Bee."

"Alright. One final thing. Are there any remaining families with the name of Kaiwiki?"

"Never   found   the   name."

That's why hard, Auntie Bee thought as she listened to Kelcie Shephard's concern about her great-grandfather as they drove up to Kurtistown. *Lolo!*

"I love Tutu-vo. He's been like a father to me for a long time. Always there for me, always strong—he was a *paniolo* for many years, then a ranch foreman, but the last few years, nothing seemed to make him happy," Tawnie lamented, "not even our trip to the Azores six years ago to see where our family came from. This past year, he got worse. Finally, he told me what was wrong."

"Was it the CCC boy who was blamed for the death of another? Like in the envelope you gave me?"

"Yeah, yeah. It was." Kelcie sighed, gripped the steering wheel tight. "*Mahalo* for coming to talk to him."

Bee looked out the window wondering what she would say. What happened at Hilina Pali was a long time ago. What Lolo did was wrong. As they drove along the Volcano Highway toward Volcanoes National Park, she tried to imagine that time, but all she could see were the changes in the land passing by. So much growth in the last few years. Older homes with tin roofs, wide, mown lawns, banana trees, skinny coconut trees and open flat fields with clumps of wild sugarcane still lined the road, but overhead highway lights and stop lights intruded on a once sleepy road to Kilauea Volcano. *The land changed, but what was right would never.*

"What do you know about the CCC?" Bee asked

"I think it's plenty cool. I love all the pictures Tutu-vo showed me."

"What do you know about your grandfather's time there?"

Kelcie shrugged. "He didn't talk much about it. Not until recently. When he looks at the pictures from the camp, I can see he was happy, but then he gets silent. He kept his secret so long, that he was hurting."

Bee turned to Tawnie. "What you mean, secret?"

"He never testified. Yet the verdict went through anyway. Tutu-vo told me everything."

Looking at her, Bee put a hand on the dashboard. "How old are you, Kelcie?"

"Old enough. Nineteen."

"My granddaughter is nineteen." Bee snorted. "I'm the one who is creaky. You're too young to carry someone's secrets. How old is your great-grandfather?"

"Ninety-four. Looks ten years younger. But I think he's getting tired."

Bee pulled her rain jacket tight around her. Before they left, Bee insisted that she needed to put on warm clothes and fill a thermos with coffee for the both of them.

"Are you cold, auntie? We're almost to the house."

"I'm fine." Bee settled down again. "Where you stay?"

"Here with my grandmother. My parents are divorced. Tutu-vo moved in over a year ago. My grandmother is his daughter."

"Does she know what's going on?"

"No, that's why I'm worried. I'm alone at the house all this week. She went to California to visit friends."

"Why you think he wanted me to have those pictures and articles? I was a little girl then. Don't remember much, except one time when Jimmy brought his friends down."

"Tutu-vo knew you were a school teacher and the sister of someone he knew at the Camp Kilauea. He wanted you to help clear the man's name. You and as many others he could think of. You weren't the only one who got envelopes."

"There were others?"

"Yeah, yeah. Five, I think. Tutu-vo asked me to help put the envelopes together, then mail them. One went to the Mainland. Some to help, some to remind what happened at the Hilina Pali."

Bee put a fist to her mouth. She was too stunned to say anything.

Kelcie slowed down as the car in front of her turned right onto a side road. Not long after, she made her own right down a long road bordered by acres of grassland on the left side and the occasional homes landscaped with tree fern and banana trees on the right. Further down, trees and scrub bushes took over on both sides. Eventually, Kelcie pulled into a neat yard with a large cream colored house with a brick red tin roof set up high above the ground. A plastic blue swimming pool was in the backyard. Kukui nut and coconut trees lined the grounds.

"I don't see my grandfather's truck." Kelcie jumped out of the Jeep and ran around to the back. "Tutu-vo. Where are you?" Kelcie disappeared from Bee's view, then suddenly the girl came running back. "He's gone. He left a note. He said he was sorry." Kelcie's eyes filled with tears. "He's gone up to the *pali.*"

Tawnie was at the entrance to the main road from Bee's house, when a white Toyota Highlander swung onto the road next to Tawnie. The driver stopped and rolled his window down. "Miss Takahashi? Tawnie Takahashi, the TV crime reporter?"

Tawnie powered her window all the way down. "Yes."

"I'm Jason Chee with the Hilo Fire Department. I'm one of Bee Takahashi's former students."

"Are you looking for my auntie?"

"Actually, she wanted me to get in touch with you. Not sure exactly where she called from, but she said not to worry. Just wants you to go up and meet her at the Hilina Pali."

"The Pali? Who's driving her? Her car is in her carport."

"She didn't say." Jason cleared his throat. "I going up there now. Happy to drive you."

Tawnie frowned. She really wanted to drive herself, but the last time she was up in the Volcanoes National Park, she was chasing a potential murderer in a vast rugged region she knew little about. Best to go with someone who was with the fire department.

"Alright." Tawnie pulled her rental car over to the side and parked it. Grabbing her bag, camera and a KWAI-5 News fleece jacket, she got into Jason's SUV.

Jason tapped a Hilo Fire Department ID tag hanging down from his rear view mirror. "Just in case you're worrying about getting in a car with a serial killer. I'm legit."

"And I'm a crime reporter. Be careful. I might be recording you." When Jason Chee hesitated, she chuckled. "No worries." She strapped herself in. "Did my auntie say anything else? It's so unlike her. I called her neighbor and she said Auntie Bee never said anything about going out. She had planned to wait until I got in. My flight was late."

Jason pulled onto the main road and headed toward the highway going to Volcano. "Well, I ran into her yesterday at the UH campus. She was concerned about pictures and news articles someone dropped off. All tied in with some accident up at the Hilina Pali a long time ago."

"Wait. Were they about the CCC?"

"Yeah, yeah. How did you know? She was worried about her brother's role in the trial that followed."

Tawnie swore, then apologized. "How did my auntie sound? Are you sure she said everything was OK?"

"Yeah, yeah."

"I saw those pictures on her chair. They are similar to others sent around the state and Mainland."

Jason frowned. "I don't think she knew anything about that, but I did find out where Miss Shepherd lives."

"Who's she?"

"She's the one who dropped the envelope off."

"That's not Kelcie Shepherd?"

"You follow Vulcan basketball at UH Hilo?"

"No, she's the great granddaughter of a man who may be behind the accident at the *pali*. Auntie Bee could be in danger."

"Not   if   I   can   help   it.

"Thanks, man." Tom Harleson said to Liko Hanale as they came out of the Volcano House Restaurant. "That was a pretty spectacular place for breakfast. Kilauea, the drive-in volcano. It lives up to its reputation. Drive up, have buffet and watch it glow." They were dressed in layers for hiking in the cool morning air, Liko in his park ranger jacket, Tom in fleece and hiking shorts. He wore hiking boots on his prosthetic legs. Each man had a day pack.

"Gotta see it when you come to the Big Island," Liko said. "Pele is here. Kilauea's a living thing. She demands our respect and attention."

"I can believe that. You said this hotel is a newer version?"

"Yeah, yeah. There was a fire here in 1940. Oil burner caused the old Victorian hotel to burn down. This one was built in 1941, not on the original site which is just up that way. The park remodeled it a few years ago."

"I wonder if my grandfather saw the fire. He was working on the Hilina Pali Road and the irrigation projects there in 1940."

"Could be. It would have lit up the skies like Pele. Let me take you around the Crater Rim Road—should go out and see the steam flats—then we can go down to the Hilina Pali overlook you want to see."

"Let's do it." Tom climbed into Liko's park SUV and strapped himself in. He was grateful that Liko offered to pick him up in town and take him out to see where his grandfather had worked with his CCC buddies. On the way up to Volcano from Hilo and during breakfast, Tom filled Liko on why he wanted to see the outlook.

"Crazy," Liko said. "I know that area pretty good. The park did a survey of all the CCC projects in the Hilina Pali a few years ago. But I don't remember hearing about that particular story. We've had fatal accidents in the park over the years, but nothing of a criminal nature. Do you think the guy sending the envelopes is dangerous? Wanting to do some harm?"

"Hard to say. More like wanting to clear Henry Oh's name. The gal at the museum and Officer Moke both said there were other envelopes sent out to various living members of the CCC company who were working here. Maybe the sender wants to at least get the ones responsible for giving false witness to admit what they did by lying."

Liko started up his SUV. "You said your wife sent some letters last night."

"Yeah, she did. From Harry Sato to my grandfather. They were in different squads but were apparently close friends. In the last letter, Harry said Gary Kaiwiki's death was accidental. Just guys horsing around."

"Geesh."

For the next hour, Liko gave Tom what he called "The Grand Tour." Out to the steam flats, and around to various viewpoints along the Crater Rim Road. Eventually, they came to a stop sign by the road. "We can come back to go through the Thurston Lava Tube later, right now, let's head down to the outlook before the crowds show up."

Tom didn't see anyone this early in the morning, not even a tour bus. "Figuratively?"

"Well, we might meet see some *nene*. Our state bird." Liko made the turn onto the Chain of Craters Road. "Oh, if you look back to your left, you'll see a trail. That's the way to first site of the CCC camp at Byron Ledge."

"You have to hike in?"

"Just like the CCC boys did, only they came down from park headquarters."

They started down the two lane between a mixed alley of koa and *ohia lehua* trees, ferns and grass. The morning light cut through the trees' leaves and branches making lacework of light and dark on the road.

"Did the CCC built this?" Tom asked.

"Nah, it's been around since the late 1920s, but you'll see where the boys worked. You'll see Pele's work too." Almost as soon as he said that, they came bursting out onto an old brown and broken lava field where trees and rounded mounds of grass were making spotted inroads. Tom immediately felt the sun's heat. Yards later they were back in woods until they hit open grassland for a stretch. Liko stopped being tour guide and they talked sports for a while.

"Hilina Pali Road," Liko announced.

Tom sat up. He had such a strange feeling as they approached the entrance to the road. An emotional jag of grief hit Tom as he thought of his grandfather, age 18 showing up here in 1939. A stranger, a *malahini* in an exotic land. *What did you think, Gramps? What was it like?* The woods opened up with more open spaces, scraggly trees spaced apart, fern and grass, but the road narrowed to a battered, single lane. Someone mowed each side to keep nature from taking it all back. "Not the most titillating view."

"Wait until we get out there. Totally worth it. Right now we're just going along the inside of the Pali. It runs for twelve miles and pretty much looks like this the whole way."

"Reminds me of Maine. Scrub brush and skinny trees. Blueberries."

"Ohelo berries here. Sacred to Pele." Liko started to add something when his cell phone rang.

"Liko Hanale here, Volcanoes National Park. Oh, Maile. Howzit?" He came to a stop and put on the brake. He listened intensely, then said, "Alright. I'll keep my eye out for her. I'll let the park police know. *Mahalo.*" Liko hung up.

"Was that Miss Horner at the museum?"

"Yeah. She's worried about Bee Takahashi. Missing from her home. Not sure if she went willingly."

"Where might she be?"

"Hilina Pali. She got an envelope full of stuff too."

Auntie Bee took one look at Kelcie Shepherd and decided that the young lady was in no shape to be driving. Tears of panic and fear rolled down her cheeks, carrying black mascara with them. Vulcan Number One Shooter looked as scared and confused as the teenager she was. Bee got out of the Jeep and went around to the driver's side.

"I like think I should drive."

Kelcie sniffed back tears and sputtered that she was OK.

Bee waggle a finger at the teenager. "You are not fine. Don't worry. My husband was in construction. I can drive all *kine* stuff."

For a brief moment, Kelcie protested further, then gave Bee the keys. Bee climbed in with a "omph," then called Jason Chee and told him to go to her house and get Tawnie. When she was done, she adjusted her seat and with everyone belted in, took off.

It didn't take long to get back on the highway. Though she was small in stature, Bee had a good view over the steering wheel and dashboard. She just wasn't used to all the gadgets that were in this car. Like backup screen with colored lines. She adjusted her wire-rim glasses and gave the accelerator a little push. "What is your grandfather driving?"

"A Ford truck. It's blue."

"OK. We'll go straight to the park. When we get there I like you look out for Chain of Craters Road sign. I know we'll find the way to Hilina Pali from there."

Kelcie sniffed again. Her nose was red, matching the streak in her hair. "I'm sorry I was rude. I'm just scared for Tutu-vo."

"I know you are. That's why I called my friend. He's one fireman. He'll get people. Why don't you tell me more about your grandfather? And basketball. What you like about basketball?"

***

While Bee and Kelcie made their way to Volcano, Tawnie drilled Jason Chee on how he knew Auntie Bee.

Jason drummed the steering wheel with his fingers. "Your auntie was my fourth grade teacher. Everyone called her Mrs. T. for turtle in the classroom because the green turtle was our class mascot, but for some of us, she was Tutu T. because she had *aloha* for those of us who had troubles in our families. My father was an alcoholic. My mom had MS. Anyway, that's why I'd do anything for her. She encouraged me to finish school, go to college. I decided to serve the community like she did— and still does—by going for the fire department."

"Did you ever meet my grandfather, Jimmy Takahashi when he came to visit her?'

"Actually, I did. He was a guest in our classroom once on Veteran's Day."

"When was that?"

"That would have to be around twenty years ago." Jason pointed to the sign that read cutoff to Mountain View. "We're getting there. Traffic's light."

Fifteen minutes later, they arrived at the stone house gate to the national park. Jason showed his pass for free entry and he chatted with the man in the booth.

"No time to talk story, Kea" Jason said, "but you didn't happen to see Bee Takahashi come through? She's in a red Jeep."

"Auntie Bee? She went through a half hour ago. Said she was going down to the Hilina Pali."

"Was she with someone?"

"Yeah, yeah. Vulcan UH Hilo number one shooter." Kea frowned. "Is everything alright? Bee seemed to be in a hurry."

"Not sure. We're headed that way right now."

Tawnie leaned across Jason. "Auntie Bee is *my* auntie. Everything's not alright. Your basketball star is related to a person of interest. Call the park police. Bee could be in danger."

Chapter 28

"How much further?" Tom asked Liko as they drove down the paved, one-lane Hilina Pali Road. As far as he could tell, they were on a winding eight-mile road to nowhere. Flat and desolate with the occasional ghostly gray tree standing guard, Tom was having trouble imagining what it was like for any CCC boy working out here on the old flat lava flows. *Hotter than hell.*

"A few more miles. Getting seasick?"

Tom chuckled. "Trying riding in a Humvee in a desert landscape." He shifted in his seat and tapped his thighs to increase circulation. "What's that smooth looking mountain ahead of us?"

"Mauna Loa."

"How many kids worked out here?"

"Couple of thousand over the years. They might have had a side camp here so they didn't have to go back to the main camp. Mess tent, tents to sleep in. It can rain hard out here. That's why the irrigation project. In 1939, there was massive flooding—flash flooding. Took out what soil there was. Put some historic petroglyphs in danger. As you see, it's just grass growing on *pahoehoe* and the occasional shrub."

"What about that campground back there?"

"Had to give it up when *nene* started nesting there. We still keep a fire shed nearby. It's extremely dry up here. Careless hiker can start a fire."

The road turned again and narrowed down to a lane just wide enough for Liko's Range Rover. Mauna Loa was now on their right. Light flashed to their left.

"That ocean?"

"Yeah, yeah. We're driving along the edge of the *pali* now."

A half mile later, the road dropped slightly between low hills greener and more vegetated than previously. Tom's heart began to pound. He caught a glimpse of turquoise-blue ocean and brown-gray land far below. Signage appeared and suddenly a tin roofed shelter made of lava rock. A hitching post for horses and an outhouse sat close by. *We're here,* he thought. *Here is where Gary Kaiwiki died.* His mouth went dry.

Liko pulled into what passed for parking lot spaces—some withered logs marking where to head in—and parked next to a red Jeep. A blue old model Ford-150 parked beside it.

Liko turned off the car. "Let's take a look."

Leaving his fleece jacket behind, Tom got out of the Rover and was immediately blasted with a breeze carrying humidity and heat. They walked across the dirt parking lot to the shelter. "Nice. Did the boys build it?"

"That's what they say. Park did some improvements in the last few years."

"Wow. That's some view." As far as Tom could see left and right, a wide of expanse of lava desert far below and ocean beyond. White clouds overhead made patterns on the desolate land like the changing moods of a living thing. A trail descended down through dirt and dry grass. At the end there was a large stone cairn reflecting silver in the sunlight and small wind-blown tree.

"*Anu,*" Liko said. "It has place name information. Let's go look."

Tom pointed at the land below. "Trails go down there?"

"Main one to your right goes all the way down to the Ka'u Desert. Think the CCC kids worked on it as well as other trails around here."

"My grandfather said they were taking a lunch break here." Tom nodded toward the cairn. "I wonder if they sat down there." He felt again a surge of grief and impending doom. "And Gary Kaiwiki fell."

"Maybe so. Your legs going to be OK? There's another drop below it. An *ahu* for the people who died in the 1975 earthquake. Part of the *pali* broke off. You get a sense of the drop. Worth a look."

"I'll be fine. I've got good hiking boots on."

As they walked out to the *anu*, Tom could hear women's voices lifting up from below. When they got to the place name monument, he was surprised how the wild beauty of the view struck him. He was even more surprised to see below a small, spry-looking Japanese woman wearing sunglasses standing dangerously near the edge of the *pali*. A tall young woman was next to her. On the ground, an elderly man slumped by an *ahu* with bundles of offerings tied up in *ti* plants. "Help us, please," the young woman said. "It's my tutu-vo."

There was no one on the Hilina Pali Road as Bee drove down. Only the rugged terrain and the memories of the last time she was down here: the week before George collapsed and died. *Two years ago.*

They had come down here with their son Kiro and his family who were visiting from Germany where he was a doctor in a medical unit. It had rained hard earlier in the day, so the meandering asphalt road was slippery and pockmarked with puddles. The flat, brown and tan landscape appeared endless, accented by the occasional yellow of a *mamane* tree flower or the red blossoms of an *ohia lehua* tree.

At one point, Kiro asked to get out. He wanted to point out some plants to his teenage kids. George got out too. Watching the men side by side, Bee had felt a powerful surge of love. Kiro was as tall as his father and except for his dark hair and his eyes shaped like her own, Kiro looked exactly like George. He hunched his shoulders against the light wind like George; gestured with his hands like George; laughed like George. Above all, he was smart, kind and loyal. *Like you, George.* As Bee remembered that time, she felt that surge again, both of love and sorrow. *You are like my brother Jimmy.*

"Are we almost there, Mrs. Takahashi?" Kelcie Shepherd leaned forward, her hands on the dashboard. She had stopped crying when they got to the park and now was taut with anticipation.

"By the way the bushes are growing here, almost there. I'll let you out and you can run find him while I park." Almost as soon as she said it, the road dipped, the area opened out with views of the ocean to the left and the lava desert below and wind-stunted trees on the remains of an old lava flow to the right.

"Is that the shelter? Oh, Tutu-vo's truck is there."

"Yeah, yeah. Now you get out and run." Bee stopped the Jeep just long enough to allow Kelcie to do that. The girl took off at a sprint to the shelter, then past it, calling out her grandfather's name. Bee's heart took a hard thump, fearing that they were too late.

She drove to the end of the parking area and parked at two worn logs by the asphalt path that led past the shelter and out to the viewing area. The sun had come out behind high white clouds, causing the ocean beyond the Ka'u Desert far below to dazzle like shattered diamonds. She put on her sunglass clips and got out. Kelcie had disappeared. Bee limped out to the grass in front of the shelter. She knew a trail took off beyond signage posted in front of it, but she was drawn to the *anu* at the edge of the *pali* on her left. A lone tree guarded it.

"Tutu-vo!" Kelcie's frantic voice flew at Bee on the wind. Bee limped as fast as she could to the *anu* where a shiny half circle with place names sat on it. From there a path dropped down the grassy hillside to a bench of land marked at its end with another *anu*. An elderly man with salt and pepper hair thinning at the crown and a thin mustache stood there arguing with Kelcie. He was a spare man, but Bee could see that he was strong in his own way. He held a package wrapped in *ti* plants in his hands. Bee studied the steep trail down through rock and grass to where they stood, judging her ability to get to them. She picked up a weathered tree limb some earlier hiker had dropped and used it for a walking staff. Kelcie continued to argue with her great-grandfather, her voice full of pain.

Half way down, Bee decided to get their attention as she worked her way down. "Lolo Garcia, what *kine tutu-vo* are you to talk to your great-granddaughter like that? She only wants to help, give you *kokua*."

Oscar Garcia looked up at Bee in shock. His face went white. He turned to Kelcie. "What did you bring her for?"

"To help you, Tutu-vo."

"Too late. It's too late to help me."

Bee kept coming, taking careful steps down the sharply descending, rocky dirt trail. She finally reached an area where the ground leveled out. Bee took a moment to catch her breath and shook her finger at him. "I didn't come all this way to tell you it's too late. I think you want me to help you. Why send me one package full of pictures and travel money?"

Kelcie looked at Lolo. "I did what you told me to do, Tutu-vo, but now I am afraid. I don't want to lose you."

Lolo shrugged. He put the *ti* package on top of the *anu* and put a lava rock on top to hold it. He kept his hand there. Bee thought he was too close to the edge where the *pali* dropped off.

Bee came by Kelcie and patted her arm. "I think I know what happened. Gary Kaiwiki was your best friend. Is this where you were taking lunch break?"

Lolo worked his mouth, but said nothing.

"I have sons." Bee said. "Sometimes they played hard when they were *keiki*. Once Clarence pushed his brother out of the tree. But no one pushed here, yeah? It was an accident."

Lolo swallowed and turned to her. For the first time, Bee noticed a pin on Lolo's short-sleeved tan aloha shirt. A brass pin with three capital letter C's. Jimmy had one. CCC. Lolo's eyes glistened, but not from old age.

"I think you are feeling bad for Henry Oh," Bee said. "He said in the newspapers, "I didn't push him. I was trying to help him," but you said he *did* push him. Now you want to take it back, so you write, "Remember Hilina Pali." What do you want me to do? Do you want to say something to me? Or the others who get these *kine* envelopes that Kelcie told me."

Lolo looked down, then directly at Bee. "Henry was a hero. I was nothing."

Kelcie reached over to Lolo. "But Tutu-vo, you told me you didn't testify."

"Yeah, yeah. But it was too late. Like right now, things are too late."

"Why was it too late?" Bee asked.

"I was angry with myself for causing Gary to fall, so I blamed someone else—Henry. I was jealous that he was going out with a *wahine*—Alice Kapuna—we all met her at a dance. I honestly didn't think it would go so far, but I got my mates to say they saw him do it when the police came to investigate—even though they didn't see me jiggle Gary's leg. By then, we were all afraid that we'd get kicked out of the CCC for telling lies—our families needed the money they got each month. I—I tried to take back what I said, but by then Henry was charged with manslaughter—got two years." Lolo grew silent and tapped the *ti* leaf bundle with his hand. A light wind coming up from below ruffled his hair.

"That was a very bad thing you did, but it's good you take responsibility. Now people will know about Henry Oh." Bee cleared her throat. "The newspaper clippings you gave me also said my brother, Jimmy Takahashi and another man got in trouble. I never knew that. Why did you want me to know that?"

Lolo smiled faintly. "Because Jimmy Takahashi did the right thing. He got angry because he wasn't allowed to say anything in court. When Henry Oh got sentenced, Jimmy fought with mates from my squad in the courtroom. He was right to do that. My mates had made up some evidence about Henry stealing cigarettes and all that, but it was that bastard—sorry fo' say that bad word—Wally Chin that who got the *wahine* to testify that Henry had been more than fresh with her." Lolo spat. "I found out later Wally had planted evidence in Henry's trunk. And he married Alice Kapuna."

Lolo started to go around to the front of the *anu* with its gifts. Bee recognized it as the monument honoring those who had been killed and injured when a part of the *pali* had collapsed in 1975. Maybe it was fitting for what had happened here decades earlier.

"Tutu-vo, be careful."

"It's OK, *anjinho*. My little angel. You are the one good thing, I've done. You and my daughter."

Bee came close to Lolo still holding her walking stick. "You said right now things are too late. Why was it too late? You are doing a good *kine* thing."

Lolo made a soft sound in his throat. His eyes filled with tears. "Henry Oh died this morning. I don't know if he ever knew how sorry I was. I ruined his family, you see. They lost his allotment. His mother got cancer while he was in jail, died when he was away in the war—he was allowed to join the Navy. His father was disabled and killed himself after she died. Drank too much. Now Henry is gone. My fault." Lolo continued going around to the front of *anu*, using its top to steady him. He paused. "Everyone called Henry Oh 'Duke' for Duke Kahanamoku. Henry was one good swimmer and he could catch the big waves. I'm just Lolo. Crazy." He stepped away from the *anu*, going for the edge of the *pali*.

"Tutu-vo!" Kelcie screamed. "Don't! Oh, please don't!"

Auntie Bee wasn't thinking when she came around and swung her stick right into Lolo's scrawny belly. She was only glad he fell against a bush to cushion him before slumping to the ground. She just hoped he didn't   break   his   hip.

Chapter 30

Two weeks after Auntie Bee confronted Lolo Garcia at the Hilina Pali Lookout, a small caravan of vehicles returned. The afternoon was warm and clear, white clouds high in a turquoise blue sky. On Bee's side of the car, a light wind came through the open window. In her lap, she carried leis.

"That too breezy for you, auntie?" Tawnie Takahashi asked as she drove down the narrow asphalt road.

"I like it. It's like forest bathing which is a good *kine* thing, but this is *pali* bathing. Just as good." Bee sighed. "So good to be out in nature. Maybe we'll see *nene* this time. Did you bring your camera?"

"I'm all set, auntie," Jim Milstead said from the back seat. "We'll do our report from there." Asami, next to him in her doggie booster seat, barked approval.

Bee put a fist to her mouth in thought. Her book club-teaching friend, Eleanor Kane, had been right. Maile had figured things out: the real names of all the young men in the three squads, contacted and got warm responses from their families scattered throughout the islands and on the Mainland, and started a petition to get Henry Oh's dishonorable discharged paper changed. If that didn't happen, she'd make sure people would remember him for his honor awards at Camp Kilauea and his valor in WW II. Maile did that.

But I saved someone, Bee thought.

Bee was glad Lolo didn't break his hip, but he was angry and upset until a man on prosthetics arrived with Liko Hanale. When Lolo saw him, he gasped.

"Haole," he said in a soft voice. "You look like Haole."

At first, Bee thought Lolo was being rude, but something in his face changed when the stranger said he was Tom Harleson, Dick Harleson's grandson. Lolo began to weep.

While Kelcie Shephard explained to Tom what was going on, Liko tended to Lolo. Bee looked for a place to sit by Lolo, but had to stand, so she just talked story to him. Talked about the good things the CCC did in the park, how it made people proud, even though they may have forgotten that time when the work was done.

Soon the grassy ledge was filled with concerned people when Tawnie and Jason arrived. Liko called the park aide car to take Lolo to Hilo to check him out. Jason came with his emergency medical kit from his car.

Bee remembered how intense and angry the air felt around them as they stood by the *anu* and the wide world below the *pali*. It was Tom's kind words as he told Lolo how his family had found the envelope in his grandfather's dresser that changed the air to forgiveness.

"I came to see that justice was done," Tom said, "just as you wished, Lolo. As my grandfather would have wished. He talked about some plan. I guess this was it." He said it with tears in his eyes, his voice thick.

Bee had looked at Tom again, an old memory stirring. The *haole* at the supper table in her family's dining room. Long ago. He did look exactly like his grandfather, Dick Harleson—Jimmy's friend who got in trouble with him for fighting in the courtroom.

Bee sighed. Now they were going out to the lookout to gather and say goodbye to the boys who had worked here before the war. In the caravan were vehicles holding the families of Tom Harleson, Harry Sato, and Lolo Garcia. Maile Horner and Liko Hanale followed in a national park Jeep. Coming to the *pali* for the first time, was Henry Oh's daughter and a great-nephew of Gary Kaiwiki. Other members of the three squads eating lunch on that day long ago were also invited.

We are almost complete, Bee thought. Except for the men nicknamed Popeye and Wimpy.

Wally Chin was dead along with his wife, Alice. Maybe the contents of the envelope made him feel shame or he was afraid of being found out or maybe, he truly loved his wife and didn't want her to suffer any more, so he killed her, then himself. Alvin Oliveria, Wimpy, was in home detention for assaulting Officer Moke. Lolo told Bee later, he was not sorry for what happened to Chin and Oliveria, but promised he would never again attempt to jump off the *pali* or any other thing like that. He would seek forgiveness in good ways.

The caravan filled the parking lot at the *pali* lookout. It took a few minutes to get everyone down to the *anu* dedicated to 1975 earthquake victims. Along with the families, Liko brought a friend who was a *kahuna*. A Protestant minister and a leader from the Buddhist Mission in Hilo were also invited.

Words and prayers were said. Leis thrown off the *pali* and more *ti* packages laid around the *anu*. Tom and Henry Oh's daughter each spread some of their relative's ashes. Afterwards, the group went up to the shelter where potluck dishes were laid out on portable camping tables. Pictures and stories were shared. Ukulele and guitars brought out. Under a dry, hot sky, the celebration couldn't have had better weather.

Bee sat on a folding chair, holding Asami in her lap. She looked toward the stunted tree that guarded the place location marker at the overlook. Someone had laid a lei there.

Tawnie came and squatted by her. "Jim and I got what we needed for the evening show. Did you hear what Lolo said about that one hundred dollar bill you and others got?"

Bee stroked Asami's back. "Yeah, yeah. Five dollars a month for the CCC boy. One hundred dollars in today's money. I think Lolo wanted us to earn it by finding out the truth."

"You seem pensive. What are you thinking, Auntie Bee?"

"I'm thinkin' I understand what the CCC was all about. It was about work, doing good things, getting money to families in hard times, but most of all, it was an *ohana*. What happened here was that this *ohana* got broke, but now it is whole again. I'm so happy for Jimmy. This is what *aloha* means."

Bee turned around to look at the families eating and talking together in the shelter. "This will be the new *ohana*. And people will remember Hilina   Pali."

When I lived in Hawaii in the 1970s, I hiked across Haleakala Crater twice. One time we spent the night in a horse shed, another time in a pack tent, always next to a long barrack-like building used by visitors to the national park. Imagine my surprise to learn years later that the building was built in the 1930s by members of the Civilian Conservation Corps. One of the greatest programs to come out of the Great Depression and the FDR's New Deal, the CCC not only put millions of young men back to work over an eight year period, but planted three billion trees, built ranger stations, campgrounds, fire lookouts, trails and so much more. Some of our national and state parks would not be what they are today. Just because Hawaii was a territory, didn't mean that the CCC wasn't in the islands.

The CCC commenced in Hawaii in January 1934 and began projects at Volcanoes National Park. Over the years under Park Superintendent Edward Wingate, they built a road up to Mauna Loa, housing for park employees, the visitor's center, interpretive museum, overlook stations, "comfort" stations, retaining walls, road berms, and the Hilina Pali Road along which they built several shelters. One of the most interesting projects, was goat eradication. The wild herds were destroying plants and trees. In 1939, flash flooding washed away fragile soil and the Hilina Pali Erosion Project number 327 commenced in 1940. Many of the CCC boys' work can be seen today throughout the park.

Resources:

The Civilian Conservation Corps Legacy

The Civilian Conservation Corps Legacy represents the alumni of America and strives to bring awareness to the heritage of the CCC, CCC alumni, their programs and accomplishments. http://www.ccclegacy.org/

The CCC at Volcanoes National Park

Documents   and   articles   at   HAVO
https://www.nps.gov/havo/learn/historyculture/civilian-conservation-corps.htm

A great video/talk on the CCC at Volcanoes National Park

http://bit.ly/2G1YEhy

ABOUT THE AUTHOR

A UH Manoa grad, award-winning author J.L. Oakley writes historical fiction that spans the mid-19th century to WW II with characters standing up for something in their own time and place. Her writing has been recognized with a 2013 Bellingham Mayor's Arts Award, the 2013 Chanticleer Grand Prize, the 2015 WILLA Silver Award, and the 2016 Goethe Award for Historical Fiction. Her time living in the Hawaiian Islands made a longtime influence on her writing. In addition to her Hilo Bay Mystey novellas, a recent full-length novel, *Mist-chi-mas:A Novel of Captivity* explores Hawaiians in the Pacific NW in the 19th century. When not writing, Oakley demonstrates 19th century folkways and gives "hands-on-history" talks and workshops in schools and museums.

To reach her other novels, go to: http://amzn.to/2eMkSH9

Website: https://jloakleyauthor.com

Twitter: @jloakley

Facebook Author page: https://www.facebook.com/JLOakleyauthor/

Made in the USA
Columbia, SC
08 January 2020